The Education of Dixie Dupree
An Indie Next List Selection!

"A searingly honest coming-of-age story with a heroine
unlike any other I've met in a long time. I read this
book through from start to finish in one sitting,
simply unable and unwilling to put it down. Here's
to another beautiful novel from Donna Everhart."
—Holly Chamberlin, author of *All Our Summers*

"Secrets, lies, peach cobbler, grits, a hot Alabama sun, and
a girl named Dixie Dupree who shows courage in the face
of betrayal, strength when all falls down around her, and
shining hope in the darkness. This is a story you'll read well
into the night." —Cathy Lamb, author of *All About Evie*

The Forgiving Kind

"Reminiscent of the novels of Lee Smith, Kaye Gibbons,
and Sandra Dallas, Everhart builds a firm sense of place,
portraying the tiredness and hope of a dry Southern
summer and voicing strong women." —*Booklist*

"With a diverse cast and layered themes, *The Forgiving Kind*
may be Everhart's best yet." —*Historical Novels Reviews*

The Saints of Swallow Hill

"Everhart's latest Southern historical novel is full of
tragedy and abuse with characters who initially aren't
easy to like, but the story becomes much more
appealing as Del and Rae Lynn grow into protagonists
to root for, in a unique setting." —*Library Journal*

Books by Donna Everhart

THE EDUCATION OF DIXIE DUPREE

THE ROAD TO BITTERSWEET

THE FORGIVING KIND

THE MOONSHINER'S DAUGHTER

THE SAINTS OF SWALLOW HILL

WHEN THE JESSAMINE GROWS

Published by Kensington Publishing Corp.

WHEN THE JESSAMINE GROWS

DONNA EVERHART

KENSINGTON
PUBLISHING CORP.

www.kensingtonbooks.com

In memory of Keilah Kuzminski Goff
March 25, 1966 – July 24, 2021

We shall never any of us be the same as we have been.

—Lucy Buck
American diarist,
Front Royal, Virginia

*For even the small piece of bread and
the molasses were things of the past.
My larder was empty.*

—Mary Boykin Chesnut
March 6, 1865

Chapter 1

Somewhere near Whitakers
Nash County, North Carolina
1861

Joetta McBride could not stomach conflict. What was transpiring in the country was certainly troubling; however, the growing discord within her own family was most concerning to her. Like her evening primrose, it had bloomed swiftly overnight, and what had been merely a nuisance grew into a matter of significance. Her father-in-law, Rudean McBride, was who she blamed. The topic occupying Mr. McBride's mind of late was war. He spent a good deal of time nattering on about the shoddy job Lincoln was doing now that he had been voted in. Lincoln was to hold resolute to his word and not interfere with the institution of slavery. Despite this, he was distrusted by many, including Mr. McBride. These issues would only have been a distraction to Joetta except for the effect it had on fifteen-year-old Henry. To her dismay, Mr. McBride reveled in the details of Northern and Southern dispositions, while Henry's questions began to fixate with uncanny interest on the possibilities of a war.

Only the other day a sunbeam cast light across her eldest son's face, highlighting the dark hair sprouting on his upper lip and along his jawline. He was becoming a young man, and with that, Joetta supposed, came a desire to think for himself. Henry was not the only one Mr. McBride captivated with his talk. Eleven-year-old Robert paid attention too, although Henry was the one who plied his grandfather with questions. Mr. McBride, enthused by his rapt audience, went on about heroic deeds and a soldier's bravery, describing how they ran full tilt toward their adversary and engaged in mortal battle in the name of honor. What he never brought up was no matter how virtuous he made it, winning should never be assumed. Men were not invincible. War was anything but how he depicted it with his elaborations on the cause and seeking justice, the grandeur of a righteous struggle. He left out the misery of exposure to extreme temperatures, hunger, thirst, disease, horrific injuries, and the ultimate price, death. He treated it like some fanciful fairytale life.

Mr. McBride expounded on the chance to see new places, meet new people, as if war were a social event. Henry's eyes glowed, his imagination ignited by what could be discovered beyond this patch of land where he had grown up. This troubled her immensely. They were yeoman farmers. They raised pigs and chickens, owned a beautiful golden milk cow named Honey, and a cooperative plow mule named Pal. They sold white corn and sorghum in order to purchase sugar, flour, salt, and coffee. They wanted for nothing and they owed no one.

One cool evening on the cusp of spring, the boys and their grandfather were gathered in the sitting room while

Ennis worked in the barn repairing a harness. The boys took turns using a whetstone to sharpen their jackknives. Mr. McBride, his hands draped over his small paunch, spoke softly, like he was picking up where he had left off from some previous conversation.

"No sir. If you can't own lots of land, life on this farm and what you see here is your future. You might be all right with that, what do I know? Now here's something I often thought I should do. I believe I'd have made a fine soldier. Point is, there will come a time when you'll have to make up your minds about what you'll do in life. Don't look to this. This ain't your future."

The boys stopped what they were doing and looked at her, expecting a response. Joetta flushed with irritation at her father-in-law's statement, and yet, she said nothing. He would love nothing better than to spar with her, so she kept her head down and hummed as if she had not heard a thing while she stirred a pan of gravy. Robert rubbed the edge of the blade with his thumb.

"But, I like it here."

Joetta smiled inwardly. Mr. McBride leaned forward and put his elbows on his knees.

"Take Mr. Poole down the road yonder with his thousands of acres, and hundreds of slaves at his beck and call. He's living high on the hog over there. Making enough money to travel and go places worth seeing. He recently come back from Europe. You got to have acreage along with slaves to handle that kind of work and to have that sort of life. He's able to travel 'cause he can afford it, but he'll go flat broke if Lincoln has his way. He's got that new carriage with them horses to pull it. Why wouldn't anyone want the finer things in life?"

Henry said, "If there's a war, Mr. Poole won't be rich anymore?"

"It's about money, more 'n anything. The South's too successful according to some. He's successful, wouldn't you say?"

The boys nodded. Mr. McBride appeared to ponder his own question.

"How can you be too successful, one might ask, and why is the South richer? Cheap labor, for one. But here's the reality. If them darkies go free, how's Poole gonna manage all that crop he's got? Imagine. Work all your life to get where you are only to have the government and the damn Yanks telling you what to do. That's why it can't happen. It ain't right."

Robert said, "What if we win?"

"Why, things would go on like always, what with everyone knowing their place and such. That's the God's honest truth. Listen to me now. I'm telling you, farming like this"—he gestured out the window at the rich land, which gave Joetta comfort, but apparently fueled his derision— "ain't doing nothing 'cept breaking your back day in and day out. If you have a lot of land, and the slaves to run it, you got something then."

Joetta banged the lid onto the pan. Where did he think his food came from? It was difficult to watch as he sat stuffing himself full with that which had been planted, picked, and prepared by her hands. What she and Ennis did was nothing to be ashamed of. She began setting the table, loudly placing supper plates, glasses, and silverware on the table, then interrupted the infuriating discussion with a question.

"How about *Idiot's Delight* for dessert?"

She stared at Mr. McBride and he paused. Then, as if she had not spoken, he moved on to recount a bloody battle, this time with Indians. She shut him out and his voice became a drone. This was how she managed even as she dwelled on the insults, and the meaning behind them. However, the more she reflected on what he said, the more indignant she became. She would certainly speak to Ennis about his horrible influence, and how he was tainting their sons' minds.

Once they finished eating, with Mr. McBride holding his plate out wordlessly for a second piece of dessert, Joetta noticed, she took up the plates and began washing them. Ennis came to her side, and she spoke quietly to him.

"He is poisoning them against our way of life. I do not understand it. As if all this"—she swept her hand around—"is not worthwhile or admirable."

Her husband leaned against the worktable.

"Pa's always been like that. He ain't never been happy with where he's at, or with what he's got. He's always had it in his head what would make him successful was to own more land, and slaves. I'll speak with him."

"Good. He certainly will not listen to me."

Ennis draped an arm over her shoulder, and squeezed.

"Does he listen to anybody?"

"Himself."

Ennis smiled, kissed her cheek, and went back outside. In the evening light, she noted, like she did on many occasions, the way he walked, his long-legged stride, his height, his hair, and his shoulders. His shape was as familiar to her as her own form. She wished when they were together like husband and wife it would result in another child. She could not see this taking place, not after so long. She did not want to think about the babies she had lost, most too small to know their sex. It did no good, but it made her ever more grateful for Henry and Robert.

She moved into the sitting room and sat in her chair, reaching into the basket she kept beside it for her sewing. After she selected some thread and began working, she looked at her sons.

"Henry, Robert, your great-grandfather actually fought in that other big war, remember?"

Mr. McBride looked at her, and huffed.

"We already heard about this."

"Not everything."

She faced the boys again.

"My grandfather, your great-grandfather Smith, died in the War of 1812 before I was born. Do you recollect my family once lived near the Albemarle Sound?"

Robert moved closer to her, while Henry remained where he was, his expression aloof.

Joetta went on. "He was working at a port when a press gang forced him into service. Do you know what a press gang is?"

At this Henry paid attention, and both boys shook their heads.

"They were men from the British Royal Navy who took sailors and other men against their will. They would grab anyone with any amount of know-how about ships and sailing the seas. It was an underhanded way of going about it, but Great Britain was at war with France, and as it went on, they took whoever they could get. For a long time my mother and grandmother held on to the possibility he was near Canada, where fighting was going on. He was not in Canada. He died overseas. They never knew where he was buried. We never forgot how he went to work one day only to never come home. I tell you this because war is not a glorious affair."

Henry, his tone bordering on rude, said, "I know that."

The way he spoke caught Joetta by surprise, and while she was still digesting his tone, he shared a bit of news that further alarmed Joetta.

"Benjamin says if he got the chance he'd go fight."

Benjamin. Of course. His tendency to brag and make

such declarations was typical. Bess and Thomas Caldwell, his parents, were friends with Joetta and Ennis. Harold, their thirteen-year-old son and their youngest, spent time with Robert. The Caldwell farm lay two miles to the east and abutted the McBride farm, and because the properties were divided by dense woods and several acres of uncultivated land, the boys often hunted in that area together.

Mr. McBride said, "By God, I'd sign up to fight too, if I won't so damn old, and didn't have this bum knee."

Henry said to no one in general, "I'd sure go."

Joetta frowned.

"Enough about this. Your grandfather is too old, and you are too young. Besides, what is going on has nothing to do with us."

Robert scrutinized his older brother.

"They wouldn't want you anyway; you're too puny."

That led to a small-scale scuffle, more of a shoving match. Henry, ever sensitive about his height because the younger Robert was already taller, shoved his brother while Mr. McBride slapped his knees and laughed, enjoying the fracas. Joetta stood, and clapped her hands.

"Stop it."

After one final shove, they obeyed, although each continued to glare at the other. She pointed at the door, and they slumped away to do their evening work, crossing the yard peacefully enough. She turned around to find Mr. McBride peering at her from over the rim of his cup. He lowered it and wiped his mouth.

"You can't keep'em from doing what they want forever."

It was the way he said it. His comment was not about this small clash; it went beyond that. She did not respond because deep down, she knew it to be true, and like any mother, she did not like having to face the fact of their autonomy one day. But they were not there yet, and though the time would come, she did not expect it for a few more years. By then, they would be more mature, able to make decisions based on facts, not the urges or notions of an old man's mind. Mr. McBride picked up his cup and slurped. She decided to set aside her sewing for now and go pull weeds. It was always a good way to vent her vexation when he was right.

That night as she and Ennis prepared for sleep, she worried out loud about Henry. Ennis sat on the bed, patting an empty space. She dropped beside him, laid her head on his shoulder, and he snugged an arm around her waist.

"He's only a boy talking big, trying to figure himself out."

Joetta could not resist.

"Your father?"

Ennis snorted in agreement, and then set her mind at ease.

"Don't fret about the boys. Henry and Robert know how their grandfather is, how he goes on and on. More important, we know our Henry, right?"

Joetta believed what her husband said was true, even while some of Henry's latest behaviors gave her reason to question this. She chose to believe Ennis was right, and that Henry was merely trying to find his way.

The next morning as Ennis read *The Farmer's Almanac*, he talked about the crops as she put breakfast on the table. Mr. McBride was already in fine form, having started in on Robert, telling him he needed to eat because he looked like a starved cat. Robert's lankiness matched Ennis, while Henry's shorter, stockier stature was more like Mr. McBride. Robert sat with a glum look, wordlessly picking at an old stain on his overalls, and Mr. McBride quickly lost interest. He snapped open a newspaper, procured on a trip to town, and within seconds began reading aloud, his derision over the latest news spilling forth.

"Lincoln won't keep his word, I'd bet on it."

He took up a snifter of whisky and dumped some in his coffee as Joetta set eggs and grits in front of them. Ennis closed the Almanac and tossed it aside.

"Pa, let's eat in peace."

Mr. McBride waved his fork in the air and mumbled, distinctly aggravated.

"Peace. Best get used to not having it. Ain't gonna be much peace around here, not if them bastards get their way."

Ennis stopped eating and stared at his father intently.

"How does any of this affect you, or us?"

Mr. McBride's mouth dropped open and a bit of egg fell out.

"What? You can't mean that! Of course it does! Where the hell you been?"

Ennis calmly responded, "I care nothing about what's going on. Neither should you."

"Good God. You teach these boys such, and they'll grow up ignorant!"

Henry and Robert watched this exchange with great interest, while Joetta banged a spoon around in the kettle of grits, her annoyance growing by the minute. It was utterly ridiculous the things he said. They did not need anyone to tell them what to do, or how to do it. They were on their land, minding their own business. Let the ones who wanted go and fight. The McBrides would be having no part of it. Ennis pointed at his sons with his fork.

"As long as they know how to keep a family and livestock fed, that's all they need to worry about."

Joetta scooped grits onto Henry's plate and paused, spoon hovering in the air, astounded by the look of derision he aimed at his father. This was something new. She glared at him, and noticing her irritation, he ducked his head to eat.

Ennis did not see this exchange, but Mr. McBride had. His smug look was condescending, and she was all too aware her opinions were valued by him no more than what Lincoln himself thought, even in her own home. Whether he liked it or not, she would speak her mind. She dropped a blob of grits on his plate.

"It is ignorant and a waste of time to argue over things that do not matter."

She continued to move around the table, serving the food. Mr. McBride shoved his chair back and wagged a finger at her and Ennis.

"Watch and see don't them boys grow up middlin'. Like somebody else I know."

His gaze swept over Ennis as he snatched up his plate, and stomped out the back door, heading for his cabin. Although his father had insulted him in front of his children, Ennis kept eating. The tension in the air diminished, and Joetta sat down.

"Looks as if we will have peace after all."

With Mr. McBride out of the house, her mood eased. It would be fine. Ennis would handle his father, the sooner, the better. She tasted the eggs. Not bad. Food always tasted better without the company of Mr. McBride.

Ennis went to Whitakers around midmorning and took his father with him. Joetta appreciated this gesture knowing full well it was done to give her a bit of peace. She sat on a squat stool in the kitchen doorway, sorting through the vegetables she had brought in from the garden, then dropping them into a pail of water. The boys walked back and forth in a distant field, creating a checkrow of hills to hold corn seed with the variety their father preferred, gourd seed. After she'd cleaned the vegetables, she moved on to the wash, and with her mind free, she enjoyed the peacefulness of the farm. Other than the rhythmic scrubbing sounds she made, and an occasional bird chirping in a nearby tree, it was a quiet spring day.

Joetta paused in her scrubbing and inspected the order of her domain, the swept yard, the bright spot of color from the crocuses and daffodils pushing up out of the ground while breathing in the familiar heady, sweet scent of jessamine. Her gaze moved on to the new barn built last year with the help of the Caldwells and the Browns. Nearby, the smokehouse was filled with ham, sausage, and bacon from the fall slaughter. There were her chickens pecking about the yard, including her two Pilgrim Fowl, Josephine and Agnes, gifts from Ennis a couple of weeks earlier for her thirty-fourth birthday. There was the shed filled with wood and finally, the orderly fields where they planted everything they needed. How could anyone be critical? Frankly, what they had done in sixteen years of marriage filled her with pride and immense satisfaction.

She gathered the material of Ennis's overalls and scrubbed, the suds making them move easier against her washboard. With the warm sun on her back, she began to hum a little tune. In these found moments of serenity, she recognized there were a few troubles here and there, but overall she was happy, contented. After her morning's work, she set about preparing the noon dinner expecting the return of the men. The squeaking of wagon wheels announced they were back, and she pulled the pot of beans and ham hock from the stove. She went through the house and stood at the front door watching as Ennis halted the wagon. As he climbed down he threw her a telltale look before he went to the back to unload flour and cornmeal. In from the field, the boys in their dusty clothes and faces red, hair damp with sweat, began to help their father. Mr. McBride carefully lowered himself down from the wagon's seat, relying heavily on his cane and rubbing his bad knee. He wasted no time sharing what he had learned in town.

"I tell you what, I knew if it ever got started, it was gonna be a Confederate win! We got them on the run 'fore they could even git their muskets half loaded. I bet we could beat'em with popguns and cornstalks!"

Henry hefted a sack of newly ground cornmeal onto his shoulders, but his grandfather's comment got his attention.

"There's fighting already?"

Ennis pointed at the fields.

"Did you get done what I told you before I left?"

Robert said, "Yes sir," while Henry sent an impatient look toward his father and did not answer.

His gaze returned to his grandfather.

"Are we at war?"

Ennis kept working, and Joetta did not understand why he permitted such impudence. Mr. McBride banged his cane on the ground with enthusiasm.

"Them damn Yanks thought we wouldn't stand our ground. Well, we showed'em at Fort Sumter! Now Lincoln's calling for seventy-five thousand men to 'quell the' . . . what's he call it, *'the Southern rebellion.'* Ha! He can go to hell! Ain't nobody with the good sense the Lord gave'em gonna help him fight his war and if they do, they ain't nothing but traitors, and we're better off without'em."

Henry acted as excited as Mr. McBride. "Our side's bound to win!"

Ennis was quick to respond. "Son. We ain't *got* a side in this thing."

Henry dropped his head. This kept his face partially hidden, but Joetta had seen enough. Ennis was right; they did know their Henry, and his expression said there would be trouble.

Chapter 2

What had flared in Henry's eyes contradicted what Joetta and Ennis had always believed, that through their hard work and example, their children would respect them and their chosen way of life. Always willing and obedient, Henry's transformation had been subtle, as obvious as seconds passing in a day, until it was not. Joetta was steeped in these thoughts as she left the hen house, where she had been gathering eggs the following morning. Mr. McBride, favoring his bad leg, limped by her. She greeted him as always for she never liked holding grudges.

"Good morning."

He grunted a greeting—of sorts. Ennis spoke to his father as well, but Mr. McBride had no time for niceties. He was headed for his grandsons, who worked near the wood pile, chopping and stacking to replenish the day's supply. He called out to them.

"Listen! I been thinking on this most of the night. We have a side, and it's the very same one as them rich planters. Don't matter we ain't got their kind a money."

Henry paused to look at his grandfather, his interest flickering and growing, the way the flame on a wick lengthens when extended. Mr. McBride stopped near him. Before Henry could react, his grandfather scraped his shirt sleeve up to expose his forearm.

"Look a here. What do you see?"

Mr. McBride's big knuckled finger jabbed repeatedly the area he'd exposed. Ennis interrupted, his warning like a rumble of thunder.

"Pa. That's enough."

Mr. McBride twisted around to look at him.

"What. Henry here, he's sensible. I'm teaching him something. What's the harm in that?"

"I know what you're doing."

"No, you don't."

He turned his back and his voice became urgent as he poked Henry's forearm again.

"It's this here white skin! Same as them big planters got, don't'cha see? Them Yanks get their way, they'll elevate the Negro to the same dispensations as you, me, any of us. Next thing you know, they'll be coming after our women-folk, doing all manner of terrible things."

He pulled Henry close to him, murmuring in his ear as Ennis raised his voice.

"I said enough!"

Mr. McBride sputtered with outrage.

"It's the very reason we got to fight. Ain't no way 'round it. They abolish slavery, they'll be roaming about the countryside, and any woman, whoever she is, will be in danger, mark my words!"

Mr. McBride resumed whatever he had to say, keeping hold of Henry by the back of the neck. Henry's eyes grew rounder with each passing second until he began to struggle to pull free. Ennis was beside his father now, and thumped him on the arm.

"Let him go, Pa."

Mr. McBride shrugged Ennis off, and whatever he said next made Henry go still the way a rabbit caught by a hawk gives up. His face turned ruddy, the color deepening with each passing second. He flicked at his ear as if bothered by a gnat.

"Stop saying those things."

Mr. McBride scowled.

"You got to know what this war means. Wouldn't you want to do something about that? Hell, I'm done. You got a good understanding now, I reckon."

Mr. McBride released Henry, who swiped at his ear as if he could remove what he had been told. He avoided his mother's eyes and went back to work. Ennis went to Joetta and let out a sigh.

"He'll be fine."

"And you?"

The corner of his mouth curled, and he tried to lighten the mood.

"That's always been questionable."

They watched Henry yank the maul free from the stump before swinging it over his head and letting it land with force against a piece of wood. Joetta's arms filled with goose bumps. She involuntarily crossed her arms as if she had caught a chill. Such anger. Was it directed at them, or was it what his grandfather said? He brought the tool down swiftly again, splitting each piece in two on the first try. The change was remarkable. He did not behave like her Henry anymore. Joetta faced Mr. McBride. He had talked this nonsense time and again, the value of his white skin something he put above money. She pointed at him.

"For shame talking of such things."

Mr. McBride sniffed.

"What's a shame is y'all gone ruin that boy."

Ennis approached his father again with a determined look and Joetta backed away. She did not need to hear this. She went inside, pulled her skillet out, and restoked the fire, wondering what Ennis might say this time that would make any difference. She dared to glance out, and he was gesturing like he would when frustrated while Mr. McBride stood with his arms crossed. He shook his head and grinned like a fool. He actually laughed a time or two until Ennis said something that made him stalk away, waving his hands in anger. Ennis pointed at the boys, who became very busy with the rest of their wood chopping. Finally, he appeared in the kitchen doorway, and Joetta paused in her cooking.

"What did you say to him?"

"I informed him he wouldn't be allowed around the boys, or to eat with us, if he kept it up."

Joetta cracked some eggs into the pan.

"Good," she said.

That day Mr. McBride kept his distance, quietly working on his whittling, and did not come to the table at noon. *What a pleasant change,* Joetta thought. Of course it was noticeable to everyone when he limped into his cabin later that evening as they ate supper. Joetta sighed, put food on a plate and took it over to the cabin. She knocked, and he opened the door, whining immediately as he took it from her.

"He said I couldn't eat with y'all."

"That is not exactly what he said."

"Sure it is. Ask him."

"Breakfast is at the usual time. See you then. Sleep well."

She made her way back across the yard, the silence behind her as loud as a gunshot.

For a while, calm was restored. Mr. McBride behaved and Joetta was pleased. One morning she sent the boys into Whitakers to pay on the bill at the store, and when they returned, they huddled together and spoke in subdued voices. Joetta smiled, noticing Robert's mouth tinted dark from eating licorice. She had allowed if there were any coins left over, they could buy some candy. Henry, however, eyes glassy bright and face flushed in such a manner he appeared as if he had taken on a sudden day fever, kept one hand clenched. Perhaps he held the remaining money, or candy, only his expression yielded an uncommon excitement. She stopped beating the rug she had draped over the porch rail. He almost vibrated with whatever it was, excitement or nervousness, she could not tell.

"What is it?" Joetta asked.

There it was, so obvious, yet so subtle only a mother might notice the shift from exhilaration to caution. He spoke carefully, signaling an effort to not sound any particular way.

"Secession. North Carolina's left the Union."

Robert spoke around a piece of candy still in his mouth. "Everyone's talking about it. Everyone. Will Papa go fight?"

Joetta supposed she should have expected it, the way things had been going since Lincoln's election, yet the news gave her a moment of uncertainty. Even so, she held no particular feelings of alarm. She shook her head.

"Of course not."

She wanted to follow this assertion with more reassuring words, if only for herself. The doubt on Henry's face made her feel he knew more than she did, and she found herself looking away, searching for Ennis. She spotted him in the nearby field, walking between the small hills the boys had created, positioning his jab planter every so often. She knew from previous years of planting corn, there would be four seeds to each mound. *One for the blackbird, one for the crow, one for the cutworm, and one to grow.* Mr. McBride limped out of his cabin and came toward them. Joetta sighed inwardly. He would be happy about this, she was certain. He called out.

"What's the latest news, boy?"

He never said their names. They were "boy," the both of them, and it was one more issue Joetta found particularly irritating. Henry eagerly informed him.

"North Carolina's seceded, Grandpa!"

Joetta picked up the rug beater and went back to work. She did not want to hear about this, and certainly did not like Henry's eagerness over it. It was only talk, though, as Ennis said. Ignoring them, she went inside and brought out another rug from the hall, observing straightaway Mr. McBride scrutinizing a small object in the palm of his hand. Henry saw her looking, and took it back. She heard him address his grandfather.

"Most everyone's wearing them."

Joetta caught a flash of red, and gold. Was that what he had done with their hard-earned money?

"Henry, where did you get that?"

Robert, not wanting to be left out, reached for the item.

"Let me see it again."

Henry handed it to him, reluctantly.

"You ain't keeping it."

His eyes stayed on the odd little symbol, even as it rested in Robert's palm. Joetta knew it to be a cockade. They had appeared suddenly to show who supported the South seceding from the Union.

Joetta walked over.

"Neither are you."

"I paid for it, though."

"Was it your money to spend?"

"You said . . ."

"Not for that."

He did not have the audacity to look at her, and by ignoring her, maybe he thought she would leave him be. That was how she felt. Like Henry wanted her to leave him be, let him do as he pleased, let him revel in whatever fanciful notions he was having. She would not.

"Hand it to me."

She held her hand out, and when Robert went to give it to her, Henry snatched it and, with great deliberation, pinned it to his overall strap. His grandfather hooted and slapped his knees.

"Won't you look at that? This boy's got spunk, now! Why, I believe you'd make a fine soldier. Shoot, I'd swear on it!"

Henry's chest expanded, and he appeared to grow taller with his grandfather's praise.

Joetta was furious.

"Is that so? How strange. Do soldiers not follow orders from their higher-ups?"

She held her hand out again. Henry took a step back, and his chin came forward. Joetta pointed to the field where Ennis worked.

"Fine. We can let your father deal with this."

Henry's sunburned face paled a little and seconds later, Ennis called out, motioning for the boys.

"Get your hoes, and let's get to work! Come on! You've had the morning off!"

Henry looked at the bright cockade, fingered the edges of it, perhaps debating whether he should remove it. He dropped his hand, and without a word, set off for the field. As he went, his stride lengthened and his shoulders squared. His behavior had turned daring, impetuous even. It was clear to Joetta he was itching for something to happen. Itching for trouble. Where had their easygoing, lovable Henry gone? The one so helpful, who brought her spring flowers, who considered others before himself? Robert hurried along beside him while Mr. McBride trailed behind.

He muttered how this was "a whole lot of fuss over something so small."

Joetta stayed where she was, sorely troubled over the quick progression of events. Her sense of peace and well-being was overridden by a new fear, fear for this life they had stitched together and what might come of it. While she believed they would go on doing as they had, and come out of it unscathed, the uncertainty was not comforting.

Even more unsettling was what she witnessed the moment Ennis spied Henry's defiant cockade. Henry had his hand held out for the jab planter, but Ennis pointed at Henry's chest and his raised voice came to her faintly. There was a distinct question to it, while Henry merely shrugged. Ennis reached for the cockade, and to Joetta's disbelieving eyes, Henry knocked his father's hand aside. Ennis dropped the planter and grabbed by Henry the arm, and Joetta set out running toward them.

In the past year Henry had certainly grown more muscular, but Ennis was still stronger and bigger, plus, he had at least twenty or so more years of hard work on him. Henry struggled, twisting and turning to keep his father from getting the cockade.

Joetta shouted, "Henry! Stop!"

Ennis ripped the cockade off and threw it on the ground. He backed Henry up against the split rail fence, and Henry decided that was not to his liking. He began to struggle, grunting and heaving, until they were battling it out, arm to arm, shoulder to shoulder straining against one another. Robert, his mouth and eyes wide with astonishment, did not move. Such a thing had never occurred. Henry, furious, yelled at his father.

"You won't always be able to tell me what to do!"

When Joetta would think back on this scene later, she would understand it was in this moment the relationship between son and father altered. Mr. McBride, for once, appeared uneasy and began rubbing his chin nervously. The fence cracked as they strained against the top rail before splintering and giving way. They fell and rolled on the ground until Ennis abruptly let go of Henry. He shoved himself to his feet and backed away, staring at his son like he did not know him. Henry jumped up too, fighting not to cry, from embarrassment, rage, or both, Joetta was not sure. She lowered her gaze as he ran by her. Mr. McBride, hands on his hips, furiously worked his chewing tobacco from one side of his mouth to the other, his agitation plain to see. Flustered, he gestured in the direction Henry went.

"I don't know if what he done called for all that."

Joetta refused to grant him her attention. This was mostly his fault, and she went to offer Ennis comfort, except he was already in the process of getting back to the work at hand. She stood helplessly, hands by her side. Ennis pointed at Robert.

"Finish up this field. Henry's going to get started on the other one."

Robert was quick to obey.

"Yes, sir."

Mr. McBride said, "Aw, leave the boy be. He needs time alone."

"We talked about this. I'll handle it and you'll stay out of it. He's getting too big to run off pouting. He's got to learn to take what he asked for, and he's going to get back to work, and that's all there is to it."

Mr. McBride fell into an uncanny silence. Joetta stooped to pick up the little ornament, mashed into the ground, now wilted and pitiful. She tucked it in her apron pocket and headed back to the house, highly disturbed by what had taken place. Everyone was angry except poor Robert. Ennis went into the barn where Henry had escaped, and she dreaded there might be another exchange between them, worse than the first one. She drew water at the springhouse, keeping an eye out. They came from out of the barn, heading back to the field. The simple fact Henry walked with Ennis allowed her some optimism, although her son's stride was stiff and his features tight. Maybe by suppertime the incident would be over with, if not forgotten altogether.

For the rest of the afternoon, she worked in the garden, watering, weeding, and tying up bean plants. She sorted through her bounty of seeds deciding what she might plant next, and as always, found solace in turning the soil and caring for the seedlings. She was satisfied with how they were thriving, the leaves bright green and the vegetables vibrant, showcasing a rainbow of color. As the sun started to set, she stretched her cramped back and brushed her hands off. From the looks of it, they would have a munificent harvest and that was the good she took from the day.

She washed up, and soon she was calling everyone to come and eat. When they gathered around the long wooden table, Henry was noticeably absent. Undoubtedly what had taken place earlier was not over. They carried on, quiet, aware of the empty seat. Ennis said a prayer, and she began serving. Their eyes stayed on their bowls, eating the stew she had prepared, while Ennis and his father calmly discussed various possible reasons behind the secession, as if the events of the afternoon were forgotten.

Joetta was familiar with their topic, a law created in 1850 regarding the return of slaves who escaped into a territory or another state. It was rumored this is what Lincoln would renege on. She remembered it because of what she had seen once right after she and Ennis had married. It had been at the end of the day, and she was walking out in the yard, her skirts swishing through the knee-high grass, imagining how everything would look years later, God willing. She was not feeling her best as she was recovering from her first miscarriage. The sun offered a bold sliver of amber over newly cleared meadows, and streaks of orange flared through a thick copse of trees.

She sipped on a cup of coffee, her gaze roving over the landscape. Whispering came from somewhere nearby. She set the cup in the saucer, and out of the corner of her eye, caught a flash of brief movement. She stared in that direction and they materialized like apparitions. They saw her too, the distance only three hundred feet or so. They were still as the warm night air and the woman clutched a baby to her chest. A family on the run. She wished she had not seen them because their fear reached over the expanse of the yard and all that lay between. She dropped her eyes, lifted her cup, and took a sip. Without lowering it, she peeked over the rim, and in that split second, they had vanished. She placed the cup back in the saucer, brushed her hair from her face, waited a few seconds, then walked casually to the other side of the house. Ennis was hammering on a windowsill. She was about to tell him what she had witnessed, and changed her mind.

She did not know why except maybe it had been because she perceived herself as they would, a danger. An obstacle. Her pretending not to see them might give them hope. And with that hope, they could concentrate on their next move. That summer, three more families passed by the farm. Nash County sat close enough to the Virginia border to be part of a way north, and since most were headed there, she did not feel surprised. She never said a word about any of these sightings. She felt remorseful since she and Ennis shared everything. Not this, though. She thought of them on this journey, toward a different kind of life, maybe one like she and Ennis had. It was a good life, one anyone would want.

Except one of their very own.

Joetta left the table while everyone finished eating. At the kitchen window, a view of the land the same as it had been back then offered a sky of deep violet and stars budding one by one. Beyond the faint light cast from the lantern on her worktable, she detected a soft yellow glow coming from the barn. She would fix a plate and take it to him. Now that she had had time to reflect on the earlier incident, she wished Ennis had let Henry wear the ridiculous little cockade. What difference would it make? Let him think what he wanted. It meant nothing really. She stuck her hand into her apron pocket and withdrew it. She placed it onto the shelf where she kept her dinnerware, pushing it to where it would not be seen.

She began dipping some stew into a bowl as the men moved to the sitting room. Robert went to the window and looked out the back door. He had been subdued all evening, and Joetta was sure he would take note of the light like she had. He would likely want to comfort his brother. Instead of taking Henry the food, she handed the bowl to Robert.

"You want to take this to your brother, along with some water? See if he needs anything else?"

He took what she offered and spoke softly. "Is it okay if I stay out there with him tonight?"

"I think that would be good. And, Robert?"

"Ma'am?"

"Please do not talk about this afternoon."

"No, ma'am."

"Not unless he brings it up."

"Yes, ma'am."

She watched him walk to the barn for only a moment before turning away. Maybe he could help smooth the way for Henry to swallow his pride. They would spend the night out there, and it would be all right by morning. If not, she did not want to think about what might come next.

Chapter 3

It seemed to Joetta she had no more than shut her eyes when she awoke to the gray light of morning. She sat up just in time to see Ennis as he was about to leave the bedroom.

"Ennis?"

He paused by the door.

"I didn't know you were awake."

Hesitant to speak because she was not sure he would agree with her, she moved to the side of the bed and glanced at him, trying to gauge his mood. She could not tell, so she took the chance.

"Maybe we should allow Henry to have his opinion."

His eyebrows met in a disapproving frown, a definite indication he was not partial to this idea. She pushed on, anyway.

"Why not? It will not change anything."

"It has already changed him. Did you not see how he acted when I tried to take that ridiculous ornament off of him?"

"I know. He should not have behaved the way he did."

Ennis rubbed at his face, his voice soft, thoughtful.

"It's come to my mind I was about his age when Pa and I got out of sorts with one another."

Joetta remained quiet because he had never shared much about his upbringing. He came and sat back down on the edge of the bed.

"Ma was always so quiet. If Pa's hands had worked like his mouth, we'd have wanted for nothing. Ma, and sometimes my sisters, had to step in when things got out of hand. Soon as they could get married and get away from him, that's what they did. Amy tolerated him best, yet even she got fed up after a while."

Amy, the youngest of Ennis's sisters, had come to visit a time or two, and Joetta had observed she was polite to Mr. McBride, respectful, although not necessarily loving.

"I think I was five the time he put me down the well."

Joetta was stunned.

"What?"

"It was punishment for something I'd done."

"What happened?"

"Amy fetched me out. Told me to hang on and ride up the way I'd gone down."

"What did your mother do?"

"Nothing. Looked me over, then went back to work."

Joetta's mother-in-law, Anna Louise Hicks McBride, rarely spoke. She labored in a quiet and efficient way, pointing here and there to communicate her wishes. It had made Joetta uncomfortable at first. She was certain the woman cared nothing for her until she noticed she was like that with everyone. Mr. McBride appeared to love his wife, but all he had to do was give her a look and whatever she was doing, she would stop and get what he wanted.

After observing this several times, Joetta thought of Mrs.

McBride like the little trained monkey she had once seen when she, her sister, Faith, and brothers, Leland and Wilbur, had gone to a county sideshow. There, a man in strange garb kept the tiny creature on a small rope. He rotated the handle on his music box and the monkey performed tricks. People would then toss coins and the monkey scurried about picking them up before taking the money to his owner for the reward of a few peanuts. At least the monkey got peanuts. Mrs. McBride was never offered a simple thank-you from her husband. Henry was still a baby when his grandmother passed after a brief illness, and Joetta swore she was smiling as she lay there in her pine box. She could not help but wonder if it was because she was finally free of that invisible tether held by Mr. McBride. Joetta's family farmed as well; however, the exception was her parents' relationship. It was close and affectionate. Her childhood home, near a town called Hamilton in Martin County, was a day's ride to the southeast, and family gatherings were not as often as she liked.

Ennis continued his reminiscing, as if pondering his past might give them an answer to their current dilemma.

"He won a slave in a card game once."

"Really?"

"I never knew his age. To me he looked ancient. Ma, me, and my sisters, we'd been doing the field work all along 'til Pa got Ezra and after that, he wouldn't allow it. Said that's what the slave was for. That old man struggled to plow a row, so I decided I'd help him since I'd been doing it before. Pa was furious. I kept on because Ma told me to, that he was going to die out there at his age. It was the only time I'd ever seen her go against anything Pa said. It was kind of peculiar how it ended."

"Why?"

"Not long after they argued, Ezra was gone."

"Gone? He died?"

"No. The shed where Pa kept him was empty one morning. He locked it at night because he was afraid he'd run off. The door was still locked. I'm sure Ma had something to do with it. She told him it was African hoodoo, and he'd better watch his back."

Ennis laughed at this memory and Joetta smiled. He rose, squeezed her hand, and left the room. She got up and prepared herself for the day, washed her face, brushed her hair, twisted it tight, and pinned it up. Next, she pulled on drawers, stockings, chemise, corset, and one of her work dresses, a pale blue with darker blue stripes. She attached a clean white collar and cuffs. After she straightened the bed, she entered the kitchen and tied on a clean apron. Pulling out her biscuit pan, she opened the back door to let in the morning air before she worked to rekindle the embers in the stove.

Out the open door, she spied Henry at the fence talking to a group of men who carried all sorts of gear. Obviously, they were volunteering to fight, and she did not know what to make of them. Muskets, canteens, tin cups, blankets rolled up and hanging off of them in various ways, by twine, ropes, or leather straps. Like peddlers, Joetta thought, with their wares suspended off their person. Henry waved them through the gate, inviting them to the well for a drink of water. Ennis and Robert worked to carry bags of seed from the barn and paused to watch the curious sight.

As the strange men ambled by, Joetta moved to the back door and gave a friendly wave. Was this not something, these young men leaving their families? The sight set her back as there had only been talk about a war, without any actual steps taken toward it. What she could not understand was, what good would fighting do for them? They were yeoman farmers too; she could tell by their clothes.

Shaking her head, she went back inside and began slicing fatback. Henry was easily heard through the open window.

"Where y'all headed?"

"Raleigh."

"Shoot. I ain't ever been there. Ain't never been nowhere really, 'cept to town and my grandmother's over to Martin County."

"Me neither. I'll go 'bout anywhere they want for eleven dollars a month.

"I reckon so."

The men finished drinking their water. With a lot of scuffling of their feet and clatter from their accoutrements, they made their way past the fence and out to the plank road put in only a year or so ago. Their boots on the wood sounded steady and strong, not quite marching, but close. It did not go unnoticed by Joetta that Henry watched the men until they disappeared. Only then did he go to the barn to join his father and brother. The entire way, he held his head down like he was apt to do when he was thinking. Before long, he returned, carrying a side of ham.

"Papa said to bring you this."

Joetta pointed to the worktable.

"Thank you. Put it right there."

He set it down, then fiddled with a button on his shirt, obviously wanting to speak. Joetta gave him her attention.

"What is it?"

"Them men that stopped by a little while ago? They're volunteers going to Raleigh."

She played ignorant.

"Oh?"

Henry's voice went soft.

"Wonder what a place like that is like?"

"Like Whitakers, only bigger. More people."

"You been before?"

"Yes, I went to Raleigh a long time ago with my father to see about attending a school called Saint Mary's. He thought education very important, and encouraged us, your aunt Faith and your uncles, Leland and Wilbur, to present ourselves as knowledgeable and be able to articulate our thoughts clearly."

"You didn't go?"

"No, I did not want to be that far from home for so long."

Henry did not meet her gaze directly as he spoke his mind.

"I'd have gone. Grandpa says Papa's got his head up his arse."

Such talk! It was hard to believe he would say such a thing, especially after all the good his father did for them each and every day. She held her temper and spoke quietly.

"Your grandfather should know better, and you ought to know better than to repeat it. If your father does not agree about this war, it does not mean he cannot see what is happening. Do not let your grandfather fill your head with his nonsense." Without giving him a chance to respond, she changed the subject. "Are you going to help plant that field?"

Henry, his mouth curved down, said, "I reckon."

"Then you best get on with it."

Stiff-legged, he went out, crossed the yard, and squeezed through the fence to enter the field where Robert and Ennis had started planting corn. She did not understand him. They all worked so hard, had so much to do, how did he find time to contemplate such topics?

Each day more men began to drift by the farm, dusty booted, and with the well visible it did not necessarily take an invitation for them to stop. They would often hang about the fence until they caught someone's attention, then ask for a drink. Henry, who never seemed to be too far off, would find a way strike up a conversation. Sometimes it was a single person, sometimes they were in twos or threes. Over the course of a few days, Henry distanced himself even more once he started talking to the volunteers. To Joetta, it was as if he was participating in his own secession, one from his family. Robert spent every night out in the barn with him. She was glad the boys were close, as there was hardly a day they had not been side by side since they were born.

The divide within the country grew. Joetta became sad for these men and their intentions. Sad and anxious. Any chance of reconciliation was unlikely given the no concessions, no backing down nature so obvious in the swagger of their walk, the confidence in their mission, and such pugnacious attitudes on display. The constant flow of men coming by the house was not unlike Fishing Creek breaching the embankment after a heavy rain. Like a coming flood, if war swept over the land, it would leave desolation in its wake. These were *her* innermost thoughts, ones she dared not speak about, for saying it might make it true.

A week after the trouble with Henry, the family gathered at the breakfast table in the early morning, everyone except, of course, Henry. Ennis sat at the head of the table and once everyone was seated, he spoke.

"Robert, go get your brother. It's time to put a stop to this foolishness." To Joetta he said, "No more sending food out to him. If he wants to eat, he will have to come to the table."

Mr. McBride interjected. "You can't be letting the boy go hungry. He's got to work."

"No one is letting him go hungry. He can come to the table and eat what he wants."

Robert did not do as he was asked. His eyes remained riveted on his lap, his hands knotted together. A tear fell off his nose. Deep within Joetta came a familiar fear, like when she had started to bleed too early and her stomach would cramp, and she knew. *She knew.* Her voice held a trace of alarm.

"Robert?"

She spoke his name with a knowledge of what he did not want to admit already sinking her heart, even as the words left his mouth.

"He left."

Ennis abruptly jumped up and went out the back door, followed by Mr. McBride. Robert stayed, while Joetta felt as if she was moving in slow motion as she rose from her chair and placed a hand briefly on the back of Robert's bowed head in the lightest of touches. She went to her dish pan where clean, hot water was ready and waiting for the dirty dishes. Her worktable held spilled flour, a crock of lard, the bowls she had used, evidence of her morning's work, including the vegetables she had brought in earlier from the garden. The cheery, colorful pile of greens, yellows, and reds seemed startling to her now, and out of place. These labors, done with ease only moments ago, meant nothing at all as the peace and satisfaction of the day vanished upon hearing those two words.

She was bewildered. The pains she took to make a happy home, to feed them, clothe them, and most importantly, to love them; had none of that made a difference to Henry? Mr. McBride came back in and sat with his hands propped on his thighs, elbows jutted out. He did not speak, which to Joetta was almost as astonishing as Henry taking off. He dumped a good bit of whisky into his cup of coffee. Ennis followed a few minutes later. He sat down and picked up his fork.

Joetta spun around and with presumption, said, "You will go after him."

Ennis began eating his plate of eggs, but at her statement, a rare reaction, shadowlike and foreign, settled over his features. She had seen Ennis truly angry only once before, and that was most recently, with Henry. Without sparing her a glance, his response was unexpected.

"I will not."

Mr. McBride emitted a grunt. That Ennis would disagree shocked her, and she was not sure she heard him correctly. Robert raised his head and reacted outwardly to the emotions she held in, gawking at her, then his father. No one spoke, and the silence that followed was heavy and unnatural for the family. Ennis set his fork down carefully.

"He needs to learn a lesson. They'll send him back when they see he's too young. Let him understand it was his choice, his impetuousness that has made him look the fool."

Joetta folded her arms. Ennis's eyes met hers and she recognized this was one of those rare instances they disagreed. It was not a pleasant realization because this was significant. It was about one of their children, not a farm animal, or the house, or the crops. It was not a quibble about whether to buy materials for more fencing, or whether it was time to move the outhouse, for the love of God. It was about *Henry*. Their firstborn. Ennis diverted his attention to Robert, who, under that unwavering stare broke down bit by bit, struggling over his loyalty to his brother and the respect he held for his father.

Before his father could speak, he declared, "He'll know I told."

Ennis said, "Do you think what he did is right?"

Robert sat a moment, then shook his head.

"Well, then?"

Robert would not look at any one of them as he explained how Henry had been quietly, subtly preparing to leave for several days. That he had snuck small amounts of food here and there, nothing that could be detected. He took the blanket he had been using in the barn, his rifle, and the water bag they used for hunting trips, essentially putting together some semblance of what the volunteers carried when they rambled by their house. He swore Robert to secrecy, taking the pocketknife he spent so much time sharpening, and cutting Robert's finger, then his own. Robert held his cut finger up, the wound yet tender looking.

"We swore on our blood! Now I broke my promise!"

Ennis went back to eating his eggs. Mr. McBride looked everywhere except at her, or his son. Joetta was managing a rampage of emotions. It would do no good to blame him and his incessant talk of war, and of being a soldier, and whatever other nonsense he had filled Henry's head with. The door off the kitchen stood open to the backyard, and beyond it lay the cleared land. She pictured three figures working the acreage. How was she going to keep herself from agonizing about where he was, how he was? These worries had started already, along with her fervent wish for Ennis to go find him and bring him home. His refusal would only fester within her and grow more urgent as time passed.

Somehow, that first day, the family worked. Joetta merely tried to get through it. She was mechanical in her actions, sometimes forgetting what she had been doing, and if someone spoke to her, it was doubtful she heard it. They came in for a noon dinner she did not remember preparing, and the same with supper. All she wanted was to go to bed so it could be the next day, and her hope would be renewed. If Ennis would change his mind, or if Henry came back of his own volition after having a change of heart, all the better. Her imagination gave her the happiness of such a return again and again, yet each time she allowed a moment's pause to look down the lane, it remained empty. Finally, she was in bed, and as she lay in the dark, she was painfully aware of Ennis and his own unnatural silence.

Chapter 4

She was often brought out of sleep throughout the long nights, and when she swung her feet over the side of the bed each morning, she was confronted by one singular thought: *Henry is gone.* In hindsight, the first day had been the easiest to get through because she felt more secure in her optimism. As more time passed, she tried to shore herself up, remembering how she had fared after her miscarriages. She had felt this kind of hurt before, this sense of loss, and she had withstood it, but this, this was different.

When she had detected the first spark of a presence deep within that had been Henry, she and Ennis had been so happy. After Henry's birth, and a few months later, she was again pregnant. Soon she could tell, however, even before her bleeding began, she had lost that one. Three years after came Robert. She lost another when he was a year old, and again, a particular mood had descended, telling her by a sense of nothingness. Her last one she had barely been able to get out of the bed. The morning sickness was so debilitating, along with headaches, she had wished to die. Unable to keep food down, she lost weight and at five months, her body gave up trying to hold on to the small life within her. The little girl slipped in and out of their lives without ever taking a breath. Joetta had held her cupped in the palms of her hands, unable to comprehend such perfection already in place.

After she had lost the first, her mother came to her, held her hand, and offered a bit of wisdom. "When they're not fit to survive outside the womb, the Lord takes them, and He always sees fit to give something back."

She had suffered three losses, and had distinctly thought, *no more, no more*, especially after the little girl, where she considered she might never be the same again. As if God heard her plea, there were no more pregnancies. After she healed, she often sat in a certain spot on the embankment of Fishing Creek, where the solitude she needed to cope eventually restored her. Henry's disappearance created that same tiredness, cloying and unrelenting, while settling into her bones as if it would stay. His leaving was more upsetting. She had held him against her chest, felt the pull of his mouth on her nipple, and had sniffed the soft sprouts of hair on his head while smiling at his bandy little legs as he kicked. She had marveled at how fast he grew.

After fifteen years, she could read his expressions, gauge his moods, and though he had changed in the past year, he had still been her Henry. That was why this felt bigger, more significant, because it was his choice. Did he not love his parents? Her? How could he have left? Robert, with his sad eyes and quiet sorrow, trudged along doing his work. Then, there was Ennis. It soon became clear where they each stood with regard to Henry. His attitude was quite different. Whereas she, Robert, and Mr. McBride, why yes, even Mr. McBride, were distressed, Ennis grew more angry by the day.

On the fourth morning, she went out into the yard where Robert was brushing Pal before his father put the harness on him. She waited a moment, her instincts telling her to test the atmosphere before approaching the subject again. There had been not one word out of her husband's mouth about Henry since he took off. This incensed Joetta. For the first time since she could remember, she was angry with him and resented his lack of concern. Mr. McBride sometimes speculated out loud about where he might be at any given moment, and Robert had mumbled a few things here and there, mostly about his remorse for not telling them what Henry had been planning to do. But Ennis? His distancing grew by the day. She followed him around the barn as he gathered up what he wanted to take to the field, biding her time.

Finally, she spoke. "Ennis. It is the fourth day."

Her emotions took over as she braced for his answer. She knotted her fingers together, stared at him with a mother's yearning. Waiting was so hard. She wanted Henry back, and right away.

"I know how long it's been. When he comes home, he'll be singing a different tune. You wait and see."

She went hot all of a sudden and words bubbled up from deep within, like water in that old black pot of hers about to boil over. She spoke loudly, in an uncommon outburst.

"I cannot believe you! What if he does not come home, what then?"

"I'll go look for him after he's had time to get there and get back home."

"That is eight days! He could get into trouble, or even get accepted because no telling who is making those decisions, or where this is all going."

She tried to calm down, her voice shrill with a combination of anguish and ire. She never spoke this way, and

Ennis's calm made her feel foolish. She held her arms rigid at her sides, hands in fists. He tried to hold them and she jerked away from him.

"Joetta. Listen to me. It'll take four days for him to get to Raleigh, which means he's there now. They'll ask him some questions, and you know Henry was never the best fibber. They will point him back in the direction he came."

"You cannot be sure of that."

"If he isn't sent home, whatever goes on won't hardly last longer than a blink. I think it's a bunch of a bluster, and bravado, each side waiting to see what the other's willing to do. They're dancing right now, circling the floor. Let him get a taste of his decision. He has to learn."

She did not understand how he could be so apathetic, how he could go about his day as if Henry had only gone into town without permission. A few feet away, under the shade of a beech tree sat Mr. McBride, the only sound coming from him the occasional ping as he spit tobacco juice into a can. He was doing the one thing Joetta found surprising, a talent that, had she not known him, would give her a different perspective of the man she knew him to be. He whittled on a chunk of wood, the shavings littering his pants and the ground around his chair. Every now and again, he stopped and studied the piece. This loud, obnoxious man carved the most beautiful little birds and was quite good at it. He paused in his work, sat back, and brushed his pants off. His voice carried over to them, and to Joetta's amazement, he actually sided with her.

"You ought to go on and do as she says and look for that boy. No telling what kinds a trouble he might get into, and I ain't saying he'd be the one causing it."

Ennis gave his father a dubious look.

"Seems to me he might still be here if not for all your fancy talk about how great that life is."

"You can't be blaming me. How was I to know he'd take off?"

Ennis said, "I told you to stop, but no. You kept on with your half-truths and outright lies. He took it to heart and decided to go see it for himself. That's how I see it."

Mr. McBride's whole body stiffened, and he grabbed his cane to steady himself as he stood.

"I'll be damned if you'll blame me. Ain't nobody told that boy to go nowheres. He made his own mind up, and that's all there is to say about it."

"You told him farming wasn't worth his time. Not unless he held slaves. And that wasn't the whole of it."

"How was I supposed to know he had such a hankering for something more than field work? Hell, it ain't so bad. Maybe he'll get a taste of whatever's eating at him, and he'll be doing his work all humble-like once he's back. Maybe you'll be thanking me for opening his eyes."

Joetta was already thinking on every possibility of what could go wrong.

She said, "If he isn't maimed, or killed."

Both men stopped talking and stared at her, until Ennis waved in a nonchalant manner.

"Aw hell. He won't be up to par quick enough for them to use him in any particular manner. Might have him peeling taters."

His voice faltered at the end. She heard it, and he knew she had. She turned on her heels and went back to the house. If he would not go after him, by God she would. She would give it one more day, two at the most. She really had no idea how she would accomplish this, but she would certainly try.

News of Henry's disappearance made it to the Caldwells and brought Bess to the house the next day. Joetta suspected Mr. McBride had talked when he went into town.

He announced his decision to walk to Whitakers right after breakfast the day before, now here was Bess, wearing one of those fancy cockades. She had always been one to like a cause, particularly one such as this. It gave her the chance to mingle with the likes of the well-to-do Hammonds and the Garners, while it rankled Joetta because their need for slaves had created this debacle in the first place. She swung her door wide in greeting.

Bess said, "I'm terribly sorry about Henry. Any word yet?"

Joetta shook her head. Even with Bess's obvious position, she was appreciative of her visit. A distraction was called for, and this would do.

She said, "Come and have coffee. I have only just made some."

They went to the sitting room, where two chairs on either side of a small wooden table offered a nice quiet place to talk. Joetta brought in the cups and the small porcelain pot she saved for company. Both women sat for a bit, sipping the hot liquid carefully in their usual companionable stillness. Eventually Bess's eyes scanned Joetta's person. With one finger tapping the cockade perched beneath her chin, she approached a subject only briefly discussed in the past.

"These are quite nice, don't you think? I made a couple extra so as to match my dresses. I've brought one for you. I fashioned it myself. The green is quite lovely, and I added the pine cone there off to the side, do you see? Oh dear, Joetta. Henry shouldn't have run off in such a manner, but at least you can show your support for him."

Poor Bess had no idea how the cockade, not only for its symbolism but for what it had caused between Ennis and Henry, would result in Joetta's firm refusal. Joetta was certain, notwithstanding it being the reason for Henry's leaving, she would have rejected it anyway. She set her cup down.

"Thank you. I choose not to wear one."

Bess drew back, eyes serious.

"Whyever not?"

Joetta put her hands in her lap and looked out the window. This visit might not be such a good idea after all.

Bess prodded her for a reply. "Joetta, you and Ennis, certainly you all are supporting the Confederacy? You're not Southern Unionists, are you?"

Joetta challenged her friend.

"Of course not, but what reason is there for us to be involved? There is not one that I can think of. We work our land to feed ourselves and our livestock. We ask for nothing more, only to live our lives as we see fit."

Bess leaned back, flummoxed. She picked up her cup and took a sip before setting it back down with a clatter.

"We can't have those Yanks telling us what's what, now can we? It could change everything."

"For who? Certainly not us." Joetta pointed toward the window and the door she had left open to allow a bit of a breeze. "What do you see, Bess?"

"I know what you're getting at, but it's unseemly if you think about it. It's about more than just slavery, as I'm sure you know. It's about you, me, and . . ." She stopped.

She stared down at her hands, then furtively peeked about the room as if reassuring herself they were alone. Her manner reflected the need for privacy. Voice hushed, Bess leaned in toward Joetta.

"Are you not afraid of being savaged by"—and here her face flushed deep red like she was working out in the sun—"one of *them*?"

She sat back, flicked her fan open, and waved it about her face as Joetta contemplated her friend, eyebrows arched.

"Honestly, Bess. You remind me of Mr. McBride and some of his outlandish thoughts. Have you ever seen such behavior? Even a hint of it?"

Bess drew in her breath, and Joetta was not sure she fully let it out as she gathered herself to leave. Joetta stood too, and Bess scurried toward the door quickly, the hem of her dress swinging like a head shaking no. Before she went out, she wagged her finger in Joetta's direction.

"Mark my words. This will not come to any good, and the more of us that stick together, the better off we'll be for it."

If Bess wanted to think like this, Joetta could not dissuade her. The best way to handle the awkwardness was to remain silent. Bess adjusted this and that, as if waiting for Joetta to concede, before finally tugging on her driving gloves. She whooshed out of the house, climbed onto her buckboard, clucked her tongue at the horse, and off she went without saying goodbye or giving Joetta her customary "so long for now" wave. Joetta remained in the doorway, arms crossed, watching as the wagon grew smaller until it was nothing more than a dot.

After a moment, she glanced about the empty room. There sat their two cups, signs of company, but the usual good feelings after such a visit were overshadowed by a sense of loss. Bess too? First Henry, now perhaps her friend. As she contemplated what had taken place, she wondered if she and Ennis were the only ones who felt this way. She did not want to lose Bess's friendship. They had done so much together over the years, from raising children to helping one another on their respective farms and in the community. Joetta's eyes filled, surprising her. Quickly she wiped her cheeks. Enough of that.

She gathered the cups and took them into the kitchen for washing. Between Bess and Mr. McBride, soon everyone would know. Joetta could not allow herself to worry about what others thought. It was their business and theirs alone. In the kitchen she set the cups in her wash basin and found herself growing upset again. This was ridiculous. She was not one to cry, and her sadness left her wondering why Bess's reaction weighed so heavily. She heated water while she thought of their conversation and all of a sudden, she understood. Bess appeared unwilling to tolerate this difference between them, and would permit it to ruin their friendship, which was as old as Joetta's marriage. The truth was, she was as stubborn as Bess. She did not plan to change either, and that was just the way of it.

Chapter 5

Back when they had lived with Mr. McBride in the beginning of their marriage, when the building of their home took longer than anticipated, Joetta's character was sorely tested. She had always been the patient sort, understanding and without complaint, yet there were limits to what one could tolerate. Ennis believed it would still be at least six months before they could move in, and his father's response, intended to suggest generosity, instead created a whole new level of anxiety within her.

He said, "Hell, the framework needs to cure at least a year, and what's the hurry anyway?"

Her eyes grew huge at that, but her back was to the men, so she was giving this alarmed look only to the butter she had turned out of a wooden mold onto a plate. The yellow square had butterflies on top to coincide with the butterfly-like fluttering in her stomach set off by his comment. She wished to ignore the idea of another whole year in such close proximity with Ennis's father, whose personality proved quite challenging in more ways than one, while her mother-in-law was so quiet, she sometimes forgot she was there. Joetta picked up a knife to smooth out the sides, wishing she could do likewise to her frayed nerves. An idea struck, and without hesitation, and with some urgency, she had turned to Ennis.

"What if I helped?"

She did not think she had sounded any particular way until Ennis shot a questioning look at her, coupled with the shift of his gaze to his father and then back to her. She quickly put her attention back on the butter, finishing with a final swipe down one side before covering it with a cloth. Mrs. McBride nodded at her handiwork. At least she approved of Joetta's efforts. Their marriage had been so new, and Joetta had not wanted it to begin with any hint of criticism of his family. After all, they had been living under his parents' roof for only the past few months. Nothing more was said about how long it might take to cure the wood, but this set in motion how they came to meet their neighbors.

Ennis disappeared one afternoon, and the next day, Thomas Caldwell and Hugh Brown arrived to help. Mr. McBride loved having more people to boss around, and he enjoyed judging their work while pointing out what they were doing wrong, mostly everything. Meanwhile, Mrs. McBride, Joetta, Bess, and Mary cooked in the shade of the trees, and the group enjoyed meals while getting to know one another. Finally, the house was completed, and they moved in. In return, Ennis helped Thomas add stalls to his barn and assisted Hugh in clearing another couple acres of his land to expand his crop field. These neighborly endeavors created the foundation for their relationships. The men worked, and the women talked about having babies, their families, and most anything that came to mind.

The bonds formed in those early years had always seemed

indestructible to Joetta, but now with Bess, she was not so sure. Not long after Bess's visit, Mary Brown came in a plume of dust, riding high on her rickety buckboard, pulled by an old mule that looked as decrepit as the old oak in front of Joetta's house. For the first time in days, she smiled.

"Mary Brown, you are a sight for sore eyes."

Mary stopped in the shade, climbed down, and brushed off the front of her madder print skirt.

"I'm a sight for sure. I believe I brought most of the road with me. My word, we could use some rain."

She sneezed as if to emphasize the point. Mary was a tall woman and filled with energy. She bounded up the steps and grabbed Joetta in a big hug. When she let go of her, she kept her hands on Joetta's shoulders and leaned back to survey her friend's face.

"How are you?"

Joetta's eyes quickly filled with tears and her voice shook as she gave an honest answer. "As well as can be. It is hard. I keep thinking how young he is. Undoubtedly those in charge will see this."

Mary patted Joetta's arm with one hand and fanned her face with the other.

"I think you're right."

"Oh, my manners. Come in, I have the very thing you need on a day like today."

Joetta led Mary into the kitchen and got two glasses off the shelf. She poured a pale brown liquid into each until they were full. Mary had flopped down onto a chair in a rather unladylike manner, still fanning herself, but sat up when she saw what Joetta poured.

"Switchel!"

Joetta smiled.

"I made it this morning."

Mary took a big swallow and closed her eyes.

Before she could respond, the uneven pace of her father-in-law's steps came in a thump, shuffle, thump. Mr. McBride gestured in the direction they faced.

"He went to get the boy?"

Joetta, troubled over the way Ennis departed and Robert's comment, spoke her mind for once.

"Henry. His name is Henry. And this is Robert. Stop calling them boy."

Mr. McBride harrumphed and mumbled a thing or two, which she ignored. Ennis's anger at Henry had spilled over to her, and now Robert was upset. She could not blame him, she was too. If Ennis thought they should let Henry suffer from his decisions, she would rather it be over anything other than what Ennis had chosen to make a stand on. Cursing. Drinking. Gambling. Lying. Those, while not ideal, would not create such pain and disquiet. She had no choice but to get through the days until they came home. She looked down and became aware of her state of undress, her bare feet. This was most unseemly, even while Mr. McBride had not noticed. He rubbed his belly, his expression inscrutable.

She said, "Let me get dressed, and we will have something to eat before we get started on work."

Robert said, "I'm not hungry."

Mr. McBride was in the same frame of mind.

"I'll just have coffee. I ain't much for eating nothing this morning."

Despite what they said, Joetta was determined to keep everything as normal as possible. She hurried into the house and at the doorway to the bedroom she stopped. Though Ennis had left only moments before, his few items stored neatly around the room gave her a longing and heartache that felt centuries old. The indentation from his body was in the mattress, as was the imprint of his head on the pillow.

She lifted it and breathed in deep before carefully placing it back onto the sheet.

As she dressed, she thought the best thing to do was stay busy. She would work hard, so she could sleep soundly at night, and before she knew it, they would be home. She would be fine. *They* would be fine. She repeated this to herself until the reality of what might happen crept in, unwanted thoughts she could not prevent. She wanted to sink into oblivion and stay there, unaware of what was before her, her days empty of Ennis and Henry.

Robert called to her from the other room. "Ma."

Joetta brushed her hands down the length of her dress. She pulled on her shoes and buttoned them up. Ridiculous thoughts. No more of those. Now was not the time to succumb to self-pity, or poor thinking. She replied, "Coming," and prepared herself to set an example of confidence and strength, to act as if it were any other ordinary day.

Chapter 6

Joetta did work hard, attempting to ensure their days went along as usual. She soon found the more time she was required to spend in the fields, the more difficult this became. Mr. McBride did not do much except critique her exertions, making comments about crooked rows, and the like. Specific tasks normally maintained for each day of the week to manage her household, along with the everyday work of hauling water, keeping a fire at the ready in the cookstove, floors swept, and the house in some semblance of order, slowly disintegrated. The first Sunday without Ennis, she concluded their morning worship would not be one of these casualties.

They ate a quick breakfast of corn bread in buttermilk and though she did not much feel like it, she went into the bedroom to get ready. She wanted to look her best, to look able and proficient, so she sat down in front of her dresser with the looking glass, given as a wedding gift from her parents. She dipped a cloth into the basin of cool water, wiped her face, neck, and arms, but she could do nothing

to diminish the look of unease. She picked up her Sunday
dress, a madder dyed calico print, sniffing it before accepting it was not as fresh as she would have liked. It would
have to do with some toilet water, used liberally. She did
have clean undergarments at least. And thank goodness she
had washed her hair a couple weeks before. She patted the
sides, ensuring they were smooth before donning her bonnet and gloves. She picked up her small parasol, and that
completed her preparations.

Robert came down the steps, and she met him in the
hallway with what she trusted was a bright smile.

"Ready?"

He gave her a gloomy stare and pulled at his shirt, which
Joetta noticed with regret looked dingy. His hair had not
been brushed either, but she did not reprimand his obvious lack of effort. They were each doing the best they
could. As he hitched Pal to the wagon and Joetta stood
on the front porch watching, she prayed he was not going to become like Henry, silent and brooding. Perhaps
church was the very thing they needed. She looked forward to a day relatively free of work, and she was anxious
to see Bess. Maybe they could set their differences aside
because they now had this one thing in common: their
boys were gone. She would get to see Mary, and Hugh, as
well as the others she had come to know, even the rich Mr.
Wilmot Poole and his aloof, sickly acting wife, Clovis, and
their thirteen children. Thirteen! It could hardly be imagined, but so it was, and surely the Lord's blessing was upon
them.

Mr. McBride hobbled toward them, his overall appearance not much better. Feeling ashamed of their bedraggled
state, Joetta almost changed her mind then and there. She
dawdled with her gloves as she mulled it over, wondering
how they might appear to the others. Had anyone else suf-

fered such an unfortunate outcome before the effort had really started? If so, they would clearly understand. How they looked was one thing, but what of their views? Of this, she was most curious. Mr. McBride would not have a problem as his opinion was as common as dirt. Now was as good a time as any to find out, she supposed.

She got in the wagon beside Robert and Mr. McBride dragged himself up beside her, and off they went. Before long, he was pointing at the field of the Browns' farm.

"Look at them straight rows. They know what they're doing."

Robert exhaled, and Joetta tapped his arm, noticing her blistered hands felt especially tender today. She had been obliged to hide their condition with gloves. It took them about fifteen minutes to arrive at the small church, and Felton Newell, one of the church elders, came forward to place a wood stool to step out on. Mr. McBride went first.

"Felton, that's mighty kind of you. This old knee of mine's a real bother."

Elder Newell's voice quivered given he was afflicted with the shaking palsy.

"Mr. Mc–Mc–Bride, g–good to see you. Mrs. Mc–Mc– Bride. R–Robert."

Elder Newell stood with Joetta and Mr. McBride while Robert guided Pal over to his usual spot in the shade of a sweetgum tree along with a couple horses, a mule, and wagons like theirs.

Joetta said, "How are you, Mr. Newell?"

"F–fair, I'd say. Y–you?"

She smiled, her answer whitewashed. "Fine, thank you."

Mr. McBride interrupted with a question. "Felton, what you reckon Preacher Rouse will talk on today?"

"His m–message is on r–reliability, how w–we d–depend on o–one another."

Mr. McBride cut a plug of tobacco and tucked it in his mouth.

"What's your view about what's going on?"

Elder Newell scratched his head slowly as he answered, "It w-wouldn't be right to l-let them ride r-roughshod over us, now w-would it?"

Mr. McBride clapped a hand on the Elder's shoulder. "No, it wouldn't."

"S-some ladies are f-forming a sewing group sp-specifically for m-making socks to send the m-men. B-Bess Caldwell is h-heading that up."

Mr. McBride said, "Now she knows how to support a cause."

He gave Joetta a crafty look before he began his hop-step toward the church doors, not bothering to wait on her or Robert. She did not care. She only wanted to sit and listen quietly to someone else for a change. Elder Newell offered a polite nod before he hurried off to help someone else.

Joetta clicked the parasol open, and she and Robert began ambling toward the small white building, along with the others. Built by early members of the congregation one hundred years before, she and a few other lady members, including Mary and Bess, had been the ones to plant new flowers around the foundation some years ago. The steeple, set against a blue sky, needed a paint job, but the windows sparkled, and the flowers were bright and colorful.

She entered the sanctuary and to her left were Bess, Thomas, and of course, Harold. If Bess noticed her, she did not acknowledge it. She stood near the pew where Vesta Fern sat, chatting with her while Thomas talked to Vesta's husband, Zebulon. Mary and Hugh were already seated with Mary's head bent toward her husband, talking quietly. There was Samuel Spivey, who owned the general store, and Alice Atwater, who ran her late husband's milliner shop and wore a rather fetching little black hat adorned with one of those troublesome cockades.

Joetta glanced about and began to notice most everyone had one pinned to their clothing. She could not tell if Mary did because she could see only the side of her face and her bonnet. The cockade's popularity proved she and Ennis were in the minority. Joetta tipped her head in acknowledgment to those who looked her way, and later on, when the mistake of coming was clear, she would recall there had been no return nod, nor even a greeting. She would remember in vivid sharpness the subtle shift of eyes downward so as to not have to speak, the slightest nudge of elbows, the whispers as she went to their usual place. Robert slid in beside her. A couple rows up, Harold Caldwell's intense stare caught her attention. He was too obvious to miss as he faced the opposite direction of his father, Thomas, and Bess, who had finished speaking to Vesta and now sat beside her husband. Robert thumbed through the hymnal. She nudged his arm.

"Harold looks to be trying to get your attention."

Robert lifted his head and gave a small wave. Harold did nothing except continue to stare. Robert waved again. Nothing from Harold. Joetta glared at the other boy whose eyes slid to hers and back to Robert. He fingered the cockade affixed to his shirt, challenging them. She leaned in and spoke to her son.

"Pay him no mind."

Harold continued to stare rudely, a smug look about him that made Joetta want to march down the aisle and give his ear a good twist. Robert sat back and stared at the pew in front of them. Preacher Rouse entered the sanctuary and quietly waited as the congregation settled down. Bess finally tapped Harold, and only then did he face forward. She did not bother to see who he was staring at, but Joetta believed she knew. Preacher Rouse's eyes circled the sanctuary. Was it her imagination, or did they rest on her a bit longer? All went along as usual in those few moments at least, and Joetta relaxed and began to enjoy the service. The hymn was one of her favorites, "Come Thou Fount of Every Blessing." She sang, and this always thrilled her for some reason, the voices coming together in harmony and friendship.

Once the congregation settled back in their seats, Preacher Rouse began his message. Joetta was poised to listen, to be fulfilled, and to renew her internal strength. She wanted to hear something inspirational, significant, to help sustain her as she returned home to face a house with half her family gone. She sought peace and comfort, what she had received here many times before. At first, Preacher Rouse talked about dependability, the need for constancy in trying times. Soon after came a clever twist that took her a moment to realize the sermon had wandered from its original intent. Or, so it sounded to her.

"But what if you find someone you once thought loyal, now untrustworthy?"

His gaze circled the room and when he came to her, it most certainly did linger before moving on.

"What if that once-faithful servant begins to falter, to turn against the flow of righteousness? What are we to think then? And perhaps that individual even stubbornly refuses to acknowledge right over wrong?"

He lowered his voice, leaned over and pinned them with a hellfire look as he recapped the story of Judas Iscariot. He posed pointed questions about what to do when one in their midst was lost, perhaps on the wrong path, and how it took only one to weaken all. They must be persuaded to come back into the fold, to a clearer way of thinking, he declared, pounding his fist dramatically on the wooden stand before him. There was shifting on the benches and mumbling while Joetta held quite still. Mr. McBride was to her left, and without moving her head, she dared a peek at him. He sat with his arms crossed, nodding. Perhaps she was being overly sensitive. Maybe because of her own troublesome times, she was misreading today's message and feeling defensive given the turmoil she had experienced lately.

Joetta decided it was her state of mind, and that she was taking too much to heart. Preacher Rouse then closed his sermon with a new addition to the program. He began to call out a list of members alphabetically who had volunteered, asking they receive the church's prayers. Benjamin Caldwell's name rang out, and Bess smiled her approval and looked about with pride as Thomas Caldwell stood abruptly and shouted, "I would leave tomorrow, by God's grace, and join the fight with my boy if I could!"

There were "hear, hears" and "Amen, brother," and "I'd be right behind you!"

His eyes held a fierceness Joetta had not seen in him before. Perhaps he was so staunch because it met Bess's approval. Preacher Rouse raised a hand for quiet and continued. The list went on and Joetta was suddenly startled at the pronouncement of Henry's and Ennis's names. Robert stared at her stupefied. She gripped her hands together, twisting her handkerchief, and stood. Somehow she found her voice.

"Their names should not be on that list."

Preacher Rouse stopped reading.

"You wish they not be prayed for?"

"Of course, but . . ." and she stopped.

There was not a cough, a rustle of clothing, or the creak of a pew. It was as if the congregation held themselves as one entity, waiting and wondering what she might say next. Preacher Rouse came down from the pulpit with a questioning look.

"Sister?"

"They should not be on it. Someone"—she looked at Mr. McBride, who sat red-faced and sweating—"filled Henry's head with nonsense." Her hand trailed up to her bonnet, to the ribbon under her chin, which suddenly felt too tight. "I am sure it is common knowledge by now he ran off hoping to volunteer." Bess flipped her fan open and fluttered it about her face furiously, and even so, Joetta persisted. "Ennis went after him. I expect them to return home."

Murmuring filled the church.

Preacher Rouse said, "You're saying they have not volunteered?"

"Ennis and I . . . well, no, he had no intentions of volunteering. Henry, as I've said, was ill-informed and like any other boy at this age, prone toward impulsive and reckless actions. My husband is only going to find him, and when he does, he will return home."

That same harmony found in song began again, a rising murmur by a congregation put off by these remarks. Joetta overheard "shame" and "disloyal" and "must be Unionists." She grew uncomfortable. Every eye was on her, and most were not friendly. She moved from the pew.

"Come, Robert."

She hurried down the aisle, escaping outside into the sunshine, and she did not stop until she was by the wagon. It was hot and sticky already, and the low hum of a few bees circling the roses that crawled along the fence reminded her of the humans buzzing about inside. Robert was by her side seconds later.

"What about Grandpa?"

"We will wait."

He looked back at the church.

"Seems like it would be easier to just go along with everyone else."

Joetta stared at him long and hard until he dropped his eyes.

"They are welcome to their war, but we do not have to be a part of it."

Robert kicked a wagon wheel, the action revealing his anger.

"But we already are. Because of Henry, and now because of you."

"What?"

"We *are* part of it, in spite of what you say."

"Robert. Henry does not know what he is doing, and your father did not leave to volunteer. If he cannot find your brother, he will be back."

Without responding, he led Pal onto the path and stayed by the animal's head. The church bell rang and the congregation filed out. Some stared in their direction, like the Caldwells and the Ferns. Mr. McBride drifted among them, lifted his hands a time or two and shook his head like he did not know what to make of what happened. Observing this, Joetta became angry. Let them be confounded, let them think what they wanted. She climbed onto the wagon seat, and Robert did as well. She tried to talk to him.

"You do not think your father should have gone after Henry?"

She was talking to the back of his head and unable to hear what he said. She gave up and watched the congregation socializing. It was quite animated, with a lot of gesturing and pointing at her. Mr. McBride finally broke free and arrived at the wagon out of breath. With some effort, he pulled himself into the seat. As soon as he was situated, Robert flicked the reins. No one spoke as they began the ride home, though Mr. McBride was undoubtedly agitated by the way he kept shifting about on the seat and mumbling as if he was responding to some internal discussion with himself. It got the best of him halfway there.

"Now, why'd you have to go and say all that?"

"You mean the truth?"

"I don't like them thinking like they are right now. That we're turncoats."

"I am quite sure they know exactly where *you* stand. You need not worry."

"Not worry? I worry what you will bring on the rest of us with this obstinate opinion of yours."

"It is not only mine. It is Ennis's as well, and no telling who else, they just will not say."

Sitting between the two of them made for an uncomfortable ride home. When they arrived, Mr. McBride hopped down and without offering her any assistance, made a slow trek to his cabin. She guessed he did not want Sunday dinner, and she was not going to ask. If he wanted to eat, he was well aware food had been prepared.

With a cheerful tone that took some effort, she turned to Robert and said, "Let us take our dinner to Fishing Creek and have a nice afternoon there. We can have a little picnic, and you can fish, and I will bring a book. Would that not be nice?"

Robert slapped the reins back and forth against his leg, his eyes on the ground.

She said, "Robert? Would you want to go fishing?"

"I don't think so."

"Oh."

He finished undoing the harness and led Pal out to the pasture. Troubled, Joetta went inside and changed into her everyday dress. Despite what he said, she entered the kitchen and put together a small basket with food. Within minutes, she was ready. Back outside, she looked around and could not see him anywhere. She crossed the yard and entered the barn.

"Robert?"

Nothing. She waited a moment listening, sensing she was being watched. Maybe he was in the loft, looking down on her. That made her look up. It was eerily quiet. She went back out. She looked around and the fields were empty. Finally, she went to Mr. McBride's cabin and knocked on his door. After a few seconds he yanked it open and stared at her grumpily.

"What is it?"

"Is Robert with you?"

Mr. McBride leaned against the doorframe. "Nope."

"You have not seen him?"

"I said no. Why?"

"He . . ."

"He what?"

"He is not happy with me."

Mr. McBride's eyebrows went up in an exaggerated manner.

"Well now. Looks like you done gone and pissed off not only most of the good folks in town but your entire family to boot."

He certainly knew how to rile her. Once again, she defended herself and Ennis.

"You never talked about how grand it was to be in a war? Or how farming is not a good enough life? Henry gathered all that on his own, is that right? You agreed Ennis ought to go after him too, or did you forget that? That is not volunteering. I did nothing more than set the matter straight."

"You did a little more than that."

He shut the door in her face. Fine. She would have the afternoon to herself. It had been so long since she had done anything like this, she did not know how she felt about it, part of her relishing the idea, the other part of her guilty. She kept to the edges of the field where it was easier to walk, and when she came to the creek she stopped to watch the water. It trickled softly, and it was certainly cooler under the trees, as well as calming and peaceful. Precisely what she needed. She began to think this is where they should have come instead of church. She sat down and even removed her shoes and socks to dip her toes in the water.

It turned out to be so relaxing she stayed as long as possible and did not start back home until the sun started to set. As she made her way there, she hurried along, suddenly anxious about the time she had been gone. She came through the field and when she was past the fence, she spied Mr. McBride sitting outside on the small porch of his cabin, a dark lump rocking back and forth. She stopped and called out, "Would you like something to eat?"

He pushed himself up from the old broken-down caneback rocking chair and tottered down the steps.

When he reached her side, he said, "I don't see how you could go off for the afternoon by yourself. It ain't suitable."

"Well, it suited me fine."

He spit in reply. She was in a better mood and feeling magnanimous, even if he was not.

"Come on to the house and I will fix you something. I believe there might be some ham with brown sugar glaze."

She went across the yard and there sat Robert on the back steps, his expression as foul as his grandfather's. She took stock of his clothes, covered in leaves and mud stains.

"Where were you this afternoon?"

He twitched a shoulder. Like Henry, Robert was revealing a new side, one that was disconcerting and out of character for him. He got to his feet, and as his father had taught him, he waited until she went into the house. As she went by him, she wanted to reach out, smooth down the cowlick on his forehead he had had since birth, but was quite sure he would not have tolerated that from her, not right now. Thirty minutes later, they sat at the supper table, Robert and Mr. McBride eating fried potatoes and ham as if there was no tomorrow. Maybe it had done them some good for her to not be so available. She certainly knew it had served her well.

The next day, the grueling work began again. Robert took his time hitching Pal up to the plow, despondent and silent. Joetta concentrated on what lay ahead, not her son's mood. After an hour of work, she lifted her head from chopping weeds. Pal stood in the middle of a row, head down, switching his tail against the flies and gnats. Robert was nowhere to be seen. She swiped off her forehead and did a slow turn, scanning the field. She did not see him. Mr. McBride sat in his usual spot in the shade, his head lolling as he slept. She walked to the end of her row and searched the woods. Panic went through her. What if he had done the same as Henry?

She made herself return to her work, and went at the weeds again with the hoe. She did several more rows and stopped. Poor Pal flicked his tail and stomped a hoof. Still no Robert. Joetta tossed the hoe aside and went to the plow. She threw the reins over her shoulders and began to cut a furrow. The mule was eager to move, having waited patiently all that time. She kept going until the sun was highest in the sky and it was time for noon dinner. Mr. McBride woke up and stretched as she went by him. He followed her to the house, where she pulled a pan of cold corn bread off the stove and put the pitcher with sorghum on the table. Mr. McBride complained about there being no meat.

"Corn bread and syrup is all?"

He sat at the kitchen table drumming his fingers while wrinkling his nose.

Joetta said, "Blame Robert. He took off, and I do not have time to cook *and* do the field work."

Mr. McBride flopped into a chair and begrudgingly waited for her to serve him. Have mercy, she thought, as she cut two big pieces of corn bread, buttered them, poured the syrup, and gave him a glass of buttermilk. He ate like he was terribly hungry, and she felt a pang of remorse. She sat across from him and talked about what she still needed to do. After all, at this point, they apparently only had each other. Mr. McBride chewed, and mumbled here and there in reply. She worked the field by herself that afternoon, stumbling over clumps of dirt and stopping to break them up. She kept at it until she was certain she would drop right there in the rough and uneven row.

She was unhitching Pal when Robert reappeared. He would not look at her, and her earlier fear was quickly replaced by irritation. She stopped what she was doing and made her way to the house without speaking to him. Every single muscle ached, and the skin of her hands was torn and burning. Robert came in moments later as she was her dipping her ruined hands in a basin of water. She controlled her annoyance and spoke quietly.

"You may not want to help because you blame me for your father leaving; however, this is what he has asked of you. Are you going to defy his wishes?"

Robert became motionless, head down, thinking. When he spoke, he remained ill-tempered.

"I'll help. Only because he said to."

"Fine," she said.

It wasn't; it hurt.

Chapter 7

Two weeks had passed since Ennis left, and there was no word from him. In the meantime, she and Robert went out at sunup and labored until sundown. When the day was done, and she wished to sleep through the night, she would startle awake. Once awake, she could not get back to sleep. She missed Ennis's warmth, his breathing, the way he slept on his back, one arm or the other thrown over his head. Her thoughts lingered on how he would sometimes wake her with a light touch, and if only for a few minutes, she was his and his alone. That private time had always suited her even if some women believed it disgraceful, and only bound by a sense of duty would they accept it.

This was why this uncommon disagreement between them worried her to the point she had started back on an old habit from her childhood, one that used to aggravate her mother to no end. Cracking her knuckles. She found herself snapping her joints one way and the other. She would engage in the mindless activity while waiting on pots of water to boil, while she sat on the porch during any rare, idle moment, usually before it was light enough to get into the fields. She could not explain how randomly squeezing and pulling on her fingers gave her relief, it just did.

Robert begrudgingly helped with the work as promised, and she tried not to make anything out of his behavior, so reminiscent of Henry. One morning he rushed to assist her as she struggled to hitch Pal to the implement needed. The mule got antsy and shifted his back end about, and it did not take much to disrupt the whole process. A fledgling thought entered her mind that she needed to be able to do this on her own. It made her wave a hand, stopping Robert from taking over. He stepped back and let her struggle. She succeeded and could not help but feel a bit of self-satisfaction.

As the days slipped by, Mr. McBride's complaints about the lack of attention to meals, and to which Joetta had grown as accustomed as the birdsong overhead, diminished. Oh, he still threw out remarks here and there, but mostly he took to sitting nearby, watching them plow the creeping jenny, cockleburs, and bindweed under. She ignored the pain in her shoulders, back, and hands as she fought to keep the implement straight. For her, it required more strength and determination to keep the point down. She paused now and again to look down the rows, shaking her head in wonder at how Ennis had always made this work look so effortless. Her blisters deepened and bled and even so, she had to keep on because soon the corn would have to be thinned out.

The never-ending cycle of field work faced her each day like the tallest of mountains. Their clothes were not washed regular, and the house was in disarray, taking away from the satisfaction of what she accomplished outside. One hot, sunny day when she was on her way in from the field, the sight of weeds, not to mention the bugs and worms overtaking her kitchen garden, stopped her midstride. Overwhelmed by all she had already done that day, she had the thought, *Let it go.* Seconds later she emitted a sound like one of the hogs. What foolishness. Let it go? She might as well start digging their graves while she had the strength. They needed those vegetables from that garden, and she scolded herself for such nonsensical thinking.

She quickly entered the kitchen and began the tedious process of mixing flour, soda, lard, and a bit of milk to make biscuits. She placed them in a pan to bake and went back out to stare morosely at the pitiful plants. Mumbling a few words of self-recrimination, she first picked a good bowlful of snap beans and field peas. Along with the biscuits and sorghum syrup, it would have to do. She put everything on to cook and went back out to yank more weeds. By the time supper came, Joetta sat, her plate before her. Eating had become something of a chore, and she did it only to keep up her strength and get through the days. There was no enjoyment in it. She merely went through the process of bringing the fork to her mouth, then chewing and swallowing to get it over with.

That night she collapsed into the bed, barely taking the time to wash the grime off, certain she would not be able to keep her eyes open. Despite the fatigue, she lay staring at the ceiling, wide awake. When Ennis was home, they would fall asleep quickly, the day's work giving them peace of mind and bodies that needed rest. The indignant harrumph of a couple of tree frogs nearby flooded the room through the open window. She waited and waited, rolling about this way and that, her unease always intensified at night. She finally drifted off around midnight, or later, and this was evident the next morning when her eyes felt like someone had tossed sand in them.

With every sundown, her apprehension grew. She had to

face the ugly fact Henry must have been allowed to join. As for Ennis, the time he had been gone caused considerable anguish, and she could only pray for his safe arrival back home. She would gladly acknowledge his efforts had been wasted, and while her concern over their firstborn would continue to cause great worry, that Ennis return was tantamount to her peace of mind. She awoke one morning to a dreary, rainy day. It was a relief, a day free of field work, yet it allowed too much thinking. After drifting from one room to the next, she sat at the kitchen table to write her family. She stared for a bit at the sheet of paper, pen in hand, a small pot of ink nearby. She did not have much paper, so she needed to keep it short and factual. After some reflection, she finally dipped the nib into the ink and began. Her first letter was to her mother.

> *Dearest Mother,*
> *I pray all is well as the forces of those who would split the country in two expend great energy to do so. Ennis and I were content tending our farm. Now I must write to share a bit of news, and I wish I could say it was good. I am sorry to trouble you with my worries; however, I feel you must know should outcomes differ than what I pray for. Unduly influenced by Mr. McBride, our Henry yielded to his grandfather's fancy embellishments of war. He took off to volunteer and at the writing of this letter, has been gone a little over a month. Ennis and I did not agree on when was a suitable time to fetch him back home, he thinking to let him manage the penalties of his choice, while I, as any mother, had done nothing except worry. I wanted Ennis to leave immediately. He finally did so on the morning of the tenth day of Henry's absence, albeit not in the most favorable of moods, and now he, himself, has been gone three weeks. I don't know what to think, but I would do some*

*better, perhaps, to hear from you and your thoughts on these
difficulties. Please give my love to all.*
  Your dutiful, loving daughter, Joetta

She wrote to Faith next, a letter that was almost verbatim and the only change to ask after her sister's husband,
Marshall, her nieces, Cora and Ellen, and nephew, Flynn.
Last was to Ennis's eldest sister, Amy, requesting she share
the news with others in his family. Now this was done, her
mood improved a tiny bit. She set the pages flat and blew
on them to dry the ink. She would take them into town
at once, now the rain had stopped. She folded the papers
carefully and put them in the pocket of her dress, then went
outside to ask Robert to hitch up Pal. He did so wordlessly,
and by the time she was on the wagon seat, he was already headed for the barn. She wished to connect with him
somehow and could hear Ennis in her mind, *Leave him be,
he'll come around.* Mr. McBride, having seen her get up into
the wagon, came out and handed her some paper money.

"Get me some chew, if you would."

She stared at the strange-looking bill in her hand.

"That's the new Confederate money. Graybacks, they're
called. Every time I hand over the old money, that's what I
get back in change. Why not, I say. If we're going to have
our own country, we got to have our own currency."

Joetta dropped the bills into her reticule and took up
the reins. As she went along, she assessed her neighbor's
farmland, comparing it against theirs, and was happy to
note no one would notice anything amiss. While it was
hard, she and Robert were keeping up with the work. She
did not want to tarry, but she did not rush either. A slight
breeze blew, fortunately in the right direction, and kept her
from arriving too dusty. In town, the Hammonds' cotton
mill, the hat shop, and Mr. Spivey's store revealed the usual

flurry of activity with patrons and workers going in and out. In front of the store, she climbed down and entered. Familiar smells and sights greeted her. There was a distinctive scent from the ropes hanging on the walls, the pungent odor of tobacco, and the acrid richness of coffee beans. It was dim inside, the only light coming in from a large window beside the entrance.

She approached the counter, and said, "Hello, Mr. Spivey, I need tobacco for Mr. McBride."

"Nice to see you, Mrs. McBride."

Mr. Spivey was middle-aged and wore wire rim glasses. His gray hair had thinned so much on top what little was there around the sides looked to her like a seeded dandelion with the top part missing. She pulled the letters from her pocket as he set the tobacco on the counter.

"Ah, you have mail to send, too, like so many wanting to get messages to their loved ones."

She tried not to sound desperate.

"Is the mail coming in all right? No delays?"

"No delays as of yet, though I fear it will become difficult, at least with regard to correspondence coming from the North."

"Would you check if you have anything for me?"

He sifted through a pile stacked behind the counter. Joetta's heart sped up, and her hands grew sweaty inside her gloves, stinging the torn skin. *Please, please, please.* He found nothing in the first pile and moved to a different area, his hand floating over small wooden boxes before him.

"Well, well. I do have something here."

He handed her an envelope, and she tried not to snatch it, instantly recognizing Ennis's handwriting. The address emblazoned across the front jumped out at her. She placed a hand over her racing heart as she read, *10th Regiment, 1st Artillery, Company D, Camp Mangum, Raleigh, North Carolina.*

Mr. Spivey said, "It appears your Ennis did volunteer after all."

Joetta could not respond. Like she was blind, he pointed out the obvious.

"See? It says 'Soldier's Letter.' They do that so there's no need to worry about trying to find stamps, and whatnot. You'll need to pay for it."

Faintly, she said, "How much?"

"A dime. Anything else?"

As she reached for the coins to pay for the tobacco and the stamp, she remembered the letters she needed to mail.

"I need three stamps, too, please."

She barely heard him when he asked again, "Is there anything else?"

She slowly shook her head, affixed the stamps, and gave the letters and the necessary payment to him. She tucked the tobacco pouch inside her reticule, going through the motions with little, if any, thought. She made her way toward the door when he said something so softly she could not hear it. He gestured for her to come back to the counter. She did so, and leaned in close even though they were the only ones in the store.

"There's talk about what happened at church the other day."

"Yes?"

Mr. Spivey looked uncomfortable.

"I urge your caution, Mrs. McBride."

Joetta gave him a stern look.

"Is someone threatening to do something?"

"No, of course not. It's only, these are strange times, and folks are getting anxious, mistrustful you might say."

For goodness' sake, and really. It was not like she had gone into the church waving a Union flag and calling for the arrest of those in favor of secession.

"How utterly ridiculous, all this talk. It is none of their business."

He gave her a winsome smile.

"Perhaps news of your Ennis will quell their unrest."

"It is of no concern to me what they say, think, or do. They should follow suit."

"Of course. You might be interested to know this, however," and he paused, searching to see if he had raised any curiosity from her.

"Go on."

"Were you aware of states who stayed neutral, well, at least as long as they could? Imagine. They were the Border States, the ones stuck between those who seceded and those who were for the Union."

"Oh?"

"Delaware, Missouri, Maryland, and Kentucky, while Kentucky appears to be holding out. As least as it stands right now. I figured you might like to know it's not an uncommon way to think, though everyone's got their own reasons."

Joetta felt the beginnings of a smile.

"Why, that *is* interesting. I do thank you for sharing," she said.

"You're most welcome."

It was then she noted Mr. Spivey did not have on a cockade. She tipped her head at him politely and left the store. Once in the wagon, she urged Pal home into a brisk pace, and the entire way, Joetta fingered the letter, thrilled Ennis had written, while simultaneously juggling her unease over what his correspondence might contain. There must be a good explanation. Soon she was back at the farm, where Mr. McBride and Robert sat under the oak.

"You get my 'backer?"

She climbed from the wagon seat and, distracted, handed

it over. He kept his hand out and she looked at him puzzled until he prompted her.

"Change?"

"Oh, yes."

She retrieved the coins and he took the time right there to count them.

"You're short."

She had used a dime to pay for Ennis's letter. Joetta drew out the letter and showed it to them.

"I had to pay for this from Ennis." She looked over to Robert. "Your papa has sent a letter," she added, as if he would not have heard her. She was so rattled, she could hardly think straight.

Mr. McBride scrubbed at his beard. "Pay for a letter you're getting? That makes no sense. Since when does a letter get mailed first, then paid for?"

"When a person has enlisted. Mr. Spivey said so."

Mr. McBride's mouth dropped open, and Robert came close, pointing to the letter in her hand.

He said, "Read it."

"Put Pal up into the pasture first while I make some coffee."

He jerked the reins from her and Joetta spoke sharply. "Robert!"

With a dark look, he quietly led the mule away. Inside the kitchen, Mr. McBride lowered himself into the chair with a groan and rubbed relentlessly at his bad knee.

"Ain't this a strange turn of events? I reckon the Good Lord tells us what we ought to do even when we don't see it for ourselves."

Joetta could not bring herself to respond. How he could look at this in any positive way was beyond her. Robert rushed in, and while the pot boiled, Joetta carefully opened the folds of paper. She wanted to study the writing, the date, everything about it, yet her audience exhibited extreme impatience, so she began.

Dear all,
As you might remember, I am not much of a writer, so bear with me. I arrived in Raleigh after a long five-day walk.

Mr. McBride interrupted, "Five days? Hell, ain't nobody I know takes five days to get there. What was he doing? Sleeping in? Dillydallying along the way?"

Joetta had already read the next sentence and said, "If you would let me finish, he explains."

Mr. McBride dropped his head in his hands, and Joetta read on.

It should have been only four; however, I was first directed to Rocky Mount by several men I come across when, misguided as I am, I took a notion to state my views. I might have been angry as I explained myself to them. I believe it was trickery on their part. Who can say?

"Now see. I wouldn't have done that. My motto is to keep important issues to myself. Ain't no telling who you gonna run into."

"I will never finish if you keep interrupting."

Impatient, Robert said, "Keep going."

Once here, I asked after Henry at the volunteer station. Men had come from several counties in this great state. All were eager for a piece of the action. One kind soul said if I were to be successful in my search for our boy, I would need to enlist, otherwise I would be no better off getting information about him than if I were a Union soldier. I pondered on

*this a great deal. Believing you would want me to exhaust
every available avenue, enlist I did. I am told I am part of
the 10th regiment of volunteers, Company D. I only tell
you this so you know. Of course it means nothing to me.
I am not fit mentally for this, nor am I willing, but here
I am. I am told we will go to Virginia soon. I purchased
paper, ink, and all needed to write this from a sutler in this
encampment. It will be taken out of the eleven dollars they
plan to pay us. It is a great help to know some of my costs
are covered by payment on your end for delivery. Therefore,
I will keep my correspondences minimal so as to not drain
finances there, and will send you what I can.*

    Yours, Ennis

Robert said, "That's it?"

Joetta flipped the note over, and back to the front again. Robert's comment echoed in her mind. *That's it.* Robert stood.

"He didn't even ask about me, or Grandpa. Or you."

His mouth trembled as he fought not to cry. He went outside and Joetta got up to watch him from the window. The summer air shimmered with heat waves as he hurried across the yard, and for a moment, Joetta was caught up at the sight, his running shape captured as if in a mirage, giving her the sense of seeing him like Henry and Ennis. Leaving.

She rushed to the door and called out to him.

"Robert?"

Already he was at the edge of the fields, the tree branches reaching for him, taking him into the green shade, and then he was out of sight. She put a hand to her throat, and her breath came harder, like she was the one running. Mr. McBride limped to the back door, to peer out despite the fact there was nothing to see.

"Sure didn't think it'd come to this."

Joetta was too tired to have the old argument about his grandiose talk creating a domino out of Henry, setting something into motion they could not stop now.

"It is going to take a lot of strength and prayer to see this through until they are home."

Mr. McBride did not reply and left her to her contemplations, going out the door and off to his cabin. Joetta drifted from one room to the next, the boy's rooms, back down to the sitting room, and to her and Ennis's bedroom, where she eventually sat on the edge of the bed. She took the note out and read it again, and again. After a fourth time, the paper fluttered to the floor, and she sat staring at her hands.

He had volunteered because he believed that was what she would have wanted. She could not say if it was or not. Could it possibly help? It was impossible to know. On top of that, there was little, if any, emotion other than an edge of resentment noticeable in the clipped sentences. He could have been writing to anyone. She could not detect any sentiment whatsoever, not even in his signature. Such a heaviness came over her, she did not know if she could rise from the bed, go into the kitchen, and begin her work. Whether they had wanted it or not, they were now involved like everyone else. She wished to deny this and could not.

Chapter 8

Joetta wearily sorted through vegetables she had picked from the garden, and tossed them into a wooden bowl, their dull thump alternating with the pounding of her head. She was exhausted. Earlier that morning when she dragged the milk stool over to Honey, she almost fell asleep with her forehead resting against the creature's warm side. As she gathered eggs, two fell out of her hand and broke. Mr. McBride, who always demanded his breakfast before he went into Whitakers, grew irritated when somehow she forgot about the biscuits and burned them. Robert pulled the darkest pieces off and ate them anyway.

Joetta said, "I can make more."

Mr. McBride, clearly put out, said, "Never mind! Sam Spivey will have something at his store."

He scraped his chair back and left. A while later as she was about to go into the field, Mr. McBride's uneven footfalls signaled his return. She braced herself. What news would he bring this time? She only allowed his talk of the war efforts because of Ennis and Henry, while what she wanted were letters because with those might come words that could settle her heart, and her mind. Since the first and only one from Ennis a little more than a week before, and with the knowledge of his decision to keep his correspondence at a minimum, her wait already seemed everlasting. Mr. McBride appeared, sweating, hair standing on end, and wild-eyed.

"Saw Elder Newell 'fore I even got to town, and he said the Confederates and Federals went head-to-head in Prince William County, Virginny! Some place called Bull Run Creek. We were able to get reinforcements in, and the Rebs sent them packing back to Washington!"

"There was fighting in Virginia? Why, that is where Ennis was headed."

Mr. McBride pushed by her and collapsed into a chair. He pulled a handkerchief from his pocket and wiped at his reddened face. Joetta picked up a pitcher of water she had just drawn from the springhouse and poured him a glass, which he promptly drank. Neither one spoke. Joetta took the glass, refilled it, and spoke with certainty.

"He is fine. I would know."

Mr. McBride gave her a sideways stare.

"Huh?"

"If something happened to Ennis, or Henry. I would know."

She was convinced of this. Surely she would feel it if they had suffered in any way. It would come over her the same as when she had lost the babies. That intrinsic sense of barrenness, a nothingness instead of serenity and contentment. Her heart would ache as if of its own accord, and she would be bound by a sorrow so intense, it would steal her breath. Such as this had come over her back then, and she somehow knew her unborn children were no longer with her. Her mother said it was maternal instincts, yet she and Ennis shared such a strong bond, she was resolute it would be the same should he, God forbid, ever leave this earth.

"Where's the boy? Robert, I mean."

"Out there, where he usually is."

She looked toward the door to where she had last seen him. There was no hat, no movement, nothing but a field of early corn. While this made her want yell his name, she remained quiet. She had done that once already a couple days after receiving Ennis's letter, when she could not find him right off, and a sick dread took hold of her. She had screamed his name over and over, turning left, then right, frantically searching, only to have him slowly rise from where he had been kneeling between rows, not hardly twenty feet from her. He had looked at her like she was some kind of fool. She would not repeat that mistake. Mr. McBride heaved himself up and went back outside.

"He might care to hear about it."

Joetta doubted this. Robert only wanted to know about his father and brother. She pulled on her sun bonnet and tied it under her chin, her mind back to the place called Bull Run Creek. She kept her fear hidden. She would not allow it to push its way through, to think of her loved ones engaged in the fight. She went to work thinning the corn, a process that required checking each plant coming up and clipping the smaller ones at soil level so bigger ones had a chance. Her failsafe plan was to always fall back on the work that needed doing, and there was no shortage of that.

Days after the news of Bull Run Creek, two wagons came into view. Joetta, her bonnet shielding her eyes against the midmorning sun, waited to see who had come. Unbelievably, Bess and Mary rode in the first one, and Bess drove in such a manner as to suggest urgency, while Mary hung on for dear life. In the second wagon was Vesta Fern and Alice Atwater. Joetta glanced down at herself, wishing she had time to freshen up, to at least put on a clean apron, collar and cuffs. The women climbed down from their seats and Mary grinned at her while flapping the skirt of her dress to knock off the dust. Joetta smiled in return as the others made their way toward her. She immediately noted they were all wearing homespun dresses of cotton and wool instead of the usual store-bought material. Mary continued smiling big and bright.

"Look," she said. She twirled around and performed a small curtsy. "What do you think?"

"It is quite nice."

Bess had yet to speak and gave Joetta an expressionless stare, as if they had never met.

Joetta said, "Bess, nice to see you."

Bess cleared her throat. "Joetta."

Joetta nodded politely at Vesta and Alice, who regarded her with the same blank expressions, although Alice at least dipped her head toward Joetta. Whatever they might have thought about the incident at church, Joetta was pleased for some company and the unexpected change in her usual routine. She moved up to her front porch and held her door open. She would invite them in and see what this particular visit was about.

"Please, come in."

Mary spoke with a gay tone, her voice light and friendly.

"Wonderful! It's already so hot."

Vesta and Alice tugged on their bonnets and smoothed down their skirts, then made their way up the steps. Bess came behind the other women and was compelled to share more.

"We are here to discuss something of great import."

Bess was apparently on a mission and could be quite single-minded. The women filed in, and it was at this moment Joetta remembered that aside from her own disheveled appearance, she had not swept properly in days. Mortified, she looked at the sitting room and the hall in the same way they would, with the dust, dead spiders, and various bits of weeds dragged in by her, Mr. McBride, and Robert. Her rugs needed beating, and a fine coat of dust had settled on the small tables in the sitting room. The sun happened to hit it all just right, emphasizing the clutter. There was nothing she could do about it, so she straightened her shoulders and gave her guests a smile.

"Ladies, please. Make yourselves comfortable. What would you have? I can make coffee. Or if you prefer a cooler drink? I have switchel."

Mary said, "I'd love to have that. You make it better than anyone."

After Mary's endorsement, Vesta and Alice said, "The same, please."

Bess shook her head and stared about the room with a critical eye.

"No, thank you."

Joetta hurried into her kitchen, shoved the vegetable peelings off the table and into the slop bucket. She hurriedly wiped the table off, then gathered up glasses and poured the liquid into her cut glass pitcher. While she was uncertain what the visit might involve, she could guess. She would be fair, listen, and make decisions accordingly. No one was chatting in the usual way about their families, their crops or even the weather as she carefully walked back into the sitting room with everything on a tray. They sat, fiddling with gloves, hair, and skirts. They all wore some sort of cockade. Why, even Mary. This did not necessarily impart any concern to Joetta, but as she poured, her hands shook a little. She handed the glasses around and after she sat, Bess gave Joetta her full attention, and to Joetta's surprise, offered a tentative smile.

Bess said, "We have come to invite you to our home-spun parties. Myself and those here, plus a few others, have decided to go back to making our own materials, such as this."

She pointed to Mary's dress. Mary fluffed the skirt to better showcase the work.

Joetta said, "The dress is very nicely made, but why are you doing this?"

Bess glanced at the others and cleared her throat.

"It is our patriotic duty, same as with the other war. We will show we don't need the North and their textiles, just as we showed the British! What the North produces is cheaply made as it is, in a factory. I understand how you feel about this"—she stopped, studied the other women, then leaned close to Joetta—"nonetheless, one's loyalty must not be questioned. It isn't safe. I'm telling you this because of what I hear. If you're a part of our little cause, it will stand as proof you are on our side, the right side. We meet once a week, midafternoon, on Thursdays. We will also knit socks and the like for our boys. It is important they have dry feet at all times, so I'm told. Socks are of utmost importance."

Bess sat back and said no more. While Joetta wished to be a part of gatherings as she had always been, and she certainly understood the atmosphere was prone to change by the day, she had to take into account what Ennis would do, if there. She knew. They would continue to live as they always had. She could not do this. Would not. It was a be-trayal to him, to their way of life. She would not pretend for the sake of everyone's comfort, or expectations. She set her glass down, tucked her hands into the folds of her skirt, and stared at her lap. She could use the excuse of having to run the farm, she supposed, but that did not sit right. She either believed the way she did or she did not.

"I am afraid I am about to disappoint all of you. I am

sorry you have made this trip for nothing; however, I do not see the use in taking part even for the reasons you give. As I stated in church, Ennis only volunteered to have a better chance at finding Henry. That is all there is to it. What I think or believe will not change now or in the future."

Bess sucked in air and blew it out.

"Why, I'm simply at a loss for words."

"I cannot help myself. It is a matter of morality. I choose to uphold my husband's values."

"Morality? Values? How can you not support the Confederates? Your husband, after all, is fighting with them!"

"It is different than how you see it."

"Wouldn't he want you to be safe?"

"Why would I be in danger on my own property?"

Bess became exasperated and stood abruptly.

"She's not secesh and never will be. For all we know they support the North."

"I am of neither persuasion, as I have said."

"That may be, but, if nothing else, it signifies you're disloyal."

Joetta, with genuine confusion and sincerity in her voice, asked, "How can I be disloyal if I have not chosen a side? Who am I disloyal to?"

Bess, rendered speechless, could only clutch her throat where her cockade was pinned. She made her way to the door, and there she spun around to point at Joetta.

"The only thing you're right about? We *have* wasted our time. This is my final attempt. Now, I must bid you goodbye."

She walked out, leaving the door wide open, prompting Vesta and Alice to quickly set their half-empty glasses on the table. Vesta shook her head at Joetta like an adult dismayed at a child. Joetta returned her indignation with a bland look. The women followed Bess, yet Mary remained seated, sipping and apparently enjoying her drink despite the arguing. Joetta sat down while keeping an eye out the window as Bess flounced into her wagon seat, obviously peeved. Mary calmly drank until she finished.

She said, "Oh my, that was good. How do you make yours? I'd love to get the receipt for it sometime, but I expect it's time for me to go if I'm to have a ride home."

Joetta said, "I use brown sugar. Then, of course, water, vinegar, and grated ginger."

"It is delicious." She gave Joetta a sly grin. "That went as you might have expected."

"I do not understand why it is so difficult."

"Because Bess Caldwell is involved."

Joetta pointed at Mary's shoulder.

"I see *you* are wearing a fancy ribbon of approval."

Mary angled her head to look down at the small red and white decoration.

"Yes. Hugh believes it is for the best. He doesn't like to go against the grain, which is why I admire you so. It would be so very hard to be one of the very few, maybe the only one around here, who hasn't declared a side."

"I have always been quite mulish in my ways."

"It's an admirable trait to stand for what one believes."

"A lot of good it has done thus far."

"Even as I wear this funny little thing, always know how deep my admiration goes. You're brave, Joetta. That's how I see it."

She grabbed one of Joetta's hands and squeezed. Joetta winced, and Mary turned Joetta's hand over and stared at her palms.

"Oh my. These blisters look awfully tender."

"They will heal. What I am most worried about is Ennis and Henry, and Robert, who is quite miserable. Of course, Mr. McBride reminds me daily of his assessment on things."

"We're all worried. The unknown is a frightening thing."

Mary gave Joetta a small hug and headed to the wagon, where Bess waited with the patience of the devil. She had hardly settled in the seat when Bess slapped the reins across the mule's rump and the wagon took off with Vesta, Alice, and a brown plume of dust following close behind. Joetta shut the door, gathered the glasses, and took them into the kitchen. To her surprise, Mr. McBride sat slumped at the table, his fingernails tap, tap, tapping on the wooden top.

He said, "You will bring trouble on us with this insistent way of thinking."

"You were listening? Do you not have anything better to do?"

He waved a hand toward the back door.

"That boy's about as ornery as a cat with its tail tied to the fence. Can't say two words to him hardly."

"He will be fine."

"You best hope he don't go and pull the same stunt as Henry."

He had to go and say the very thing she feared. He picked at the material of his sleeve, unraveling a thread. She went to the back door and looked out across the farm. Robert was at the farthest point of the field, bent over, yanking out the smaller corn plants. A slight breeze ruffled the leaves and the pines murmured. Though the sun was out and the new corn was coming up well, giving off a crisp, brilliant green color, everything about it put her off, particularly the sight of her son working alone. It depressed her.

"I will be out in the fields."

Mr. McBride stayed put, arms crossed over his chest, mouth working around a wad of tobacco. His response was the typical grunt, but she knew that look well and escaped before he could harp on what had been said. She made her way into the rows, where she began to work one over from

Robert, and she did not stop for some time. Eventually she raised up to stretch her back and realized they had missed dinner altogether.

She stood, brushed her skirt off, and called out, "I am going to fix some dinner."

Robert's response was negligible. As she began making her way toward the house, a rumbling sound grew, and to her right came men in uniforms, marching quickly. This was startling to see. Robert jerked upright, and like scarecrows, neither of them moved.

The men filed through the fence and into the yard, and one on horseback called out. "We'd like to water our horses and fill our canteens. We've a long ways to go. Trying to get to the coast."

She gestured toward the well right as Mr. McBride barreled out of the house as if shot from a cannon, his shoulders hitching up and down to accommodate his bad knee, moving faster than Joetta had seen in a while.

"No! No! No!"

The men stopped while Joetta stared at him in surprise.

"What is wrong?"

"They're Union!" he yelled, pointing at them before he confronted the same man who addressed Joetta. "I know a Yank when I see one!"

The man, a captain, dismounted and faced Mr. McBride.

"I ain't no Yank. I'm from right here in North Carolina. We only wish to have some of your water. That is all."

"Permission not granted!"

Joetta moved in front of Mr. McBride and said, "You have *my* permission. These horses look jaded."

Mr. McBride was apoplectic.

"You can't be aiding the enemy!"

"I am allowing *men* and their horses who are hot and

thirsty to get water, which is the Christian thing to do." She turned to the man and said, "Please. You and your men fill your canteens, and the trough is right there for your horses."

They moved forward as one unit and Mr. McBride was forced to step out of their way. He was so distressed, he trembled all over. His mouth worked furiously around the wad of tobacco, and his chest heaved up and down. He glared as they filed by, most not looking, while a few grinned at him. They pulled their forage caps low on their heads and swaggered a bit.

He shook his fist and declared, "I ought to get my gun and shoot you, and you and you!"

The men started to have a bit of fun.

"Aw, come on, Grandpa, no you wouldn't. What if we're cousins? Could be for all you know."

"Hey, Grandpa, you shaking so hard you couldn't hit the broadside of that hog yonder."

Mr. McBride took off for his cabin, not paying attention to where he put his feet, and tripped over a divot in the ground.

When he stumbled and fell, a few of the soldiers laughed until the captain raised a hand and said, "Enough!"

He approached Mr. McBride and extended his hand to help him up. Joetta winced when Mr. McBride made as if to slap it away.

"I don't need your damn help. I'm getting my rifle to shoot all you sons-a-bitches, and if I'm lucky I'll get a couple more."

The captain pushed him back down as he struggled to get up.

"In that case, stay right there until we leave. Private, make sure this man doesn't move."

One of the soldiers who jeered at Mr. McBride drew close and held his musket on him. Joetta went toward Mr. McBride. She addressed the soldier holding the long rifle on him.

"Please, let him stand."

The soldier shook his head solemnly.

"I have my orders, ma'am."

If she could be thankful over one thing, it was that Robert was too far away to see his grandfather suffer this humiliation. The men drank, taking their time while she waited with Mr. McBride. She tried mollifying him.

"Do not let this bother you. They are only trying to assert authority in a meaningless way."

He ignored her, staring morosely toward his cabin. Finally, the soldiers were done and reorganized themselves into some semblance of a marching line. They began a steady trudging, off the McBride property.

Some small part of Joetta regretted allowing them to use the well given their treatment of her father-in-law, until the captain tipped his hat and said, "Much obliged. If we can continue to be civil to one another, we might all fare the better for it. You've been most kind. Good day now."

Joetta turned to Mr. McBride to say, "See?" only to have the word lost to the air as he limped toward his cabin. He probably would not come out for a while after having suffered such shame. She could not blame him. She watched the last of them disappear, blue coats providing a stark contrast against the green of the trees. They reached the road, where the sound of their boots against the wood planks, rhythmic and firm, eventually grew faint. This was their foe, so they were told, young men from the very same state. *Imagine.* Mr. McBride went by her at a fast clip for him, rifle in hand. He dashed into the road and calmly put his weapon to his shoulder, aimed, and fired. It was a useless,

wasted shot. They were out of sight. He fired again anyway, and nodded with satisfaction before glaring at her and
gesturing in the direction they had gone.

"That's what you do to someone who ain't on our side!"

"Our side? You mean yours."

He cursed into the air, and the fact that any kindness
would not be accepted or given, was what gave her every
reason to fear for them all.

Chapter 9

Joetta's need to know what was happening was mixed up with the hope of no news. Word of a Confederate win in Missouri, the Battle of Wilson's Creek, made Mr. McBride happy. As long as what he shared did not involve Virginia, she breathed easier and trusted Ennis was safe. Of Henry, she was in a constant state of agitation. It was as if he had disappeared altogether. As time went on and they discovered more about what each side was doing, she grew ever more fretful. The conflict deepened, reached different areas, and grew more invasive by the day, like an illness with no cure. In between all of this, Robert turned twelve, and Joetta apologized for not having made him a cake, to which he replied, "A cake ain't what I want anyway."

"Is not."

He glared at her correction. She understood his feelings more than he realized, but there was no need to regress in one's manner of speech. She could not help herself. She was like this because of her own upbringing. Her father, a reader, and one who considered himself more of a gentleman farmer, had instructed her, her sister and brothers in elocution. This was why she paid such close attention; she had been taught to speak with precision since she had first babbled "mama." It was a small thing, perhaps, but it was one thing she could ensure Robert had.

At the end of August, a battle at Fort Hatteras, right off the North Carolina coast, fell to the Union, and Mr. McBride raged for days.

"They're trying to strangle our supply lines. That's their goal. You wait and see."

September came, and the corn and sorghum continued to do well. Joetta would look at the rows, and her sense of accomplishment gave her immense satisfaction. The plants were beginning to transition for fall, with the corn husks yellowing and the sorghum tassels turning burgundy. She had seen Robert pinching the seeds, testing them for readiness. Reports about Lexington, Missouri, coming under control of the Confederates once again reenergized Mr. McBride. He was like a flag waving proudly in the wind. When there was good news, he was filled with bluster and bravado, and when there was a loss, his body seemed to shrink, his posture gone poor. He lived and breathed the latest word, and was in town more than at the farm.

The uptick in war activity had Joetta taking her pen to paper again instead of waiting for Ennis to send word. She sat at the kitchen table to write him while Robert and Mr. McBride ate their breakfast. She kept her letter filled with positive, reassuring information, intensifying her need for him to reciprocate in kind.

> *Dear husband,*
> *I was ever so pleased to receive your letter, although dismayed. You are now in danger, and while it is perhaps the only way to find our Henry, my heart trembles with the*

knowledge of what is required of you. Of course, I have had no word from our son, but perhaps by now, you have some of your own? Robert and I have done as you bid, and the crops are growing well. Robert is peevish these days as he is missing his father and brother. Just the other day, Union soldiers passed by the house. Can you imagine? They struck quite a posture in their fancy uniforms, making the Confederate volunteers we have seen appear rather shabby and unkempt in their dress. I allowed them to water their horses, and to quench their thirst. This did not set well with Mr. McBride. I must say, all in all, even in spite of a show of fractiousness from him, no one suffered any ill harm. Husband, please send word of your health that I might be at ease.

Your faithful and loving wife, Joetta

Robert watched her write as he mindlessly forked eggs into his mouth.

"Is that a letter to Papa?"

"Yes. I wanted him to know the crops are doing well. I think it will make him glad that the work he asked us to do is being taken care of."

His shrug was noncommittal, as were most of his exchanges with his mother these days.

"I wish he'd write."

In the past, she would have reached out, touched him in some reassuring way. Not now, not while it appeared as if any contact were repulsive, as if she were some horrible person he did not want to know. She had to settle for conversation. At least he was talking to her.

"I know."

Mr. McBride let his fork clatter on his plate.

"That's the least of his worries, I guarantee."

This struck Joetta as possibly true. That was not going

to deter her from sending her message on, however. She folded the piece of paper.

"I am certain he would want to know what is happening here at home, how we are managing."

Mr. McBride scrutinized his fingernails.

"Looks to me like he'd write and ask."

"He will. This has taken all of us by surprise. Even you, I imagine."

Her quiet certainty cut off any further commentary. Mr. McBride stood, pulled at his waistcoat, and held his hand out.

"I'll take it to town for you."

Joetta placed the letter in his palm.

"Would you get me some thread as well? I have several shirts to mend. Dark brown, if possible."

After Mr. McBride left, Joetta turned back to Robert.

"Can you tend the fields today?"

"Yes."

"Good. I need to put this house in order."

She could not have anyone showing up again with it in such a state, making it appear as if she could not manage. By midmorning she took a break and carried food out to Robert. She found him in the middle of a field and waited patiently at the end of a row, but instead of stopping, he went by her as if she was not there, his slouch hat shielding his eyes. She called to him and held up a small bundle of cloth.

"I brought you some dinner."

He kept on.

"I will set it by the fence."

He had to have seen and heard her. Some part of her wanted to take a hickory stick to his backside, while realizing how ridiculous the idea was. Aside from the fact he was bigger, and stronger, did she want him to resent her even more? And look what happened between Henry and Ennis, a rift unparalleled, and the actions to match it. Their sons had always been well-behaved and loving, the sort who had not required much discipline. Adjusting to this new world had all of them acting different. She went back to the house and found herself in Henry's room, and there she lingered. She straightened the summer medallion quilt, dusted off the small wood bureau, and pushed a chair back into the corner. She swept the floor, then stood in the middle of the room, her chin lowered, fighting back her emotions. Her memory still carried the sound of his voice through the years, how he had screeched in joy as an infant, the first words he had spoken, and his laugh. Overcome, she left the room and shut the door behind her. Doing so felt as if she were closing an important chapter in her life.

Later that afternoon she came from the dank, musty cellar to find Robert in the yard holding up two skinned squirrels.

"I got'em both just a bit ago."

Joetta smiled and though he did not return it, the fact he had contributed was a significant improvement.

"Oh, how wonderful. They will be good with these vegetables."

He hesitated, like he wanted to say something, and she waited, wanting him to open up, become the Robert she remembered, the boy who would talk about anything and everything. Instead, he handed them to her and walked off to take care of the livestock. Perturbed, she started for her kitchen when Mr. McBride's distinctive whistle came and he rounded the corner of the house, hobbling fast and looking over his shoulder. He acted as if he was being chased. He stopped, bent over, and tried to catch his breath. Joetta sensed something wrong.

"Whatever is the matter?"

He raised himself a little and pointed down the lane.

"Some of'em's coming."

"Who? Who is coming?"

"Some men from town."

"Why?"

He straightened up, and his eyes skipped about as he cleared his throat and twiddled with his hat. Finally, he thrust his chin forward and clamped his mouth tight. She had seen this expression before, belligerent and defiant, similar to when she and Ennis had pointed out his part in Henry's leaving. He raised his shoulders.

"I reckon they didn't like what they heard."

"From who?"

"Well, see. I got to talking to a few men over to the store about them Union devils and what they done when they come here. How that one held a gun on me and all. They got to asking questions, wanting to know how they come to be on the property, and I said you allowed they could have some water."

"Meaning, they did not like what *you* told them." She looked down the path and then back at her father-in-law. "Who are these men?"

"Ain't sure. One of'em said he couldn't understand why you helped Union soldiers. I said 'cause you was stubborn as the day is long."

Joetta made an exasperated sound. Seconds later, a low rumbling sound on the road signaled their arrival.

Mr. McBride said, "Hellfire. I was hoping they was only mouthing off. Look, you tell'em what they want to hear, and that'll settle'em down."

"Tell them what they want to hear? What does that mean?"

"That we're Confederate supporters. Tell'em that."

The men rode onto the farm as if they had every right to

do so. She waited calmly while her insides were in a turmoil and her mouth was as dry as if she chewed a piece of cotton. A man got off his horse and pushed his way through the group. His eyes, shadowed by the brim of his hat, were dark and unfriendly, and with a thin, unsmiling mouth and a squint like he faced the sun, Joetta was certain he meant to intimidate her. She returned the stare.

"Who are you?"

"You don't need to know my name."

"Why are you here, then?"

There was shifting of feet and muttering amongst those who had come with him. Joetta glanced at where Mr. McBride had been standing only to find she was by herself because he was slinking toward his cabin. The man gestured toward the well and the water trough.

"Heard you allowed the enemy to fill their canteens and water their horses. Now, why would you go and do a thing like'at?"

The way he said it gave Joetta pause. She did not want trouble. She would do as Mr. McBride suggested and was about to do so until the stranger looked around at the others and smirked. That did not set well and her tone turned sharp.

"Why would I allow thirsty men and horses to drink? What an absurd question."

His eyes swiveled in her direction, apparently amazed she would defy him.

"You blind, or maybe a bit addled?"

"I am perfectly fine. Now, what do you want?"

"You ain't addled, and you ain't blind. Yet, you saw what they wore. Saw them colors, and all."

"What I am telling you is I allowed them to use my well and water their horses. Nothing else. What they wore was inconsequential to me."

This drew more murmuring, and he held his hand up.

"And that is openly aiding the enemy."

"Actually, if you think about it, that is not feasible."

He gawked at her, seeming perplexed.

"How so?"

"I have no opinion about these issues one way or the other."

"Wonder what your husband might say to that? Ain't he off fighting for the Confederacy?"

"No."

His face flushed, and he stepped closer to her. She stayed where she was, praying the fear boiling inside her did not show.

"You ain't fooling nobody with this sham. I saw the letter. That man right over there, he showed me, said his son was fighting with the Rebels. Ain't that man your kin?"

She did not turn around to look where he pointed, assuming Mr. McBride must have remained outside his cabin. She kept her voice reasonable, albeit measured with a touch of sarcasm. "I suppose I must claim him since I married his son. My husband is looking for our oldest boy who became smitten with the idea of being a soldier. That is the only reason he signed on. If our son had joined the Union, my husband would have volunteered with them. It is as simple as that."

The man twisted around to stare at his friends with incredulity. He lifted his hands as if to say, *Now what?* Another man came forward.

"Now you look here. We ain't got a lot of tolerance for such as this, and if you ain't on the Confederate side, far as I'm concerned, you're a traitor, through and through."

The rest of the group concurred with rumblings of "yeah" and "that's right."

There was a growing restlessness, and one from the back

said, "We didn't come to chitchat with no woman, much less no turncoat. Let's handle it or move on."

Joetta's stomach knotted. Since their arrival she had picked up on their mood. They had already made some sort of decision and were not here to listen to anything she might say. The first man nudged the man beside him, and they rejoined the group and remounted their horses. The group cast their eyes around, as if taking in the layout of the farm. One gave a signal and without any warning, they surged forward. The horses thundered through the property, and the riders began whooping and hollering. They sent the chickens scattering, and the hogs squealed and grunted in alarm from their pens.

Joetta, realizing what they were about to do, ran after them, screaming, "Stop!"

Mr. McBride waved both his arms in the air and yelled along with her. "What the hell? I'm a Confederate! What're you doing? Stop this minute, I tell you!"

In seconds the horses had leaped over the fence into the fields. The men slapped their reins on their rumps to urge them on. They ran up and down, and back and forth, trampling the corn and sorghum plants row by row. Joetta watched in horror as the crops were flattened into the soil. She was so stunned, she could not move from where she stood. Robert came running out of the barn and headed into the field. He zigzagged back and forth, waving his arms and yelling to try and spook the horses. Joetta recovered and took off her apron, while running and screaming and waving it over her head. Her long skirt hindered her, and she fell multiple times, but she got back up, scurrying here and there, doing what she could to distract the horses.

After a few minutes the men tired of their game, and the ringleader urged his horse back over the fence and the rest of them followed, galloping off the farm and out of sight.

Joetta spun in a circle, taking in the devastation. The scent of churned soil reached her nose as she stared in disbelief. She retrieved a crushed ear of corn at her feet, and seeing its condition, she let it drop back onto the dirt. She put her hands to her face. How could she have been so filled with ignorance as to not know what might happen, to not detect the destruction they intended? She was certain anything she said would not have mattered. They had heard enough from her father-in-law. A choking noise from Robert drew her gaze to him as he gestured at the ruined fields. He stood by his grandfather, fighting tears.

"Why did they do this?"

Mr. McBride pointed to her.

"Ask your mother."

Joetta's mouth dropped.

"Oh no. Those men would not have come if it had not been for you. You caused this by talking about what was none of their business."

"Let me tell you something. I didn't need to say a word. The folks in town know how you think. All of 'em. You think this is going to get any easier? All you had to say was you were Confederate, and none of this would've happened."

"You told them about those Union soldiers. *You* should have kept quiet."

Robert's gaze passed from one to the other, then stayed on her. She saw him come to a conclusion right before his face shuttered. She could not look at him, unable to bear his judgment. Her sadness and worry were inevitable, and maybe too was the decision she must make.

Chapter 10

She walked up and down the trampled rows, picking up a crushed ear of corn here and there. After her initial shock wore off, she started scouring the field, attempting to salvage anything she could. Most ears still held too much moisture and would sour and grow mold if kept. The drier ones she dropped into wooden pails before moving on. Eventually Robert joined her, and when the buckets became full, mother and son walked to the corn crib and emptied them. Because the corn had not been allowed to dry down properly for milling, the only thing she could think to do was gather up the best of the worst and perhaps feed their animals. They worked until dark before stopping. Without speaking, it was understood they would resume tomorrow.

Inside they ate by lantern light, not much, only what was already cooked from earlier, cold biscuits and some fatback. At least it was enough to stem the pangs of hunger. The tension was as palpable as the heat of the sun as blame and remorse permeated the small space where mother and son sat together. Mr. McBride had not been out of his cabin since he and Joetta exchanged words. Joetta finished eating and offered another biscuit to Robert. He refused. She then split two of them, filled them with fatback, wrapped them in a cloth, and handed the bundle to Robert. She began to collect the few plates they dirtied, but he remained in the kitchen as if trying to figure out how to say what was on his mind. She stopped pouring hot water into the dishpan, and with her eyes averted, she waited.

Finally, he spoke. "All you had to do was tell'em we were on the Confederate side."

"It would have done no good. They were bent on destruction. We have always stood by what we believe in, Robert."

"Even if?"

He pointed out the open door, where the air remained redolent of a ruined livelihood, a wet, sweet odor strangely reminiscent of the mill in town. Even from where she stood, the destruction was evident, the tall plants flattened, the long green leaves no longer rustling softly in the breeze. Here and there a shredded section rose and fluttered before collapsing, as if signaling surrender.

"I had no idea they were going to do that. Certainly, they had no right."

"But they did, and all you had to say . . ."

Her voice grew loud, her weariness and worry mounting as the realization of what they faced once winter came was foremost in her mind. "I know!" She lowered her voice. "I know. I see it has to be that way, and that is what I will do, at least until your father is home."

Robert made a derisive sound, like she was ridiculous. Joetta reached out to him, wanting to explain. He denied her, turning away and going out the door to his grandfather's cabin, the twilight casting his shadow long. She stuck her hands into the hot water and began cleaning off the few plates and cups. When he did not come back right away, she pictured the two of them commiserating over her obstinacy. He was too young perhaps to understand the importance, the reasons you held on to your way of thinking, even if it was hard. She had been raised in this principled way by her own father and mother, not only in their faith, but with regard to their work ethic and traditions. This was why she and Ennis got along, why their marriage had worked. His own mother, as he had admitted in the past, had the most influence on him. His father had nothing to do with what he stood for other than to present a clear sense of who or what he did not want to be. Together she and Ennis realized what guided their actions, what made them who they were, who they had been all along. Robert did not understand because his life until now had been unassuming and dependable. Even worse, and equally confusing to him, were the inconsistencies she displayed, and already she was beginning to struggle mightily with this one.

She finished her work in the kitchen and went to the bedroom, where she sat on the edge of the bed. The realization about what she could have done, if for no other reason than to save their livelihood, tormented her. Her mind was in a turmoil, her entire body ached with fatigue, and she had a pounding headache. She would not sleep well, if at all. She poured water in the wash basin before pulling the pins from her hair, and it fell in a cascade down her back. She pulled the length of it around and began brushing, hoping it would ease her headache. As she worked through it section by section, she stared at the color caught by candlelight, infused with highlights of gold and orange against dark brown, with a muted gray intertwined here and there. Generally, she did not feel old; tonight, she did.

She set the brush on the dresser, washed off her face, and finally pulled her nightgown on over her head. She blew out the lantern, then laid down, listening to the tree frogs and a distant owl through the open window. Her awareness of the empty side of the bed was worse tonight than others, and it made her turn onto her side, take hold of Ennis's pillow, and hug it to herself. There was no moon, and the pitch-black of the night drew her attention to the stars spattered across the sky. She explored the heavens' tiny pinpoints of light to distract herself while keeping an ear tuned for Robert, expecting to hear him any minute climb the steps to his room. Her only knowledge of passing time was the nightlife ramping up, and expected or not, she slept.

Joetta awakened the next morning to the hoarse crowing of the rooster. Abruptly, she sat up, puzzling over the apprehensive feeling she had until she remembered the events of the day before. A hard knot formed in her throat. How she longed for the days when she and Ennis would lie in bed and discuss their plans. She threw the sheet off and walked to her door to peek out and up toward Robert's room at the top of the stairs. His door stood open. Either he was already up or he had not come back to the house last night.

That initial sinking feeling she had when she first awoke and remembered did not deter her. She readied herself for the day, her mood improving, shifting to optimism, despite the fact she could see the ruin from the bedroom window. She hurried to fix her hair and put her work clothes on. She went outside, where a pink-edged sky greeted her as she made her way to the barn to milk Honey. When she was done, the bucket of milk reassured they would at least have this. They would have the bounty from her garden, and they would have eggs and chickens. Meat from the hogs. It would work out. Back in the kitchen she fried sausage and made gravy. In no time she had biscuits done and the table set. Robert finally showed up at the back door. He had not bothered to wash his face, and his hair was pointing in a myriad of directions. He avoided looking at her and sat at the table, head bowed, habitually waiting as he had been taught. She quietly set a plate of biscuits in front of him, along with a bowl of sausage gravy. Mr. McBride came in and Joetta held the pot of coffee up, her gesture a question. Mr. McBride dropped into his chair and held his cup out.

So far, all this and not a word between any of them. Her optimism began to fade as her guilt took over yet again. If she declared herself loyal to the Confederate cause, it certainly was not going to change the fact the crops were already ruined. Mr. McBride set his cup down to let his coffee cool, and cleared his throat, indicating he had something on his mind.

"Men like them who showed up here yesterday? More will come. They ain't going to stop if they know you ain't secesh. You got to decide what's more important, sticking to your guns, or saying what needs saying so we don't end up dead."

It irked her to no end he refused to take responsibility, yet his words held a ring of truth she could not deny. It seemed hard to believe they could be killed, though the men who came did not look too far off from committing such an act.

She said, "I will say or do whatever is necessary to keep us safe. Will you?"

Mr. McBride scoffed at her question as he heaped his plate. He waved his fork at her, then stabbed a bite of biscuit and smeared it through the gravy.

"Meaning you'll declare loyalty to the Rebs? Hmph. I'll believe that when I see it. Boy, pass me that muscadine jam."

Joetta's brow puckered as she split a biscuit and nibbled. A few seconds later she got up, went to the kitchen, and reached up on the shelf, searching for what she had put aside weeks ago. Her fingers encountered the satin edge, and she brought it down. The cockade rested in her palm, and she brushed off the dried dirt that clung to it. She experienced a pang of regret once again, like she was betraying herself, and Ennis. It reminded her of the incident between Henry and his father, and how adamant Ennis had been about Henry not having it, much less wearing it. *This is something I must do, if only for now.* She returned to the table and sat down, placing the bauble by her plate. She poured herself some more coffee.

Mr. McBride did not notice it until Robert said, "Isn't that what Henry had?"

Mr. McBride wiped his mouth off on his sleeve, a habit Joetta detested, and leaned back in his chair, his expression inscrutable.

She sipped on her coffee and then answered Robert, "I will only wear it when necessary." Joetta then changed the subject. "Was there no mail yesterday?"

Mr. McBride's eyes grew round, and he looked momentarily confused.

"I reckon I forgot about that after I got tied up talking about them soldiers."

Robert continued to stare at the cockade, such an innocuous-appearing item, yet it held substantial meaning, a sign of who you were, where you stood. In her heart, Joetta fancied burning the thing.

Robert said, "Why did you keep it?"

Joetta picked it up again.

"I am not sure. I suppose it will come in handy at the moment, though, so I can carry out this charade."

Mr. McBride spluttered and coffee droplets hit his shirt.

"Charade? Best not let them think you're fooling. It won't do us a bit of good. You got to have confidence to see it through."

Joetta stood and began gathering the dirty dishes. She

was not sure she had it in her. It was as bad as telling Ennis she hated him, and it did nothing in teaching Robert
about standing for his principles. With breakfast done, she
and Robert went back to the work they started the day before, neither one of them speaking, yet she could not say it
was uncomfortable. With only a break here and there, they
managed to get what they could, and by late afternoon they
had gone row by row through the entire field, and what
they'd dumped into the corn crib was still a pitiful amount.
Considering how the winters could sometimes drag on,
this was not encouraging, not when the crib was typically
full to the top. She drifted over to the sorghum and studied
the broken stalks and panicles.

Robert pointed and said, "Maybe we can leave it and see
what it does?"

Joetta waved with a tired air at the forlorn field. "Yes,
there is nothing else to do that I can see."

Glumly she followed him back up to the house and began to cut squash off the vine in her garden while pulling a
weed here and there. Mr. McBride was quick to come out
of his cabin, and she figured he would complain about the
lack of a midday meal. Instead he waved something in the
air, a small white square. She stood up from where she had
been kneeling under the tomato plants and hurried toward
him. He handed it to her, while he explained how he came
to have it.

"Spivey come by here on his way from Rocky Mount.
Good thing 'cause I didn't feel like going back into town. I
ain't had enough to eat to do that kind of walking."

"I am about to fix supper."

"Good. A man can't go hours and not eat something."
He threw an arm out and continued. "He asked what happened to them fields there."

"And I am sure you told him."

She was so tired she did not care she sounded as petulant as he, and walked off before he could respond. Her mother's familiar handwriting stretched across the top of the cover, and while Joetta was excited to have received it, she was also sorely disappointed it was not from Ennis. She reminded herself of the reason he did not write frequently, as he was having to use every bit of his soldier's pay for his own necessities. She suddenly realized paying for his letters might prove difficult for her as well, what with the ruined crops. Some of what they grew had always supplemented them with the cash flow they needed. There would be none of that. Robert drew near and peered over her shoulder, his voice wistful when he saw who it was from.

"Grandmother, not Papa."

"Yes. But he will write soon, I am sure."

She intended to read it after supper, only she could not wait. She retrieved the opener from the small desk in the sitting room and quickly slit the cover. A few petals from her mother's favorite flower, verbena, floated to the floor. Joetta smiled at the very idea she would send these and lifted the paper to her nose, catching the flower's scent. Her memories awakened and she imagined her mother as she had last seen her, a smallish woman, gray braids wrapped about her head like a crown, bespectacled, with an affinity toward humor, as well as a soft heart toward every small woodland creature about the farm. Her mother had once befriended a fox squirrel she amusingly named Stew, which had irritated Joetta's father to no end. He claimed she had turned a perfectly good meal into a family member.

Joetta read through the first part about normal daily household activities, along with a lament over her father's failing eyesight, the state of the gardens, and other mundane concerns involving church activities. At the end of the page, and in only the way her mother could, she advised Joetta as such:

> *Daughter, dear, it is horrible to hear this about Henry. Keep your faith close. Turn to the Lord and seek Him in the moments when your greatest doubts threaten. Know there is nothing else to be done now except bear what you must, do what you must, and give yourself over to prayer. Ennis is a cautious, smart man, and he will do his best to find Henry. You will prevail in this, as any loving mother would. You reacted out of concern, and that is admirable. As you know, you are always welcome for a visit, and your father would love to see each and every one of you, as would I; however, I strongly advise against travel at this time. There appears to be minimal activity toward this effort they undertake, and I sense this will soon change as we have already seen many men marching toward the coast.*
>
> *Sending love and prayers, Mother*

Joetta pressed the paper against her chest and closed her eyes. Her mother's words, soothing and supportive, made her feel better.

"What did your mother say?"

Mr. McBride stood with Robert, and both were waiting for her to share the contents of the letter.

"She said to pray."

"Oh? Well now. That's the smartest thing I've heard lately."

Joetta began thinking of how to manage the farm going forward. Her mother's assurances encouraged her to make decisions. She looked at Robert when she spoke, hoping to reassure him too.

"We will reduce the livestock feed. It is doubtful we will

have enough corn for very long, maybe two months or so. We should plant fall oats, and if the sorghum recovers, it might be enough to get by. We will slaughter a couple of the hogs now, so we do not have as many to feed. Keep the boar from the sows and gilts so there are no more piglets for now. Those that remain might get a little thinner, but they will live."

Robert appeared hopeful, until Mr. McBride scoffed.

"All fine and good, 'til you plant them fields again. They'll come back soon as anyone finds out. It ain't 'cause of what I said neither."

He poked himself in the chest emphatically to make a point. If only he could keep himself quiet and Joetta could get someone on her side to advocate for her, they might be left alone. The most likely person was Bess. Bess and all of her grand displays of loyalty and devotion to the Confederacy. If Bess stood with her, there would be no question of allegiance.

Chapter 11

The change of season brought a distinct coolness to the air as she drove the wagon toward the Caldwell farm. She bobbed along on the front seat telling Pal of her woes, and his ears flicked back and forth at the sound of her voice. Her latest concern was Robert's unexpected decision to stay with his grandfather. He made it sound like his grandfather's idea, and maybe it was, although Joetta had her doubts. She imagined her relationship with her youngest as a taut thread that might snap at any given moment with the slightest touch. Robert refused to meet her gaze when he told her. Told. Did not ask. That left her by herself in the house, like an unmanned ship at sea, all those empty rooms and only her footsteps echoing throughout. At least Pal appeared attentive, with his soft brown eyes that blinked as if in sympathy.

The little cockade sat perched at her throat, decorating the white collar above her blue calico print dress. She had assessed its appearance by way of the floor mirror, a lively spot of bright red and gold. Very patriotic, indeed, she decided. It rested harmlessly against her neck, and while Joetta did not like it there and remained dismayed by its placement on her person, she trusted she would have the wherewithal to say the right things and somehow pull off this bold-faced lie with a tinge of success. Bess was shrewd. She missed nothing and would be hard to convince, more so than anyone.

Joetta had picked the day the sewing group would be gathered, and while she had no idea if anything had changed since Bess's visit to invite her, she could at least present herself and see what might happen. Neither Mr. McBride nor Robert reacted much when she announced her visit; however, when she came out of the bedroom, Robert stared at the ornament in surprise, while Mr. McBride shook his head as if having already judged the effort a failure. She dared either one to say a word as she swished her skirt aside to whisk by them and out the door, and they wisely kept their mouths clamped shut.

She carried her sewing bag with her, a sign of good intentions, to prove she was sincere in her efforts. To that end, she brought her old wooden hand carders, last used when she was living back home in Martin County. She, her mother, and Faith used to spin and weave cloth for their various household items, as well as most of their clothing back then. The carders sat in her sewing bag near her feet, rattling each time she hit a bump. She was actually enjoying her little jaunt with the sun shining, even as her thoughts circled neurotically around the reality and purpose. Her mood remained cautious as she pulled onto the long dirt drive to Bess's cabin. She took her time along the tree-lined path, noting and envying the perfect cornfields. The contrast was so stark compared to their fields, she set her eyes forward again, watching Pal's head as it bobbed up and down, his plodding gait quieting her. Beyond the cornfields the Caldwells' sheep dotted the pastures, white cloudlike shapes moving against the green.

The cabin came into view. Nervous as a young girl about whether her friends would be nice to her or not, she gulped in a few steadying breaths. How ridiculous to have to go through such schoolgirl-like emotions at the age of thirty-four. Joetta pulled at her collar, her fingers brushing against the cockade.

"You will either be my savior or a troublemaker, which is it?"

She almost giggled, the absurdity of talking to an inanimate object striking her as funny; however, she was close to the house now and her amusement subsided. If she knew Bess, the sound of her arrival would have her friend watching from a window, and she did not need her witnessing anything to gossip or speculate over. There were two other wagons present, which meant the sewing group was gathered. She stopped in a nice patch of shade under a massive hickory tree near the other wagons where Pal could graze and socialize with the horses. She stepped down, then leaned in to grab her sewing bag. The front door opened and Bess called out, her voice shaded with surprise, and suspicion.

"Joetta?"

Bess quickly descended the front steps and Joetta was suddenly unsure if she would be welcomed, or even how she would begin to explain her sudden appearance. She opted for being straightforward.

"Hello, Bess. I am here to join your sewing group. Since you invited me a while back, I gave it some thought and, well, here I am."

She held up her bag, and while Bess acknowledged the bag with barely a peek, it was what Joetta had at her neck her friend ogled with skepticism. If Joetta had shown up drunk, she did not think she could have surprised Bess

Caldwell any more. Bess, in that rather annoying manner she tended to adopt when feigning ignorance, pointed at the cockade.

"Why, I am purely taken aback. What has caused this sudden change of heart? Pray tell and for the love of God, have you converted? Are you secesh?"

This was going to be harder than Joetta imagined. Not because of what Bess asked, rather it was the pitch of her voice, a marked characteristic she attributed to another penchant Bess had aside from her causes, and that was for scandal and rumor. Joetta had known Bess long enough to hear the falseness to a question in which she already knew the answer. Without a doubt she knew what transpired at the McBride farm, for how could she not? Joetta tipped her head and gave her a forthright look.

"You must certainly know what happened at our farm."

Bess's cheeks flushed, and she had the decency to look away, and when she fixed her gaze back on Joetta, sympathy had replaced suspicion.

"Yes, yes. I am truly sorry about that. They go too far, these young men with their lawlessness." Bess seemed to catch herself and straightened up. "My dear, you should have known this could happen! Now is not the time for equivocation. What a hard lesson, but if you put it behind you, recognize it as an error in judgment, I am sure you and the rest of us will be all the better for it!"

Bess motioned at Joetta's cockade again. Joetta could not bring herself to acknowledge, much less agree with Bess's assumption. Instead, she referred to the work being done by the sewing group. This was something she could get behind without feeling as if she were giving herself up, body and soul.

"It occurred to me what is being done here is an act of goodwill. Indeed, I can stand by that."

She prayed Bess would leave it alone. In the meantime, Vesta and Alice had come out onto the porch and were perched by the railing like two birds, clearly listening in. Mary, on the other hand, hurried down the steps and came to stand beside Joetta.

"My goodness, this is a wonderful surprise."

In spite of the words she spoke, Mary sounded alarmed.

"Hello, Mary."

Joetta could not meet Mary's eyes. It was hard to imagine what she must think of her, and while Joetta felt contrite, she kept her attention on Bess, who pointed at Joetta's neck.

"But, what of this? Certainly it means your loyalty?"

Joetta let her breath out, put her hand to her throat, and rested her fingertips there.

"It was Henry's. He only wore it the once, right before he left. I found it, and I kept it without really knowing why. I expect now I do."

"And here you are now, wearing it."

"I long for my family's safety and well-being. If, in order to achieve that, I must wear something that guarantees it, then that is what I intend to do."

Joetta's choice of words drew Bess's mouth down. Despite that, Joetta met her gaze and hoped her own did not reveal how troublesome she found those words. Bess appeared torn, somewhat expectant, yet doubtful.

"I would love for you to join us, it's just, those men, what they did. We don't need that sort coming here."

"Of course not."

Joetta waited. It was up to Bess after all. A few tense seconds passed, and Joetta was on the verge of relinquishing Bess from this obviously difficult decision, when she relaxed and acted, if nothing else, at least partially satisfied. Her face transformed, became the Bess of old, her mouth softening, her eyes crinkling with her smile. Here was the Bess Joetta knew, and she could not deny it made her happy. She greatly missed the camaraderie and companionship. Bess spoke to Mary and the two women on the porch who had watched the exchange with great interest.

"Well, ladies, we have an extra pair of hands! Do come in, Joetta."

Bess moved up the steps, and Joetta started to follow, then stopped when Mary laid a hand softly upon her arm, urging her to wait a moment.

She whispered, "I was certain nothing would sway you, that you would never concede your position."

"Have you not heard about what happened?"

"Everyone has, of course. I'm truly sorry. Who denounced you?"

"Who likes to hear himself talk?"

"Mr. McBride? Why on earth . . . ?"

"His pride. His lack of forethought, perhaps. Who can tell?"

"Didn't he realize what might happen? One has to be careful, more so than ever these days. You can barely even hint of thinking otherwise, and they're on you quick as a fly to a carcass. I know. Some are making remarks because Hugh hasn't volunteered."

"Mark my words. As we discussed, it will be conscriptions before long."

Mary shook her head, glancing around quickly.

"It's not fair, is it? As for you, I can see why you'd want to prevent anything more from happening."

Bess poked her head out the door, and said, "Are you coming in? Whatever are you whispering on about?"

Joetta said, "Mary has filled me in on what we are working on." She patted Mary on the arm, leaned over, and said, "We do what we must, even when we do not like it."

The two women entered the house, where Vesta and

Alice were already busy working, one at a loom and the other at the spinning wheel. The cabin was laid out as one large room including the kitchen area, and through the opened back door sat a large pot near a fire in the backyard for dyeing. Near the working women, finished socks were piled to one side, along with mittens and a scarf or two.

Joetta said, "What would you like me to do? I brought along my own carders, or I can do whatever is necessary."

Bess pointed at the work in progress.

"As you can see, we really need more hands in order to accomplish the amounts our men can unquestionably use. For now, I'd say card that pile of wool over there, and, Mary, you do the same. We will move on and do the dyeing once we've made the yarn."

Joetta and Mary began swiping hunks of wool against the carders, one side to the other, and over again. For the time she was there, Joetta listened to the women rail against the North, and their efforts to inhibit a way of life none of them had ever experienced, and likely never would. They repeated the beliefs of Mr. McBride, talking candidly of the superiority of whites, and what on earth would it all come to if the Negro were ever allowed to vote, for God's sake! Much of their commentary was peppered with their husbands' thoughts, not their own. "Thomas says this," and "Zebulon says that," and Alice, because she had no husband to tell her what mattered to her, took in what the other men had told their wives, and trembled with fear while making sucking noises of worry at what these women proposed might happen.

Joetta and Mary worked silently, casting wary looks at one another occasionally, and Joetta found she might as well be at home listening to Mr. McBride. It did not help that a time or two, Bess asked Joetta a question directly, as if testing her.

"What do you think, Joetta? How do you think the Ne-gro should be treated? Time and again, Lincoln has said they should be colonized elsewhere, as if that would resolve the issue at hand. There is work to be done, after all, and who would do it, I ask?"

All eyes were on Joetta and they waited to see what she would say. Joetta set her carders down, sat back, and considered the women before her, trying to think of a way to answer without undoing the effort she had put into this outing thus far. She opted for safety by addressing Bess, appealing to her penchant for flattery. If nothing else, Joetta understood this implicitly about her friend. She blinked at Bess and made sure her voice was strong.

"My word, it would appear you know so much more than I, Bess. I defer to your wisdom on these topics as I am sure we can learn what we need to know from you."

Bess raised herself an inch or two and cast a knowing glance at the women in the circle.

"It is true I have made myself aware of the facts, as we all should, but frankly, since when have you ever followed suit if you didn't agree on something?"

"There is always a time for change."

"Well, then, what would you say to colonization?"

Bess was in a tenacious mood. Joetta decided stating a fact did not reveal anything in particular, one way or the other.

"That would seem counterintuitive to the North's purported goal, is it not? How would putting slaves into colonies free them?"

Bess wagged a finger while nodding.

"It would keep us safe!"

Joetta focused on the wool, taking her time to select some, and Bess moved on. After two hours of listening to them talk, she stood up from the stool, where mounds of carded wool sat around her feet. She deeply questioned her choice in coming. While her façade had only begun, it was more tiresome than if she had spent the day in the fields with Robert chopping and hoeing.

Her voice scratchy and dry, because Bess had not been the best hostess, she said, "Ladies, I must take my leave. I promised Robert and Mr. McBride I would be home in time to cook supper, and if I do not go now, I will be late in getting it on the table."

Bess stood too, wanting a commitment.

"When will you be back? We were doing this once a week, but it isn't nearly enough. We're meeting as much as we can. I suggest Monday, Wednesday, and Friday."

Joetta could not imagine how they were able to complete normal household chores if most of their time and energy were engrossed with this effort. She not only had field work, she had yet to make butter for the week. There was the wash to do as well. Cooking supper was really the simplest of her everyday tasks. Those things aside, how could she bear a repeat of today?

"I will endeavor to come as often as I can."

Before Bess could pin her down, she made her way to the front door while trying not to appear as if she was fleeing. Mary started to get up, and Bess was quick to stop her.

"Mary, I believe you said you were staying the afternoon, is that right?"

Mary sank back down and resumed her work as Bess hovered over her like some sort of odd taskmaster. Joetta shut the door and hurried across the front yard to where Pal slept in place, one leg slightly bent. At the sound of her footsteps he roused and swung his head to look at her. Joetta leaned her forehead into his neck and rubbed the soft hair. She did this only a few seconds before realizing she must get going. If Bess looked out, she would assume there was a problem or that her claim of needing to get back was not quite as urgent as she had professed. She climbed onto the wagon seat and to her dismay, the front door flew open and here came Bess.

"Joetta!"

She started to flick the reins so Pal would move, but Bess would know Joetta heard her. She waited until Bess was by the wagon, staring up at her with a mixture of fondness and frustration. Bess stuck her hands in the pockets of her dress and did not speak right away.

Finally, she said, "I have worried on this more than you can imagine. You don't fool me, Joetta McBride. Tossing about milquetoast comments, wearing the symbol of Southern patriotism as a prop. I understand why you would go to such lengths, I do; however, I can see through it, and the others won't believe you either if you're not sincere."

Joetta's face heated up in an embarrassed flush.

"That obvious, then. Well, what else would you have me do?"

Bess lifted her hands and let them drop.

"No one will be able to stop people like those who came and ruined your fields. Not me. Not anyone. If they even sense you're not secesh, there will be trouble. It's dangerous to continue on in this manner of thinking! Can't you see that?"

Joetta said, "Of course I realize it. I'm trying to do what I can to avoid anything else from happening. If Ennis were here—"

Bess cut her off with an impatient gesture. "If Ennis were here, he might have held them off, but we will never know. I don't want the guilt of knowing if something else happens, it's because I wasn't able to persuade you to come to your senses. I have to think of my own family too, you know."

And, Joetta thought, *I have mine.*

"Please. Do not concern yourself over this."

She slapped the reins lightly against Pal's rump, and he promptly pulled her away.

"Joetta!"

Joetta did not stop. She had done her part to try to get along, yet she questioned herself, and whether she had somehow caused more harm than good. All she could do was go home and face Mr. McBride's scrutiny and Robert's doubt. They would wonder how it went, and if her effort had been worthwhile. She needed to hear from Ennis more so than ever before, but there was little he could do from so far away.

Chapter 12

As a dedicated and regular member of the sewing group, Joetta proved herself faithful in that regard at least, even while she remained elusive in her allegiance to the Confederacy. She opted to go on Wednesdays, and everyone seemed truly thankful for her help. Bess, in her eagerness to prove she had not allowed a defector in their midst, continued to pepper Joetta with questions. While awkward, and at times painful, Joetta skirted direct answers, or stated obvious facts. The time she spent there built a foundation of trust, and her worry someone would accuse her subsided. Still, there was no question it was displeasing she had to placate and mold herself into a particular role befitting her friend's ideals.

Rather than think on this, Joetta threw herself into the season's work of preserving as much food for the winter as possible. She and Robert continued to sift through the cornfields each and every day, taking their rakes and hoes with them, moving the ravaged stalks this way and that, continuing to search for any ears still salvageable beneath the trampled foliage. They found very little after sweeping the fields several times. Luckily, they had more success with the sorghum. Eventually the season wore on, and the seeds transitioned to a deep burgundy color, in the same way they did every year. This crop had certainly fared better than the corn, and by early October, Robert and Joetta began the backbreaking work of hacking the leaves off the stalks and cutting them down.

After taking loads to the barn and emptying the wagon, Robert hitched Pal to the sweep that would work the press. To Joetta's surprise, even Mr. McBride helped. He got himself a chair from the kitchen and sat by it and fed the long cane pieces into the box where the rollers grabbed on to them and crushed them as Pal went round and round. Joetta placed a barrel on the other side of the press covered with a piece of burlap where a hole was cut for a spout. The grinder wheels inside the box crushed the stalks and the juice flowed from the spout into a large metal pan, and Joetta smiled. They had not beaten her. No. There would be sorghum syrup despite the deeds of those horrible men. Not only were they able to make the syrup, the pressed stalks were gathered up and stored for the animals. Neither the salvaged corn nor the sorghum fodder were enough to see the animals through the entire winter, yet Joetta was determined they would somehow make do.

On a cold crisp morning toward the end of October, Mr. McBride took his pistol and killed a boar and a sow. Soon after, the scent coming from the smokehouse brought memories of Ennis sitting up all night to tend the fire with the boys when they were young. Robert still hunted every day, and they ate his fresh kill if he was successful, to conserve the other meat as they could. Joetta had done as she had in the past, taking what came from the vegetable garden—the potatoes, squash, turnips, cabbage, and onions—and stored them in the root cellar. She and Robert picked apples off their trees and dried the fruit out by spreading it in single layers on wooden planks on the western side of the house where the sun hit the strongest in the afternoons.

As she had expected, and before long, the cornmeal and flour dwindled, and she grew conservative to the point Robert and Mr. McBride complained about the infrequency of biscuits, corn bread, or grits when they sat down to eat. She was adamant, and they grumbled but became accustomed to her rationing it. It went along like this with Joetta involved in the usual farm tasks, then donning the hateful little cockade once a week and making an appearance at Bess's to, as she thought of it, fortify the farce. Bess continued to act satisfied, and even Alice and Vesta warmed back up. Joetta and Mary had moments of mutual commiseration they snuck in before returning to their respective homes. Joetta was pleased to know at least she and Mary were of like minds.

As time passed, her unease began to wane. She allowed the ruination of their crops had been a singular occurrence, mischief by individuals who thought it a lark to stir up trouble. One night, in early November, she went outside to empty the chamber pot. She always did so along the edge of the woods. As she emptied the bowl, there came a distinctive noise, and she spun around, peering into the darkness. A feeling slipped over her the way a breeze would—there, but nothing to see. She was certain she was being watched. She looked into the dark woods, alert and attentive, then behind her. The hairs on her head and back of her neck tingled, and her instincts sent her rushing back across the yard and into the house. She banged the back door shut and barred it. Never, in all her years on the farm, had she ever felt this way.

She retrieved the musket from over the door with no idea

if she needed it, but she would be ready if she did. How had it come to this, her alone in this house? She had only ever acted out of love, yet she had somehow become something of a pariah. She used to sit with her sewing basket of shirts, pants, and whatnot that needed mending, filled with utter contentment with her family gathered around, and yes, even Mr. McBride in his corner chair grumbling about this or that. She looked over her shoulder at the circle of empty chairs. To even contemplate sitting in there by herself only emphasized her solitude.

From the kitchen window, she stared into the blackness beyond and felt as if she were on high alert, waiting for what, she did not know. She held the musket at the ready, for some unknown amount of time, until she began to feel a bit foolish. She replaced the weapon and went into the bedroom, where she lit the oil lamp and began to get ready for bed. She was becoming too high-strung. It was probably a deer, or a fox. It was highly unlikely someone lurked about as her mind wanted her to think. Even with these reasonable assumptions, she tossed this way and that all night and into the hour before dawn. Finally, she rose. After getting dressed, she went out to feed the chickens and just before reaching the chicken coop, she stopped. Right in front of her was proof of her suspicion last night.

Near the corner of the small enclosure and hanging from a pine sapling, where she was sure to see it, a small replica of the Confederate Stars and Bars waved in the cool morning air. The sight of it was so out of place that once again she looked behind her and all around. She yanked it off the branch and stuffed it into her apron pocket. Josephine and Agnes peeked out, saw her, squawked, and came strutting down the ramp, and rest of the flock were not far behind. She tossed them a bit of corn and scraps of vegetables from supper the night before. They flapped and fluttered about while she deliberated if someone was still hidden away, spying on her. She acted normal, gave no clues she was aware of anything unusual.

She moved on to the hog pen, still highly tuned in to her surroundings. Boot prints were around it, and she was convinced the flag was a message, an obvious attempt to scare her. In the barn, she milked Honey and let her out to graze. Back at the house she set about making breakfast as usual. Robert and Mr. McBride came in as she was setting the table. She hesitated, but was so unnerved by what she had found, she pulled the small flag from her apron pocket and put it by Mr. McBride's plate. He plopped into his chair, picked it up, and frowned at it.

"Where'd this Rebel flag come from?"

"I found it hanging by the chicken coop this morning."

He banged his cane on the floor.

"You best be careful, Missy!"

Joetta, startled, dropped the piece of bacon dangling off the fork and grease spattered onto her apron.

Robert said, "Secesh don't have much tolerance for those who ain't true to the cause. Harold said so."

Mr. McBride said, "It's called sympathizing with the enemy."

They stared at her, and Joetta placed her hands on her hips.

"I have done nothing except go to Bess's, sew socks for the Confederates, all the while with that absurd ornament hanging off my person."

"But what're you saying when you're there?"

"Nothing of significance."

Mr. McBride pointed at her.

"Listen, now. It's getting serious. It was in the paper

about some woman up near to Washington, D.C., where the Union done took her, her two daughters, and her sister off to prison, accused of spying."

Joetta absorbed this latest news. Despite the seeming goodwill toward her, Bess made it clear she held doubts about Joetta's motivations, yet needed her help badly enough to allow her some leniency. Joetta did not *think* she would be denounced by the other women. She did not believe she would be allowed to come if they had any inkling she might present some sort of trouble to them. That was what made this particular incident highly disturbing. She served the food. Robert picked up his fork and offered his mother a tiny bit of encouragement.

"That's mostly happening in the Border States, like Virginia and Tennessee."

Tennessee, where Faith, Marshall, and her nieces and nephew lived.

Mr. McBride said, "Don't be too complacent, my boy. The same could very well happen here too." He scowled at Joetta. "You best be singing the right tune at them sewing meetings. You could get us into more trouble than you ever seen."

Joetta's appetite left.

She said, "I need to get more buttermilk from the springhouse."

She rushed out the back door and around the corner. There she leaned against the house, trying to gather her thoughts. A minute later, Mr. McBride yelled.

"Where you at with that buttermilk? I'm about parched!"

She straightened up. She must keep calm and not appear worried. She hurried to the springhouse, and once she was back inside, Mr. McBride, eyes narrowed, stared at her with suspicion. To distract him from whatever he thought, she sat down again and pushed the food around on her plate.

Finally, they finished and went out. She dumped her food into the scrap bucket. She needed to eat more, only her insides were always in a turmoil, not to mention her mind.

A few days later, Mr. McBride came back from town as downtrodden and demoralized as she had ever seen him. He entered the kitchen, where she was straining muscadine juice to make jam. He sat in a chair, his hands braced on his knees, and his expression glum. His white hair, rearranged by anxious fingers, was as frizzy as the tattered ends of a rag.

"Folks in town's acting mighty peculiar."

"Oh?"

"Won't nobody hardly talk to me none, barely a how do. I go into Spivey's and them who was there got up and left. I go on down the street, and damn if most don't cross to the other side so as to not have to speak, or plumb change to the other direction."

"Maybe you're imagining it."

"I ain't imagining nothing. And I sure as hell know I ain't spoke to nary a soul the entire time I was there. Except Spivey, himself."

"Maybe they are only worried. There is plenty to be worried about these days."

"Well, who ain't? Don't mean they can't have a word or two. I give up and come on home. If there ain't nobody wanting to talk to me, ain't no point in staying. Hell, I get overlooked here by my own."

Joetta wanted to roll her eyes. He had to be exaggerating, as he did have a tendency toward the dramatic. People were concerned. Everyone had the same questions on their mind. How long was this going to go on, when would it end? Women were yearning for their men to come home because they were needed, and the ones who were not fighting were nervous they might be called. As well was the fact the longer men were gone, the greater the risk they would never return. Joetta was painfully aware of this.

She said, "Maybe I should write to Ennis again."

Mr. McBride quickly reached into his pocket.

"Oh, I almost forgot. I brung you this."

Joetta grabbed for the letter he tossed to the table as he went off mumbling to himself. It was from her sister, Faith, and while glad to have it, she had the same reaction to receiving this correspondence as she had from her mother. Happy, yet disappointed. If Ennis were here, he would reassure her she could not have stopped the men who crushed their fields. He would tell her they had not been harmed physically, and this was what was most important. Well, he was not here, and she was beginning to feel more and more forsaken by him. Two letters between them in all this time. She need not have worried about the cost. One from him, and the one she had written was all there was. She had since waited. And waited. She did not want to inconvenience him, but it would have helped immeasurably to have some word from him.

She tore open Faith's letter and read it quickly the first time, and more slowly the second. Faith was short in her details. Marshall had volunteered for the Union. The *Union*. Joetta did not know what to think of this. She read it a third time. She had not seen her sister in a good while and there were certainly Union sympathizers in North Carolina's western area and beyond. Marshall's decision made Joetta feel even more alienated, and cautious. When she wrote again, she would have to keep her news as routine as the Monday wash. If she were asked about her family's involvement, she would feign ignorance. Joetta took her sister's letter, and as hard as it was to do so, she opened up the door to the cookstove and tossed it in. She stoked the fire, and it roared. She returned to her jam making, contemplating the country's divisions and the similar fractures it created within families.

The air changed quickly, becoming nippy, shadows lengthened and the warm rays of the sun left them earlier and earlier. Thanksgiving was only a week away when Mr. McBride pulled a flier from his pocket one morning.

"Why don't we take a little ride into town? They're giving out hot cider down to the courthouse square. Heard there might be a speech or two from some of them gov'ment types."

He wanted reassurances he remained in good standing, to be certain his previous experience in town had been an anomaly. He was raring to go. It was an outing they could all use, particularly Robert, who had not been anywhere all summer and was as gloomy as an overcast sky. She would like to go too, except she was certain it would be best for her to stay home.

"Maybe just you and Robert go. I have plenty to do here, yet. My sewing is way behind."

Mr. McBride raised an eyebrow.

"Don't trust the welcome? All them visits to the Caldwells ain't paying off?"

"I would be just as welcome as you, from the sound of it."

Mr. McBride spit on the ground.

"Wear that little fancy doodad. I'll carry that flag. We will make an appearance, as we should. Word gets around we weren't there, could be suspicious seeming."

Perhaps he was right. Perhaps it was best to be seen at such an event.

"Fine. However, I need time to look presentable."

"Ain't got to go just this minute. We can go in an hour."

He headed back to his cabin yelling to Robert they were going to town. Joetta heated water and began scrubbing her arms, face, and neck. She took her hair down, brushed it a few times, re-braided it, and wrapped it back around her head. She put on a clean collar and cuffs. She buffed her shoes. Last, she fastened the little knot of ribbon to her neck. She got her bonnet, some of the Confederate money for coffee, and her reticule. She was ready. Mr. McBride had hitched Pal to the wagon, and he and Robert waited for her. Both had brushed their hair, and when she appeared, she believed she saw a hint of admiration in Robert's gaze. Mr. McBride motioned for her to climb up, and she did so with a hand from Robert. She almost gripped it longer than necessary as this was the first touch her youngest son had bestowed upon her in weeks. This in of itself made Joetta glad she had consented to go out for the jaunt.

The fit was tight on the seat, but there was a nice cool breeze and an overcast sky, yet the seasonal change of the leaves made up for the lack of sun. The landscape, painted in patches of burnt orange, fiery red, and bright yellow, glowed against the dull, gray clouds. After they arrived in town, Mr. McBride parked at the front of Mr. Spivey's store. Elder Newell walked slowly down the wooden walkway that ran along the main street and stopped to speak. Mr. McBride shook hands and clapped him on the back. When Elder Newell faced Joetta, his reaction was not unlike Bess's the first time Joetta wore the decoration of support. His eyes opened big as they could go, he warbled out a greeting, his voice quavering along in time to his head.

"Why M-Mrs. Mc-McBride, my eyes did s-sorely need to see you to-today."

It was a bit amusing as his eyes were on her neck rather than her face. She deduced it was the cockade he was happy to see.

"Elder Newell."

Mr. McBride said, "What's the latest?"

"Aw, a-ain't much news on the war. W-what all I know, armies are starting to build th-their w-winter encampments."

"That so?"

"Y-yep."

Joetta was relieved. Safety. There was safety for her loved ones for at least a little while. Mr. McBride and Robert headed for the square, while she went into the store. Mr. Spivey, behind the counter as always, did a double take as she approached, quickly recovered, and smiled.

"Mrs. McBride, how are you on this fine day?"

She took a chance.

"Well, and doing what I must. You?"

"Same, same."

"I have come for some coffee."

Mr. Spivey said, "We will soon be running out, I fear. They're fortifying the blockades on the coast, and less is coming this way. How much do you need?"

Joetta said, "I heard. Two pounds, if you have it."

Mr. Spivey went to the back and Joetta drifted about the store, noting a few items here and there that might make a good Christmas present for Robert. A new pocketknife, perhaps. A store-bought scarf. This was frivolous thinking, of course. She had to be careful with spending. When Mr. Spivey returned, he placed the coffee onto the counter. He then held a finger up and went over to where mail was kept. Before he even sifted through what he had, her heart began pounding. He turned to her holding several letters. He flipped through them, and she expected him to shake his head that they were not for her. Instead, he walked over and handed all of them to her. She gazed in wonder, caught up in the moment. There were three (three!) long-awaited letters from Ennis. One was dated only three weeks ago!

His familiar print set her heart racing, and her hands shook as she slapped the money down, grabbed them up, and rushed from the store. Outside she held them tight against her chest, as if hugging the very person who sent them. She did not care who saw or what they might think. Elated, she simply could not help herself.

Chapter 13

With the treasured letters tucked safely in her reticule, she strode along with energy, smiling at everyone and nothing. The day was now perfect, and even though she did not know what they contained, she was filled with a renewed optimism. She went in search of Mr. McBride and Robert, and as she approached the square, a small crowd had already gathered. She surveyed those standing on the outermost edge of the throng and did not see them right way. There. There was a familiar shirt sleeve in the air, and a hand waving the small, yet distinctive flag back and forth with enthusiasm accompanied by a raucous cheer. That would certainly be Mr. McBride. The crowd swayed one way and the other trying to see the stage and who would speak. She edged by a variety of different individuals, some dressed as if they had just come from church, others in their everyday wear.

She squeezed by, mumbling "excuse me, pardon me," and drew closer to the waving arm.

There was Robert, turning this way and that, looking

to see who else was there. A few others waved flags similar to the one she had found and given to Mr. McBride. This had her curious, wondering who might be selling them. Others had whistles or noisemakers and were using both enthusiastically. She finally reached Mr. McBride and stood between him and Robert. The crowd grew impatient, and their eagerness to hear the speaker fueled a ripple of energy unlike anything she had ever experienced. No one had yet approached the lectern, and Joetta could not imagine the reaction they would have when this person materialized. She looked for the Caldwells. Surely they were in attendance for such as this. Even after craning her neck to look, she did not see them.

She began to concentrate on those around her. She was furtive, not wanting to draw attention, yet wanting to know if she might spot the men who came to the farm. No one looked even vaguely familiar, so it held to reason they had been strangers passing through. She returned her attention to the front when those around her started murmuring and pointing. A man stepped onto the erected stage and held his arms up to get the crowd to settle down. Why, it was Wilmot Poole, dressed as if he were going out for an evening, his expensive suit like a polished stone among the rubble. He waved at a few people in the front, then turned to a man off to the side and bowed, as if paying homage.

Mr. Poole shouted, "That cider y'all are enjoying? It come straight from my apple trees, made only this morning! But! For those of you who want something with a little extra kick, go on over to the back of my cotton warehouse ri'tch yonder. Y'all know where it is! Have you something that will put a fire in your belly for this effort against our enemy!"

He stepped down amidst cheering, and Joetta was able to make out his progress through the crowd as they parted to let him through. Several standing nearby hurried in the direction of the cotton warehouse. The man Wilmot Poole bowed to stepped onto the stage and clapped until Mr. Poole was no longer visible before he focused on those gathered.

"Good citizens, I see your dedicated loyalty on display here!"

A boisterous cheer resounded through the crowd.

"Let me tell you all who I am. My name is George Lidell, and I have been sent to let you know there's a bonus for those willing to sign up!"

A disgruntled rumbling went through the crowd.

"Yes, yes, I know. Many of you got farms, and you need to feed your families. But, listen to me! As upstanding citizens who go to church, who only want to keep their kinfolk safe, now is the time to protect them and what you have! Rich or poor, you will lose your freedoms unless you fight!"

A disturbed murmur began and Joetta found she was paying attention.

"What if one day someone not from 'round here came and took what you worked so hard for as their very own?"

Boos and hissing.

"What if them Yankees came here and staked a claim on land that had been in your family for generations? Said they were taking it over for the gov'ment?"

The jeering sound grew louder.

"What if they get what they want? What if our land, our families, and *our women* are violated?"

The mass moved as one, surging toward the stage with various denouncements ringing out.

"Never!"

"It won't be allowed! Not here!"

"To hell with them Yankee devils!"

The speaker motioned again to quiet them down.

He shouted, "This! This is why we fight! Why we must fight! We are here for volunteers! Come, good, brave men! Fight for your way of life! Fight for this moment in history against those who would dare tell us we are wrong, those who expect us to falter. Not if we can help it, by the Almighty God!"

Every bell, whistle, and voice sounded, creating a rowdy din that had Joetta covering her ears. Could their land be taken? How could that happen to individuals not part of any dissidence? Their only desire was to raise their boys to be good, hardworking Christian men and to live amicably among those in the community. They did not want to see harm come to anyone, but this was not *their* fight. Mr. McBride shouted with the others.

"Let them dare to come on my property again, and I'll shoot every damn one of them!"

Robert jumped up and down, and to her dismay, yelled a threat, too.

"I'll shoot them Yankees dead!"

She snatched his arm, wanting to separate him from the belligerent and volatile. He pulled against her grasp, and she gripped even tighter, shooting an angry look at him. He stopped resisting, and together they weaved through the throng and away from what was turning into a mob. When they were clear of the crowd, she stopped, put her hands on her hips.

"Robert McBride, what do you think you are doing? You are but twelve years old!"

His eyes shimmered with remorse, the first hint of the old Robert since Henry and Ennis had left.

"I thought we were on their side," and he pointed back toward the group of rabble-rousers who were jostling one another. "Because of Henry, Papa, and your wearing that.

Ain't I supposed to show whose side we're on? I don't understand."

Joetta yielded, her impatience dissolving with his bewilderment.

"We are only doing what we must to stay safe. The way they are acting"—she tipped her head toward the square where the shouting went on—"they fear for what might happen. What that man was saying, we do not know if it is true or not. I do know this, your papa would not be part of it, not if he could help it."

"What are *we* going to do? Nothing? Look what happened to our fields!"

"We are going back to the farm, and what we are going to do from this point on is to stay out of sight as much as possible. No church. No trips to town. It is safer that way."

At this revelation Robert quickly resumed his previous disposition, one of detached miserableness, but Joetta could not worry about Robert's mood. She had to do what was best, and given this experience, and the fervency and disposition of the town, what was best was to make themselves scarce so as to not anger anyone or put themselves in harm's way. She quickly pulled the letters from her bag and held them up.

"Look. I have good news. We have three whole letters from your father to read. Let us go home and see what he has to say."

The change in Robert was not unlike her own. His eyes rested on his father's handwriting, and the alteration was immediate, a similar yearning to hers unfolded right before her, and her heart ached for him. He held his hands out and she gave the precious letters over to him. She waited, a little smile playing about her mouth as he looked at the dates on each one.

"He wrote."

"Yes."

Joetta did not say anything more because Mr. McBride had made his way over to them.

"What happened? Why'd y'all disappear all of a sudden?"

Joetta pointed at what Robert held.

"We have letters from Ennis. I want to go home and read them. I have heard and seen enough here."

Mr. McBride stared over his shoulder, studying the gathering. His gaze followed several men who broke away from the crowd to make their way toward Mr. Poole's cotton warehouse.

"Y'all go on. Maybe Caldwell or Brown can give me a ride back partway."

"Do you not want to come home and see what your son has to say?"

"I'll hear about it when I get back."

"You are sure?"

"Hell yes, I'm sure. Damn. Why all the questions?"

"I thought maybe you would want to know how he is doing."

"He wrote, didn't he? He's alive, I'd warrant."

Joetta frowned, and even Robert reared his head back and scowled in his direction.

"Come on then, Robert. We will go."

Joetta could not be disappointed in the outing, even while it had shown how strongly many felt. She finally had what she had been waiting for, letters from her beloved, and nothing could take that away. She climbed onto the seat while Robert unraveled Pal's reins from the wooden railing in front of the store. Once they were on their way, she sat back to enjoy the ride. They had gone about halfway when behind them came the sound of the staccato, rapid strike of hooves, and they twisted about to see who rode so fast. A man, partially obscured by a handkerchief over the lower half of his face, quickly bore down on them. To Joetta, he looked like a bandit on the run, but his looks became inconsequential compared to his intent. He came close, so close, it was as if he intended to ride his horse into the sides of the wagon. Over his head he waved a Confederate flag, and as he passed them by, he shouted words neither of them understood.

Pal spooked and Robert pulled up on the reins, yelling "Whoa! Whoa!" in vain.

Into a shallow ditch they went, the wheels bumping over the uneven ground and jostling Joetta so badly she came close to being thrown out. They sat bewildered and breathless, staring after the rider. He looked back, and because he did not stop to see if they were all right, it made her certain his erratic maneuvering was intentional. They climbed down, and Robert took hold of the reins and carefully led Pal back onto the road, all the while murmuring to the mule and reassuring him. Soon, they were back on their way. Robert's comment caught Joetta off guard.

"That was 'cause of you."

Incredulous, she said, "Me? What do I have to do with the crazy actions of that man?"

"I didn't get a good look at him, but I recognize that green coat."

"How?"

"I saw him."

"Where, in town just now?"

He nodded.

"Seemed like he was always nearby. I didn't ever see his face, though."

Exasperated, Joetta stared at Robert.

"Why did you not tell me?"

Robert did not answer, and Joetta stared at her hands. After a while she spoke again.

"Do you see why I said we ought to stay out of sight?"

Robert did not look at her when he made a comment Jo-etta would have sworn came straight out of Mr. McBride's mouth. "Maybe it's you who needs to stay hidden."

She adjusted the skirt of her dress with a quick jerk as anger beset her.

"Is that so? From the sound of it, maybe you are spending way too much time with your grandfather."

He smacked the reins against Pal's rump to get him to speed up. She did not want to argue, but this seemed to be the way of late. Once they were back at the farm, Robert stopped so she could climb down. She exited swiftly, her mood simmering. As quick as she was to step down, he was just as quick to urge Pal toward the barn, barely giving her time to get out of the way. She was dismayed at such insolence and disrespect. She let her breath out and went to the springhouse for milk and butter. When she came out, Pal had been let loose in the pasture and Robert was nowhere to be seen. She went up the back steps, shoved the back door open, and came to a sudden stop at the sound of hurried footsteps coming from the direction of the sitting room.

"Robert?"

There was no answer and she got that same feeling she had the other night, a prickly sensation down her neck and spine. She reached for the musket over the back door, shouldered it, and listened. The house was quiet. She approached the hall and stared into the sitting room. It was empty; however, the front door was wide open, and the view just beyond to the front of the house made her breath catch. The very same rider in the green coat was hunched over the neck of his horse, flying down the road like the devil was after him. The idea of someone in her home, where she had always believed she was safe, gave her a sense of vulnerability she had never felt before. She still had the gun to her shoulder, and while she was a pretty good shot, he was already too far away.

She lowered it and ran across the yard, looking for Robert. He was not in the barn. She went to Mr. McBride's cabin and knocked on the door, glancing to her left, right, and behind her, suspicious and mistrustful of her surroundings. She was at odds with so many—her sons, Mr. McBride, even Ennis, given the way he had departed. Her own sister supported the Union, and her brothers? She did not know about them. What she understood was this cunning hostility and behavior was a message sent as decisively as the blast from a cannon.

Robert did not come to the door. She opened it and stuck her head inside, calling out.

"Robert?"

She gave up and shut it. She made her way back across the yard and reentered the barn on the off chance she had somehow missed him.

"Robert?"

The scent of hay, redolent with memories, filled her nose and made it easy to picture how they had once been, a family working through the harvest to store feed for their livestock. She wanted so badly for their lives to be that way again, with her alongside Ennis, Henry, Robert, and yes, even Mr. McBride, laboring together toward a common goal. She lingered briefly as voices of the past echoed along with a vision of her husband and their two sons, side by side.

She sensed Robert there, waiting, wanting her to leave. Slowly, hoping he'd change his mind, perhaps soften, if only a little, Joetta went out with nothing accompanying her but the sound of her own sigh. She took refuge in her kitchen and brought out the letters. She could at least console herself, and thanked God for them. She prayed Ennis's words would restore her spirit and renew her will to hold steadfast, her head held high.

Chapter 14

Dear one,

At that, Joetta stopped reading. Those two words alone did wonders to heal her aching, desolate heart. She bent her head and allowed a few miserable tears to dampen her cheeks and drip from her jawline. The endearment reverberated in her head, as if he were right beside her.

Dear one, dear one, dear one . . .

Her throat tightened, and she allowed herself a moment, long enough to feel the release before she wiped her nose, and continued. She was reading his letters in order, and this was the oldest one, which meant he had already had a change of heart since the one and only correspondence she had received, the one that had given her reason to worry over their relationship for the first time in their marriage.

I write to you on a warm summer's eve, having marched for many miles since my first letter. During these long treks I have reflected on the day I left, and heavy, cumbersome

*thoughts have taken hold of me. I wish to say I am sorry. I
wish I had not left angry, but had the grace to understand
the love of a mother for her child. There is nothing like distance and days apart to correct a mood. I hope you can and
will forgive me, my love.*

Joetta sank back against the chair, her relief enormous,
and joy swept through her, wiping away the emotional
strain she had felt since he left. She placed her hand over
her heart and patted her chest lightly, gulping air as if she
had run for miles.

Oh, Ennis. How I wish you here with me.

She continued on, happy and eager for all he might share.

*We set up camp each night, then drill some. All along
we have been in a few skirmishes here and there. Most were
over with quickly. This is all well and good as it is obvious we are not well-trained despite the fact we work hard to
improve and do as we must. It is a rough lot, undisciplined
and with a minimal understanding of rank. Men don't like
taking orders, having spent most of their lives working to
provide without account to anyone but themselves, their family, and God. I don't mind being told what to do, for I am
ignorant of the ways of these efforts, and only yearn to get
through this and back home. I inquire about Henry to everyone I can. I am sorry to say I have not been given much
hope of finding him.*

I must get some rest. Please write. All my love, Ennis

Joetta lowered her hands, the paper resting on her lap.
His words stitched her soul back together and she felt more
herself than she had in a while. While she could not completely shake off her uneasiness over the intruder, she was
not as afraid as she had been a few moments ago. Ennis

was asking her forgiveness. She smiled to herself at the fact he loved her as he always had. How could she have ever doubted this? While his words at the end about Henry tamped her mood somewhat, she could now rest easy that her husband was all right, and all was well between them. She moved on to the next one, which was dated in early October, shortly after she had sent hers, begging him to put her mind at ease.

My love, have no fear. As you would have gathered from my last letter, I am ashamed of my behavior as I love you, and always will. We have arrived at our encampment for the next several months. I am told we will winter here. My efforts to find Henry will be delayed as I have ascertained all I can for now and know he is nowhere in the vicinity. As you will note on the cover, I am in Centreville, Virginia. This is where a battle took place in an area called Bull Run Creek in July. Perhaps there was news of it there? As we'd not yet arrived, we missed the action, as my new friends would style it. They don't know how glad I am we've not been called upon too often to fight in any significant man-ner in this effort which matters not to me. I count this as a blessing, as I know you will, too. I try to stay to myself, and don't say much.

We've been engaged in building our shelters, and none too soon. The weather is turning, and soon, I fear, the days I spend in this wretched effort will be long, and cold. All is done in a very strict and orderly manner. Reveille is at six in the morning. We form lines in the streets and there is roll call. We commence with a bit of drilling before breakfast at seven. It is not much to my liking, what they give us. It is sometimes bread, salt pork, salted beef, and coffee. I've had to partake of some oddity called desiccated vegetables. A cake of shredded vegetables that have been pressed and dried.

*Most everyone calls them desecrated vegetables. I tend to
agree as they are tasteless lumps of something not recogniz-
able when water is added. Soon it will be Thanksgiving,
and I try not to think of the feast you would prepare. Send
whatever you can. It will be devoured with appreciation.*

*Guard duty is determined by eight. From nine until
twelve we are engaged in the learnings of soldiering. Dinner
is at one. More in the ways of learning how to be a soldier
follows until supper at six. It is under very strict orders that
any man, and not more than five, be allowed to leave the
camp for a short time. Such is the life of your poor husband,
thus far.*

*Now that I have shared a bit about my days, I would
ask after you, Robert, and Pa. It is my fervent hope all is
well at home, the harvest plentiful, and you are situated well
for the upcoming winter. I'm certain Robert is as helpful as
ever. He's always been that way, and I would expect he's
been useful. Please tell him his papa is proud of him and
all he does to help you. This stagnating in camp has taken
a toll, and what gets me through my time here is to foresee
the day I come down the lane, delivered into your arms once
again. Please keep your faith and your prayers coming.*

All my love, Ennis

Of course she would not tell him of what had occurred
with the crops. There was no need to worry him with it.
Robert should read this one, with certainty. Perhaps these
words from his father would help in adjusting his conduct.
She picked up Ennis's last letter. In this one he updated
her on the progress of their encampment fortifications and
shared family stories told to him by his fellow volunteers.
He had met men from other parts of North Carolina, as
well as Alabama and South Carolina. She could tell his
good humor was restored, although he still complained

about the food while poking a little fun at himself for his cooking skills, or lack thereof.

Since Ennis had left, Joetta had not allowed herself to ponder on memories that might send her in a state of despondency. She did so now, thinking back to the day they met. It was late January in 1845 and she had been with her family at the stockyard, where they had gone to buy a milk cow after the one they had for years died. She first saw him standing by himself near a fence and thought how handsome he was with his longish hair and tall frame. Faith, already married to Marshall the year before, was home for a visit from Tennessee.

She bumped Joetta with her hip, and said, "That is not a cow you are looking at."

Joetta, her voice lowered, came out like a hiss. "Be quiet! He will hear you!"

"And what if he does? Have you not started thinking of marriage?"

Joetta would soon be eighteen years old, with a couple of suitors here and there, but no one had caught her eye, much less her heart. She wanted someone to love, and her parents did not care how long it took as long as she was happy.

She returned her attention to the cow, tuning out Faith and her comments until Faith leaned over and said, "Oh my. He's coming this way."

Joetta's senses went on high alert. Someone came close and stood to her left. She did not need to look to know it was him. She smelled leather, wood smoke, and something else she could not put her finger on. Soap? He leaned down, pointed, and spoke to her in a low voice, his breath making a tendril of her hair move.

"I like that Jersey over yonder."

It was the same one she considered worth the money. She smiled, keeping her gaze on the cow. He asked her name, and she allowed herself a peek at him from up close. She should not have. *Eyes like smoke.* It was the only coherent thought she had.

"Joetta. Bowen."

He reached for her hand, and said, "Well, Miss Joetta Bowen, I'm pleased to make your acquaintance."

He did not give her his name.

"And your name?" she prompted him.

He smiled in such a way Joetta was certain he had been playing a little game with her.

"Ennis McBride, ma'am."

She lowered her head and did not speak, however she stole several more looks. She found him exceptionally charismatic. He succeeded in derailing her usual nonplussed reactions to interest shown her by the opposite sex when he boldly took her hand, her left one, and looked pointedly at her ring finger. The hand, as if with a mind of its own, promptly became sweaty. Embarrassed, she pulled it away, wishing her body had not betrayed her. She made some flimsy comment about finding her parents, ignoring Faith and her big-eyed stare. He walked along with Joetta to where her parents were now engaged in bidding on the very same cow. Faith followed behind wearing an impish grin.

Joetta's mother gave Ennis a forthright look and nudged her father. Joetta grew hot around the collar of her dress, the warmth going right down her back. She introduced him and believed her voice sounded off-putting, and jarring. Her mother continued her acute assessment, while her father asked his opinion about the Jersey cow. Ennis McBride knew his cattle and pointed out the cow's possible age, her straight back, dished head, and broad nostrils. Joetta's father was not looking at the cow. He was studying

Ennis McBride with the eye of a parent wanting only the best for his daughter.

"Thank you," he said when Ennis finished his appraisal.

Afterward, Ennis and Joetta walked a few feet away, and he said, "Where do you live?"

"Our farm is about two miles east. One cannot miss it. The barn has a red roof."

"May I come and see you?"

Joetta looked across the stockyard, hesitating, while he waited patiently.

"Yes," she said, finally.

She had known her answer but had not wanted to seem eager. He came as he promised. Each time Joetta found herself more drawn to him. He was almost a year older, and they liked the same things, had the same ideas. It was no surprise, really, when a few months later they gathered on a Saturday afternoon in May of 1845 to marry, one month after her eighteenth birthday. Her mother and father gave her a hope chest filled with the items she would need to start her own household. A new skillet, handsewn napkins, a tablecloth, and a beautiful appliqué quilt her mother had worked on for some time in a madder red print Joetta adored. Joetta stored her things in Ennis's wagon, and they made their way to his father's land due west, and a day's ride from her childhood home. From then on, they had suffered few disagreements throughout the years, up until this incident with Henry.

Joetta tucked the letters into her apron pocket and began cooking supper. She cooked green beans, fried some pork tenderloin, and put sliced peaches in a bowl. She set the food on the table. She had some milk from the springhouse and butter too, because she had made biscuits for the first time in several days, a treat due to her buoyant mood. The sound of wheels rolling over the hard-packed dirt at the front of the house meant Mr. McBride was home.

She arrived on the porch in time to see him more or less fall off the seat of Elder Newell's wagon, and this caused both men to laugh hysterically. She realized both of them were drunk. Mr. McBride propped himself against the side of the wagon to catch his breath. He saw her, pushed himself off, and lurched toward the house. His limp was worse, like he had walked too much for one day, or perhaps twisted his knee. Elder Newell struggled to get his wagon aimed at going back down the lane. He finally had to climb down, take hold of the harness, and lead his horse so he was pointed in the direction he wanted to go. If he took note of her standing there, he did not let on. Finally, he was off.

She faced Mr. McBride. The sharp scent of corn liquor wafted off of him as soon as he came within a foot of her, and his words slurred when he spoke.

"Ish shupper done?"

He looked so bedraggled, and even spite of all that had happened that afternoon, she almost laughed. Her mood was light as air due to Ennis's affirmation of his love, so she felt generous, and went down the steps to take her father-in-law's arm and help him into the house.

"Yes, supper is done."

He hacked and coughed, and Joetta turned her head, grimacing at the noises he produced.

"Where'sh the boy?"

She did not bother to correct him.

"I am not sure. He took off as soon as we got home."

She wanted to tell Mr. McBride about the stranger in the house, but one look at his slack mouth and droopy eyes told her if he even made it through supper without his head falling into his plate, this would be an achievement. She led him to his chair and he promptly dropped into it. He sat staring at his empty plate. She studied him a moment.

"Can you eat?"

"Sure, sure."

She began serving and poured him some coffee. He sat weaving, fork clutched in his hand. He was able to spear a piece of meat, ignoring the knife she had placed by his plate. Joetta sat down as well and attempted to eat with him, deciding not to concern herself with Robert's absence. His continued inconsiderate behavior ought to be dealt with, but she did not want to ruin her good mood. Abruptly, Mr. McBride let his fork drop.

"I got to get home. I'm feeling a mite off."

Joetta did not say it served him right, even though it did.

"I will wrap your plate. Maybe you will want to eat later. Go on and have some coffee. That might help."

Mr. McBride picked up the cup with a shaky hand and slurped, while she rose from her chair and got a cloth to put over his plate. She waited a few minutes, busying herself and hoping the coffee would do enough for him so he could walk with a little assistance.

"Okay," he grunted.

She went to his side and offered her arm. He gripped it hard and tried to pull himself up.

"Whoops."

He flopped back into the chair, grinning like some kind of fool. Joetta propped her hands on her hips. He tried to look at her straight-faced.

"What? Can't a man enjoy himself every now and again?"

"Certainly. As long as that man can walk on his own. After all, now is not the time to be caught with our guard down. Not after what happened to me and Robert on our way home, and afterward."

This had a tiny sobering effect on Mr. McBride. He sat up straighter and attempted to focus.

"Whatever are you babbling on about?"

The corn liquor made him more rude than usual.

"A man on a horse came by us, spooked Pal, and caused us to run off the road. I might have believed it an accident, except when we got home, that very same man was in this house. He must have heard me because he ran out. By the time I got the gun, he was riding away."

They both jumped as the back door flew open with a bang and Robert came in.

Joetta said, "Where have you been? You should have told me where you were going. That man was in the house. The one who ran us off the road. And your grandfather has had too much fun at Mr. Poole's warehouse and is not feeling his best at the moment."

Mr. McBride belched, and grumbled, "I'm fine."

Joetta ignored Mr. McBride and said, "Where did you go?"

Robert would not look at her and instead turned to his grandfather. "You need help getting home, Grandpa?"

The old man grunted and lifted his arm for Robert to grab.

"Robert, I asked you a question."

He hesitated, then continued as if she had not spoken. He pulled his grandfather to his feet. Mr. McBride held himself steady with a hand placed on the edge of the table, his stare in her direction unfocused.

He said, "Aw, hell. Leave the boy alone."

Joetta paid him no attention and insisted she have an answer from Robert.

"Where have you been? Did you not hear me? That man was inside the house, and here I was, alone."

Robert had the decency to look ashamed before his re-morse became something else, there and gone in a flash. It was so quick, she was not sure of it, but Joetta knew her youngest, and this was a side of Robert that should not be there, shifty and sly. Mr. McBride sat back down, bracing his hands on his knees, and looked ill.

She stared at Robert, waiting, and finally he said, "I went to visit Harold. He wasn't at home, though."

"You should have told me. As if I would care about that."

She let it go. Mr. McBride looked as if he would keel over if Robert did not help him to his bed and soon. He struggled to get back to his feet, and Robert was quick to assist, gripping his arm and his waist. He helped him along as he moved painfully toward the door. The attention and watchfulness he gave the old man created a mix of emotions in Joetta. His compassion for his grandfather reminded her of the old Robert, while creating a wistfulness in her for the days when he looked at her in adoration, as if she could do no wrong. On the other hand, when she thought about how he was acting, she returned to being infuriated with him. He needed his father's guidance more now than ever. He would want to read the letters, and she would say nothing about what was in them. Let him see for himself his father's expectations.

When they had disappeared inside the cabin, she made him a plate and set it aside. As she cleaned up, she softened toward him, her aggravation replaced with understanding. He was going through a lot, as well. They were all going through difficult times, even Mr. McBride. One day Robert would realize she was the same mother she had always been, and she would be waiting for him when he did. She placed his father's letters by the plate and went to bed, praying they would speak to him in a way she could not.

Chapter 15

Eliza Garner and Rebecca Hammond came to participate in the sewing group, and while Joetta was only slightly acquainted with them through church, she was aware they each lived on large farms of several hundred acres and were friends with the eccentric Clovis Poole. Rebecca Hammond's husband also owned the cotton mill and, aside from the Pooles, was next in line as the most well-to-do of anyone else in Nash County. Bess's sewing group was the one outing Joetta allowed herself because it was important to continue her appearance of loyalty for the sake of the farm, and themselves. However, it did not take long before she found being around these women quite difficult. She had nothing in common with them, while all they wanted to do was discuss what the war might do to their livelihoods. Generally, they did not mingle with those who farmed, like Joetta and Ennis, the Browns, or the Caldwells. Theirs were the sort of farms that grew cash crops, cotton and tobacco, and had many slaves and overseers to run the day-to-day work, including household slaves. These women spent time in Europe each summer.

The first time they came, she took note of the fancy barouche wagon with a driver sitting in the front dozing in the sun as she pulled up. The contrast between it and the old buckboard wagon she rode in was like comparing a rock to a precious jewel, satin to burlap, sweet tea to champagne. Her to them. She had entered Bess's sitting room with the thought, *Why not let them come and make homespun and sew a few socks*. The rich *ought* to feel compelled to participate in the cause given it was their lifestyle at stake more so than anyone else. Soon they brought up the rumor about the manumissions that took place at a landowner's cotton farm a couple of counties away. The women were quite informative about what their husbands said, how there was talk about retribution against the landowner. By the next visit, they "were happy to report," that very same landowner was found hanged at the entrance to his property along with several of the slaves he had freed. Eliza Garner was particularly proud of her overseer, a man named Miller. She made sure they understood he was the one who took charge and the appropriate measures were taken.

"He saw to the whole affair. Mr. Garner was so pleased, he has increased his pay because of it."

They had seemed quite satisfied with this result, and even discussed how the buzzards had come to peck at the bodies. Joetta was horrified. She found the both of them highfalutin' and highly disagreeable individuals who relished the telling of those morbid stories. What sort of person derived pleasure over such events as this?

On another typical Wednesday visit right before Christmas, she drove over on a cold, brisk day, and was thoroughly chilled by the time she arrived. Anxious to sit by the fire, she hurried up the steps and entered. As she pulled off her gloves, Mary, Alice, and Vesta greeted her as usual, while Rebecca and Eliza nodded at her, as if assessing her differently from the visits before. They sat wordlessly, reserved and detached, their skin smooth with good health, their hands plump and soft. Joetta put her hands up to the fire briefly, their redness from work and the cold ride boldly apparent, at least to her. When she faced the group again, the two women continued to study her. It bordered on rude, their stares longer than necessary. Or, perhaps she was being too sensitive.

Eliza said, "How do you do, Joetta? So, here is our little nonconformist. Or, so I've heard."

Rebecca patted her friend's arm, and said, "Now, now, Eliza. Look. She has on the Rebel symbol. It must not be true. Is it?"

They turned to her in one motion and considered her very carefully, even Bess, like the mother who hopes her child will behave properly in front of the company. There was a skip in time as Joetta refused to answer. Bess offered up a nervous little laugh while twisting a lace handkerchief. Mary, Alice, and Vesta kept their heads down, busy with the socks, fingers flying, the sewing receiving their utmost attention. Joetta finally pointed decisively at the cockade.

"Here I am, prepared to sew all while wearing the stamp of approval."

Bess bobbed her head vigorously.

"See? Nothing to be alarmed over. Don't forget her wonderful husband has volunteered for the cause as well, isn't that right, Joetta? Of course, Henry too, which is certainly worrisome because of his age, but what a fine and brave boy! Then there's my Benjamin. We are certainly blessed to have such courage from our menfolk, aren't we, Joetta?"

Bess peered at her expectantly, nodding ever so slightly. Joetta yearned to speak the truth, hers and Ennis's, to push the boundaries and watch what unfolded on the faces of these shallow-minded women, to see what impact her words might have. Perhaps she could get them to understand what the McBrides did, or that their personal beliefs should not be of importance to them. It changed nothing for them, while what they wanted had changed her world entirely. She would like to explain how it was not as cut-and-dry as they believed. But, no. Instead, she had to play along, swallow down what she wished to say. It rankled, and she almost choked on the word she was forced to vocalize in order to uphold what she had come to call her loyalty lie.

"Yes."

Bess glanced worriedly at Rebecca and Eliza, as if they might breathe fire when they spoke again, but they only shared a knowing look with one another. Bess hurried to get a chair from her kitchen so Joetta could sit. She placed it beside Eliza, and Joetta, reluctant to sit next to the woman, sat anyway. She blew on her still-frozen fingers, while the rest continued on with their chatter. She began to work and listened while they scorned freedom for their "property," carrying their outrage like a banner. The topic was one where she could offer very little, while Bess, Vesta, and Alice displayed an equivalent righteousness she did not, and could not understand. Mary did not speak, and Joetta took her silence as a personal condemnation of the topic, and Joetta remained reserved, doing her best not to arouse any suspicion by working diligently. Eliza moaned about what would happen should the North win.

"Oh, how complicated it is to run a farm the size we have. I simply do not know how Clovis manages all she does. Just the upkeep of the kitchen staff in of itself is horrendous. Think of what might happen if she did not have the help?"

Rebecca added her opinion. "Yes. Yes. Then what? It would be disastrous."

The words were out before Joetta could stop herself.

"You could always sell some land, reduce your acreage, and farm for yourselves, if it came down to it. Like I do," she said, eyes innocent as a fawn's.

Eliza and Rebecca paused for a second, not unlike sparrows who quickly fall silent as soon as a perceived threat approaches the bush they have inhabited. Rebecca cleared her throat.

"Tell me. How many acres might you and your husband have?"

"Enough for what we need and to feed our farm animals."

"And . . . you, you . . . do all the work. Your family?"

"Yes."

"My, my."

"Until my eldest son, Henry, as Bess mentioned, decided he was not fit for that sort of life."

"Ah, the impetuousness of youth," said Rebecca, as she examined her stitches, the material practically held against her nose.

Eliza said, "Perhaps his wish to be a soldier is not so bad. It would elevate him, if he wishes to aspire to greater things."

Eliza was like a female version of Mr. McBride. The cavalier comment only underscored what she knew about who was actually fighting this war. It certainly did not include the Garners, Hammonds, or the Pooles. Eliza smiled at her, and Joetta did not return it.

Eliza said, "Of course I did not mean to imply anything by that, my dear."

The conversation moved back to the slaves and Rebecca made clucking sounds of disappointment, while Joetta held on to an internal and totally entertaining thought of sewing certain mouths shut.

"The very idea they would be allowed to roam about freely, it's outrageous, for pity's sake! What would they do all day without some occupation? How would they live? Where would they go?"

There was a lull in conversation as the women absorbed this, then Eliza sat back with a huff. She said, "Oh. That is not all. That is not even the worst of it."

She leaned forward, and Bess, Alice, Vesta, and even Mary did so as well, understanding by this posturing, she was about to impart something not meant to be spoken aloud, some sordid detail for their edification. Joetta remained upright, measuring a length of yarn while wishing she had not come this week. Her stomach roiled as she knitted, and she kept thinking she could have done this in the peace of her own home. Eliza proffered a delectable scandal.

"I heard, and do not, I repeat, do not say where this came from. I heard one somehow got hold of that lovely Lucy Ann Lewis over in Little Creek, and I heard she is now pregnant! This, this *disgraceful act* will happen more and more, is what I heard, if we allow them their freedoms! It is an abomination! Mr. Garner offered to send Mr. Miller to help determine the culprit because Mr. Miller, well, he certainly knows how to apply the lash most effectively, to coerce the truth from lips that refuse to speak."

Joetta, disgusted these supposedly refined women would allow such brutality, and even encourage it, could not help herself. The words came forth as they would, and with force.

"I heard, I heard. I heard. Why, everything you have said

is nothing but hearsay. Such behavior from one human to another, it is barbaric."

Both Rebecca and Eliza drew in their breath so quick, Joetta was certain they would pop the lacings of their corsets. Bess gave her a wretched look, while Alice and Vesta stopped knitting and sat with mouths drooping, their expressions akin to smelling rotten turnips. Mary hid an unexpected smile behind a fake yawn. Joetta resumed her work as they absorbed the comment while trying to determine her exact motivation by saying it. She could have told them, but she had decided not to waste her breath. Eliza got her wits about her and responded with an indignant tone.

"My *dear*, Preacher Rouse would not say something of this nature to my very own and dear husband, who told me, mind you, unless it were true!"

Joetta raised her eyes to the other woman's and challenged her.

"Preacher Rouse? And, who told him?"

"Well. I, I, I don't rightly know. But, he is the preacher, after all!"

"Precisely. How very Christian-like."

Eliza sat back and looked around the room. Had they followed Joetta's insinuation, they would realize how ridiculous they sounded. The preacher ought to be ashamed of himself for perpetuating gossip. Rebecca and Eliza leaned their heads together and muttered. Rebecca abruptly stood and stated matter-of-factly.

"It appears now is a good time to take our leave. We must be off."

Bess flustered, urged them to stay.

"But I've an apple pie, and plenty of coffee. Won't you stay and have some? I am known for the pie. It is favored at church functions."

Eliza said, "Thank you. However, I believe we have well overstayed our welcome."

Rebecca added, "Food will not settle well on my stomach at the moment, of that I am certain," and delivered a sour glare toward Joetta.

They gathered bonnets, wraps, gloves, and sewing bags and were about to make a swift exit when Rebecca paused and stared over at Joetta.

"Be mindful, Mrs. McBride. I'd hate to see something happen to your farm—again. It is bound to happen if word gets about. One just never knows."

With Bess fluttering behind them, and back to wringing her handkerchief, Joetta and Mary watched their departure from their chairs by the window.

"Off they go," Mary said, before whispering to Joetta, "Well spoken."

Joetta's mood floundered after Rebecca Hammond's comments. Bess returned to the sitting room, sank into her chair, her mouth turned down. She wagged her finger at Joetta.

"Joetta McBride, you will rue this day."

"I only spoke the truth."

"Those women, along with the Pooles, why they are the very bedrock of this county."

"I pray to heaven not. What I say should not make a difference to them if they are all that important. I only pointed out there was nothing to back up what they shared, and how is that a bad thing? Besides, the preacher ought to be ashamed of himself for furthering such talk."

"But, don't you see? It makes you sound like you're not on *our* side."

Joetta gave her friend a pointed look. Bess threw up her hands.

"Joetta McBride, you are quite obstinate and hard-headed."

"I said nothing against one thing or another."

Bess blew out an exasperated sigh. The remainder of the afternoon went along without any further discussion about Eliza and Rebecca, and Joetta found she enjoyed it, while Bess was withdrawn. She served the pie and coffee, which Joetta also ate with pleasure. She watched Bess now and again, noting how she stabbed her knitting needle through the material of every sock like she wanted to jab them into someone. Perhaps Joetta. The women had moved on to discuss the upcoming holiday and what they might send to their men, and the soldiers in general.

Eventually the late-afternoon sun filtered into the room signaling it was time to go. Joetta gathered her things and made her way to the door. Alice and Vesta made haste in leaving, glancing nervously over their shoulders as if they expected Bess to erupt now her guests were gone. Mary lingered, carrying coffee cups into the kitchen and straightening up the sitting room.

Bess trailed Joetta to the front door, and said, "I worry for you, and what might happen. It's not as if you have not had enough trouble."

"We had another odd incident recently."

Bess turned wary and watchful.

"Oh? What happened?"

"Robert and I were run off the road. We have no idea who did it; he went by so fast. It took some time to get the wagon free. After we were back home, that very same man had been in the house. He ran out the door and took off on his horse. I surprised him, and perhaps that stopped him from doing whatever he was planning. That is my guess."

Bess crossed her arms and looked away, leaving Joetta with the feeling she wished to speak, but instead gave her attention to the harrowed land at the front of her house, where Thomas and Harold had tilled the soil under for the winter season. There was nothing out there but a few crows pecking at the remnants of a successful corn harvest, from what Joetta could see. Bess cleared her throat.

"Once you are denounced, you're an adversary. Unfortunately, your father-in-law foolishly talked about what happened with those soldiers, and now it is hard for some to accept anything you profess as truth. What happened in your fields, and with that man, it's of utmost concern, but I fear you haven't seen the last of your troubles."

"I would ask, what would you have done if thirsty men and animals needed water?"

"I would not have allowed our foe any advantage whatsoever. I would have pointed them to a nearby creek."

Adversary. Foe. Joetta opened her mouth, then closed it. The truth was, she was weary of it all. Bess was not done, and as she continued, her tone turned even more ominous.

"Be forewarned, families like that of Clovis Poole, Eliza Garner, and Rebecca Hammond, they have much at stake, more than any of us."

"Oh, really? Are their husbands and sons off fighting this war? That is what is at stake for you, for me, and many others. The worst part of it? Ennis and I wanted nothing to do with this, this, effort, yet here we are. Torn asunder, while the rich have their families, and the only threat they suffer is to their pockets!"

This gave Bess pause, and Joetta hoped she had finally made a difference, had actually broken through to her friend. She had not, as proven when Bess appeared to come to a decision.

"As much as I want you helping us, it puts everyone in peril. I can't afford to take such a chance, and truthfully, neither can you. The damage is done now. Eliza and Rebecca will not take lightly to what transpired today. They will say what they will, and I hope for your sake nothing comes of it, but, should they decide to return, I prefer you not be here. I must not invite trouble to my own home, where none is warranted."

"Fine."

"It is not what I want, believe me. But . . ."

"No need to explain."

"When this is over . . ."

Joetta took Bess's hand, while shaking her head.

"Please. Do not make promises you may regret. We think differently on this. It cannot be helped."

Joetta released Bess's hand and made her way to the wagon. As she left, she looked over her shoulder to see Mary on the porch, but Bess was not. Mary gave Joetta a dejected little wave and Joetta offered a tiny smile. It was bound to happen, this fracture between her and Bess. They could not see eye to eye, and everyone was nervous, afraid for themselves and their families. She struggled to determine if what she had done to keep out of the fray, even as the act festered within her, had worsened their circumstances. This was highly possible, but there was nothing to be done about it now.

She flicked the reins and huddled down against the wind. Her thoughts stayed on Eliza Garner and Rebecca Hammond, women who could cause more trouble for her. She should have stayed home, kept out of sight like she had told Robert. She would miss the weekly outing, yet deep down she felt relief for no longer having to play a part. The ride home was as cold and desolate as any she had taken. The sun grazed the earth allowing golden light to fill barren fields. Her shape, Pal's, and the wagon cast dark, slanted shadows on the road. Even with the freezing temperature, it was a beautiful time of year. The trees, having lost their crown, revealed the shapes of their branches, gray limbs beseeching the heavens in prayer. The farmland was wiped clear of the season's toil and lay in a state of rest.

Normally, she would take stock of what had been accomplished once their crops were in. Having spent half the harvest season without Ennis, and with the realization their cornmeal and flour were virtually gone, and feed for the animals would be in short supply, she was not in the mood for such reflections. She wished the issues that kept them apart would come to resolution in some favorable way for all concerned. Given what she had experienced thus far, it was difficult to believe possible. The divide of the North and South was like a great crack in the earth, a gaping maw of distrust, and the self-righteousness and determination that grew with each passing conflict only served to expand the differences. And here she dwelled, in this land divided, impartial, nonaligned, and hoping to remain thus until it was all over.

As Christmas approached, she sent Ennis food twice, filling each package with what they had the most of—bacon, smoked ham, molasses, and some muscadine jam—to eat with the hardtack he had complained about. She sent them so one would arrive before Christmas and the other right after, or at least she hoped. She included socks from her time with Bess's sewing group and a quilt she no longer used. She made a solitary trip to Mr. Spivey's store, ducking in to mail the first package and to buy oranges for Mr. McBride and Robert. She parted with precious coins for these extravagant items, but she did not let that worry her. It was for Christmas, after all!

Mr. Spivey eyed her with a hint of worry. "Everything all right?"

"Yes. Why?"

"I heard about your visitor."

"Oh? Who told? No, let me guess. Mr. McBride or Bess Caldwell."

"You need to be more careful, Mrs. McBride."

"By that, you mean keep my mouth shut unless I am peddling Confederate praise."

"It's only because of things you've said, or maybe not said. Many believe you're an opponent of the Southern cause."

"That is only because they cannot see beyond their own selfish noses." She softened her tone. "Thank you for the warning. It is kind of you to be concerned."

She took the oranges and left.

The holiday season had become a bizarre and strange affair for Joetta, even while she tried to do most everything she would typically do. She strung dried cranberries, gathered pine cones, and found bits of old lace to decorate a tree Robert begrudgingly cut down. She placed a few evergreen branches on the mantel above the fireplaces. When she hung the stockings on Christmas Eve, she put Ennis's and Henry's stockings out too, and though they would hang empty, it was symbolic, and meaningful, at least to her. Those stockings spoke of her faith they would return, that they would be there for Christmas next year. To not have them out felt like bad luck.

Christmas morning arrived, an overcast day with a bitter wind. Joetta had breakfast ready when Robert and Mr. McBride came through the back door, an icy draft sweeping in with them, and Robert's behavior not much warmer. He did not bring up what his father said in the letters. She had found them on the kitchen table the next day, and that was the end of it. On this chilly morning, they ate quietly, then moved to the sitting room to be near the fireplace. Joetta had put the oranges and some sugared pecans in each of their stockings earlier that morning when she got up.

She had wrapped their gifts, each a new shirt sewn from the wool she had carded, all accomplished while she was at Bess's, plus the socks. These she wrapped in brown paper tied with red and green string she had from the year before.

Robert opened his and stared at the warm, chocolate-colored wool shirt, fingers rubbing the fine stitches. He admired the new socks the same way. Joetta watched him and nothing needed to be said, because the small gestures of appreciation revealed told her the Robert of old was still in there, somewhere.

Mr. McBride said, "Well, ain't these mighty fine. I thank you."

Surprised by his words, she smiled, while knowing the best gift she could receive would be any acknowledgment from her son. He had not even wished her a Merry Christmas, and it was one more little hurt she inadvertently collected and added to the assortment. At least he was participating, even if more dutiful than enthusiastic. They set their presents aside and began talking about pheasant hunting while Joetta went into the kitchen to check on the roasting hen. She had made a dressing, too. Out of her scarce, precious flour she had baked a loaf of bread, let it get old, and after crumbling it up, she had then added in chicken stock and savory. She returned to the sitting room and was dumbfounded to see a small wrapped item in her chair. At first she smiled at Robert, but he shook his head and turned to stare into the flames in the fireplace. Mr. McBride sat reared back in his chair, and with a grand gesture, motioned at the small bundle.

He said, "Go on and see what it is."

"This is from *you?*"

Joetta could not hide the disbelief from her voice. She picked up the package, sat down, and unfolded the cloth to reveal a little wooden box he had made. In it, nesting on some straw, was the carving of a tiny bluebird. She lifted it out of the nest, where it sat perfectly in her palm. He had taken the time to stain it, adding delicate feathered features to the wings and breast.

As if she was not already taken aback, he said, "It's supposed to represent happiness, or something like 'at."

She could not have been more moved, or more stunned, so unexpected was this offering, given with such consideration. She carefully held it against her breast, overcome with emotion. She reached over and put a hand on his shoulder as he tucked his into his armpits and shifted about on his chair, discomfited by her reaction.

"I had it a while. It ain't like I made it special, or nothing."

She sniffled, and said, "Thank you. Anyway."

Mr. McBride scowled at his feet while she went back to admiring the little bird, and truly loved it. It was the first present he had ever given her, the first nice thing he had ever done for her. Robert held out his hand and she put the bluebird in it. He turned it this way and that, before handing it back wordlessly. His capacity to get over his anger, his ability to give and receive with any grace had gone missing since his father left. She could have prompted him about his father's wishes he act accordingly, but not on this day. Not when she only wanted to be as festive as circumstances allowed, and to enjoy the goodness intended at this time of year.

Soon, the time was gone and the weather became even colder if that were possible. With the sap frozen hard, the trees cracked at night, and Joetta worried about Ennis, and Henry, and what they might be going through. For the remainder of 1861, they entered into a state of almost hibernation-like existence into January of 1862. A letter came from her mother with well wishes for the holidays while expressing grave concern for the country. Several came from Ennis, and his words of love and appreciation for everything she sent lifted her spirits. While there was plenty of misery in the encampment with rain and frigid temperatures, he stayed busy drilling and preparing for battles to come. For the first time in her life, she dreaded the spring, and what would happen when it became warm again because it meant the war effort would resume, dragging all of them with it.

Chapter 16

But it did not take until the spring. In late January of 1862, President Lincoln issued orders allowing the Union to commence hostile actions against the Confederacy. Fortunately, at least to Joetta, newspapers wrote General McClellan was a man who apparently did not like taking Lincoln's orders. McClellan thought Lincoln a fool and therefore did nothing he commanded. Doing nothing meant her beloved Ennis and Henry were safe for now. Despite the inaction, her dread grew, to the point she became as obsessed as Mr. McBride, wanting to hear everything of what might be happening in Virginia and elsewhere. When the Union general continued to snub his Commander in Chief, Mr. McBride cackled with glee. Joetta smiled too, even while knowing this would not last, something was bound to happen and soon.

Of course Ennis's and Henry's safety was not all that consumed Joetta's mind. Robert's moods altered like the seasons, hot or cold, angry or remote, there in body, but not in mind. He worked as always, feeding the animals, chopping wood, doing repairs on the fence and other structures around the farm. She would see him enter the woods to throw out scraps that kept the hogs nearby. Sometimes she encountered him when she went to milk Honey or gather eggs, and it hurt to see how he would change direction and go do something else until she was done, then come back to finish. She had to remind herself of his age, and that he had taken on a lot of responsibility. She attempted to tell him this one afternoon.

"Robert?"

He held a hammer, lightly tapping the head of it against his leg.

"I appreciate you working as hard as you are. It is a lot for the both of us. I have written your father telling him all that you do."

Robert's hair was the only part of him that moved, the wind lifting it off his forehead. He stared over her shoulder, as distant as Henry had been. She might as well have been speaking to herself for all he seemed to care.

"I wanted you to know how appreciative I am and that I am proud of you, and I know your father would be as well."

He gave a single nod, and on impulse, she went to hug him. He backed away so fast he stumbled over his own feet, fell, and somehow the hammer ended up under his thigh.

When he landed on it, a look of pain shot across his face, and she cried out, "Oh, I'm sorry!"

She tried to help him up, and he jerked away.

"I'm fine!"

He favored the leg as he went to the barn, and Joetta brought her hand up to cover her mouth, as everything before her went blurry. She tried not to think about how he had recoiled from her touch, as if she carried some sort of malady. After that, she began to spend most of her time by the fire in the sitting room, repairing their clothing.

She worked on new cuffs and collars for their shirts from old shirt materials she had saved, hunched over in the dim light of the front window. She made more socks to send to Ennis. She cut up an old bedsheet for the new collars and cuffs for her work dresses, and made a new apron. She stitched little flowers on the pockets, then ripped them out, her mood not one for the likes of pretty little blooms. It was too cold for visitors, but she really did not expect any. She was a potential threat. She doubted even Mary would come, not if she had told Hugh what happened, as he might forbid it. No one wanted to associate with someone who could be accused of treason. The only thing she had to look forward to were letters from Ennis and her mother, and the meals Mr. McBride and Robert still took with her. At least Mr. McBride talked. He had always liked to hear himself and did not notice her or Robert's silence.

February came, the month of Henry's sixteenth birthday. Joetta passed the days quietly, glad when the month was over. In March, she received a letter from Ennis saying they had broken from the encampment and were now heading toward Richmond.

Correspondence from me will possibly be delayed, or very sparse. Please try not to worry. I am too stubborn to die on one of these miserable battlefields.

Mr. McBride grew ever more engrossed on what was happening due east. With the growing blockade along the Southern coastline, the opposing sides had engaged in the first battle between two great iron warships. It resulted in a draw, albeit with a small victory on the Confederate side after a couple of smaller wooden Union ships were sunk.

Mr. McBride said, "Even the smallest victories are worth the sacrifices."

Joetta stewed over his blithe statement. Easy enough for him to say as he sat idly by the fire. The weather turned foul with more rainy days than not. She grew increasingly miserable, and decided the window with its rivulets of rain running down the glass represented her internal state. The bare ground became sodden and a few coyotes nosed around at the edge of the woods. She hurried outside to make sure her chickens were put up, and the coyotes moved closer instead of running away, emboldened by hunger.

Finally, the rain ended, and on the first sunny day she took the small box off the shelf in the kitchen where they set aside money for the various household needs. She sifted through the few coins and a few graybacks wishing to plant something, anything really. Despite the heavy work required, Joetta was eager to have the fields growing again. It would erase the memory of what had taken place, and she wished to see them lush and green, signaling success. There was solace in a fresh start, and surely it would be a balm to their spirits. She placed the box back up on the shelf and considered how Ennis received a monthly stipend, yet she could not bring herself to ask him for some small part. It would only worry him, make him wonder what was going on.

In early April, more soldiers marched by. They wore a mixture of browns and blues, which meant nothing to Joetta. She happened to be outside near the springhouse and the sound they made was like some huge animal lumbering closer and closer, hundreds of feet tramping along. Her reaction was to set her pails of water down and bolt for the house, as she did not wish to give them any reason to stop. She entered through the back door and hurried through the kitchen to the front sitting room, where she could keep watch. They had seen no militia since last year, and at the sight of them, her heart began to pound. She prayed they would keep going, and quickly.

From the relative safety of where she stood, she noted how they assessed everything, exploring the fields, the barn, the outbuildings and the house, but they did not stop, and for that she was relieved. She waited until they had passed by before she ventured back outside and found Robert bringing the pails of water she had left and his grandfather following behind him, his head cocked strangely. Mr. McBride waved a hand.

"Shush! You hear that?"

The rhythmic step of the soldiers' boots was faint, but noticeable. Joetta pointed down the lane.

"Soldiers went by a minute ago."

Robert looked in the direction she indicated. His hair had not been brushed, there was dirt on his neck, and he wore the pants and shirt he had had on for some time now. She detected a strong odor coming off the both of them, the sharp tang of unwashed bodies and clothes. Her mouth pressed tight to keep the criticism in. Undoubtedly she had not expected Mr. McBride to be the best influence, but Robert's unkempt appearance made her feel even more like a failure as a mother. Mr. McBride walked to the fence and looked down the lane. He pulled his chewing tobacco out of his pocket and stuffed a plug into his mouth.

"Soldiers, you say? What'd they have on?"

Joetta had to think for a second.

"Brown, gray, different shades of blue."

"Sounds like these were Confederate, if I was to guess. Did they say anything?"

"I went into the house. I believed it best not to be seen."

Robert kicked at a clod of dirt and made a disparaging sound while Mr. McBride offered his assessment.

"They're getting a hunnert dollars in gold at the end of their enlistment, and I suspect this road's bound to turn into a common thoroughfare in the coming weeks."

Robert turned again to stare in that direction, and to Joetta ears, spoke somewhat wistfully. "Wonder where they're going?"

"Prob'ly to the coast to try and keep them Union devils from impeding our waterways even more. Let's hope they do."

He continued to grumble as he turned to go back to his cabin, leaving Joetta and Robert standing together. She took the opportunity to ask her son whether or not he had read the mail sent by his father.

"Have you read any of your father's letters?"

She could have been some unfamiliar person for how he acted, and he clearly did not want to talk about it. He barely nodded in answer and the silence that went on made the small distance between them much larger. He fiddled with a button on his shirt.

"Robert, I have been patient while you have been rude, behaving as if you have forgotten who I am. I would remind you, I am still your mother. And because I am your mother, I love you, but I also require your respect."

He shifted his shoulders in the way one does to dislodge some irritation. Before he would have hugged her, his thin, boyish arms around her waist while resting his disheveled head on her chest. As tall as he was getting, that would no longer be possible. Joetta was certain if he could have figured out some way to vanish, he would have. She waited quietly for him to respond, her memories giving her images of the boy who saw the good in most everything, who laughed with her, who brought her wildflowers.

Her mouth lifted with a smile at these private thoughts, and when she came back to the present, it was only to realize as she dwelled in the past, Robert had walked off and was no longer there. He had crossed the field and was almost in the woods. If nothing else, at least she felt better for insisting on some modicum of respect while affirming her love for him, as a mother would to a child who is hurting. He would come around, eventually.

As April progressed, rain kept the ground soaked and too wet for field work. Robert gladly stayed in the woods, hunting and fishing, while Mr. McBride rode into town as much as possible for news and the mail. Letters from Ennis had virtually stopped, and she was in a constant state of concern. Finally, Mr. McBride brought her two, one from him and the other from her mother. Now she could breathe for a bit, relax from the mental antics she put herself through that kept her on edge. Ennis's arrived in a colorful cover with the design of a flag that bore the Confederate president's name, Jefferson Davis, and Alex H. Stephens, Vice President. Mr. McBride poked at it with a gnarly finger.

"He must not be doing much, got all this time to write."

"He writes at night, when he can."

"Hmm."

Ennis's love always showed in the careful words he chose, meaningful and with deep reflection. She had not slowed in her own writing, believing her correspondence would eventually catch up to him, wherever his destination. Her letters professed her own love but were otherwise filled with lies. Lies about the crops, Robert, and about what she had witnessed and experienced since he left. She stayed on topics that were typical, prattling on about everyday tasks, acting as if the farm had not changed, and even while doing so made her feel better, the life she communicated on paper was only as realistic as her dreams. She wrote about planting the kitchen garden from the seeds of the previous year, painting a picture of bounty, and normalcy. Her mother's letter, aside from sharing about her usual day-to-day tasks, came filled with worry about progression on the warfront.

*Daughter, upon waking and upon going to sleep, my
thoughts are filled only with this war. I fear for our old
friends on the Albemarle. It and the Pamlico Sound are now
held by the Union and I have not heard word from them in
weeks. The Union have taken control of the White Oak
River. Your father worries, because for some time, it has
been difficult to find what is needed. Please let us know as
soon as you are able how you are faring.*

Joetta was quick to pen her reply, almost verbatim to
what she wrote to Ennis, elaborating on a glorious, abun-
dant garden, adequate crops, and a smokehouse filled with
hams, bacon, and sausages.

*Do not fret, Mother. We are a bit farther West, and
while I too have seen movement of troops, they pay little, if
any, attention to our small farm.*

The spring rains finally stopped, and Mr. McBride came
back from town one afternoon in May, complaining of the
dry, dusty walk. He hacked and spit, then dropped a letter from Ennis beside her where she knelt on the ground
pulling weeds from around the foundation. She thanked
him and smiled, anticipating what her beloved might say.
She tucked the envelope into the pocket of her apron and
kept working. Their seventeenth wedding anniversary was
coming up this month and his correspondence was timely.
Instead of leaving immediately, Mr. McBride leaned against
the fence, watching her with an expression of solemnity.
She stopped working.

"What is it?"

"The gov'ment started enforcing conscription in April.
Hugh Brown's got to go. It's for them who're eighteen to
thirty-five. They got to sign up for three years."

Joetta's voice went high, filled with alarm even as she tried to reassure herself. "Surely Ennis did not have to. He turns thirty-six next month!"

Mr. McBride pushed off the fence as he answered. "I don't know. I don't know nothing except what I hear."

"Dear Lord."

He had never asked what was in Ennis's letters. This time he inclined his head toward her apron, where she had stowed the letter.

"Why'nt you see if he says anything about it."

She rose from her knees, her nerves suddenly tingling with anxiety. In the house she sat at the table and pulled the pages free. Despite the colorful paper, the cover was in terrible shape, as if it had been carried for a while, although none ever showed up in pristine condition, given the miles traveled. It was written on April 25th, a month ago, but mail was not delivered as before, and delays were expected. Her unsteady hands made the papers shake. She always gave Ennis's words her attention, and even as she began reading out loud, she could hear him in her head. She skipped the parts where he professed his feelings, and read only of his miseries. They were marching in an early heat, dust filling their lungs. There were worms in the dry goods, and on his person, an infestation of lice on his body and in his bedding. Keeping his socks dry was a daily trial, and could she send him a few more pairs? He signed off as usual, *All my love, Ennis.* Behind the April 25th letter, another page had been added. She flipped to it, and the date was May 1st.

My love, you may hear of this newly created Conscription Act, an ungodly three-year commitment. I heard of it back in December but did not want to trouble you. At that time came word of providing bounties and sixty-day furloughs to keep men longer, though many already deserted some months ago. While I long to come home, and it is not in me to quit my search for our Henry, it was mandated I sign on, despite the fact I would have been beyond the age limit in a short time. Understand this, if I am successful in finding Henry, we will come home, regardless of my status. Fighting in various states has intensified. Our orders are we will head into battle as soon as we are in position. We are as ready as we can be for what is to come. Pray for me, my dear wife, pray that I am able to fend off harm and make it home to you and my family. It may be a while before you hear from me.

    All my love always, Ennis

She struggled not to break down in front of Mr. McBride. She put her fingertips to her eyes and rubbed. Angry, distressed, and without any recourse, she must accept this latest news even as she only wanted to toss the papers straight into the stove fire, as if turning them into ash might change the inevitable. Mr. McBride slumped in his chair, moving one leg back and forth in an agitated manner.

He said, "They need to go on and fight like hell and win this thing, so he can come home."

Joetta did not trust herself to speak. She wanted to blame him, blame Henry, but it was as much her fault as anyone's, maybe more. She alone had insisted he search for Henry until he gave in. She had to reconsider what this meant. She got up and began washing dishes, mechanically scrubbing plates, forks, spoons, and cups, dunking each piece in water and placing them on a towel. A few seconds later, Mr. McBride slid his chair back and went out the back door. She quickly wiped her hands down the front of her apron and hurried after him. She must be the one to tell

Robert though she did not relish the idea. It was important he knew the truth, and she needed to tell him in her own way, explain how no one had known this would happen.

Robert was already with his grandfather, an undeniable look in his eyes. He dared her with that first glance to try and explain this latest calamity. Wet streaks on each side of his face revealed pale skin beneath the grime. She lifted a hand toward him, wanting to reassure him it would be all right, that his father was a smart and courageous man. Before she could utter one word, he jumped the fence and took off across the wind-swept field, running, running from her.

Chapter 17

Robert came to the back door that evening, hesitating at the threshold as if unsure he wanted to be there. He stood awkwardly, waiting, for what she did not know. She continued to stir potatoes and spring onions in the frying pan, sensing his criticism as noxious as the pig sty, permeating the atmosphere. Well, she could not produce miracles. She was only his mother. In the grand scheme of it all, her role was rather mundane: to feed and clothe him, to tend to him when he was sick or injured, and more importantly, to love him, even when he did not return it. Nothing more, nothing less.

She was as distraught as he was, and only capable of doing what she could in that moment. She fed him. He tracked her movements as she seasoned food on a plate, then placed it on the table in front of his chair. She stepped back, her hands folded against her apron, a silent invitation. He entered the kitchen, his hunger prevailing, and she began cleaning up. He did not tell her his thoughts, and she did not ask. She was tired. Of fighting, of explaining, of worrying. Subdued, he ate what she set before him, but she did not join him. Instead, she went to bed. As far as she was concerned, unless Robert chose otherwise, the subject of his father's tenure in the war was one she would rather not discuss. It was too heartbreaking, too difficult, and she was having a difficult enough time managing her own confusing emotions.

She went through her nightly rituals, and when she finally sat on the bed, she gathered up Ennis's pillow, the one with the casing she had not changed since he left, and hugged it to herself. Somehow sleep found her, and she was granted the rest she needed. The next morning as she left the bedroom, she stopped at the bottom of the staircase and looked up. The door to Robert's room was closed, indicating he had decided to stay in his own bed for a change. She took nothing from this other than he was spent, and perhaps did not care to listen to his grandfather's exhaustive speculations. She went outside, milked Honey, and tossed a bit of scraps to the chickens and pigs, her mood gloomy. Conscription was entrapment, the act of being held by a device Ennis could not break free of, and by association, neither could she. To take her mind from this, she began to assess what still needed to be done in the fields. Before too long, Robert came outside, gnawing on a knucklebone. He surprised her by speaking first.

"I'll do some tilling today," he said.

"Wonderful."

She did not discuss how they were supposed to get by, how difficult it was going to be, or how daily living would likely get worse before it got better. Joetta was beginning to understand the challenges ahead, but Robert did not. He could maintain a fresher outlook because of his ignorance of financial matters and naïveté due to age. He still had the bravado of the young, only marred by the most immediate disappointment.

Robert was good as his word and they began working dawn to dusk as normal, day after day, plowing the rows and working to keep the weeds at bay. Joetta held on to a renewed hope as progress was made in the fields. Despite how tired she was, she began losing sleep. She lay awake most nights, only to get up while it was still dark, make a bit of coffee, and go out to sit on the back steps. The night air at this time was pungent with turned soil, and she spent this time thinking too much about their predicament. As soon as she could, she went to the chicken coop where Josephine and Agnes gave her quizzical looks from golden eyes, crested red heads bobbing in time to mincing dainty steps. They pecked and pranced, coming close while the other chickens kept some distance, always mistrusting her intentions. The feed was low, and she carefully measured what she gave them. The pigs squealed and huffed too, urging her to fill the scrap pails. Ham bones, or wild game bones and offal, along with potato and yam peels and vegetable scraps was all she had, and still they grunted, slopped, and gobbled what little there was happily enough.

At first light she was in the fields, wrangling the unwieldy plow, but Pal was accommodating so she kept at it until her back and legs ached. Robert would find her and take over, and she would go into the house, drink some water, and force herself to eat an egg, a slice of ham, and return to help. Other than the necessary conversations they had to coordinate their efforts, the easiness of conversation from days gone by remained nonexistent, signaling to Joetta this was how it would be from here on and until who knew when.

Because of Ennis's conscription, her previous wish to

know everything about the war had changed. Mr. McBride wanted to continue to sort through detailed accounts of battles he had read about in the town square, where the newspaper was tacked onto a wooden frame each day, and where those interested could read the latest events. Joetta had to set boundaries.

"I only want to know how much of the fighting is in Virginia."

Mr. McBride stared at his feet.

"There's some in and around Richmond."

Joetta raised her hand.

"Please do not tell me anything more. I will wait to hear from Ennis."

Before long it was July, and growing ever hotter. Joetta continued to be grateful for the work, using it as a distraction. Though the fields remained dry, the sorghum from the seeds of the salvaged acreage gave her a gratifying sense of accomplishment as the plants grew. Meanwhile, Mr. McBride ignored her wishes and talked extensively of campaigns and theaters—the Peninsula Campaign, and the Shenandoah Valley Campaign, and the Eastern Theater, the Western Theater, and more. These terms, while understanding they were merely a bloody effort to force one side to succumb to the other, gave her the impression of a grand ballet, like dancers in a field, calculating their next move before charging, swerving, and lunging.

Joetta took the last of the money and suggested they go into town to buy what corn they could. He stared at what she had.

"That won't hardly make it worth the effort to plant. It's too late, anyway."

"It is worth it to me."

To her surprise, he said nothing more. Her reason for going along had more to do than with just corn. She had been too busy to check on Mary to see how she was holding up after hearing of Hugh's conscription. They left Robert preparing the field, and quite honestly, Joetta was happy to be doing something else. The heat of the sun on her back was enjoyable, as was the occasional light scent of wild honeysuckle. Halfway into town he dropped her off and she meandered down the well-kept path to a small wooden gate. The Browns lived in Hugh's deceased parents' farmhouse. With Hugh gone, Joetta was certain Mary had to feel as lonely as she did at times. At least Joetta had Mr. McBride and Robert close by, while Mary had no one. She crossed the swept yard, and at the front door, she knocked softly. Seconds later, it opened, and Mary's face showed surprise.

"Joetta! How nice to see you."

"Hi, Mary. I heard about Hugh and I wanted to come earlier to see how you were faring, but we have been busy with field work."

Mary stared past Joetta, her gaze sharp and searching, making Joetta turn to look behind her, and a sudden realization gave way to a blush on her cheeks.

"If you're nervous about me being here, I can leave. I would understand."

Mary glanced about her property again, then stepped back, opening the door more.

"No, no, please. Come in, come in."

Joetta barely got herself inside before Mary shut the door and leaned against it as she faced Joetta.

"It's really good to see you. It's just that Hugh told me before he left I would do well to keep to myself. No one suspects our position, but all it would take is . . ." She dropped her eyes, and her cheeks went pink. "Well, it's not hard to imagine those who came and destroyed your crops wouldn't do the same here."

Mary waved a hand toward a window where Joetta could see pristinely planted rows.

"You are right, and I did not think about that. I came because Mr. McBride has gone to buy corn. A first for us, but given what happened, there was none left to plant. It is good to see Hugh was able to get yours in before he left."

"Just barely. Once they decide to take someone, they want them quick. Come into the kitchen. I was making biscuits for dinner, a treat given the expense of flour. I don't know why when I'm the only one here to eat them, and since Hugh left, I have no appetite. But, look at you. You look as if you could use a biscuit or two yourself, Joetta McBride."

Joetta followed Mary, sniffing the air as she went, catching the wonderful floury aroma coming from the oven. Her mouth watered and she swallowed. It had been a while since she had enjoyed a buttered biscuit. She sat at the table as Mary pulled the pan out. She split two, slathered them thick with butter, set them on a plate, and put that in front of Joetta. Joetta was mesmerized by the sight, the white fluffy centers filled with a warm yellow puddle.

She did not need much encouragement when Mary said, "Eat."

Joetta tapped the place at the table next to her.

"Please, sit and eat with me. You need to keep up your strength too."

Mary did as she asked and took up one half of a biscuit. For a while it was like any other ordinary time, without a world of woes to consider. Both knew it was only pretend.

Mary brushed the crumbs off her lap, and said, "Ennis has been gone a year now, hasn't he?"

"Yes. We thought he would have better luck finding Henry. Now, he too has been caught by this draft."

"Three years is much too long."

"Yes. But we must not let that keep us from hoping it will work out."

"You're right, only I can't help but worry how I will manage alone."

"Robert and I could help you with whatever is necessary."

Mary said, "I can't ask that of you. You already have enough as it is. And—"

Joetta finished for her. "You cannot take such a chance."

"No, it would go against what Hugh wished."

A familiar whistle sounded, and Joetta stood.

"Is that Mr. McBride already? I feel as if I just got here."

"Wait. Let me be sure."

Mary looked out from one of the windows at the front of the house while Joetta remained in the hall, adjusting her bonnet and pulling on her gloves. Mary did not identify the person right away.

Joetta said, "Is it not him? Who is it?"

Mary's voice came quietly, her back to Joetta as she peered out the window.

"It's him. The Caldwells too, and some man I don't know."

Joetta moved to stand beside Mary and looked out. Mr. McBride sat slumped on the wagon seat, a hand over his eyes while the Caldwells waited behind him, sitting very still. The man she did not know was at the side of his own wagon, tending to his cargo. Joetta paid close attention to what the stranger was doing. He checked the straps on a long box with some sort of stamp on it. Mary stepped away from the window and gave Joetta a puzzled look.

"What is going on?"

A cold chill crawled along Joetta's back, and with it, the sense of doom and dread. She went outside and made her way slowly toward Mr. McBride. She stared up as he gazed down at her, the look on his face unlike any she had ever seen. She could not decipher it. Bess had a hand over her mouth, eyes shut, while Thomas focused on his boots. Joetta moved toward the other wagon, and the scent of death greeted her. She knew this odor. She had smelled it when they had buried their babies. It could not be helped because the act of grieving and acceptance of the loss took time, often long enough for nature to begin taking its course. Mr. McBride had stepped down from the wagon, and he placed a hand on her shoulder. She turned to him, and he took her own hands in his, an odd tenderness in the gesture, something she had never experienced as they had rarely ever touched one another.

He sort of shook them, and said, "Now, now. Look here at me."

She did as he asked, wide-eyed and heart racing. The stranger, the Caldwells, and Mary waited, just as she waited. Mr. McBride cleared his throat. Keeping hold of Joetta's hands, his chin trembled as he tried to speak. She began to conceive what this meant as a trace of awareness unfolded in her mind, and before the thought was fully clarified, she was already denying it. She tried to pull her hands free, and he tightened his grip. There was a desperate urgency to it.

"Wait. Listen, now. I got something to tell you."

Becoming more unnerved by the minute by his manner, by the bizarre behavior of the others, her voice came out sharp.

"Well, then. Tell me."

Her mind was ahead of his. Could it be what she always dreaded? Was it Henry, or Ennis?

"It's Ennis."

This time Joetta was successful when she jerked her hands from his. She stepped backward, shaking her head no.

"What are you saying? What do you mean?"

Mr. McBride breathed in and out. His nose ran, and his

eyes had gone watery. He pointed at the wagon with the box.

"In there. It's Ennis."

She clapped a hand over her mouth, and one over her heart. She could not suppress her cry of anguish. She peered wildly at the stranger as he edged closer to speak to her.

He mumbled, "My condolences, ma'am. You're one of the lucky ones, I reckon."

His remark was so out of place, so preposterous, she could only formulate simple questions.

"Who are you?"

"Name's Reginald Stout. I work over to the Wilmington and Weldon rail. I brung you your husband, ma'am. He's come home today. Don't many get their loved ones back, is what I mean by lucky. Sorry."

Joetta felt the air whoosh out of her lungs, and she doubled over, his words as vicious as a punch to her belly. Mary, Bess, and Thomas rushed to her side. They held her elbows, but she pulled herself free as another agonized cry came from the very center of her being. She faced Reginald Stout. It was not possible. He was lying. With a trembling hand, she pointed at what she now realized was her husband's coffin.

"I would see for myself!"

Mr. McBride said, "Here? Now?"

Joetta's voice went an octave higher. "Here, and now, by God!"

The man hurried to do as she wished, grabbing a hammer from behind his seat. Joetta read what was stamped on the box: *McBride, Ennis, Whitakers, NC, 10th Infantry.*

Her mind went blank; her leg muscles turned gummy, yet somehow she stayed on her feet, waiting. After the man had loosened the top, he faced her. She closed her eyes briefly, swallowed hard, and gave him a curt nod. He lifted the top, and she stepped over to the side of the wagon to see her beloved. The ugly, foul development of decay along with bloat distorted familiar traits and characteristics, and only a lustrous wave of brown hair resembled anything normal within the container. She backed away, putting a hand over the lower half of her face. She promptly understood Ennis would need to be buried as soon as possible.

Mr. Stout said, "I'm real sorry about his . . . his condition. It's been a few days, of course."

Rendered dumb with shock, Joetta's gaze remained fastened on what she could still see of Ennis. The tip of his blackened nose, the movement of a strand of hair. She could not utter a word. Mr. Stout began to lower the lid when Bess spoke, her simple comment charged with disbelief. "Why, he wears the Union colors!"

Despite Joetta's devastation and distress, she found Bess's comment crass, and uncalled for. She lifted a hand to halt Mr. Stout. Mary's soft crying, Bess's high-pitched whispers, and Mr. McBride's heavy breathing came to her as she peered over the side of the box once again. She shut them out, until all that remained in the realm of her awareness was the sound of her heart and the sight of her beloved. Bess was right. Her husband wore a coat in the colors of a Union soldier, as if that was important when he lay there dead. The cloth was mostly unmarred, in fairly good shape, but who cared about that when he was gone from her forever. As if this was of some import and made a difference. Her breath rasping in her throat, and certain she would soon be sick, she whirled around to face Bess, her voice hoarse with emotion.

"And, what of it?"

Chapter 18

For her, the moldering was irrelevant. She wanted to remain with Ennis as long she could, and her wish was to keep him with her. He was her adored husband, therefore the strength of her love overcame the workings of nature. They took him anyway, despite her wails, despite her fighting to hold on to him. They would not, could not allow her what she wanted. What they did was proper, and necessary, and somewhere deep down, she understood this. Her desperate behavior, while it created consternation, was also understood. After he was in the ground, she took to bed. Familiar voices came and went, unheeded by her. Bess, Mary, Mr. McBride, and Robert. There was only one voice she wanted to hear, and it was gone forever. They said she would be all right, and hands patted her. Even in her despairing state, their words signified nothing, and her misery increased because life as she knew it had ended. She turned over on her side so she could better ignore them.

Time passed as it does, whether one wants it or not. She slept mostly, because doing so took her into the oblivion she craved. She often dreamed of sitting by Fishing Creek. Another time she was at the edge of a massive empty field with the moon suspended overhead, the color of butter-milk. An owl in a distant pine asked, *Who?* And she sobbed the answer, *Ennis*. She would awaken to find faces looming over her in the bed, concern etched in their eyes. She was given small bites of soft food. Sips of water. She took in the nourishment, but it was with little or no recollection of doing so.

She lost track of Robert. He would sometimes appear briefly in the bedroom doorway, but when her tear-laden eyes went searching, he was no longer there. She could not determine how or if he was managing this dreadful, hor-rible outcome. She was too distraught to tend to him, too lost to find her way out of her sadness. She had no recollec-tion of what she did, or what she said, or how it came to be that one morning she awoke, more clear-headed than she had been in some time, only to discover the house empty. Those who had been there were gone, and all was quiet except for the songs of a white-throated sparrow singing cheerfully in the magnolia rose bush outside the bedroom window.

She sat up in the bed. Her mourning dress lay over the back of the chair in the corner. Someone had found it in the trunk at the foot of the bed and had taken care to ready it for her. The sight of it sent her back to the last time she had worn it, when their baby girl was taken. She wilted where she sat, overcome by the memories. She did not want to get up, and yet she rose, washed, and dressed herself, aware the dress hung on her as if it was still draped over the chair. In front of the standing mirror in the corner of the bedroom, she had the appearance of a walking skeleton. She adjusted this and that, only to sit back down again, the effort making her light-headed. After a few minutes, she went into the kitchen only to sit down again. She needed food, and water. On the table across from her sat two letters, each from her mother. She fingered them but did not pick them up.

Mr. McBride shuffled in, his clothes stained with spills, face unshaven, and his eyes reddened by fatigue or something else. He gaped at her as if he were seeing a haint. He bent down and waved a hand in front of her face.

"You there?"

She jerked her head back.

"Stop shouting. Can you not see?"

Mr. McBride straightened up.

"Well, you ain't been exactly right, so to speak. I was afraid you might be sleepwalking again."

He dropped into a chair across from her. That might explain some of her bizarre dreams.

"Sleepwalking?"

He gave a slow nod, and a grunt. She cracked her knuckles a time or two, disturbed by this idea, then, with her knees stiff like she had been kneeling on the floor for days, she stood. Her movements mechanical, she went to the stove and pulled the skillet forward. A tiny pinprick of memory tried to come, a vision of Ennis sitting at the table behind her, reading. Her eyes filled. How was she supposed to get on? How was she supposed to live without him? The realization the passage of her life would continue like this, void of his presence, expanded before her as blank as a universe without stars, empty and flat.

She swallowed and in a shaky voice, she said, "Where is Robert?"

"With the Caldwells. Bess said she'd look after him."

Joetta's stomach soured further with this news. Under

Bess's thumb was not where Robert needed to be. She feared he might turn on her even more, if that were possible. She faced Mr. McBride.

"Ennis. He was wearing Union garments?"

Mr. McBride scrubbed at his chin.

"It appeared so."

"What does that mean?"

He shook his head.

"Not a thing. They probably been taking what they need. Confederates, they ain't outfitted like them Yanks. Ennis left when it was warm, and he'd been through a cold winter. Must've wore out what he had. Rebels ain't got standard uniforms."

She digested this, then went over to her worktable. Eggs were sitting neatly in a bowl. Pails of fresh water sat nearby. Wood was stacked in the box by the stove. The floor had been swept. Fresh butter was at hand. Someone must have done all of this during her fugue.

"Who did these chores?"

She gestured about the kitchen.

"The Brown woman, mostly. I tried to pay her, with the money you give me for the corn. She wouldn't take it. I put it back there on the shelf."

He rubbed his neck, appeared smaller somehow, older. She felt ancient herself. Her head itched terribly, and she could smell that she needed a bath.

"When did Robert leave?"

"A month ago, or thereabouts, I reckon."

"A month."

It could not be. She looked out the window at the sorghum, which had already entered the hard dough stage. What month was it?

Mr. McBride, as if reading her mind, said, "It's on into August. You ain't been of a right mind in a while."

Joetta directed her attention to the one thing she believed necessary.

"I want him home, here with me. With us. We have much to do."

Mr. McBride's head bobbed in agreement. Joetta looked about her kitchen and out into the fields. How precarious her emotions were. It took all she had to keep her mind from wandering in the direction it wanted, to dwell in her memories of Ennis. Her mind was not on the state of their crops, not on the things that were most important to their survival. She would have to watch herself, because if she did not, she could very well sink into that despair once again and she would be useless. She would mourn only at night, once she was in bed. That would be her time. The rest she owed to what was left of her family.

She made herself crack eggs into a bowl. Peeled a couple potatoes. Cut up an onion. Mr. McBride watched as she put bacon into the skillet, licking his lips, although he remained quiet for a change. She would feed him, and maybe she would eat too. It did not take long before she was setting a fragrant plate of bacon, eggs, and fried potatoes and onions before him. He hunched over the plate and began immediately, sometimes using his fingers to cram food in. The sight made her chest ache. She could not stand to see anyone so hungry. She picked at the food on her plate as Mr. McBride swiped his clean. He leaned back, patting his belly, watching as she shifted her food around.

"You want me to go get'im?"

"No, I will go."

"I ain't got nothing else to do."

"You want this?"

She tipped her head toward her barely touched food.

"If you ain't gonna eat it."

She dumped what she had onto his plate, and he went at

it again as if he had not eaten at all. When he was done, he grabbed his cane.

"I reckon I'll go see if that boy wants to come on home."

"No, let me. I need to talk to him."

Mr. McBride leaned on his cane, speaking with caution.

"You ought to know, he seemed eager to go with them. To be gone from here."

"Here reminds him too much of his father."

"Yes. I . . ." He stopped speaking and wiggled his cane in a disturbed fashion. "I find it difficult to get hold of myself."

It was the most he had ever admitted when it came to expressing feelings about his son. Joetta's heart swelled with empathy.

"It is difficult. I do not know what it means for us, but we still have one another. Robert, you, and me. Maybe even Henry one day."

He stared out the window, frowning.

"Way I see it, I wouldn't have got myself shot like 'at, and sure wouldn't have put on no damn Yankee uniform."

Joetta's brief moment of understanding shriveled.

"You have no idea what you would have done, and you, you do not get to judge him, especially not now."

Mr. McBride wiggled his cane in agitation again.

"I don't mean nothing by it. I'm only talking."

"Do not say another word about him unless you sing his praises."

She abruptly turned on her heel and went out the door. The sight of the sorghum gave her pause. Mr. McBride clumped along behind her and pointed at the field.

"Ain't been no rain the entire time you were laid up. We're bound to lose this crop, too."

Joetta could not believe what she was seeing. She could

not focus on this right now. First thing was to bring Robert home. Without having to ask, Mr. McBride put Pal into his traces and got him hooked to the wagon. He did not look at her, appearing ashamed of his earlier comment.

"I could go yet. Or go with you?"

She thought about it, but she needed to be alone, to clear her head. This arrangement, which had transpired while she was incapable of coherent thought, while gracious and giving, was troublesome. Even while Bess would ensure Robert's well-being, if he could be influenced to their way of thinking, then he too was lost to her.

"No. He needs to see I am up and about. That will bring him home."

She spoke with a confidence she did not feel. It worked, however. He backed away.

"All right, then."

She guided Pal down the drive and onto the lane. Disoriented and out of sorts, with her strength already waning, she realized it was only midmorning, yet it seemed as if the day was at an end. She sat back and let the mule go along as he wanted. Soon she was bypassing the Caldwells' fields. The corn bent one way and the other in the hot breeze, as dry as the sorghum. She rolled into the yard and stopped for a moment, looking around to see if someone might be working in a garden or the fields. She saw no one. She guided Pal over to the shade, climbed down, and brushed her skirts off.

She had decided to go to the front door when Harold and Robert came from around the side of the house, their heads together, arguing over something. Both carried muskets and wore mock uniforms. They stopped at the sight of her. The impact of his father's death on Robert was evident. His face was without color, his eyes dull. Harold rolled his eyes toward Robert, then back to her. He spoke politely enough.

"Hello, Mrs. McBride. I'm real sorry about Mr. McBride."

Joetta acknowledged Harold with a small nod and greeted him. "Hello, Harold. Thank you very much."

She turned her gaze back to Robert, imploring him with a look to not hold her completely accountable for what had happened. The one he gave her equaled that of a stranger.

"I know why you're here, and I ain't going back."

She dipped her head, stared at the dusty toes of her shoes. When she raised her eyes, it was like looking at him from underwater, and it felt as if she were drowning. She offered him nothing, no begging, no wise comments. She turned away, her hopeful attempt squashed by that one heartbreaking look he had given her. She stopped abruptly, her curiosity rising above her grief.

"What are you wearing?"

She waited for his answer, her back to him. No sound came. She twisted her head to look over her shoulder and with a defiant tone, he finally answered.

"We're practicing to be soldiers."

"Let me guess. Confederate."

Robert's eyes bore into hers, bright and hard.

"Yeah."

A year ago, she would not have tolerated the insolence in his tone. A year ago, he would not have spoken to her that way. She looked away, unwilling or perhaps unable to consent to his viewpoints. She spoke softly, fighting to keep her emotions out of her voice.

"When you are ready to come home and be the son your father expected, your grandfather and I will be waiting."

"You know, I'm thirteen now. A man by some's standards."

His voice faded away, signifying his own distress. Joetta closed her eyes. My God. What kind of mother was she? She had forgotten his birthday. It had come and gone as she floundered in her misery and pain. She turned back around to face him and wished she had not. He looked through her as she struggled to regain her mental footing and failed. In retaliation, her response was quick and held the same coldness he directed at her.

"Well, then, it is time to act like one."

She walked away and climbed onto the seat of the wagon. Flicking the reins, she set off down the long path. She glanced back once to see Bess standing with the boys, speaking to Robert, who did not look at her but at Joetta. She wondered what Bess thought of her rushing off. Perhaps she was telling Robert it was best he stay with them, safe from those whose honor was questionable. She was too far away to see his expression. She faced forward, her heart and mood as black as her dress.

For the next couple of weeks, she rose from her bed after sleepless, fraught nights. She was exhausted from her attempts to water the sorghum, pail by pail. She worked to the point of near collapse and in spite of her body's intense fatigue, she could not shut down her mind. It bounced from what Ennis might have experienced, to where Henry might be, and on to how Robert was doing. Often she got up and went to sit on the back steps, staring into the dark, weighing all of the complications and difficulties they faced. She told Mr. McBride to go on and use whatever money was left to buy coffee, flour, and cornmeal. He purchased what he could, but the blockade constricted supplies severely. Her mother's most recent letters had been filled with information about the Union controlling waterways along the coast, and it was the same there. No coffee or sugar. Her mother lamented, *The flour and cornmeal is mostly gone, too.* Joetta knew she ought to reply and could not, for the life of her.

Mr. McBride wandered from the house to the barn and back again, like he did not know where he belonged, or as if he were looking for something or someone. She continued to cook but was never hungry. Even he appeared to have lost some of his appetite. He began staying in his cabin and not coming to the house to eat like usual. Joetta was actually glad. She did not want to have to listen to him ponder or judge what happened to Ennis, and what he might have done different. He did not dare bring up the subject of Robert. Maybe it was something about how she had been since coming back from the Caldwells. Mr. McBride became quite disturbed when Joetta told him Robert refused to return.

"He ain't coming home? They ain't his family. We are."

"He chose to stay."

"He'll come if I go after him."

"I would not be so sure of it." She hesitated, then admitted her lapse of memory.

"I forgot his birthday, of all things."

In one of those rare instances of understanding, Mr. McBride astounded her.

"I reckon you've had plenty of good reason to forget lots of things."

She relished his uncommon sympathy, even while it did little good for her mood. She began taking food to him, and the first time she did this, he opened the door and wordlessly stepped aside as if he had expected it would come to this. She went by him and set the plate on a small table beside his chair, and then looked about at the familiar interior, which had not changed since she had first seen it seventeen years ago. She had always liked the cabin, although

Mr. McBride treated the inside no different than if he were outside. He whittled on his birds, and let the shavings drop to the floor and never swept them up. A collection of mud, leaves, and various other debris littered the corners. At least he used a spittoon.

When she and Ennis had lived here after their marriage, it had been clean and cozy. Mrs. McBride had seen to that. The fireplace where she would cook still had the cast-iron rod with the kettle suspended from it. Joetta recollected swinging it out and away from the fire to stir the stews and soups they prepared, remembering how hot it had been in the summer, and how she had warmed her feet on the hearth stones in the winter. Mrs. McBride's skillet remained on those stones even now, a reminder of the woman as tough as the cooking implement.

There was a door off that room, and that was a bedroom, added on after Mrs. McBride gave birth to Ennis. His room had not been much bigger than the woodshed, and it was in there Robert had slept. She went to it and stared at a few things that had migrated from her house to here. A shirt and a pair of pants hung over the back of a chair. A book she and Ennis had given him for Christmas one year, *Walden; or, Life in the Woods*. She left Mr. McBride eating and wandered back to the empty house.

The days followed one after the other, and Joetta did not bother to keep up with which was which. One afternoon after Mr. McBride had been into town, he came to the house and paced around the kitchen. She asked him what was going on, and he grew animated as she gave him her attention.

"That son of a gun Lincoln's planning to write some sort of proclamation to free them darkies. Just like that with one swoop of his pen. How can he do that? They're not *his* to set free. They are property, and according to the Constitution, property cannot be taken without compensation. The owners bought them with their own good money. Mark my words, there'll be all kinds of trouble over this."

"As if there has not been already? The sooner it is over with the better. I do not care how it happens. We have paid dearly, and for what? Nothing."

Mr. McBride threw his hands up.

"I'll never understand you."

"That is certainly something we can finally agree on."

Chapter 19

She did not go after Robert again. She wanted him home, but she wanted the choice to be of his own free will. Her mother's intuition said if he returned it would be because he, and he alone, had reconciled his feelings toward her. And so there they were: Mr. McBride stuffed into his cabin, and her rambling about the house. The farm work held most of her attention. She was bound to save the sorghum, even as she watched each plant succumb to the heat, in spite of her efforts. One day she was unexpectedly caught as the rhythmic marching she had come to know so well reached her. She quickly squatted among the crooked rows and withered plants so she would not be seen, and waited, feeling the sweat trickling down her face, back, and legs.

They came into sight, Confederate soldiers on their way to Lord only knew where. Fighting had escalated, and terrible tales made their way back to Southern civilians about the Union troops taking over small towns one by one, burning, plundering, and doling out punishment, whether righteous or not, to those who crossed their path. The steady tromp of those determined men never failed to make her mouth go dry, and her breath came hard as if she had been running instead of squatting in the middle of a field. The Union were not the only ones who threw people into prison. The Confederates would just as soon do the same if they heard even one word spoken of disloyalty, so she hid.

To her utter shame she had done this same thing twice before when Mary came by. Joetta understood her friend only wanted to check on her, but she had neither the heart nor the inclination for probing conversations and questions about her well-being. Mary called out and searched the farm with a hand up to her brow, shading her eyes. Joetta remained out of sight, watching her friend shake her head in despair before leaving items on the porch and climbing back onto her wagon. Joetta had closed her eyes, resigned to her sunken feelings of despair.

After the soldiers were gone, she once again turned her attention to the state of the sorghum plants, realizing she had wasted time watering with the bucket. The crop was lost. She was digesting this and still standing in the middle of the field when Mr. McBride arrived after his wanderings about town. As soon as he spotted her, he hurried over and asked about the contingent of soldiers he had seen, excitement filling his voice.

"Did you see them?"

"No."

"How could you miss them?"

He continued his enthusiastic rendering of the sight while she gave directions silently, pointing at Pal, who needed hitching up. He talked even as she got behind the plow, unaware of what she was about to do. It was only as she began to till the plants under that he grew quiet. She kept working while he stood watching in dismay. She had already moved on in her thoughts, which had turned to her sister. She was curious about Faith and how they might be faring, given their Union favor. Perhaps better, though she somehow doubted it. She was painfully aware she should write to her parents about Ennis, and still could not muster the will to do so. To put those dire, sad words to paper and share that which she could hardly believe true would be like cutting open her veins with a knife. She envisioned the ink like blood on the page, and used the excuse of the mail service to delay such an emotionally arduous task. Pulling herself out of her reverie only to hear Mr. McBride talking once more had her guiding Pal and the plow farther into the field.

Summer passed, and she punished herself with work. She went at it until her hands were raw, digging up potatoes, hauling them out of the field, and storing them in the root cellar. She harvested turnips, cabbage, and squash. Before long, she and Mr. McBride had hunkered down once again for the winter, and Joetta could not stop her descent into the way she had been during her mourning period for Ennis. Each day she awoke, she wished she had not, and then came the thought: *Get through it, just get through it. There was Robert, still.* She hoped.

Christmas was a sorry, sad affair. She cooked one of the chickens, boiled a few potatoes with cabbage, and put it on the table. Mr. McBride ate with gusto while she stared resentfully at him and his ceaseless appetite. New Year's Eve was spent staring out the window, her own reflection in it from the lamplight behind her. It was like looking at a haint. She awoke bleary-eyed, and she and Mr. McBride faced one another at the breakfast table in a sort of startled silence. For her, it was a realization Robert had not been home in six months. For Mr. McBride it was about the war entering its third year, and even he sounded like he was getting tired of it.

"I wished they'd get on with it. It's 1863, and ain't nowhere near to being settled."

The day passed uneventful, cold and dreary. The next morning, when she entered the kitchen, Mr. McBride had let himself in and was seated at the table. From the flush of his skin, it was clear he was livid. On the table beside her cup was a letter, the cover dirty and damaged. A letter from her mother! Feeling glad for it, she picked it up, but did not open it immediately, not with Mr. McBride obviously upset.

"What has you up so early?"

He was in a bellowing mood.

"That bastard, Lincoln, he done signed it!" He glared at her as if she were the one with a pen in hand, scribbling a signature. "Damn him. That Proclamation of his, won't do nothing 'cept make us dig in harder!"

She had taken to roasting okra seed and boiling it, the concoction replacing the coffee they no longer had. She placed a cup of it in front of him and sat down with her own. His fingers drummed on the table and he wiggled about on the chair, snorting through his nose.

"Ain't you got nothing to say? He's single-handedly freed every single darkie!"

Her initial reply was a loud, unladylike slurp of the odd-tasting brew. She cared only to hear, *It is over.* Setting her cup down, she told him how she felt.

"Here is what I have to say. I want Henry home. I want Robert home. I want Ennis back, but that is never going to be, and I am merely trying to get by until someone tells me it is over. Is it over?"

He sat back with a thump, the color of his face deepening as it did when he was distressed. Now he was the one to slurp loudly. They sat without speaking until he pointed at the letter.

"Ain't you gonna read it?"

Joetta picked up the letter.

"Would you like to hear it?"

He nodded. She opened it and unfolded the paper.

> *Dearest daughter,*
>
> *By the time you receive this, Christmas will be past, and the New Year will be on us. My daughter, I yearn for word from you. It worries me I have not heard from you in a very long time. I know there are difficulties pursuant to even the simplest parts of our lives during these most arduous days. Can you imagine? Leland signed with the Confederacy. Wilbur did not. Your father and I, we do not understand Leland. And then we heard Faith and her husband are with the Union, as are many in the western counties. How could this be? Perhaps it is merely for survival, yet our family is literally in the throes of this great divide, and at such a personal level. Your father and I are at wit's end over it. I do hope that perhaps by now you have sent me a letter and it is on its way. I hope you have good news from Ennis. Is there any word on Henry?*

Here Mr. McBride interrupted.

"You have not written to your mother about . . . ?"

Joetta looked away, her heart troubled.

"No, I cannot bring myself to do so."

He took a breath as if to speak, and she held a hand up.

"I will. When I am ready."

The firmness with which she spoke stayed his comment, and she continued reading.

> *I must tell you, the Confederates began construction on a fort to keep the Union from coming upriver. It is being built off of Rainbow Banks and is to be called Fort Branch. The*

building of it has made me quite nervous. Father says the
need is there, which offers me no comfort. Undoubtedly, this
will bring the fight ever closer.

Mr. McBride perked up at this news, grunting in satisfaction.

"Smart, smart."

She began reading about her mother's day to day and
stopped when he flipped his hand about.

"I don't care none about all that. Does she say anything
else about the fort?"

Joetta scanned the page.

"No."

She folded the letter and put it in her apron pocket, filled
with mortification at causing her mother such worry, but
to write of everything except the most crucial news was in-
conceivable. They went back to sipping on the odd-tasting
brew, with Mr. McBride occasionally mumbling to himself, of course loud enough for Joetta to hear.

"They ought to know about their own son-in-law, one
would think. Your family is in flux, got one this way, one
that way. Well. At least they had the sense to make up their
minds."

She slurped. Loudly.

Henry's seventeenth birthday came and went, and Joetta wondered if he was alive to even see it. She and Mr.
McBride navigated the rest of the long winter with difficulty, their dependency on one another a matter of survival,
and a great cause of irritation. She threatened to withhold
food in order to get him to help split wood and chop kindling. She pointed out she was the one who did most everything else, including breaking ice that formed over the
water buckets, feeding the animals, milking the cow, gath-

ering eggs, mending clothes, on and on. She would not even start cooking unless her wood box was full.

Winter slid into spring, and Joetta managed to get at least one field plowed, as crooked as the creek, but she was proud for having done it. She had only a few sorghum seeds to plant, although her efforts were often hampered by soldiers, again breaking from their winter encampments to resume the war. Day after day, week by week, they passed the farm, boot soles meeting the hard-packed soil, creating a sound as if the very earth itself had a heartbeat. One afternoon the ground beneath her vibrated a warning, and the doves, pheasants, and other birds perched on limbs in nearby trees took flight. She used the springhouse to hide, keeping watch through a crack in the door. Soon, like a stream, they flowed by, some looking at the farm, where, to their eye, no life was visible. She closed her eyes, prayed they would keep going. She did not want her house destroyed, things taken. They had so very little as it was.

Even from where she hid, it was obvious these Confederates were not in good shape. Their clothes hung off their thin frames, and she had seen scarecrows better dressed. She studied them, torn between wanting to help and her fear. After everything she had experienced, she took no chances, not when she was, in essence, alone. She believed it possible most were on their way to help fortify areas of the Inner Banks, to somehow disrupt the Union's control along the North Carolina shoreline. She thought this courtesy of Mr. McBride's incessant ramblings where he had explained this Union effort, the Anaconda Plan as it was called, implemented by "that lowly bastard, Scott," to use his description. Scott's intentions to cut off the supply routes to the Confederacy by way of the Mississippi, then along the Southern coastlines the way the snake would constrict its prey, was working. To that, Joetta and many others could attest.

She moved a bit so she could see Mr. McBride's cabin. The door remained shut. She had half expected him to bolt outside. She leaned against the door, head tilted, waiting. She always worried there might be a straggler or two suddenly appearing out of nowhere. Finally, she felt safe and left the springhouse to resume her field work. She walked down the rows, noting the flag leaves had emerged, and the plants would soon enter the boot stage. The panicles, still hidden within the leaf folds, would come out in the next couple of days. She nodded with satisfaction. They would have the benefit of this scrappy crop at the very least.

Joetta stayed in the field, losing time as she watched Pal's tail flick flies off his rump, and enjoyed the touch of a light wind across her face. It was late spring, yet summerlike heat enveloped the land, making the distant countryside ripple and dance as if submerged in water. When she became aware again, it was as if she were coming out of a dream. She adjusted the loose, ill-fitting dress over her hip bones, recollecting how she had meant to move the buttons over and had yet to do so. She walked slowly to the fence where she had hung a bucket of water. She took the dipper, drank a bit of the tepid liquid, and her stomach clenched with a wave of nausea. Her appetite had a mind of its own, and came and went as it pleased. Mr. McBride had recently expressed concern, at least what she believed at first was concern. He pointed at her untouched plate.

"You need to eat."

"My appetite has taken leave again."

Several more meals passed with her picking at her food until he dropped his fork, rested his elbows on the table.

"Look here. If you're gonna starve yourself to death, by

all means go right on, but at least get that crop in before you drop dead so I can make do somehow."

Joetta set her own fork aside and sat with her hands in her lap. Well, then. If he could choose to say what he had on his mind, she would too.

"Not to worry. I plan to stick around if for no other reason than to irritate you."

He jerked abruptly like she had kicked him in the shin.

"All I'm saying is, you ain't the only one 'round here who's affected by his death. I don't want to have to bury you beside him."

Joetta, astonished at this admission, leaned back in her chair and watched him wiggle and twitch. He ignored her and busied himself by wiping his hands repetitiously on his pant leg, as if revealing those innermost thoughts caused him a good deal of discomfort. What the war had done thus far to her and her family underscored actions of kindness, or malice. Everyone behaved in the way they considered apt for a moment in time. She was entrenched in her own emotions, no different than they, she supposed. She would do as she pleased; what did she have to lose? Everything that truly mattered to her was gone, had been taken, or had left.

She lifted the bucket off the fence post and came out of the field. It was only midday, but her strength had waned, and caused a bout of light-headedness. She finally freed Pal of the plow harness, all the while imagining Mr. McBride watching her on the sly, yet refusing to help. It made her even more determined to show she could do these things for herself. She only succeeded because Pal was patient and cooperated as she guided him with her hands. She turned him loose in the pasture and immediately went and sat down on the splitting stump near the wood pile to catch her breath. The sun found her before long and she rose, crossed the yard, and entered the house, where she sat at the kitchen table, doing nothing until it was almost dark, and only then did she finally rise to light the lantern.

She made supper. Each mouthful was a struggle to chew and swallow as she stared dismally about the room. She drank a cup of buttermilk while keeping an eye on the back door. She had saved enough food for Mr. McBride, but he would have to come and get it. She did not have the energy to take it over there. She sat tapping her fingers on the table and cracking her knuckles. Maybe she would do nothing whatsoever from here on out. What was the point? The desire, the worth and meaning behind it, had become much less important.

Joetta spoke to the empty room. "I am alone."

The sound of her solitary voice gave her an even greater sense of abandonment. She fell quiet, and after waiting for Mr. McBride a bit longer, she wrapped the food in a cloth and went to bed. Although exhausted, her sleep was broken and irregular. Finally, it came, and took her so far away she did not wake up until midmorning. This was highly irregular, and it disturbed her greatly to see the sun well past the tops of the trees. She got up and looked out the window, where, of course, nothing was happening, except the chickens were clustered against the fence looking toward the house with high expectations. She wanted to sink back into sleep because it allowed a reprieve. Instead, she made herself get dressed, not bothering to do more than pin her hair up and pull on the black dress, groaning as she bent to button her shoes. She went into the kitchen, got her basket and the scrap bucket before going out the back door, shielding her eyes from the sun.

The chickens took note of movement and strutted about with hopeful clucks, encouraging her to come their way.

She shuffled across the yard to their enclosure, opened the gate, and first retrieved a few eggs and placed them in the basket. They flapped about her feet and came as close as they dared while she tossed out potato peels, forage, and other vegetable scraps. After she gave them fresh water, she took care of the hogs, who also squealed eagerly. They had come out of the woods and milled about the pen, acting as if they wanted back inside, but as soon as she threw their scraps out, they demolished them and trotted off to the woods again, grunting and nudging their noses in the dirt. Joetta watched both hens and hogs go about their business, envying their simplistic existence.

Mr. McBride's cabin remained still and quiet. He was either sleeping or had gone into town. If so, he had walked, because Pal was in the pasture. She drifted toward the barn to milk Honey, thinking she would eat today while internally retching at the thought of what was available. What she longed for were fluffy hot biscuits or buttery corn bread. Rich, black coffee. Her husband, and sons. She set the stool beside the cow and began her task, stopping periodically to rest, her forehead against Honey's side. Finally, she finished and turned the cow out into the pasture with Pal.

She picked up the pail of milk and began walking across the yard toward the springhouse, setting it down a couple of times along the way. This had never happened to her before, this inability to continue without stopping. She shook her arm and picked it up again, and kept going. She was about to enter the springhouse when a thump and a floorboard creaking made the back of her neck tingle. She had the distinct sensation of being watched. Behaving as if she had changed her mind, she spoke out loud. "What am I doing? I am supposed to make butter today," and changed course to go toward the house instead.

Once inside, she set the pail down and hurried to drop

the wooden bar across the door. Fear drove her actions and she grabbed the musket from over the doorframe. Peering out the window, she waited, watching the springhouse door. After a few minutes, she began thinking maybe she had been wrong. She could have been hearing things and she began to feel silly. As she was about to set the gun back over the door, fingers appeared at the edge of the springhouse door and it eased open. Joetta was so astonished she did not think about the fact she was by herself as she lifted the bar and rushed out, yelling, "Come from out of there now!"

She paused, chest heaving, gun at her shoulder and ready to shoot. She waited, then clarified the threat to the intruder.

"I will shoot straight through that door."

The tips of the fingers whitened and she noticed they were not much bigger than hers.

She spoke calmly. "I do not plan to shoot if you come out. *Now.*"

The door opened wider, and into the sunlight stepped a person, blinking rapidly and shielding his eyes. Joetta's widened with surprise at the small man, no, a boy. He could not be older than Robert, if that. He was dressed in the uniform of the North. Her voice was sharp.

"Who are you? Why are you hiding in my springhouse?"

He took off his hat revealing orange hair, so dirty the color was dull, muted by the grime. He scratched. Twitched his head and shoulders.

"Name's . . . Ch-Charlie H-Hastings. Ma'am."

Joetta narrowed her eyes.

"Is that your *real* name?"

He scratched at his armpit and said nothing. Joetta took in his appearance. The uniform was quite filthy and torn in places, but she had a trained eye when it came to cloth and design. He wore a sack coat, with four buttons. The coat was made of cotton warp and woolen weft. These materials gave it a shiny look, despite the fact he had apparently worn it for some time. His pants, light blue, hung off of him the way her dress did. In his hands he gripped a dark blue kepi. He quivered all over, either with fear, or some ailment, perhaps both.

"How old are you?"

Oddly, as it was not cold, his teeth chattered, and when he spoke, he reminded her of Elder Newell.

"N-none of your b-business."

"You look no more than twelve. Barely that."

He glared at her, but his supposed bravery was nothing but a front given his lower lip trembled. He scratched again, this time at his belly.

"Where are you from?"

"V-Virginia." He then burst into a bit of foul language. "Gotdammitall! I'm g-gonna go m-mad. My f-feet's on fire, and th-they's itching somethin' f-fierce!"

To Joetta's astonishment, he dropped to the ground and began pulling off his boots. He sucked in his breath as he peeled away the rotting socks. Skin came with them. Joetta was stunned by the condition of his feet, the skin shriveled, raw and red, with layers now missing with the removal of his socks. She held her nose as the smell wafted her way. He gave a sigh, laid back, and to Joetta's surprise, appeared to fall asleep in seconds.

"Charlie Hastings," she called to him. She called again, louder. "Charlie Hastings!"

He did not move. Her attention was caught by a wiggling movement around the top part of the socks he had taken off. They looked alive as vermin squirmed and crawled about, searching for his body warmth. He had yet to stir even as the pests scuttled over him, his coat, shirt, and pants. It was as if his stillness had disturbed them. While he lay there, she rushed to get the wash tub and pulled it out into the yard. She got a fire going to heat water and went into the kitchen for lye soap and set it next to the tub. She grabbed a stick, and gagging with revulsion, she speared the socks and tossed them into the flames. They were gone in seconds.

She yelled, "Charlie Hastings!" and kicked his ankle.

To her immense relief, he jerked and sat up, looking confused.

"I ain't f-feeling so w-well."

He sat shivering, with a high color in his cheeks. Joetta was certain he had fever.

"Get out of those clothes. I need to burn them."

"B–burn? I c–can't be letting y–you d–do that. It's th-the only clothes I got. Wh–what will I p–put on?"

"I am sure you realize this is not Union-friendly territory. You cannot keep wearing them, not unless you want to get shot, hanged, or taken to jail. Moreover, you and your clothing are crawling with Lord knows what."

He hung his head.

"L–Lord knows m–me. Knows I ain't n–nothing but a fleck of d–dust on H–His Hand, but I am His."

"No one said different, Charlie Hastings."

"C–call me Hasty, m–ma'am. Th–that's what th–they called m–me."

"Who? Who called you that?"

"Th–them in my r–regiment."

"You are with the Union." She said this as a statement.

"Y–yes'm. Un–undoubtedly, as you can see from them colors."

"Why were you in my springhouse?"

"I, I ain't w–wanting to be p–part of it n–no more. I'se only tr–trying to . . ."

He swallowed and his lip trembled again. Joetta considered him with the shrewd eye of a mother. He was in a woeful state and certainly in no shape to cause her any trouble. She pointed at the washtub.

"Get in that hot water. It will help take the chill off. There is soap. Scrub yourself good. You cannot come into my house until I do not see anything crawling on you."

"Yes, m-ma'am. But . . . I c-can't be g-going about n-nekkid."

"Of course not. I have something I think will fit."

He turned away from her and took off the clothes, dropping them to the ground. He was short, about Henry's height only he did not have Henry's bulk. Hasty was nothing except wasted flesh pulled tight over bones. She adjusted her assessment and guessed him to be younger, perhaps not even old as Robert. Not nearly old enough for whatever he had been through. His skin was yellowish, covered by a layer of brown dirt. With the same stick, she scooped up his clothes and tossed them onto the flames. He moaned as he sank into the warm water, his position cramped, but he closed his eyes in relief. Even with the balmy air and the sun beating down on him, he had goose bumps on his arms and back. She added more hot water, then turned to him.

"I have clothes you can wear in that cabin over there. I will be back directly."

He stared off into the distance.

"Y-you g-got anything I c-can eat? I ain't h-had me n-nary a b-bite in three days."

This too she could manage. She would feed him, tend to him. He was sick, no doubt.

"I will get you something to eat. You bathe, and I will see to it."

"Y-yes'm. Thank you."

She kept the musket with her but could not imagine him causing any problems because for one, he had no clothes, and two, he appeared even weaker than she first suspected. She hurried to Mr. McBride's cabin and went in. She had no idea where he might have got off to, and did not have time to speculate. She retrieved the shirt and pants from the room where Robert had slept, and when she came back outside, Charlie Hastings had not moved. With his forehead on his knees, he remained folded up, a small, wadded form of human misery. Her maternal instincts kicked in, and she heated more water. She was in the process of dumping it into the wash tub when Mr. McBride appeared, and with him was Robert. Astonished, Joetta straightened up and stared at her son, who had grown another inch or two. Meanwhile Mr. McBride gawked at the thin, pale form crouched in the tub. He rubbed his fingers across his scruffy chin and twisted around to look at Joetta. She was glad she had burned Charlie Hastings's uniform.

"Who do we have here?"

Joetta, still staring in surprise at Robert, managed to tell him the newcomer's name.

"This is Charlie Hastings."

"Where'd he come from?"

Joetta had not thought about how to answer when young Hasty spoke up.

"H-hell."

Chapter 20

A few evenings later, Mr. McBride explained how he had managed to get Robert to return.

"I told him you were wasting away. Said he was apt to lose you too, lessen he come on home and showed you something to live for."

"I suppose he did not expect to find that boy here."

Mr. McBride rubbed at his chin, his gaze on Hasty, busy stacking wood.

"I reckon we could use the help."

Joetta did not point out the "we" part as utterly ridiculous thinking on his part. Robert must have expected to see her flailing about in the fields, and instead found her busy mothering this scrap of a boy, who called her Mrs. Joetta, and who had stuck himself to her like a cocklebur. Maybe it would do some good in the long run; the adoration of another might help him recover what he had apparently lost. For the next few days, Robert worked the sorghum, while Hasty helped her. She did her best to eat, to allow Robert to see her trying, while wondering if he really cared. He must have held a tiny bit of concern because he stayed close to the farm instead of disappearing like before. She caught him watching the other boy without giving the appearance of it, assessing the smaller kid in a way she believed came from jealousy, or perhaps even puzzlement over Hasty's noticeable desire to stay close to her. It was obvious her son carried many burdens, from blame to anger to sorrow. She worried he would never again return to his old self.

Hasty, with the opportunity to eat more regularly, did quite a bit of work. For his smallish size and evident illness, which came and went at a certain time every day, he was stronger than he appeared and was soon handling most of the more mundane chores. Along with stacking wood and keeping Joetta's wood box full, he retrieved pails of water for her, milked the cow, fed the chickens and hogs, and after a week there, even helped her churn butter. He did this work without being asked. Before she could get to one thing or another, it was already done, and he would be waiting to help her with anything else she was about to do.

The change in Joetta's household was poignant, particularly when they took meals together. Their presence at the table was reminiscent of what had once been, as she, the two boys, and the old man ate. They had ravenous appetites, while she continued to pick. At the end of that first week after Hasty's arrival, she made mention the meat was almost gone.

"That boar and sow we slaughtered last year?"

Mr. McBride's fork stopped between his plate and his mouth.

"Yes?"

"It is almost gone."

Joetta looked at him, he looked at her, and they got up from the table at the same time as if having identical thoughts. Robert pushed his chair back to follow, and so did Hasty. Robert pointed at Hasty.

"Where do you think you're going?"

Hasty froze, a trace of red eclipsing his cheeks, and Joetta gave her son a puzzled look.

"What is it, Robert?"

"This ain't got nothing to do with him. He ain't *family*. You even got him sleeping in Henry's room. It ain't right."

Joetta had suspected Robert would speak up about this at some point. She corrected his speech to give herself time to think. "Is not right."

His mouth turned down even more, and his hands became fists. Given his recent conduct and his desire to distance himself from this very family he was now so defensive over, his behavior was startling. It was jealousy, pure and simple, and this she did not understand. Where was his compassion and his consideration?

"I am glad you finally recognize and claim us as family. He is not harming anyone or anything."

Hasty concentrated on his hands, and it was Robert's turn to flush to a high color at his mother's words. Still, he continued to scowl, mistrustful and suspicious. Joetta decided to let them sort it out, and she followed after Mr. McBride. As she approached, he exited from the smokehouse, arms flapping in distress.

"They ain't but two shoulders, a bit of bacon, and sausage in there. We ain't eat all that meat already, even with an extra mouth to feed. We should've had more than enough to get us through this winter."

He glared at Joetta as if her not eating had somehow made the meat disappear. She had been so completely addled by Ennis's death, the time that followed was merely a haze of images and nothingness. She had not paid attention as she should have. He was right, one hog would typically last well over a year. In that moment she remembered the stranger who had come into the house, and the Confederate flag she found by the chicken coop. She recollected all those times when she had felt as if she were being watched.

"Someone is taking it."

By now, Robert had come outside, with Hasty trailing some distance behind him. Robert and Mr. McBride gave one another a look like she was making ridiculous declarations. Mr. McBride tipped his head toward the smokehouse.

"Taking our meat?"

"Yes."

"Who would do that? We know everyone 'round here."

"The farm, it is being watched. By someone. I am certain of it."

"Ain't nobody seen nothing."

"What about the flag that was left? And that man that ran us off the road, and then I found him inside the house? There are times I feel as if I am being watched."

"Hell, ain't nothing happened since all that."

"This. This has happened. There is no other explanation other than someone taking it."

Robert pointed at Hasty.

"Maybe he knows something about it."

Hasty quickly shook his head while Mr. McBride poked his chin out, suspicion bringing his eyebrows together. Joetta gestured toward their guest.

"He might be hungry, but no one can eat that much in such a short time."

Mr. McBride faced the boy, ignoring her.

"You know anything 'bout this?"

Joetta moved closer to Hasty, wanting to protect him while also wishing to somehow inform him not to impart too much. If he confessed he had been with the Union, it would not matter what he said. Mr. McBride would not tolerate him on their property, much less at their table. He would accuse her of harboring the "enemy," and force him to leave. She realized how badly she did not want this to happen. Wondrously, Hasty had filled some of the void in her heart. His partiality and deference to her helped her forget, if only for a little while, despite his short time on the farm. She hurried over to him and put an arm around his shoulder. His bones felt fragile beneath the shirt and she felt even more protective toward him.

"How would he know anything? He has hardly been out of my sight since he got here."

Robert exhaled with force.

"Ain't that the truth. Why, he's even got on my britches and shirt."

Hasty spoke up in his own defense. "I'll give'em back. And I don't know nothing. It ain't me."

At Robert's woeful comment, Joetta removed her arm from around Hasty's shoulder. She began cracking her knuckles until she caught herself, and crossed her arms.

Mr. McBride continued his speculations. "Kinda strange how all of a sudden we're running low on meat, though."

Hasty switched from one foot to the other, then winced. There had been no extra shoes for him to wear, and his skin, although healing, still looked horrible. Mr. McBride began to study them.

"I been wondering since you got here, how your feet come to be like'at."

"They got wet."

"You a runaway?"

Hasty looked from her to Mr. McBride. "Runaway?"

"War's got lots of deserters. You a deserter? Don't many cotton to Yanks or deserters 'round here."

Hasty, his face stricken, and fearful, went mute. Robert, who had been pacing with his hands shoved into his pockets, stopped and looked at the other boy with renewed suspicion. Joetta surged in front of Hasty, her skirts spinning around her legs, her movement quick and born of aggravation, and fear.

"Leave him be, the both of you. He is not well. Can you not see that? Look at his color. He is yellow with malaria, and yet, he has been nothing but considerate and helpful to me, to all of us. That is more than I can say for either of you."

Mr. McBride and Robert were dumbfounded by this outburst. They mirrored one another with their round eyes and speechlessness. Joetta regretted her sharp words as the hurt in Robert's face bloomed, but what she said rang true, and they knew it. Their subdued behavior and lack of argument was proof. She reassured Hasty.

"Never mind all this. You are a help to me, and you can stay as long as you wish, although, I have to imagine, your mother must worry about you."

It was the first time Joetta had seen Hasty close himself off. His face fell flat, and his eyes went blank, as if he had lost consciousness or had passed on to another life right before her eyes. He visibly shrank, and turned away from them as he fought not to cry. His emotions, whatever brought them on, moved her. She wanted to allow him time to recover from that which had taken hold of him. She faced Mr. McBride and Robert.

"We will kill another hog."

Mr. McBride was easy to get along with all of a sudden. "All right, then."

Robert too. "Okay."

How agreeable they could be when she held firm.

Robert said, "I'll go and get one sorted out from the rest."

His calm compliance made Joetta grateful, and she said, "That would be helpful."

With work to be done, they quickly finished their meal and then each went their own way to accomplish their tasks. Hasty fell in with her and, without being asked, began to help set up for the scalding. He rolled the big cast-iron pot kept near the smokehouse, then hauled water and filled it up. Joetta worried about preserving the meat. They could only smoke it as there was no salt for curing. She went into the dim smokehouse, retrieved her scraper and some rags. She was sweating when she came out. It was not the proper time of year for this. December was hog-killing month.

With a fire going under the pot, she and Hasty waited. He, on the back steps, hands dangling between his knees, soaking up the heat of the sun. She walked about the yard aimlessly. In looking at him, she suspected his fever had returned, though his voice had not tremored from it. His eyes held a glazed, heavy look, and he experienced an occasional shiver. His hair, clean and minus the vermin, gleamed in the sunlight as it clung to his scalp, damp from the sweat of work and his illness. The orange tone reminded her of leaves on a sugar maple when they turned. She had not noticed his freckles the first day because he had been so dirty. Today they stood out against the yellow of his skin like miniature constellations speckling his nose and cheeks. Poor Hasty; he presented an odd picture, the colors of fall or a vivid sunset.

Joetta said, "I will see if I can acquire some quinine. That is what you need for your sickness."

"What do I got?"

"What do I have," Joetta corrected him, and immediately regretted it. "I am sorry. It is not my place to tell you how to speak."

"What do I have?" Hasty repeated obediently while watching her with the eyes of one who longed for somebody to care.

"I believe you have malaria. It is quite common. Your skin tone says that is what it is. And the fact your fever returns about the same time every day."

"Oh. Will it help?"

"It should."

He looked away and his voice hitched as he spoke.

"It was the worst thing I ever been through."

Joetta held her breath, waiting for him to explain himself. He had not said, *it is* the worst thing, but *it was* the worst thing. He was not talking about malaria. Seconds later, he began describing his experience in the war.

"Mrs. Joetta, you wouldn't never want to see the sights I seen. I can't un-see them, can't un-hear them."

Here he pressed his hands to his ears, then his eyes, before lowering them to rest between his legs again. He spoke quiet, and if she had not known better, she would have believed she was hearing the plight of someone much older.

"It got bad at night. Those hurt, the ones missing what God give'em, they screamed. Couldn't nobody sleep. How can someone live without legs, or their insides coming out of'em? Some with that awfulness done lasted days, though I don't know how. I got to where I could tell when they were getting close to their end, and I would beat my drum for'em till they went on and didn't cry no more. I didn't know'em, but ever one of'em was owed at least that. It got to where nobody wanted me to play my drum. That's why they called me Hasty. It got took as a sign, like I's bringing Death down on'em quicker. Maybe I *was* calling it to'em. I surely wouldn't want to live like'at. Either way, nobody would eat with me. Talk to me. They were skeered. Seemed best to leave, though I guess you could say I had my own reasons for being there."

Joetta sat beside him on the steps, feeling the heat of his fever, reminiscent of the embers of a dying fire.

"I am sorry for what you have been through. This war. It has been the Devil's curse to us all. I fear before it is over, there will be more of the same, and worse. Why on earth did you join in the first place? It had to be your mother did not know. Certainly she would not have wanted that. Are you trying to go home to your parents, to your dearest mother?"

Joetta had to believe Hasty's mother *was* a dear soul to have raised such a sweet boy. Hasty, visibly tormented by his experiences, and perhaps thoughts of home, would not meet her gaze and did not respond to her questions. He stared straight ahead, beyond the pasture and on to the woods.

He whispered, "I can't see how it could get any worse."

In that moment came the sound of a gunshot, and Hasty jumped to his feet, startled. Joetta reached for him, placed a hand on his hot arm.

"That's only Robert, shooting the hog."

Hasty spun around, and Joetta did not think he heard her.

"Might be them."

"Who?"

"They might be lookin' for me."

"Who? Why?"

Robert emerged from the wooded area beyond the sorghum field. He yanked and rested, yanked again, as he gripped the back leg of a hog, struggling to drag it. It was easier back when they kept the pigs close by in the pens.

Joetta pointed and said, "See, it is only Robert."

Given his story of how he came by the name Hasty, Joetta had made a decision.

"From now on, you are Charlie, and only Charlie. Not Hasty. The name does you a disservice because it was not you who brought on the demise of those men."

He released his breath and said, "Yes ma'am," before he hurried away to help bring the animal the rest of the way into the yard.

Robert had the grace to look ashamed as the smaller boy, without any resentment, did his share. Mr. McBride joined them near the beech tree with a gambrel he rigged to a lower branch. Robert hoisted the animal up so it hung suspended a couple of feet from the ground. With his knife, he quickly opened the throat and the blood drained into the bucket he put beneath it. There was nothing to be done until that finished.

Mr. McBride said, "Ought to be a couple hours," and with that, he pulled up the old chair he kept near the fence and began whittling.

Robert disappeared into the woodshed, while Charlie stared, as if mesmerized by the dripping blood. Joetta started for the house intending to clean the kitchen, when a group of Confederates materialized out of nowhere like phantoms. They rushed into the yard, and Charlie shot her a petrified look as he suddenly took off and ran by her. A shot rang out, creating a bullet hole near the door he dashed through. He slammed it shut, and next came the clunk of the wooden bar dropping into place. Mr. McBride stared with bewilderment at the cluster of men, then Joetta.

He stood and wobbled forward, shouting, "What's the shooting about? What can I do for you?"

A tall man stepped forward, his homespun frock coat stained and worn around the neck and cuffs. He held his rifle in a nonthreatening manner, but Joetta had the impression he would use it, and quickly, if provoked.

"You are harboring the enemy."

Mr. McBride, his voice raised in alarm, said, "What in tarnation you talking about?"

"That redheaded young man you have here. He's with the Union. He has something of utmost importance."

Mr. McBride whipped around and yelled at Joetta, "He's with the *Union*?"

Joetta could not move, could not speak, and that was answer enough for all of them.

Chapter 21

Mr. McBride distanced himself from Joetta and raised his hands in supplication toward the lieutenant.

"See here, now. I ain't had nothing to do with how he come to be here. Had I known that, I'd have chased him off, or called for somebody to come get him. I won't tolerate no Union scum—!"

Joetta cut in and spoke to the Lieutenant. "He is only a boy, dressed in normal clothing."

"He is with the other side, ma'am. We have tracked him all along."

"Certainly whatever it is you think he has cannot be so important grown men need to chase a youngster down."

The lieutenant eyed her with a flat, dull stare, like that of a corpse.

"We believe he has a dispatch."

"A dispatch?"

"We too have our way of finding things out, Mrs. . . . . ?"

"McBride."

He removed his hat and swept it across his chest as he gave a slight bow and his name.

"Lieutenant Shepherd Braswell."

Joetta said, "Lieutenant Braswell, I can assure you I found nothing on him except the rags he wore and a healthy infestation of vermin. Even if he did have what you say, it was most likely burned with his rotten clothing. It was the only way to rid him of those awful parasites, and I rid him of everything he owned after I discovered him hiding in my springhouse."

She regretted the last part as soon as the words were spoken. The lieutenant quickly gestured at his men, and three came forward.

He said, "Check the springhouse, and check it good."

Joetta's heart sank as the men entered the small building. Maybe they would not disturb her milk, butter, and cream. Maybe they would not break anything. They carried the clay pitchers out along with the wooden butter form Joetta received as a wedding gift from her mother. They looked in question at Lieutenant Braswell, who gestured toward the rest of the soldiers huddled under the beech tree. They carried the dairy items over to the group and handed the pitchers into eager hands. The soldiers gulped a few times before passing them along so everyone got some. Others began breaking open their haversacks, eating hardtack slathered with the butter she and Charlie made the day before. They reentered the springhouse, and the sound of wood splintering was, of course, highly disturbing for Joetta.

She said, "Please make them stop. I have been in and out of the springhouse, and I have seen nothing."

"Of course you wouldn't. For one, he may have hidden it. And second, you wouldn't have known to look. Or would you?"

Joetta paled at the insinuation and vigorously shook her head.

Mr. McBride interrupted with a question. "What will you do with him?"

"Hold him in the Confederate prison until the end of the war. Long as he doesn't try to escape again. He does that, we will shoot him dead."

Joetta sucked her breath in, her thinking random and scattershot as she tried to figure out how to prevent any of this from happening. Mr. McBride shrugged as if it could not be helped. The men were in there for several minutes, and it was almost more than she could stand. When they came out, one shook his head and lifted his shoulders. Joetta held back the bitter *I told you so.* Lieutenant Braswell waved at the men to join the others, then faced her.

"He's got to come with us, and I aim to see he does."

"Utterly ridiculous!"

"Ask him to come out, or we will burn him out."

Mr. McBride huffed in outrage. "Burn down a *Confederate* home?"

Joetta, in a panic, raised her voice. "He is but a child!"

Her thoughts raced back to the men who destroyed their crops. This could not happen, but she only had to look at Lieutenant Braswell's face to realize what she deemed as incomprehensible was only one command away.

Lieutenant Braswell said, "Neither age nor gender matter when it comes to treasonous actions."

She tried reasoning with him, gesturing at her black dress.

"As you can see, I am in mourning. My own beloved husband served in the 10th Regiment, and he was killed not long ago fighting in this godforsaken war." She pointed toward the grave, visible from the house. "Does that not count for something?"

Lieutenant Braswell hesitated. Joetta, gaining hope, continued. "If this young boy is the person you seek, I imagine he is afraid to come out, and rightly so. I would speak with him, if I may?"

The lieutenant looked beyond her shoulder at his men, thinking. After a few seconds, he waved an imperious hand. "You have one minute."

Joetta walked toward the house, fighting to appear calm and collected, even as her legs quivered with every step. Once she was at the back door, she leaned in close and spoke. "Charlie?"

She did not know what to say to him. She wanted to protect him, but at what cost to the rest of them? She was torn. With an ear to the wood, she listened for any sound from within. There was only silence. Robert, who had been out of sight until now, gave her an intense look she could not read. She waited a few more seconds, thinking hard on any possible outcome that might spare Charlie Hastings. The lieutenant cleared his throat.

"Ma'am. That minute is up."

She took her time as she went toward him, gathering herself for what might come as she did so. Robert casually made his way toward her, and because everyone watched her, waiting to see what she would say, they paid him little attention. She scrutinized these strange men in her yard before allowing herself to look at her son's face. It was filled with confidence and calm. All would be well, is what she interpreted. She made an imperious motion at the lieutenant, much like his own arrogant gesture moments before.

"Please, can you not just search the house? There is no need for the drastic measures you suggest."

"That depends."

"Oh?"

"We will see what we find. Step out of the way."

He swept his arm forward, and because they had been waiting on his cue, the soldiers quickly swarmed and she was forced to move aside. In the meantime, a caisson was brought close to the house, giving the impression that should they find something of value, they would load it onto the wagon. The soldiers rammed the door with a piece of uncut wood, while others ran around to the front of the house. The door at the back gave way with a crack, and they rushed inside. Crashes, thumps, banging, and other destructive sounds rang out through the open windows. Joetta wanted to go in and stop them, but Mr. McBride gave her a warning look.

"Ain't nothing we can do about this, and a few broken things are better'n them shooting us."

"Really? And what if they do that anyway?"

Robert leaned over and spoke in her ear.

"Looked to me like he went through the house and out the front door, probably into the woods across the road. I closed it so they wouldn't know."

Joetta was grateful he had seen to help the young boy instead of betraying him. She was about to praise him when Lieutenant Braswell came outside, speaking to a couple of his men.

"Be sure to check the root cellar."

The McBrides had to endure sounds of destruction beneath the house, which bespoke the same outcome as what took place inside. The canned goods, to Joetta's dismay, were loaded onto the wagon. She had a tremendous urge to crack her knuckles, although her pride would not allow the lieutenant to know how these proceedings disturbed her, and or to see such weakness. Before too long, the soldiers in the cellar were back in the yard, indicating they found nothing. The rest who had searched the house now stood under the trees, and Joetta spotted one of them wearing her apron. He cavorted in and out between the others, batting his eyes and banging on her skillet with a spoon. Behaving like imbeciles, she thought, as if her property, and her family's livelihood, meant nothing.

With annoyance, she watched him frolic and at her look of aggravation, he whacked the pan all the louder, and began a chant, "Burn it down! Burn it down!"

Joetta turned away, praying the lieutenant had control over his men. Prayed he would not see fit to do as this one apparently desired. He blew a whistle, and the sharp sound cut through the racket. He walked among them, staring at each individual, until one by one, they settled down and came to attention. He stopped in front of the one wearing an apron. The man let the skillet and spoon drop from his hands onto the dirt.

"Private Riggins."

"Sir."

"Since you appear to be interested in the chores of a housewife, you will be responsible for digging latrines at the next camp."

Some of the men sniggered. Private Riggins yanked Joetta's apron off and dropped it on top of her skillet. The lack of amusement on his superior's face caused him great embarrassment, and Joetta did not spare him either. She glared at him until he had the decency to look the other way. She returned her attention to the lieutenant and addressed him once more.

"I tell you again, if this *child*," and she made sure to clearly enunciate the word, "ever had what you claim, it has been burned. By my very own hands. He has been right here until you showed up. It never made it to the destination for which it was intended. No harm done, *if* it ever existed."

"That very well may be true, but I have my orders, and it was to find him, bring him in for questioning, where he will be held until the matter is resolved, one way or the other."

"I know nothing of that, and he certainly did not act the spy. He only acted afraid."

Lieutenant Braswell said, "We have good trackers. We'll find him. In the meantime, our supplies are running low." He pointed at the suspended pig, the drip of blood having slowed significantly. "My men are in need of a good meal in order to make it to the coast. We would have that pig, yonder. I am willing to pay."

Mr. McBride did not look at Joetta as he agreed. "No need. Take it, take anything you need."

Even Robert grunted in dismay while Joetta protested. "We need that hog. We had to slaughter it early because someone is stealing from our smokehouse."

Lieutenant Braswell grew vague and distracted. Joetta sent him a scathing look. It could very well have been him and his men sneaking onto the property the night before to filch their smokehouse meats right out from under them. She would believe that before she believed anything else. He picked at a spot on his neck.

"I am willing to pay, as I said."

With a sage look, confident their meat went where she suspected, and why he now offered an amenable solution, she did not answer right away. He reached into his pocket and held out paper money. She waved a dismissive hand. Hands on her hips, Joetta narrowed her eyes. She could drive a good bargain.

"That does no one any good. The most basic of necessities have been blockaded. Do you not have anything to trade? Coffee? Sugar? Flour? Meal?"

"No, ma'am. Not much food making it our way either."

Someone coughed. Joetta's gaze landed on a soldier near the front of the line who shivered and sweated profusely at the same time. Lieutenant Braswell looked at the man briefly, then he returned his attention to her. He offered a diagnosis.

"He has consumption."

She almost laughed. She had purposefully not mentioned Charlie being sick, and was glad she had not, otherwise what she was asking for would appear suspicious.

"Would you happen to have any quinine, then?"

Lieutenant Braswell hesitated, then nodded.

Joetta said, "If you will allow me a bit to keep on hand, you are welcome to the pig. We cannot get it."

Mr. McBride said, "Quinine? For the pig? What . . ."

Joetta, urgency in her voice, said, "We will spare this one."

Robert said, "But—" and Joetta cut him off.

"Please, tell your men to take it and roast it over there."

She pointed to the beech tree, while Lieutenant Braswell smiled as if he had won.

"Wonderful."

He motioned toward his men and two of them began lowering the animal, and the butchering was quickly accomplished. Before long, they had skewered big chunks of pork that smoked, crackled, and glistened, the fat from the skin running off into the fire, causing sparks and a distinctive odor of richness, and the promise of fulfillment.

Wide-eyed, Robert asked, "Should I shoot us another?"

"Not yet."

Joetta held no remorse for the exchange she just made, nor the rationale behind her decision. Mr. McBride leaned in, hissing at her for striking a useless deal by his estimation.

"Quinine? What in hell you need that for?"

She kept watch of the lieutenant while she mumbled her answer. "If he has nothing else to trade, it is the most valuable resource. Ennis is gone, and maybe Henry as well, though I hold on to hope that is not so. Either way, I will not have another soul, including the one who has found his way to us, slip from this earth before my very eyes. Not if I can help it."

Mr. McBride went blisteringly red and croaked in astonishment.

"You would get quinine for a Union spy?"

Joetta shot him a warning look.

"Keep your voice down! If they hear you, they might do more than they already have!"

Mr. McBride was furious.

"I best not catch him here again, now I know him for what he is."

Joetta cared not a whit for his threats. If young Charlie returned, she would figure out a way to take care of him. She moved away from Mr. McBride and his anger to explain to Robert why they would not kill another hog just yet.

"Wait until they are gone. If we do it now, they will take the meat from that one too. We will wait and see how far their decency carries them."

Robert was more tolerant.

He said, "I think they're trying to be honorable. Mostly."

She squinted at him, her skepticism plain. Honorable. She had seen enough to discern where *that* took them. She stepped through the back door to see what had been done to her home, and what it would take to put it back in order. They had cleared the kitchen shelves with one swipe of a hand and moved on. As she surveyed the mess they had made, she came close to rushing back outside, regretting her generosity. She did not. She was only one woman against all of them. Looking around, she had no idea where to start, but decided right where she stood made sense as her cooking implements, baskets, wood for the stove, and other items were strewn about.

She began picking up shards of pottery and glass. The four potatoes set on top of her woodstove for baking later in the hot ashes of the stove were gone. They had probably pocketed them, and it diminished her opinion of them even further, and she did not think much of them as it was. Stepping carefully, she made her away around the chaos of upended tables and overturned chairs. It was the same everywhere as she moved through the house, noting how it was mostly furniture and items knocked over, but beyond that, the damage was reversible. She grew indignant at such high-handedness.

She marched back outside, snatched her apron off the ground, and retrieved the skillet and spoon. The soldiers had made themselves right at home, congregating under the beech tree. They sat in a semicircle around the roasting pig and paid her no mind, too busy playing cards, smoking, chewing tobacco, and talking while they waited. She could not deny it smelled wonderful, and her stomach gurgled and churned. She turned away, knowing in her heart, somehow she and her family had to get by in whatever way possible. Hardships were not unfamiliar, but this war had brought on circumstances unlike any other time in her life.

The lieutenant came toward her, his hand outstretched, and in it, the wondrous pills tucked into a small white packet that he handed over without a word. Now this had been taken care of, she wanted him and his men on their way, and soon. Her concern for Charlie mounted by the minute, and this was coupled with the idea he might not return. Joetta was filled with renewed despair, not unlike that at Henry's absence. Unwittingly, Charlie had given her back a bit of her old self, had managed to somehow shape their lives such that she was reminded of the old times, before the war, before Henry left, before Ennis was killed for naught. This made her determined to manage Mr. McBride and his threats about Charlie, if and when the time came.

She looked out the window at the foreigners in her backyard, and she found herself suddenly softening toward them. They too were the sons, husbands, brothers, uncles of a family if she chose to see them this way. Under that guise, it was clear they could have been her own, many of them appearing rather young, not quite as young as Henry, but young, nonetheless. Others looked closer to Ennis's age. They rested, joked, acted like they were at a picnic. It occurred to her she did not know where any of them might be in a month, a year, or longer. The only comfort was knowing neither did anyone else, not these Rebels, not even the Yanks. Day by day was the only feasible plan any of them really had. One only had to survive.

Chapter 22

Joetta looked out the small window of the kitchen every so often, examining the soldiers enthusiastically tearing into large steaming chunks of meat from the pig's carcass. Their appearance explained much to her, as did the way they ate, cramming the pork into their mouths and pressing hands over their lips as they chewed. They had barely swallowed before they repeated it all over again. It was hard to ignore the state of their clothing along with their visible starvation. Eventually, one by one they collapsed beneath the trees, satiated, she was certain, for the first time in a while. Although they captured her attention and she had a strong yearning for these young men to be able to return home to their families, it was Robert she noticed most as he loitered by the barn under the pretense of working so he could watch them. His frequent glances and pauses contradicted a practiced nonchalance.

She was aware, as any mother would be, of his longing, as if he wished to join their ranks, perhaps for the camaraderie they displayed. They may have reminded him of his relationship with his father and Henry. This gave her a foreboding, and it was that Robert was as lonely as she had been before Charlie came along. The loss of the two most important people in his life had changed him. While it was true he had her and his grandfather, their presence, care, and concern for him was nothing like the connection he once had with his father and brother. It would serve her well to keep this in mind when she did not understand his glum and reticent behavior.

Sometime later, instead of pitching them, the soldiers spread their dog tents across the ground and bivouacked right where they were, settling down for the night so fast, it was apparent they were exhausted. She had not expected this. She believed they would eat, gather their gear, and move on. Not knowing what to make of it, Joetta located the lieutenant propped against the smokehouse, enjoying a pinch of snuff with Mr. McBride. She was forthright.

"You are staying the night."

He swept his cap from his head, and bestowed upon her a slight bow.

"Mrs. McBride."

She smelled whisky wafting off of them in addition to the rustic odor of fresh-cut tobacco. Leave it to Mr. McBride to curry the lieutenant's favor with a little drink and chew, even after his men had destroyed her house. All fine and good that they ate their fill and prolonged their stay, while poor Charlie could very well be hiding out in the woods hungry and sick. She kept herself in check, resting her hands on her apron front, waiting to see what the lieutenant might tell her.

"We would camp here tonight, if that is agreeable."

Mr. McBride was quick to answer. "Stay long as you need. You're welcome to our hospitality. Besides, we got to show we're loyal to the cause. Considering."

He shot her a stubborn look and Joetta pinched her mouth shut. If only she could refute him, yet what could she say or do without creating more trouble for herself and her family? It was ridiculous she had to mind her tongue, even on her own property. She dutifully inclined her head and forced herself to calmly walk away. The lieutenant called out, maybe with a hint of appeasement.

"We plan to leave at first light."

She did not acknowledge him, or even slow her steps. As she entered the kitchen, she found Robert lifting the kitchen table back onto its legs.

"Where's Grandpa?"

"With the lieutenant near the smokehouse."

"Oh."

Neither had grown completely comfortable with the other yet, their behavior no more familiar than that of strangers. She busied herself checking on what was not yet done, moving across the room to the wood box, which had been kicked across the floor, scattering her kindling and a few of the larger pieces.

As she bent down to start picking up the wood, she pointed toward the staircase and said, "Your room, I am sure, was disturbed as well. Maybe you would like to get it back in order?"

Robert pushed the table into place against the wall, and Joetta went back to her task, reaching for pieces under the pie safe. He surprised her when he appeared at her side and helped her fill it, then dragged it into its rightful place by the woodstove. She wiped off her forehead. The air was humid even as the sun surrendered, illuminating the land in orange and gold. Dusk had come, yet the room felt as warm and sticky as it had earlier.

"Might you be hungry? I can try to find something."

He shook his head and acted nervous, picking at a loose

thread on his shirt while leaning in the doorway of the kitchen and watching as she began to sweep. He remained there, his thumbs hooked into the pockets of his pants. He must want something.

"What is it, then?"

With a voice barely discernible, he asked her a surprising question. "Why do you care about him so much?"

"Who? Who do you mean?"

She knew; it was the fact she had not expected this. She halted her sweeping while he struggled to answer.

"Him. Charlie."

While his directness caught her off guard, at the same time it revealed she was correct in her earlier assessment. Robert was jealous, and he also appeared genuinely curious. She considered him, his fidgeting a telltale sign of conflicted emotions. She reminded herself he could have told the soldiers where Charlie went. She reflected on how best to answer him, given this was the first chance at honest discourse. Robert could not understand how Charlie had given her the companionship she missed from her own sons. She did not think she understood it herself. She doubted he could abide hearing how a scrawny redheaded boy had replaced the sense of loss she felt as her family left her side one by one. She considered her purpose in caring for Charlie from a more pragmatic stance. He had been in dire need, and because of this, she said what made the most sense, what might be acceptable to her own grieving son.

"It is a woman's nature, if one is the mothering sort, to care for the sick or downtrodden. When someone or something is hurt, hungry, or whatever may be wrong, this is what most women feel compelled to do, to tend to them, to the best of their abilities."

Robert listened to her carefully while concentrating on the unraveling thread. Joetta made herself be still and did not say more, even while she wanted to reach out and brush the hair off his forehead, to touch him in the way to show he did not need to worry because within her was an ever-lasting and abiding love for one who had come from her very own womb. After this long pause, he gave her a scant look.

"It's just, you . . . you ain't his mother."

"No, but I also would not let anyone suffer, not if I can help them. It would go against my beliefs."

"Like how you are about the war? How you won't take sides?"

Joetta hesitated. Her answer might reignite their discord, might send him out the door and back to the Caldwells. There was no other way to respond except with the truth, not when deep inside herself she knew what she would or would not do. She locked eyes with him and admitted it.

"Yes."

Robert did not move for a full minute, digesting what she said.

"Why did you wear the cockade when you went to the Caldwells, then?"

"I did not want to cause any more trouble for us, if I could help it."

"Only you will, if he comes back here. Because you won't turn him away, will you?"

He spoke in a flat tone, stating it as a fact while dealing with the issue as he knew it, from the mangled crops and now from a position of jealousy. What would he do, her once-thoughtful and loving son, if by his own decision, he could take someone's life? It was a moment of clarity for her.

"What would you have me do? Tell me what you think should happen to him, and I will do my best to accommodate your decision."

He gave her a disconcerted look, and his voice went up an octave. "You want me to decide what to do with him? If he comes back here?"

Joetta raised her eyebrows in answer. Let him stand in her shoes, if only for a few seconds. What better way to show him. She reaffirmed her request.

"You decide and I promise, I will do as you wish. His lot, should he return here, is entirely up to you. His life is in your hands."

Robert did not move. She did not think he could. He frowned as he turned the problem over in his head. She went back to sweeping, her heart thudding with fear over this gamble she was taking. She finished the floor and began rearranging the remaining unbroken dishes back on the shelves. After that, she started a fire in the cookstove. By Joetta's estimation, thirty minutes had gone by and he had yet to speak. She began to look over what they might have for supper, as late as it was, when he finally cleared his throat.

"I reckon he could stay. If he even comes back."

Joetta did her best not to reveal her relief because she did not know if she could have kept such a promise, but that did not matter now. She began to pray for Charlie to not return in case her son was not the son she thought him to be. In case he was being cavalier only because the boy was gone, vanished as if he had never been. Robert shoved his hands into his pant pockets and paced around the room. Heaven on earth, he looked so much like Ennis in that moment. She remained quiet, wanting him to explain how he had come to his decision. He spoke quietly.

"He told me something."

"Oh? What was that?"

"He ain't got a mother. He said it was about a year ago when she died."

"I see. Well, that is terribly sad."

"When you and Grandpa went to check the meat in the smokehouse, he said if his mother was still around, he'd have never left home."

"Did he say what happened to her?"

He shook his head and before she could push him for an answer, he came and wrapped his arms about her, placing his head on her shoulder. He had to bend slightly to do so, and she hugged him back with all of the intensity of time gone by, as if the harder she squeezed the more it would make up for the moments she had missed. Her hands wandered across familiar shoulder blades and the knobs of his spine. He was growing so fast, and not getting enough to eat. He finally let her go and used his shirt sleeve to wipe his nose. Her Robert, the one she knew so well, had returned. She did what she had wanted to do moments before and brushed the hair off of his forehead. Neither could speak, and really, there was nothing more to be said. He breathed deep and let it out, releasing the pent-up anxiety he had held.

"I'll go straighten my room now."

He ascended the stairs. After a few seconds, he stuck his head out the door.

"Mother?"

She moved to stand at the bottom of the stairs and looked at him. He amazed her yet again.

"If Charlie comes back, I reckon he can go back to using Henry's room. You know, until Henry comes home."

Joetta placed a hand over her heart. Not trusting herself to speak, she nodded, acknowledging she heard.

Later that evening, after she, Robert, and Mr. McBride had eaten a couple of potatoes she found in the cellar, fried with some pieces of fatback she had scrounged out of the smokehouse, Mr. McBride scooted his chair back, and said,

"Come on, boy, let's go see what them Rebs is doing. I told that lieutenant to come on to the cabin and I'd challenge him to a real card game."

Robert did not move.

"I'm gonna stay here."

Mr. McBride tucked his chin into his chest and eyed his grandson.

"I'll keep the door unlatched for you for when you come later."

"No, I mean I'm gonna stay. With Mother."

Mr. McBride hesitated a moment before rising from his chair to stomp across the yard. Robert watched him go.

"I reckon he's upset with me."

"He will be furious with both of us if a certain person returns."

"Grandpa won't do nothing, will he? I mean, considering?"

Joetta pondered this, reflecting on the incident with their crops. She believed Mr. McBride's actions had not been intentional in that respect. This was different. She did not know what he might do, given his earlier threat. Then again, he was given to moments of grandiose statements even he did not have the heart to back up.

"I do not know."

Dawn came with an uncanny quiet and Joetta rose, her body tired, and her head hurting. She dressed in her widow's weeds, and in the kitchen, peeked out the window and noted the soldiers were gone. She lifted her eyes to the heavens and thought, *Thank you*, before picking up her egg basket and draping it in the crook of her arm.

Opening the door, she stepped outside and emitted a startled, "Oh! You're still here."

Lieutenant Braswell waited at the bottom of the step,

slapping his forage cap against his thigh. Dust came off it, and he nitpicked at some lint as he spoke. He did not meet her look and she found this odd.

"I'm leaving now, but I aim to see someone keeps an eye on this farm."

So that was how it was to be. She adjusted the egg basket, fiddled with her apron, and waited patiently, pretending his remarks mattered not. He still did not take his leave. Her lack of a response could be taken for disregard, and the lieutenant cleared his throat. Joetta was spared whatever he was about to say when Mr. McBride shouted a greeting.

"A fine good morning, Lieutenant!"

He came close enough to the other man they could have hugged. Joetta found her father-in-law's behavior most intolerable, as if what took place yesterday never happened. She gestured at the lieutenant.

"He means to have the farm watched."

Bewilderment sharpened Mr. McBride's voice. "What's that?"

Lieutenant Braswell hooked his thumbs in his lapels.

"That's right. Home Guard, or loyal citizens, either one."

Mr. McBride cogitated this information, running his fingers across his scruffy chin several times.

He said, "I was aiming to join 'cept 'cording to their rules, I'm too old."

Joetta maintained her composure even as she sniffed internally. He had never said a word about it. Maybe because he had not been allowed to sign on, an insult, she suspected. Lieutenant Braswell stared at her father-in-law.

"Well, there's ways to help even if you don't join."

"Oh, don't I know."

Mr. McBride shot a sly look Joetta's way. Lieutenant Braswell took it as a cue.

"Do not interfere, Mrs. McBride, with whatever may happen to the individual we are interested in," came the warning from Lieutenant Braswell.

Joetta's expression was as wooden as the porch boards they stood on, feigning obedience, a disinterested woman easily ignored. The lieutenant still did not move, awaiting some sort of acknowledgment from her. Releasing her breath, she inclined her head and spoke in a begrudging, low-key voice.

"Indeed."

It was a lackluster response, but it was all he would get. Oh, how he behaved! Talking as if she could somehow single-handedly jeopardize the success of their precious war by helping a child. If they were this worried over Charlie, they were doing much worse than they imagined. Both sides were bullheaded and would continue to sunder the land, the people, and civilization until nothing remotely reminiscent of what was before would exist. With an abrupt salute, he removed himself from her steps, and she was glad to see the backside of him. He mounted his horse, nudged him forward, and soon all that was left was a hot wind and the creak of crickets in the long grasses at the edge of their fields. Mr. McBride, still poised on the stoop with his thumbs hooked into his garters, observed where the soldiers had been. Joetta headed for the chicken coop, and he called out to her.

"We can't be inviting trouble, and that boy's trouble."

Joetta continued on her way.

"You hear me?"

She swung the bucket of scraps and called over her shoulder.

"I doubt he will come back. He is too afraid."

"And he ought to be."

Joetta fumed inwardly until she was close to the chicken

coop, and there she stopped. She looked about with suspicion. Something was not right. She made her usual clucks and kissing noises. Just to be sure, she inspected the inside of the coop. It was, as she already feared, empty. She could see it happening as if she had been witness to it. They had taken off with her chickens, even Josephine and Agnes, those two special ones never destined for a cooking pot.

She rushed past the barn, and with a high-pitched, "Sooey!" she tried to coax the swine out of the woods.

Not one pig came a grunting. They had stolen them too, then slunk away like no-account thieves. Whatever compassion she might have had dissipated as she scanned the fields, which revealed no sign of Pal. Mr. McBride, taking note of her frantic dashes to and fro, rushed to the barn. When he came out it was apparent they had confiscated poor Honey too. The Confederates had planned this and spared them nothing. Joetta's mind began to cycle through the implications, one by one. The lieutenant had to have known and still had the audacity to lay down even more threats. She spun in all directions, looking this way and that in disbelief. The betrayal was so great, Mr. McBride could not even speak or move.

She shouted, "What do you think of your Rebels now?"

Chapter 23

She sat on the embankment of Fishing Creek, her voluminous black skirt tucked beneath her legs, hands held still in her lap, head bowed. She prayed. She prayed to understand why some people behaved the way they did. For the war to end. To go back home and find their livestock returned by some kind soul. After a few minutes she lifted her head, aware the solitude and quiet had failed to work, as she was still distraught and unsettled. Aside from Honey and Pal, she was particularly sorrowful about the loss of Josephine and Agnes. She could not help but think of what Mr. McBride had said to the lieutenant, *Take what you need*, and the lieutenant had undoubtedly listened.

In hindsight she wished she had accepted his money instead of the quinine. With Charlie gone, perhaps never to be seen again, money might have been used as a leverage for bargaining. Even while she had claimed it useless to the lieutenant, there might have been something useful at Mr. Spivey's store. She cracked a knuckle and sorted through what few options they had. Methodically working her fingers, she ruminated on her avoidance of Mary and Bess, and how it might appear to ask for their help now. Bess was closest, and easiest to get to, but with a request would likely come expectations, because Bess would want assurances. Should she even ask for her assistance? To do so might jeopardize the Caldwells' safety. Should harm come to them, Joetta would bear an insurmountable level of remorse.

There were no good answers. She kept on with her fingers, happy no one was around to witness this singular behavior. She gleaned much satisfaction from it, despite the fact it did nothing to help solve their dilemma. She turned her mind to other possible solutions. Was there work she might do? Mrs. Hammond's husband had converted his cotton mill to a sewing factory. Sewing uniforms for the Confederacy? She would not be hired, and why she even thought of it was beyond her ken. She was too controversial, and she had seen enough staunch and unyielding dispositions, like those of Eliza Garner and Rebecca Hammond, to comprehend it was utterly foolish to even consider it.

Some distance away, Robert called, "Sooey! Sooey!"

His grandfather must have told him. She retreated back to her reveries once more, methodically working her knuckle joints, when, above the noises of her bones cracking came another sound, a rustle of movement. She stopped abruptly and swung her head around, looking behind her. No one was there. She faced forward when directly in front of her came a small, croaking voice from the stand of reeds by the creek.

"Ma–ma'am."

Joetta gathered her skirts and scrambled to her feet, clumsy and inept. She bent in the direction of the voice, aghast and jubilant all at once.

"Charlie?"

"Yes, ma'am."

His head rose like a flower emerging from the soil even while he remained flat on his belly, peering at her from a few feet away. Had it not been for him speaking, or for his movements, she would never have noticed him. He looked about, then back at her.

"Is it s-safe?"

"For now, at least."

He stood from his hiding place, trembling. The scare from the day before along with a night out in the elements had set him back, so he appeared as sick as he had when he first showed up, minus the vermin.

"I stuck around hoping they'd leave 'cause I wanted to thank you 'fore I go."

"Go?"

"Yes, ma'am. H-home, I reckon. I d-don't want to c-cause no more problems."

While she had concerns over the lieutenant's threats, and Mr. McBride's unpredictability, she instantly knew she would help him. He was undeserving of their relentless hunt. If he had been used by the Union to send a message, he would have been intent on delivering it, and would have made sure he followed orders. She spoke more to herself than Charlie.

"They have taken everything except what has not been dug out of the ground yet."

Charlie collapsed back into a sitting position, elbows on his knees. Neither of them spoke for some time.

Eventually he said, "Misery makes people do things they shouldn't. Believe me, I know."

Joetta thought about her earlier prayers, and here was this young boy with the wisdom of an ageless soul.

He got to his feet, and said, "I b-best be getting along. Only wanted to th-thank you for what you d-done."

Before Joetta could speak, he stumbled away, his balance

affected by his weakness. She could not let him go. His well-being would weigh on her, and before she could think on it more, she called out to him.

"You will never make it home, not in your condition. Charlie, listen to me. I was able to procure some quinine, the very medicine you need."

He stopped and looked at her with those needy eyes of his.

"Y-you did?"

"Yes. Even so, I could never forgive myself if I let you leave, sick as you are. We can be careful; do not worry. No one will know. When you are well, you can be on your way."

He switched from one leg to the other, his discomfort and illness causing him much distress, yet he still did not think of himself.

"What about R-Robert? Won't he mind? I d-don't think he liked me m-much."

"Robert is fine. He has agreed you can stay in his brother's room again."

Charlie persisted, needing reassurances of everyone's opinion.

"Wh-what about . . . Mr. McBride?"

"I will deal with him."

He looked so hopeful, Joetta thought he might burst into tears. She had all good reason to believe if he left, he was taking a chance with his life. He could not make it back to his home in his condition if he tried.

She said, "Let me go to the house, and when I am able, either I or Robert will come back to get you. It will not be long. Wait here and do not leave. Promise?"

Defeated, he nodded. "All right. Th-thank you."

Joetta hurried back up the embankment, skirts held high. She made her way through the woods and across the field, looking back over her shoulder. She could see nothing. Charlie had once again dropped from sight, and she hoped he would keep his word since his fear was so obvious. Robert was with his grandfather, and they were having an argument from the look of it, given Mr. McBride's broad and expansive gesturing and Robert's folded arms. They spotted her, and stopped talking. Robert frowned as he walked away from his grandfather and toward Joetta.

"He said if he shows up, he's going to turn him in."

Mr. McBride spat on the ground and yelled with conviction.

"Damn right! They done told you they plan to keep an eye on this place! Hell, they even think he's here, they're liable to haul us off to jail, or worse! I ain't about to have my loyalties put into question by some little Union pipsqueak, sick or not!"

Mr. McBride's rant did not carry with any certainty his moral convictions, even as he feigned outrage. Her own voice matched his anger as she reminded him those he professed loyalty to had, in the brief time they were on the property, acted disgracefully, and with malice.

"No thanks to you extending such a grand welcome, they helped themselves, leaving us with barely a scrap. What sort of men do that, then sneak away in the dark? I will tell you. Dishonorable men. No. Dishonorable *thieves*. And all the while, their superior had the gall to threaten us on our own property. They cared not what happened to any one of us. I do not care about their threats. This is *my* home, and I will do on it what I choose!"

Mr. McBride pushed his hands into his pockets and rolled his shoulders awkwardly, discomfited by the truth. He pulled at his hair, which had grown over his ears, tugging it into an even more unruly state before squinting at Joetta. He glared at her, but the intensity of his voice softened.

"Not dishonorable. Desperate."

"Which is how we will end up, given their actions."

He threw an arm out to the garden.

"They didn't touch that."

It was true. Inexplicably, the garden had escaped the Rebels' destructive hands and feet. Even so, it would not be enough, not without the other necessary victuals. She walked toward the plants, and behind her came a shuffling sound as they followed. She went row by row, making a mental note of the cabbages, turnips, and potatoes not yet dug up. She believed she could make what was there last for a little while. She spoke to Robert.

"If you hunt, we will make do."

Robert said, "Sure. I can fish, too."

Joetta steeled herself for an argument with Mr. McBride about Charlie. It was one she was prepared to win.

"Charlie is still here, by the creek. He wishes to go home, only he cannot make it sick as he is. I would like to allow him a brief respite here. I do not believe you wish him ill. He has worked hard, when he was able. He means no harm. The lieutenant and his men are mistaken about him."

Mr. McBride started to argue until Robert cut him off.

"Charlie's not who or what you think."

Mr. McBride grunted and rolled his eyes toward Robert.

"*Now* we get the truth."

"His mother was shot and killed before his very eyes, in their front yard."

Joetta closed hers briefly, and when she opened them, she said, "How did this happen?"

"There was fighting near his home. A Confederate soldier got shot. He was still alive, and Charlie's mother ran out to help, and she was shot too. When the fighting was over, he ran to her. Union soldiers came into the yard and took him. He told me it happened a year ago. He never got to bury her."

Mr. McBride had listened but grumbled under his breath. "Seems mighty far-fetched to me."

Joetta said, "Why would Charlie lie about such a thing?"

She thought of Ennis, of his own childhood, of her father-in-law's treatment of his grandsons when they were babies and as they grew. He was not in a position to make decisions that would affect someone's well-being. She stared him down.

"I would have him here. As soon as he is able, he can leave, if he chooses. That is all there is to it. Robert, go get him. He's near the tupelo tree at the creek."

Robert took off while Mr. McBride spoke his mind.

"You will rue this decision."

"Not any more than others I've made thus far."

He thumped his cane on the ground in anger before he went to his chair. Even from where he sat, she could feel his eyes boring into her. Minutes later, Robert came with Charlie trailing him, struggling to keep up. Wide-eyed, Charlie looked from Joetta to Robert. He did not dare look at Mr. McBride, and the old man stayed where he was, his look venomous even from a distance.

"Robert, help him to Henry's room and get him some water to drink."

"Yes, ma'am."

Robert motioned at Charlie to follow him, and Joetta went back into the garden and began to dig for the remainder of the root vegetables. She stabbed the end of the shovel into the ground. Robert came out and helped her. Between the two of them, they did their best to replace what had been, but where there had been a large mound stored in a corner, now there was only a small bump. She could not dwell on this. It did no good. She took a head of cabbage, along with a few onions. She retrieved some carrots and herbs. It would do. She could make a soup, and it would be filling, and hot.

Robert reached for the shovel. "I can finish working on this."

Joetta swiped at her face. "Thank you."

Because of these small moments with her son by her side, willing to help, she was reassured. Inside, she began preparing the vegetables, and before long, she had a pot simmering on the stove. Mr. McBride ambled in, and her hackles went up. He coughed, a sign he was bound to speak, whether she wanted him to or not.

"If them on our side take what they please, I reckon just about any damn thing can happen."

She kept stirring while wishing for salt. He yanked a chair out from the table and plopped into it.

"I suppose I could see how what he said could be true. I mean, her getting shot, and him getting taken, and such as that."

His admission was so unexpected, she set her spoon down, and relieved, she spoke her thoughts.

"He was caught in the middle. What happened to him is no different than what has happened to us. Through no choice of his own he has become ensnared in this terrible war, and is suffering the consequences. It sounds quite familiar, do you not agree?"

Mr. McBride leaned over, put his elbows on his knees, and clasped his hands between them. Oftentimes, he was not one to think before he spoke, but in this particular instance, he had given the situation some thought.

"Well, we sure don't need nothing else to happen around here, that's God's honest truth."

Joetta went back to stirring, unsure where her father-in-law would direct his latest, surprising revelations. He began to tap his foot in a nervous way, the mannerism unlike his usual bravado.

"My point is, can you fib? Can you look someone in the eye and say what is necessary without giving nothing away?"

She faced him again.

"When it comes down to it, yes, I believe I can."

"You best be sure. What I wonder is, what will you do if that Home Guard or some other trouble shows up?"

"I'm not worried about what *I* would do."

"There won't any call for them to take ever last thing, but they did. And that boy I reckon ain't to blame for where he ended up. You ain't got to worry none about me. I won't say nothing about him being here."

Speechless, she watched as he pushed himself up and went out the door. It was the first time she had ever believed him.

Chapter 24

She had to do what she could for her family, and Charlie; therefore, she took it upon herself to go and see Bess. She would explain how the soldiers came, and how they took what they had. Of course, she would not mention that Charlie was actually there. As she prepared to leave, Robert advised her to take the path through the woods.

"It's safer."

Mr. McBride agreed.

"If someone's watching, they'll think you're going to work the fields and they won't follow you."

Joetta was still piqued about the lieutenant and what his soldiers had done. She rolled her shoulders in aggravation.

"Certainly I can move about on my own property, or go see a neighbor?"

Mr. McBride flapped a hand.

"I'm only saying they'll follow."

Charlie was listening, and he repeated what he had proposed before.

"I can leave. If I did, they couldn't accuse you of nothing."

Joetta refused to even consider it.

"No, you are much too sick."

"I ain't no worse off than when I first come. I'll keep taking them pills and I'll be fine. Took care a myself once and I can do it again."

Joetta thought he must have been thinking quite a bit on this and was set to argue about it when Mr. McBride spoke up again.

"Ought to let him go on if he wants to go. Ain't nothing worse than being held against your will. He's gonna feel like a prisoner all over again."

Though she tried to not show it, there was indecision in Joetta's eyes, and Charlie saw it.

"If I leave now, they'd never know I was still around. And if I don't go now, when would I?"

She put a hand to her forehead and rubbed, while Mr. McBride continued to side with Charlie.

"He's right. Way it's going, this war's liable to last forever."

Forever. She understood forever perhaps better than anyone. Forever was waking each morning to face the day without her beloved. Forever was waiting to find out whether your son was dead or alive. Forever felt exactly like right now. They had very little choice except bear whatever came their way, and pray. This prompted her to ask Charlie if he practiced his faith.

"Do you pray, Charlie?"

"Not no more."

No one spoke for some time, digesting the weary-sounding words of the youngest among them. Joetta could not imagine what it must take for someone his age to lose hope. Charlie surprised them even more with his next admission.

"I saw a sheep in my room. I reached out to pet it, and it disappeared."

With alarm, they looked at one another as he weaved to

and fro in the chair, eyes glassy. The subject of him leaving was dropped. He had a raging fever once again, despite the quinine. She did not know how long it took to work, but it was obvious he could not go anywhere. She insisted he go back upstairs to Henry's room to lie down.

Shortly thereafter, she did as asked, and started her walk to Bess's along the footpath behind the house, covered by the canopy of trees. She was unable to remember the last time she had taken this two-mile trail between the farms. The lowing of a cow came and brought the pang of loss for Honey, and for what she had provided them. Soon the Caldwells' fields were in front of her, and in this late season, she was surprised not to see the usual vast acres of ripening corn. Joetta made her way around to the front of the house, adjusting her bonnet as she went, worrying over how she might appear.

With some bit of fortitude mustered from where she knew not, she lifted a hand and knocked. She had barely finished rapping when Bess pulled the door open, her manner less than welcoming. Her attention was on the front path, which led to the house, her unease obvious. She did not move aside to invite Joetta in, and Joetta immediately began regretting that she had come. With her hands clasped in front, she spoke first, and immediately addressed the issue between them.

"Do not worry. I came along the path, so no one saw me."

"A wise choice, given what is circulating, which is to say, please, quickly explain your reason for being here, then I must ask you to leave promptly."

"May I ask what it is that has created this high degree of alarm? What am I accused of now?"

"Surely you are aware."

With a hint of wryness, Joetta said, "Tell me anyway, so that I might understand fully."

"That you harbored a Union spy."

Joetta laughed, the sound sharp and unnatural. The lieutenant had been quick to spread the word. She did not disagree; what would be the point? Bess's skin, every spot Joetta could see, flushed as if she stood under a noonday sun.

"Joetta! For pity's sake, I can't help but question your reason for doing such a thing! And let's not even get started on the last instance of what can only be deemed traitorous as well. With all due respect to the deceased, I will not bring it up, even if I did find it abhorrent."

"If my beloved Ennis needed a coat, I care not where he got it. Neither side is without guilt, Bess. Willfully, they take what they want and claim they are confiscating it in the name of their cause. You must know this is true. For that matter, *your* Confederates were at my house not long ago, which is how this whole bit about a Union spy came about. That young man, not even a man, a mere boy, saw his very own mother killed when she tried to help a wounded soldier. A Rebel soldier, not that it should matter. I only tell you so you understand the full story. He was then taken by the Union. He escaped, and I found him in my springhouse, sick and on the verge of starvation. How can helping someone in such need be bad? Is it not the Christian thing to do?"

Bess fussed with a ruffled cap she wore over her hair, yanking at its sides, appearing deep in thought. Meanwhile, from within the house came the rich scent of meat simmering. Joetta shut her eyes, inhaled deeply, and as she opened them, a distinctive spot of color over Bess's shoulder caught her attention. She went rigid, her mind switching into panic mode, and she involuntarily let out a gasp. Bess quit pulling at her cap and stared at her in confusion.

"Why do you look like that? Whatever is the matter?"

Joetta could not move. She was planted, her shoes rooted

to the porch, mesmerized by a man's green coat. She pointed over Bess's shoulder.

"Whose coat is that?"

Bess looked to where Joetta indicated, and when she faced forward again, her cheeks held an even deeper flush, and her eyes were lit with an awareness that was quickly extinguished.

"Why?"

"Whose is it?"

"Why does it matter? It's just a coat."

In her mind Joetta saw the man who forced them off the road and then running from her house. She was certain this was the very item worn by that individual. She could not ask Bess for help. Not now. She straightened her back, and spoke rapidly, making up a different excuse for why she was there.

"My intentions in coming were to thank you for looking after Robert during my period of mourning. I realize now, given what you have heard, and what you believe, it is probably best we do not speak again."

"You could very well turn this around, if you chose to do so. You tried, once. Why not try again? Can't you see it would make sense?"

"You are asking me to put aside what I believe, what Ennis believed. I will not. It would sully his memory, and I am not inclined to change simply to suit what others wish."

"You have always been willfully stubborn. Even Eliza Garner and Rebecca Hammond commented on that the last time they were here."

"They know nothing about me."

"Know nothing about you? This position of disloyalty is not insignificant, and I tell you truthfully, it is surprising to many how you persist. Even Mary Brown says so." That revelation took Joetta off guard, but she had little time to think on it as Bess continued her tirade. "You claim you are neither this, nor that, yet your actions prove otherwise. Protecting a Union spy? Perhaps that was due to Ennis. After all, he was supposedly fighting for the Rebels, yet came home in that *that Union coat*! It only seems appropriate before he was transported home it might have been removed!" Bess raised her chin, narrowed her eyes. "Green coat. Blue coat. Turncoat. One wears what suits them, most likely."

"Do not speak of my husband in that way."

"I'm only saying you should keep in mind what is fact, and your own actions, my dear. It does not paint the most favorable picture."

"How is it either side can be committed to their principles, while someone such as myself cannot? Somehow, and inexplicably, I am the one who is in the wrong. Those who would judge me ought to remember I am at liberty to choose my own path and it is of no consequence to them."

"The Garners and the Hammonds have suffered losses. Why, they've had to let go of their overseers! Be forewarned, Joetta McBride. The one named Miller, a vile little man, I must admit, will do whatever is necessary to root out nonloyal and untrustworthy sorts."

"I have nothing, and no one, to hide."

Mr. McBride would have been quite pleased in that moment, as she boldly lied to Bess. From a distance came the sound of a horse's hooves clopping slowly down the path. Bess switched her hand about frantically, motioning for Joetta to leave.

"That's Thomas. You must leave! Go. Go!"

What Thomas Caldwell had done had Joetta scrambling off the porch in a flurry of black cloth, like a crow in flight. She picked up her skirt and ran down the path and into the cover of the woods. Had circumstances been different, she might have lingered to confront him about running them off the road, and being in her house, but it was not wise to unnecessarily bring more trouble. An unpleasant taste of acid lingered at the back of her throat, equal to the bitterness settling in her heart. Bess had become as unyielding as a suit of armor and could not see past her own fears, perhaps because of retribution from those around her. Joetta would not allow herself to be put in such a position again. They would figure out how to get by.

She stopped every so often, wanting to ensure she was not being followed, and it was only when she detected nothing, she raced on. At one point, a branch snagged her hair, causing her to stop as the neat braid she wore was jerked loose. She twisted about to untangle herself and when the branch snapped back into place, it scratched her across the cheek. Finally free, she pushed on until the farm came into view. Grateful to be home at last, she slowed to catch her breath. The field of pitiful planted sorghum, the barren chicken coop, the empty hog pen and barn, collectively brought on a dismal feeling, an impression of failure. She stopped in the yard, almost in tears. Robert and Mr. McBride stared at her from the back porch. From the upstairs window of Henry's room, a curtain moved. She wished she could have returned with something more than her fears. Robert and Mr. McBride took in her demeanor, and it was obvious they should not ask questions.

They met her halfway and Joetta fought to keep her voice steady.

"The lieutenant was good on his word. He must have alerted everyone because Bess said everyone has heard I harbored a spy." She laughed as she had at Bess's, the sound unnatural once again, and she abruptly cut it off. "Remember how we were forced off the road, and after we came home, that very same man ran out of the front door?"

Mr. McBride squinted, trying to recall the events and Robert only looked at her.

"It was Thomas Caldwell."

Robert had no reaction as he absorbed this news. He folded his arms together while Mr. McBride erupted in disbelief.

"For the love of God, what're you talking about?"

"There was a green coat, the very coat that man wore, hanging in the Caldwell house. Bess did not like me asking about it."

Robert remained tight-lipped and refused to meet her eyes. This sent a tingling of fear along her spine, and even so, she raised her hands and let them drop.

"What is done is done."

She allowed some grace, partly for him and partly for herself, after the disastrous encounter with Bess, while Mr. McBride was mystified.

"Why on earth would he have done that?"

Robert kicked at a clump of weeds while Joetta reexamined the moment she recognized the coat. It was then Robert blurted out the truth with such force, it sounded as if he were choking.

"He only wanted to send you a warning, Mother. He didn't like you didn't support the cause. Neither did Mrs. Caldwell. Mr. Caldwell thought scaring you might make you change your mind. Least, that's what Harold said."

"You *knew* it was him?"

Robert was quick to defend himself.

"No! Not right off. I saw the coat one day and told Harold what had happened to us. Harold admitted his papa had done it. Mrs. Caldwell didn't know Harold told me. He would've been in trouble."

They stared at one another, deciding what this meant. Joetta did not want another rift to form between them, and

Robert looked so upset, so contrite, she repeated what she said earlier.

"What is done is done."

He ducked his head, his shame palpable.

He mumbled, "That's mostly why I came home. It didn't feel right to stay."

That night, they ate the soup again, grateful for it, knowing it would not last, and Charlie told them about the dream he had of a black sheep eating all their food.

Chapter 25

Each day, starting with misty mornings and the hoarse caw of crows scavenging their ruined fields, they would crawl out of their beds, often accomplishing very little before the sun reluctantly relinquished its hold over a barren countryside. They mostly foraged, bringing home whatever they could find: wild grapes, dandelion greens, and curly dock. Robert fished often, saving his shells, because there was a shortage of ammunition too, and they must be able to protect themselves, if necessary.

Meanwhile Charlie became like a jack-in-the-box, ducking in and out of the house, knowing to stay out of sight, but he was young, and on days he felt well, he grew restless. She did not have the heart to speak to him about being careless when he sat outside. After all, she did not want him to feel as if he *was* a prisoner. Joetta gratefully cooked whatever she found or what was brought to her. She kept watch on the meager pile of root vegetables in the cellar, and tried not to think of the day when even that would no longer exist. It became habit when gathering around the table to not pay attention to what was being served. One day a pot of weak soup, the next day a sparse offering of vegetables, roasted or pan-fried. They ate what was there, if only to quell the gnawing.

"Eat, eat," Joetta insisted, urging them on, even as the scarcity became more imminent.

They were sick to death of the bland, repetitious diet. Even Charlie, who usually ate with gusto everything she put before him, scrutinized his bowl or plate with waning enthusiasm. She quietly prayed for better times to come while remembering the apple trees would bear ripening fruit by fall. Those she could add to the peaches she was drying, and before too long, pecans would fall and these things would help see them through.

One muggy morning as she stepped outside to get water, the toe of her shoe connected with a hard object. Caught off guard, she dropped the pail and it rolled across the porch, rattling loudly and scattering a nearby flock of wrens. Joetta squatted to see what she had kicked. At the back door sat a wooden crate, and from it came the distinctive odor of cured meat. She quickly surveyed the yard, and the path out to the road. She gazed toward the fields and beyond, eyes scanning the edge of the woods. It was as it had been, quiet.

Her mouth filled with saliva as she hoisted the crate into her arms, smiling for the first time in days. She began ticking off the possibilities. Bess? Most assuredly not. Joetta reentered the house and set it on the table. After she removed a large shoulder of ham, a dozen eggs, a small crock of blackberry conserve, and two jars of beans, she found a small piece of paper tucked in the bottom, folded tightly. She opened it and read, *Blue days, gray days, one is not so much unlike the other here on God's green earth. When this is over, I would enjoy a glass of your delicious switchel.* Mary! Ever so discreetly, kind and thoughtful Mary had found a way to not only help but to provide a small message. Joetta clasped her hands together over her bosom, relieved, not only at their good fortune but at Mary's kindness. She opened the jam and could not stop herself from dipping her finger in to sample it. Her eyes fluttered closed; the sweetness and flavor signaled the abundance of better times.

She replaced the lid carefully and went back out to get the water, and once she returned, she began cooking. Before long, a rich, familiar smell permeated the room. She happily poked at the meat while it sputtered and popped, giving her a tremendous sense of satisfaction. Not more than a few minutes passed when Robert and Charlie came down the stairs faster than usual. They burst into the kitchen, sniffing like bloodhounds at the air.

Robert said, "Where'd you get ham?"

Charlie licked his lips and could not take his eyes off the pink meat. Joetta tapped a bowl where she had placed the eggs.

"Eggs as well, and beans. We will each have a spoonful of blackberry conserve, too."

She had already decided to be careful with portions, wanting to make everything last as long as possible.

Robert repeated his question. "From who?"

Joetta had decided not to say so they would not have the burden of knowledge, just in case.

"The Lord has answered our prayers. That is all we should care about. Go and sit. It will not be long."

The boys needed no other encouragement. Moments later, Mr. McBride showed up at the back door, and by then, Robert and Charlie were eating with a sense of eagerness long forgotten. He bent over to peer at the boy's plates.

"What's this here? Ham and eggs?"

Joetta lifted her shoulders.

"An answered prayer; that is all I know. It was on the back porch this morning."

"The Caldwells, I'd bet. Probably sent out of shame."

Joetta let him think what he wanted. All that mattered to her was they would have full bellies. Each bite was savored slowly. She put water into the skillet she had used to fry the ham, added some of the treasured beans, and set them on a slow simmer. If only she had cornmeal. Robert, Charlie, and Mr. McBride reclined in their chairs around the table, and while it was only a brief respite, their contented looks made her ever so happy. She would not allow herself to think on how long she might make it last. For now, it was enough.

She was very careful, but of course the inevitable came, and the box of food was soon gone and only a lingering memory. Too quick they were back to scraping for what could be gleaned off the land, back to a state of half-starvation. Joetta pondered on what Ennis might do. Would he have had some other recourse? She did not know. What she knew was what she could see before her very eyes, even while no one complained. It was difficult watching Mr. McBride, Robert, and Charlie wolf down meager offerings, only to show signs of hunger an hour or two later, rubbing their midsections, drinking water to fool their minds, as their bodies revealed what had not been obvious the week before. Faces honed to sharper angles; teeth, noses, and eyes more prominent; arms and legs thin as a marsh reed; pants and shirts flapping about their bony frames as if hung on the limbs of a tree to dry.

One evening, the air yet heavy and laden with humidity from a late Indian summer, Joetta made herself sit at the small desk in the sitting room to write her mother. She held a handkerchief to dab at the dampness on her forehead, and neck, then took up the pen and dipped it into the ink. She was weak from hunger, but she would not mention how extreme their circumstances had become, and she certainly would not mention Charlie. She sat for a moment thinking on how to begin. There was not much she could share except to tell them her sad news, and perhaps request advice from her mother about her stubborn inclination toward neutrality, as she was wont to do.

Dearest Mother,

I had not intended this much time to pass before I corresponded with you. Once you have read this letter, perhaps you will understand why. It is with great pain in my heart and a soul crushed I write to you in utmost sorrow. My true love, my dear husband now lies in the ground. I have wanted to write to you of this horrible tragedy and found I could not bear to do so until now. Please pray for us. We were not fully informed of how he died. I only know he was brought home to me, and for this I am grateful. It is known many have gone into mass graves, and their loved ones are left to wonder what might have happened to them. I worry, dare I even write it, or even think it, this may be the case with our Henry. There has been nothing from him in over two years. However, as long as I have no word to the contrary, I continue to hope and pray for his safe return.

How is Father? And my brothers? Have you word from them? And, what of Faith? I have had no news from my dear sister either, and perhaps it is due to their Union position. It is complicated, this war, and the ramifications slip downstream, as they have with my very own family. That unwavering unification, once the foundation of our country, might not last. How would I feel about this? I do not know. I have remained one who has not chosen sides, though there is danger in this. Duly, my position, or lack thereof, has created a rift between myself and our community. Would you have any advice for your youngest daughter? Even the small-est conciliatory word from you would suffice, to know you understand my way of thinking. It would evermore encour-age my steadfastness with regard to our unassuming way of life and thinking.

Robert has returned to his old self, and this makes me happy. He grows by the day and is at least a foot taller than me, this at fourteen. He has declared himself a man, and truthfully, he is. These times have seen him mature, and his father would be so proud. Mr. McBride is as ever, cantan-kerous, and staunchly rooting for the Confederacy. His limp worsens and bothers him so. Please give my love to all.

Your devoted daughter, Joetta

She waved the paper about, drying the ink, folded it, and placed it in one of the few remaining covers she had. She would be the one to walk to town and have it mailed. Mr. McBride's usual jaunts were not only affected by his grow-ing physical limitation, his enthusiasm for news of the war was dampened by the effectiveness of the Union's ability to strangle the Rebel's supply chain. They knew firsthand the success of this mission and did not need official announce-ments from a newspaper. It would be the first time she pre-sented herself in Whitakers for some time, and she had no way to know how she might be received.

She went into the kitchen and poked about the shelves, hoping against hope a coin had somehow been missed. Of course there was nothing. She returned to the sitting room and dug into her sewing basket. She had two pairs of socks she had sewn at some point, intending to send them to Ennis. They might be of use for trade. She placed them in her reticule and moved into her bedroom to check her image in the mirror. Her mourning dress hung shapeless, and loose. It was well made with twilled bombazine of silk warp and worsted weft, and only now after a year's wear, the cuffs, neck, and hem showed signs of fraying. She raised her eyes. Her cheekbones, like Mr. McBride and the boys, formed a sharp slant toward her jawline. Beneath dark brown eyes, dabs of purple lent a distressed appearance. Who was this frail wraith of a being? Where was the robust, bright-eyed woman of the past? She had retreated, perhaps never to be seen again. Joetta drew in her breath and let it out. If nothing else, the somber clothing accurately depicted her mood. Let them see what this war did. Let them look upon her and see no one was spared, despite favorable opinions or objections, or neither.

It was midmorning when she set out. Clouds and blue sky shared the heavens equally and she found the walk not unpleasant, although she undoubtedly missed the ease of riding in the wagon pulled by ever-faithful Pal. She passed the Brown farm, but as it was set back off the road she could not tell how Mary was doing. She planned to stop on the way home to thank her for the food, and she would find out then. Arriving at the outskirts of Whitakers, she felt her strength waning as she had not eaten that morning except a nibble or two, because to her, what they ate tasted of the dirt it came from, and not much else. She walked slowly into town and saw a few changes. Advertisements in shop windows had switched from promoting the usual goods for sale to encouraging contributions to the war effort. Other signs suggested work could be found at Hammond's cotton mill, sewing uniforms.

She stopped at the board where news was posted. There were older articles, one from July, with a bold headline that declared defeat (again), at a place called Gettysburg. A battle won by the Confederates had taken place in an area in Georgia near West Chickamauga Creek only a month before, in September. There was a note about the fall of Vicksburg, and notably, a tone of despair in each article. She scanned the posted newspapers for additional headlines, and one struck her immediately, which described the severity of food shortages with people eating whatever they could get their hands on—birds, rats, snakes, frogs, anything. She was swept into the details when a distinct word separated itself from the noises of the street.

"Traitor! Traitor!"

Fear was a frivolous companion at such a time, this she knew. She furtively looked about. Everyone went about their business, walking quickly, hands and arms burdened with various items, appearing much too busy to notice a bedraggled, red-faced farm woman in widow weeds. The heat of the day turned unbearable, making her feel like she was on a desert. The black dress hung heavy, weighing her down. She became uneasy, her senses heightened and her pulse pounding in her head, and it was as if she had lost her hearing. Notifications about deserters, proof not everyone wanted this war, boldly declared the various ramifications if caught. Forced back to the front! Prison! Possible execution! She left the news board and normal sounds returned, giving her a sense of the customary. The creak of wagons, horses, and mules clopping along the main thoroughfare, the soft swish of a broom outside one of the businesses.

She hurried to Mr. Spivey's store, where a sign in one of his windows said: IMPRESSMENT BY THE CONFEDERATE GOVERNMENT. NO FLOUR, CORNMEAL, COFFEE, OR SUGAR. She absorbed what she had not been privy to in some time, the expanded efforts at whatever cost to support the Confederacy, the leaning in to the cause. She entered, and the familiar tinkling of the bell announced her. It was cooler inside, and the quiet of the store calmed her. A door opened, and Mr. Spivey appeared. He rushed forward and offered a solicitous greeting.

"Why, Mrs. McBride! It's been a good while since you graced my small establishment. I've not had the chance to offer proper condolences over the untimely loss of your husband. My deepest sympathies to you and yours. Ennis was a good and kind man."

Mr. Spivey's words made her feel less out of place, less of a foreigner.

"Thank you. I appreciate your kind words."

He peered at her closely.

"I don't mean to pry, but are you well?"

She imagined herself a little wild-eyed, disheveled from her long walk, and perhaps unhealthy looking. She was certainly too thin. Embarrassed, she bowed her head and inadvertently cracked a knuckle. The sharp pop of the joint gave her even more reason to feel self-conscious. She brought her hands together in a tight clasp and raised her head. She had nothing to be ashamed of; none of this was of her doing, after all.

"We are managing. It has been a difficult time, as you might imagine."

Mr. Spivey did not look critical, but instead, compassionate.

"Indeed, I'm sure."

"I am here to see if you would be willing to exchange these socks for the cost of sending this letter?" She retrieved the pair from her reticule and set them on the counter. "The letter is for my mother in Hamilton. I have neglected writing to her for some time."

Mr. Spivey picked up the socks.

"These are very finely made. Sadly, I can't give you actual coins for them. The government has come up with a solution, of course."

"What would that be?"

"These."

He reached into his register and pulled out some pieces of paper that looked like typical paper currency, only smaller. There were denominations from five cents to twenty-five cents.

"Heavens, what are those?"

"Shinplasters, so they're called. From the Revolutionary soldiers who used to line the inside of their boots with cheap paper to cushion their shins. The name seems to have been adopted, mostly because Confederate cash is becoming worthless as time goes on. I suppose we'll see, depending on the outcome. See here, it says, '*Six months after the ratification of a treaty between the Confederate States and the United States, the Confederate States will pay to bearer,*' whatever the cost is."

She deemed them worthless already given the state of the currency.

"I would rather exchange whatever is left for something you might have here in the store?"

"Why certainly. I can do that. You would get thirty-five cents for the socks, deduct ten cents for the letter. That leaves twenty-five cents."

He stared at her sadly over the amount, but Joetta was overcome with gratitude. Her letter would be mailed and she would have something extra. She turned to the store shelves, which were mostly empty.

"I wish to buy whatever I might afford. There was an incident on the farm, and we are in need."

"I heard about what went on out there."

Joetta's voice held a scathing quality. "Lieutenant Braswell certainly kept his promise."

Mr. Spivey leaned in and spoke in a whisper. "Talk of harboring a Union spy is quite serious, Mrs. McBride."

Joetta fixed Mr. Spivey with a look of exasperation.

"The uninformed are speaking of that which they know nothing. I . . ." And here she hesitated, then went on. "I only cared for a sick boy. *He* was their supposed spy. Have you heard anything else?"

"Just that the lieutenant and his men helped themselves to the commodities of your farm. Of course it is claimed as justified, for the cause and whatnot. A penance for what they believe you've been a part of, I suppose. I don't agree with such methods of intimidation."

"They ate most everything we had in the smokehouse. Snuck it right out from under our noses. We had just slaughtered a pig to replenish what they took, and we gave that to them as well. None of our generosity mattered. They went on to make a grand mess of everything in the house looking for this purported enemy. Then they took off with all of our livestock. We were left with very little, and are doing what we can to get by, but it has not been easy."

Mr. Spivey shook his head.

"So much is being asked of every citizen. I am required to reserve what I have for the Confederacy. That is why"—he swept his arm around the store—"as you can see, I do not have much."

"Reserve for the Confederacy? That only contributes to the shortages!"

"You haven't heard of this?"

"Without Pal, Mr. McBride has not been able to get to town for any news. He has much difficulty walking."

"Ah. Well. The directives have caused quite the stir, here

and far. Farmers are to provide ten percent of what they grow. In Richmond, a couple of women charged the Virginia governor's office complaining over the high prices, the lack of flour, among other things. The bread riot, they called it. President Jefferson caught wind and actually threatened use of Confederate forces to stop them. It was only then some of the food reserves were released. It's not enough. It will only get worse, I fear."

"I am not the only one unhappy with the state we are in, it appears."

"No, you certainly aren't. Please, look at what I do have and see if any of it would suit you."

Mr. Spivey still had no idea how bad it was for them. To even look at the hoop of cheese made her mouth water. Eighteen cents a pound. Unbelievable. She walked a bit farther. A dozen eggs, fifteen cents. She could not imagine! Why, she used to have as many eggs as she could ever want! There was not much else she could afford either because of cost, or because it was not available. She hesitated by the eggs, and Mr. Spivey called out to her.

"I need to get rid of some of those. And this cheese has become a bit hard, but a hot skillet ought to fix that, if that is suitable to you? I have some coming in later this week, God willing."

"How much for all of it?"

"What was left over from the socks will do nicely."

She glanced at him to see if he was serious, and he inclined his head at her, his expression earnest. She blew out an exasperated breath. She dropped her head feeling ashamed of her outburst.

"I do not mean to sound as if I am complaining."

Mr. Spivey expressed only sympathy.

"We are all feeling the pinch. A dozen eggs and a pound of cheese, then?"

She said, "Yes, thank you," and quickly turned away so he would not see her weakness.

He began slicing the cheese and from outside, a heavy-footed individual walked with purpose down the board-walk. Mr. Spivey leaned over and glanced out the window at the end of his counter. He turned to her, put a finger to his mouth, and flapped a hand in the direction where he had entered the store. She reacted quickly, given the stricken look on his face, hurrying to the door and ducking through it. She found herself in a narrow space with stairs leading to what must be Mr. Spivey's living quarters above the store. She eased it shut and became motionless.

The bell jangled, and a man yelled, "Where's she at?"

"Who're you talking about?"

"The McBride woman! Someone said she came in here."

"As you can see, she's not in here."

Joetta shut her eyes. Mr. Spivey had chosen his words carefully. *In here*, he'd said, thereby telling the truth.

"You sure about that? Was she here?"

"Feel free to look around, Mr. Miller."

Miller. That was the name of the overseer Bess mentioned. The man moved around the store, the floorboards reacting to his decisive, intimidating steps, vibrating beneath her feet as he went by. Something scraped along the floor near her hiding place and Joetta's hands grew sweaty. She tucked her chin to her chest and tried not to pant in fear, bracing herself for the door to fly open. Mr. Spivey began to softly whistle as the bristles of a broom made a swishing sound. More footsteps and low-key mumbling. The overseer muttered to himself. A few seconds later, the bell clanked.

Miller said, "I'm going to check a few other places. You see her, you best keep her here."

Mr. Spivey grunted in response, and the door slammed

so hard, the bell hit the floor. Then, silence. Joetta breathed in, out. The scraping noise again, then a tap on the door as Mr. Spivey muttered her name.

"Mrs. McBride."

She opened the door with caution and found him standing beside a cracker barrel he had moved.

"I didn't want him getting any ideas about opening that door. I thought he might not pay it much attention if I moved this barrel in front of it while he was here. I'll admit, he's not the brightest man I've ever known."

"I am indebted to you, Mr. Spivey."

"Not at all. Folks acting mighty strange these days, ever since Lincoln's Proclamation. Whites are offended and one by one, slaves are taking it upon themselves to leave, unless their owners have already released them."

"What is called manumission?"

"Yes. The Garners didn't release their slaves; they left. Only a couple of house servants stayed, and one or two of their older field hands. Last I heard Mr. Garner was out there trying to bring his crops in alongside them. The Hammonds took on government contracts to make uniforms, but can't hardly do what they promised because their cotton crops are mostly in the fields, too."

Joetta's attention remained fixed on the door. Her stomach churned, and she brushed a hand across her damp forehead.

"Mercy. I never thought coming to town to conduct a simple transaction would cause a problem."

"Mrs. McBride, that middle road you're traveling is mighty lonely, and treacherous. I'd suggest you leave out the back. It'll keep you off the main street. Be careful to keep your eyes and ears open."

He handed her a cloth sack filled with the eggs and cheese. She paused to look about the store, remembering when she would come with Ennis, Henry, and Robert. It seemed so long ago, an echo of a pleasant memory. Mr. Spivey led her to the back and opened the door. He looked out, before standing aside so she could leave. Joetta spoke with gratitude as she lifted the sack.

"Thank you for everything."

Mr. Spivey had a dejected look. "Be careful."

They stood quiet for a moment, each recognizing their destinies were all but bound by the success of men wearing blue or gray.

Chapter 26

Joetta skirted the backside of buildings, growing ever more indignant at being forced to creep along like some sort of criminal. Finally, she was out of town, and thoroughly frazzled by the experience. She cradled the sack of food and took her time. Glory be! At least she had something to show for the moments of panic she had suffered. Mr. McBride's, Robert's, and Charlie's faces when she showed them what she had would be worth her efforts. She was lost in the thought of their happiness when she realized how incredibly thirsty she was. Since leaving the farm, she had not had a sip of water, nor had she even dampened her handkerchief so that she might cool off her forehead and neck. What an unusual heat blanketing the land, and it already parched from drought. If there something else to be grateful for, it was that she did not have crops drying up in the fields. God had his ways.

With this thought, she continued, and soon came to the entrance of the path that led to Mary's. Anxious to see her friend, she now regretted the times she had not acknowledged her visits, remaining hidden away. That behavior had been foolish, she supposed. She carefully held the eggs and cheese as she navigated the footpath. It had always been narrow, but it was now severely overgrown, and she had to hike her skirt up over thick cocklebur, nutsedge, and thistle, all while keeping an eye out for snakes. The Browns had always kept the path well-tended with only wildflowers growing along the edges, typically quite inviting. Maybe it was like this because Mary did not have time with all she was required to do. She was managing as best as she could. After all, she too was alone.

Joetta arrived at the gate, and stopped. There was a hush all around and she tilted her head, the stillness disconcerting. The fields, like Joetta's own, were strangely empty. Across the yard, the barn door was shut. The two hens pecking near the chicken coop brought relief, even though they were the only signs of life. Like most, Mary's farm was not operating as usual either. She opened the gate, entered the yard, and called out.

"Mary?"

She tried again, and louder.

"Mary, are you here?"

A hot wind brought leaves along with bits of field debris to swirl around her feet. With it came the faint odor of spoil. She walked to the side of the house where Mary kept her garden. It looked about as dilapidated as hers. It had taken on some weeds, and there were a couple melons and squash that had drawn infinite flies and gnats, and the smell. Joetta considered, only briefly, whether some part of the fruit or vegetable might be worth eating. Almost as quick, she backed away. What was she thinking? She would not stoop so low as to take what was not hers, but forgive her, dear Lord, she certainly had thought about it.

She hurried back around to the front, where a bucket

hung suspended over the well and clanked periodically against the wooden frame, a lonely and rather desolate sound. Joetta climbed the steps to the porch as ill-kept as the yard. After knocking on the door, she stared at the corners of the windows filled with cobwebs. She knocked again, more forcefully. After a minute, she gave up. Descending the steps, she was disappointed, and worried. Mary had often talked about her mother who lived in Red Oak. She had wanted her mother to come and live with her and Hugh after her father died, but her mother, an independent woman, apparently did not mind living alone. It was possible Mary had been sent for, or perhaps she had gone to fetch her, to bring her here given Mary was waiting on Hugh's return.

"Joetta!"

Joetta, lost in her musings, jumped. She turned to see her friend, who had materialized from out of nowhere. Her appearance caused great alarm as she looked much different than the last time Joetta had seen her. Not unlike herself, Mary had lost weight, her skin was pasty, and her clothing showed much wear, no different than Joetta's mourning attire.

"Mary! I thought you had gone to Red Oak to get your mother."

"No, no. I've been nowhere to speak of. How are you, Joetta? I went to see you a couple times, but you weren't around."

Joetta peered closely at her friend. Mary acted nervous, her eyes never staying in one spot for too long, as if she were on the lookout for something. Or someone. Joetta reached for her friend's hand.

"I wanted to come and thank you for your generosity and for your understanding of . . . our unique situation."

Mary finally looked at Joetta.

"It isn't uncommon for everyone to have a secret, or two."

"Mary, is there anything I can help you with? Should I send Robert? He is strong."

Mary shook her head vigorously.

"There's really nothing for him to do. I wasn't able to manage the crops, such as they were, and lost quite a bit of them. Someone took the mules. The cow and chickens were left because they were secured in the barn."

Joetta flushed at how she had looked at Mary's garden and considered helping herself to some of it.

"I cannot let you keep giving me things without repaying you in some small way. You are welcome to stay with me, even if only for a little while. We do not have much, but the offer is there, and extended with the utmost wish you would consider it."

Mary cleared her throat, dropped her eyes, and began to wag her head, her refusal adamant.

"I would stay here, but thank you."

She then held up a finger for Joetta to wait, and hurried around to the back of the house. When she returned, she held a crock of milk in the crook of her arm. She handed it to Joetta, who, once again, was overcome with gratitude.

"I cannot express to you how much this helps, and I wish you would come and stay with me, but I know you must feel closer to Hugh by remaining here."

At that, Mary became distant and did not speak again. Joetta looked at the sun, which had started its descent.

"I best be going. It was so good to see you. I promise, the first thing I will do is have you over for that glass of switchel as soon as we see the end of this horrible time."

At that, Mary smiled and looked more herself. Joetta gave her a one-armed hug and took her leave. She went out of the gate and made her way carefully back down the path.

Juggling the milk and the sack, she looked back, intending to wave at Mary. Mary was where Joetta had left her, but was not looking her way. Instead, she concentrated on the barn door as it eased open, and Hugh Brown emerged into the daylight. Joetta's mouth was wide open, and rather than call out, she hurried away, not wanting them to know she had seen. Fear, as much for them as for herself and her own family, drove her homeward. Soon, the farm's split rail fence came into view, and it was a relief as she was hot, dusty, and tired. She hurried to the springhouse and set the crock of milk on a shelf before filling a bucket with cool water. She drank a dipper full without stopping, and did it again before making her way into the house. There sat Mr. McBride, Robert, and Charlie at the table, the wood box full, and another bucket of water by the stove. On it sat potatoes, and a couple turnips. She turned her attention to the three sitting at the table and held the sack of food up, smiling.

"Eggs and cheese, from Mr. Spivey's store. And there is some milk in the springhouse. I stopped to see Mary Brown on my way home."

Robert eyed what she had with a disgruntled look.

"I wish you hadn't brought nothing back."

Confounded, she said, "Why?"

"After it's gone, it's like starting all over again, having to get used to not having enough."

Mr. McBride agreed. "S'truth."

Joetta could not argue the point. When they ate less, it became somewhat bearable to have less. The period after eating what Mary brought was an adjustment, and actually somewhat of a misery.

"We must be thankful for anything we get until we are graced with God's bounty again."

Charlie, ever observant, spoke with his usual selflessness. "Give him my share. I shouldn't be here no way."

Joetta wagged a finger around the table. "There is enough for *everyone.*"

Charlie's eyes locked on the food as she removed it from the sack. He could say what he wanted, but clearly he was glad she refused his suggestion. Despite not having enough, he was always fidgeting with pent-up energy. His yellow-toned skin, less obvious after having taken the quinine pills, stood out in stark contrast to Robert's ruddy tinge. He needed to eat to restore his health. She would not allow any of them to make such a sacrifice.

Mr. McBride said, "Any news from town?"

Joetta informed him of what she found out and what she had witnessed.

"Hammond's cotton mill is sewing uniforms. Alice Atwater's hat shop is being used for rolling bandages. And listen to this, the Confederate government is forcing many, like Mr. Spivey, to set aside goods. His shelves were mostly empty. Even so, he is required to send whatever he can. Did you know, if we had crops, we would have to send ten percent?"

She waited for his reaction, while not mentioning anything about the overseer, or Hugh Brown. The entire ordeal had set her on edge. Her instincts told her such knowledge was dangerous, and the less who knew, the better. Mr. McBride put his head in his hand with a look of exasperation but would not speak against his Rebels too harshly.

"I guess they got to do what they can to not starve."

Joetta eyes grew round and big.

"While it is fine for citizens to do so?"

He harrumphed and scratched an armpit. Joetta went on to tell him about Gettysburg and Chickamauga. A loss. A win. Mr. McBride absorbed the news without much reaction, as if his interest was waning. The quick win he expected had never materialized, and it was possible he wanted the war over as bad as she did at this point. The one thing she could be happy over was that Mary had Hugh back, even though a twinge of envy came along with those feelings of gladness. As Joetta thought of this, Robert stood up.

"I'm going fishing. Charlie here, he'd like to go too."

Charlie gave her a yearning look even as a persistent image of Miller came to Joetta's mind. She was cautious with her reply.

"I do not think it is a good idea."

Charlie slumped in his chair, despondent, and Joetta was conflicted once again, remembering Mr. McBride's comparison of keeping him like a prisoner, right here, on this very farm. Charlie was, after all, merely a boy who wanted to fish.

Noncommittal, she asked, "Where were you planning to go?"

"That area of the creek close to the back field, not far from the house. I ain't fished there in a while. I got some worms earlier today near the springhouse. Fish with them eggs and cheese would be real good, I figure."

Charlie grew hopeful.

"I'd be real careful. I'd sit so if anyone was to come along, they'd not see me. Like how you couldn't see me till I talked to you that day."

With an avid air, they waited. She just did not know. Mr. McBride hooked his thumbs in his galluses and squinted at Charlie.

"Reckon he ought to earn some of the food going in that mouth."

Joetta exhaled with irritation.

"He does not eat enough to make a difference."

She fell quiet again and had an almost irrepressible urge to snap one of her finger joints, then came to a decision.

"Charlie, it would most likely do you some good to get

outside. Go ahead. No one can come onto this property that I would not see them."

Robert jumped up from the table with an exuberance she had not seen in some time. Charlie followed suit, both grinning big and wide. In minutes they were on their way with cane poles from the barn and the worms Robert had collected. Joetta was glad she had relented. It did her own disposition good to see them looking happy for a change. Mr. McBride followed them outside, hollering his wishes.

"Bring me some pike. Ah, I don't care. I'll eat anything."

Eat anything. At least it had not come to that yet, not for them. Reading of the necessity of eating rats, snakes, or whatever else due to the severity of deprivation haunted her. She wished she had not learned of such desperation. Mr. McBride went and sat in his chair under the beech tree and began whittling. She remained at the back door, watching the boys, Charlie a step or two behind Robert. The sight brought forward memories of Henry and Robert heading off to fish. And Ennis. Ennis who loved catfish with her onion relish. Her heart yearned for what they had lost, and would never regain. She tucked the memory into a distant corner. For now, such recollections were much too painful.

Exhausted from her venture, she settled into a kitchen chair, hands in her lap. *Idle hands are the Devil's playthings* used to be a favorite phrase of her mother's, but no one was here to witness such shiftlessness, and with the current circumstances, who would care? And there she sat until the sun began to fall from the sky and she heard the boys return. They were with Mr. McBride, holding up the fish they had caught. A smile stretched the muscles around her mouth, a foreign sensation as she did not know the last time she had done so. That night, she baked the fish along with the eggs and cheese, and they had milk to wash it all down. It was a fine meal.

As was the case with full stomachs, optimism abounded, and their outlook improved. Charlie began to go fishing more often, and sometimes even on the rare hunt. The boys would return with something almost every time. The weather finally turned cooler, and soon, the pecans were ready. With their help, quite a bit was gathered. She baked some of the dried peaches with the nuts, a real treat everyone enjoyed immensely. One clear, cool day, she did two things she believed significant. When she got out of bed, she did not put on her mourning attire. Instead, she put on a clean, regular work dress, white collar and cuffs. She tied an apron around her waist, and at the image reflecting back at her in the mirror, her mood lifted. Next, she directed Robert and Charlie to drag the wooden press out of the barn. They took turns cranking the wheel as Joetta poured buckets of apples into the hatch, and they were rewarded with gallons of fresh cider to drink. She cautioned moderation in their drinking, but Mr. McBride paid her no attention, and spent a day in the outhouse for it. They shared a good laugh over this, everyone except him.

At Thanksgiving, the food offerings began to show up again. A ham. A hunk of deer meat. Most unusual, and most appreciated, was a bag of cornmeal, half empty. There was nothing to help identify who did these good deeds. Joetta did not suspect Mary for two reasons. One, she was certain she no longer had anything to spare, not with Hugh home, and Mary so thin too. Joetta wondered out loud about the mysterious gifts to Mr. McBride one evening as they ate. He shoved a large chunk of meat into his mouth and waved his fork at her.

"Don't go looking a gift horse in the mouth."

Charlie picked at his portions while gazing around the table. Joetta hoped he was not succumbing to the fever again, or allowing guilt to overrule his own enjoyment. It was right before Christmas and early when she went out to retrieve water, and there sat part of a large ham near the back door. Joetta did not immediately pick it up. Instead, she went down the steps, checked inside the barn, the smokehouse, the corn crib. Mr. McBride's cabin sat silent and dark in the predawn light. Her search was useless; there was nothing to be seen, nothing to be heard, and other than what was on the porch, nothing to be found.

She returned and stared down at the meat. How could she catch this person? Did she even want to know? What if whoever did this only kept it up because she was ignorant of their identity? What if they stopped providing if they suspected she was trying to figure it out? The fact they were not as hungry as they had been was a blessing. She should simply accept these items with grace and let it be, as Mr. McBride had advised. She took the ham inside and placed it on her worktable, ignoring the questions in her mind. Robert and Charlie were in the kitchen, and she decided on one thing, at least.

"Charlie, perhaps you should not go fishing or hunting for right now. Not until we know where this"—and she pointed at the ham—"is coming from."

Charlie did not respond, while Robert argued against this idea.

"Nothing has happened so far. I doubt anyone would be bringing us food if they thought we were hiding a *spy*."

He poked Charlie in the arm in a teasing manner. Joetta saw the logic in this but could not bring herself to take the risk.

"We cannot take chances."

"How long is that gonna last? He doesn't want to be stuck in the house again, do you, Charlie?"

Charlie's expression was one of caution, and his eyes flitted between Joetta and Robert, as if he wished not to offend either of them. Joetta began to cook the ham while she pondered on the matter, and then reaffirmed she would be the one to make the decision.

"We will have to see."

She quickly served them, and Robert began eating while Charlie sat looking at his plate. Joetta was about to ask him if he felt all right when he picked up a piece of ham and bit into it, eating with restraint and chewing slowly. His coloring was more sallow than it had been, and it did no good to mention this because she had no more quinine. For the next few days Robert went out alone and Charlie remained inside. Mr. McBride asked him why he did not go fishing, and Joetta intervened.

"We cannot take the chance. Someone is coming onto this property unbeknownst to us, and for all we know, they could be watching this place."

"True, true."

When Robert returned he wore a sour look, and one morning he threw a challenge down. He finished his portion of breakfast and got up.

"I'm going fishing, alone again, I guess."

He stood by Charlie, and there was a dare in the look he gave him. Joetta was quite familiar with it; she had seen it often between Henry and Robert when Henry would goad his younger brother into doing something. It was as if Robert had switched into that role, acting like Henry had with him. Joetta opened her mouth to speak, but Charlie accepted the challenge and rose from his seat abruptly.

"I'm going too!"

In that moment, Joetta understood that, in truth, Charlie could do as he pleased. He was not hers. She had no claim to him. He could leave if he wanted, and if he did, could she stop him? Should she? These unexpected thoughts kept her from saying a word, and her lack of reaction was taken as acceptance. Robert motioned for Charlie to follow him, while Joetta sat very still, and very alone, at the table. Dismayed, somewhat confused by these sudden internal revelations, she had not moved for several minutes when shouting began. It started off faint, like the distant tapping of a far-off woodpecker. The persistence was what got her attention. She hurried to the door.

She spotted Robert first as he trotted past the back field, coming toward the house. He was followed by Charlie, whose dazzling hair shone like a flame as the sun struck it. On his heels came . . . Harold! Harold yelled, and Robert yelled back, but what they said could not be understood. Joetta experienced an internal tumultuous reaction caused by the realization they had been found out. Mr. McBride heard them too and came out of his cabin, leaning heavy on his cane. Joetta realized she had not seen him until now, and he did not look well, but she did not have time to think about that. Harold stalked Robert and Charlie, still shouting, only now he was close enough she could understand him.

"I know who that is! That's that spy! Papa said he was hid over here!"

Robert yelled back, "He ain't no spy!"

Robert's face held a mixture of fear and fury, and Charlie's only fear. Robert motioned for Charlie to go in front of him, and Charlie did, running past him and shooting Joetta a tragic look as he went by her and into the house. Joetta made herself walk across the yard, determined she would remain calm even as her insides quaked with foreboding. She could not believe it had happened after all this time. She would talk to Harold and explain.

"Hello, Harold."

Harold was growing up. He was, what, sixteen now? He had facial hair, and he was certainly taller. Joetta took this in, and his distressed behavior, as his chest heaved in and out with emotion. He raised an arm and pointed at the house where Charlie had disappeared.

"I know 'bout him."

"If you will listen, I will explain Charlie's story."

"Ain't no need. What my folks said is what I believe. Not you. Not no traitor. You ain't never showed no loyalty. Never."

Oh, the audacity! Harold was already turning around to go back the way he had come, and as he did, to Joetta's amazement, Mr. McBride spoke in Charlie's defense.

"You hold on a minute, you rascal. That boy's mother was killed trying to help a Reb and the Union took him. That ain't his fault."

Harold stopped, but only for a second, and in a voice laced with mistrust, he yelled at Mr. McBride, "I'm telling my papa he's here. I done seen him!" and he took off running.

Robert started after him, and Joetta shouted, "Robert! Let him go!"

Robert halted, struggling with some emotion, and while Joetta wished to comfort him, Mr. McBride emitted a harsh cough that went on and on. She ended up at his side, alarmed.

"Are you unwell?"

"It's only a little cough. I'm fine."

She noted his pallor, and his sweaty forehead. She went to touch it, and he batted her hand away.

"There ain't no time for that. Don't you see? You and them boys got to go and now!"

"What? Why?"

"My God, woman! He's on his way to tell his father, who will waste no time bringing trouble. Do you want to be here when that shows up? Let me handle it. Take what bit of food there is and go to your mother's."

"I cannot leave you here alone. I will stay with you to resolve this issue. The boys must leave."

"Don't be foolish! If we end up in jail, or worse, then what's to become of them?"

"Then, come with us."

"I'm staying right here on my property, the devil be damned. I can't hardly walk as it is, and I'd only slow them up. It has to be you and them that goes. That's all there is to it!"

Mr. McBride went to Robert. He spoke to him, and Robert looked over his shoulder at her. Then, Joetta witnessed something she had never seen. The old man grabbed the boy and hugged him, then released him.

"Take care of your mother."

Robert's voice cracked. "I will."

She was torn. She did not want to leave, even while knowing Mr. McBride was right. To be sure, nothing would be done to him as he had shown his loyalties all along. But how would he eat? He did not know how to cook. He had never done it before, and she had no idea how long they would be gone.

"There is still some dried fruit and nuts in the . . ."

He spoke to her in his old way, rudely.

"No time! Not now! Go!"

She backed away, locking eyes with him, and in that split second an emotion that only under such dire circumstances would have ever been revealed was shared. Who would have known she could feel so wretched leaving this cranky old man who had been such a thorn, always piercing her heart with his harsh words and actions? She could see past his irritability, the rudeness, to the likeness between Ennis and him, as if she were seeing her husband in his old age, and in that moment, her heart healed the area she had hardened toward Rudean McBride.

"We will come back as soon as we can."

Mr. McBride made no acknowledgment she had spoken. She ran across the yard and into the house to gather a few things. When she, Robert, and Charlie left the farm, Mr. McBride was nowhere to be seen, but Joetta was certain he watched them from a window of the cabin.

Chapter 27

They finally stopped to catch their breath, and with heaving chests and darting eyes, they waited to see if anyone had followed. The soft whisper of wind and water trickling in the nearby creek peacefully serenaded them and this was all they heard. Joetta relaxed a little and began to wish on the stars and the heavens for some way to see this through, so they might return home sooner rather than later. If followed by those skilled at tracking, they would not stand a chance of making it very far. Robert was the more knowledgeable and in the stillness, he spoke in a low voice, telling her and Charlie what they should do.

"We wait 'til dark, then follow Fishing Creek until it dips south to the Tar River. We then go to Logsboro and after that, Deep Creek. We'll have to go north a ways, around Coneeto Swamp, and by then, we'll be close to Grandma and Grandpa Bowen's farm."

Joetta listened, though she was already having strong doubts about this decision, even as she kept quiet. This must have signaled concern because Robert kept his eyes

on her, perhaps expecting her to intercede. She only nodded, accepting his plan, and everyone settled down to wait.
Each boy carried a loaded shotgun, and what little ammunition they had in their pockets. Despite the lack of food,
and shells, Joetta was more worried about getting lost.

She spoke softly. "How do you know where to go?"

"Henry and I used to go hunting here with Papa. It's an
old Indian trail."

Charlie had not spoken since they left the farm. His self-
reproach was evident in the way he distanced himself from
them. It concerned Joetta, but she let him be, believing
once they were farther along, he would come around. They
passed the rest of the afternoon quietly, with Robert leaning against the trunk of a large pine and Joetta maintaining
a subtle watchfulness. Charlie was restless and kept going
down to the creek. It seemed to take forever before dusk
came, granting them the signal for their first night of travel.
When it did, she gave each of the boys some ham while she
nibbled on a handful of nuts. They drank water from the
creek, and at last, using large sticks Robert found to help
walk along the uneven terrain, they began again, a waxing
gibbous moon in the eastern sky guiding them. Joetta had
a most difficult time due to her skirt, and it was not long
before she asked them to stop.

"Wait."

She brought the hem from the back to the front and
tucked it into the waistband of her skirt, thereby fashion-
ing temporary pantaloons. Now she could move better,
quicker, and it would keep her skirt free of the brush and
mostly dry. By Joetta's estimation, they should arrive in
Hamilton in three nights, and it helped ease her mind as to
the accuracy of the trail they took when Robert pointed out
areas he remembered, like Culpepper Branch and Daniels
Branch, landmarks his father had detailed to him. There

was a distinctive white stone fireplace from a hunter's cabin of long ago, and a uniquely shaped tree limb in the bend at Daniels Branch that Charlie sat on, or it would have otherwise been missed. Robert studied it for a moment.

"Papa told me Indians cut'em like that to show others where to cross, point to trails, or a spring."

It made Joetta happy he could talk about his father and have these memories.

Once the sun rose, they stopped, and Joetta deemed their first night of travel successful. Nothing untoward had happened, and now they could rest. She opened the burlap sack and took out apples, dried peaches, pecans, and ham. She considered the fare adequate, and while it would not satisfy them completely, it would see them through.

Charlie pushed his portion back toward her.

"I don't want nothing to eat."

Joetta protested. "You have walked all night. Of course you must eat to keep up your strength."

She held out the apple, ham, and a handful of pecans toward him, again, and Robert tried to make light of it.

"Yeah, I ain't carrying you."

This brotherly banter always pleased Joetta, while Charlie, eyes sad and contrite, only gave a little smile. Otherwise, he did not respond.

Later, Joetta would think how she should have known, but in that moment, Charlie was just being Charlie, and thinking of everyone else. Eating made her uncomfortable because he drifted about, going in circles. Despite his refusal, she made sure to put the food she set aside for him on his blanket before she lay down. Exhausted, she drifted off quickly, only to be awakened by Robert tapping her on the arm. It felt as if she had just gone to sleep; however, the sun was directly over him, showing her it was noon. Alarmed, she sat upright.

WHEN THE JESSAMINE GROWS

"What is wrong?"

"I can't find Charlie."

Confused, she frowned up at him.

"What do you mean?"

"I woke up and he wasn't here. I waited a bit thinking maybe he needed to use the privy. After a while, I went to see and I found something."

Robert began walking toward the creek, and Joetta got up and followed. Scattered along the edges of the water were rocks both small and large, and a stretch of sandy dirt. He pointed, and she made her way to where Charlie had placed rocks to form an arrow, indicating the direction he had gone. North. Robert's voice shook with distress.

"I reckon he's gone back home to Virginia."

Her heart hiccupped. *Gone.* She looked down the creek hoping he might appear, wave at them, and in that careful way of his, apologize that he had caused them concern. He would anxiously explain and do something to show his remorse for scaring them. The area remained quiet and peaceful. Joetta folded her arms. Charlie's sense of guilt had finally overwhelmed him, despite her efforts to ease his mind. Robert would not look at her. *Let blame not come between us again*, thought Joetta. She went back to her blanket and sat down while Robert paced. She kept thinking how this scrap of a boy had become such an important part of their family in a short period of time. Less than a year he had been with them, yet he had managed to wiggle his way into her heart. Charlie had meant something to Robert too. He had helped both of them, and while he could never replace Henry, his presence had given them renewed purpose and focus.

As usual, under intense moments of stress, Joetta squeezed her fingers, and in the stillness, her bones crunched together and the sound made Robert frown at her. She began yanking the weeds and grass nearby, tearing the leaves and stems into bits. This stained her fingers, but she did not stop, agonizing over Charlie and what might become of him. It made her particularly upset to think they might never see him again. She began to imagine herself at home, in the kitchen working as she always had. She pictured the bedroom's most comforting sight, the dip of Ennis's body, faint, yet still evident in the corn shuck mattress of their bed. She had not been gone but a single night, and even so, a great and huge longing for home clung to her the way the jessamine wrapped itself around her front porch posts.

She began to regret this decision, even while it had been obvious that staying was dangerous. Her biggest concern had been for Charlie, but now he had taken it upon himself to leave. He would believe he was doing the right thing, and this explained his agitation, and distancing. Perhaps he had wanted to leave all along, and was only waiting to find the right time. The more she thought on another two nights of travel taking them farther and farther away, the more she did not know what was best, given these new circumstances. She turned to Robert.

"What should we do?"

He glanced at her, opened his mouth, and shut it. Joetta waited because she truly wanted to know what he thought.

"I don't know. What if it's worse at Grandma and Grandpa's?"

How anything could be worse than what they were experiencing she did not know, but she did recollect her mother's letters explaining their own trials and advising against travel.

"It is bad everywhere. That is a fact."

"If we go back . . ." His voice trailed off, hopeful, yet reticent.

It was clear that it was Robert's wish to return to the

farm. It was hers too, yet even without Charlie, retaliation of the suspected offense might still come. Harold *had* seen Charlie, after all. Neither one moved or spoke for some time. Robert appeared uncertain, and gestured at the path toward his grandparents.

"If we kept on, when would we be able to go home?"

Joetta raised her shoulders and shook her head. She began to envision the surprise of showing up on her mother and father's doorstep. There was no doubt they would be thrilled, but she did not want her parents having to parcel out food to feed them. Torn by her own thoughts and by the hopeful look Robert gave her, she weighed everything they had discussed and more. There was Mr. McBride suddenly taken ill. She recalled the look they had exchanged, the finality of their decision in that split-second moment. There were many unknowns relative to Hamilton and what they might find once there. They had left the farm in haste, without many options. There was risk in going back, but Charlie's departure had her second-guessing continuing on.

"If we go back, we would need to be very careful. We would need to stay out of sight during the day and only stay in the house at night."

"Okay."

"Even without Charlie, there is the likelihood someone will be watching."

"I don't think Mr. and Mrs. Caldwell will do anything."

"Why not?"

"Mr. Caldwell only wanted to scare you. He said you knew your own mind, and that you were daring. He said if every soldier was like you, we'd have won the war by now."

"He said that?"

"Yes. Mrs. Caldwell didn't agree. She said you were pigheaded."

Joetta could hear them as if she had stood in the same room. It sounded like conversations she had with Bess herself. She made up her mind.

"As soon as the sun goes down, we will start back."

Robert, appearing relieved, finally stopped pacing and sat down. Joetta felt better having decided, and a tremendous weight was lifted. Not knowing what was happening at the farm, or with Mr. McBride, worried her more than she had realized. The rest of the afternoon passed, a little cooler and cloudier than the day before, and they rested as much as possible. Joetta could not help but hold out hope Charlie might yet magically appear. Her hopes faded as each hour was lost, and when the sun finally began to set, they ate another apple and Joetta got out the last of the ham. She gave it to Robert and he hesitated before eating.

"You're not going to have any?"

"I am not very hungry."

He shoved it into his mouth and chewed vigorously. Robert's lankiness was ever more pronounced given their sporadic diet, and in this moment he reminded Joetta more of her father, an exceptionally slender man, than of Ennis. The thought of her father made her sorry she would not see him, or her mother. Robert took Charlie's blanket and rolled it together with his. He shouldered his gun, and Joetta gathered what she had. They did not stop to question again what they were doing. They reversed course, the moon now at their backs. Robert led the way. She remained upset at Charlie leaving without a word, and yet they would have argued with him, and he knew this. She wondered what he would do once he arrived at his destination. He had never mentioned other relatives, and she thought of him alone, perhaps having to beg. She could not do anything about it, so she concentrated on where she placed her feet.

After a long night, and making very few stops, they arrived at a familiar section of Fishing Creek. They were close to the farm, and this knowledge drove them forward until the back field came into view. A streak of pale-yellow sunlight tinted a bank of low-lying clouds to the east. Joetta placed a hand on Robert's back, and he stopped.

"We need to be careful."

He acknowledged this with a nod. They moved forward cautiously. They had not gone more than a few feet when a distinctive odor of smoke, pervasive and pungent, made them stop again. Robert looked back at her, eyes shining in the dim light of dawn. She swept her arm about and spoke in a low tone.

"I thought it might be your grandfather's fireplace. It is smoke, as thick and heavy as fog."

"I see it."

They skirted the fence. The Confederate soldiers had taken sections of it for their fires, and they entered the field through one of those gaps and began to walk up the slight incline. The smell of burned wood hastened them, wafting across the field, and as unappealing as the metallic odor of blood when they slaughtered pigs. Joetta faltered. The house should have been right in front of her. She saw only two chimneys and the stone foundation, like bones left behind once the flesh is gone. The house lay in a blackened, smoldering heap, puffs of ash and smoke still coiling into the air. Every time a breeze came, soot floated and got in their eyes, on their clothes, and in their hair. She could taste it, and smell the ruin. The outbuildings, even Mr. McBride's cabin, had been torched. The front half where his porch had been was burned, along with the front wall, leaving the interior exposed to the elements. She was able to see inside to a chair, the spittoon, the fireplace.

Dazed and disbelieving, the shock was so great, it disabled

her. She was unable to move or speak. Her breath caught again and again as she took in the devastation. Robert was beside her, and raised his hands in helplessness, only to clasp them behind his head, as dumbstruck as she was. This house, built with love, and the very haven they sought, was destroyed. She could not define what it was that fled downward into her heart, flooded her limbs, and came to settle in her chest. Bitterness, perhaps. Anguish, most certainly. As if in defiance, the sun cast its glorious golden rays across this demolished world. Birds began to call and sing, and still she remained in that one spot, occasionally turning her head away from the stink of charred wood. To move meant she must do something, and she did not know what that should be. Strangled noises came from Robert as he began to cry in that way young men do when they do not want anyone to know. Eventually, she did move. She smoothed her skirt, straightened her back, and spoke to him.

"We need to find your grandfather."

Swiping at his nose with his sleeve, eyes red-rimmed, his reaction was not unexpected.

"That damn Harold. He ain't no friend of mine! Not no more!"

She did not chastise him for his language. Her own feelings were not much different from his. They first approached the remains of the house and stopped by a heap of smoldering wood, when from behind them came a gruff voice.

"What in the hell! Why're you here?"

Mr. McBride, relying heavily on his cane, came forward. He was quite pale, and coupled with his white hair, he exuded an extreme frailty that had not been apparent when they left. She hurried to him and when she came close, she found it necessary to place her hand over her nose. The stench was appalling, a vile odor of sickness, although he acted as if he was not aware. His eyes and nose streamed, and the words he spoke hung in the murky air, broken segments of thought.

"Look what they done." A pause, a cough. "Woke up. Everything's burning."

He was unsteady on his feet even with his cane, and Joetta believed he might collapse.

"Robert, get your grandfather a chair."

Mr. McBride's eyes roamed about wildly as if expecting to see someone. Robert retrieved the chair from under the beech tree, both astoundingly unscathed by the fire, and to Joetta's relief, Mr. McBride sat down. He placed his cane between his knees and breathed heavily. Joetta wanted to know who was responsible, but waited until Mr. McBride was breathing easier before she asked.

"Who did this?"

"No idea."

"You did not see them?"

"Couldn't see nothing but fire. They were like shadows. They took off pretty quick once I started shooting." He leaned over, coughing violently, then he straightened up. "Hold on now. Where's that boy?"

"He is not with us."

"What do you mean?"

"After the first night we stopped at daybreak to rest. Charlie must have thought it better if he did not stay. Robert found some stones made into an arrow that pointed north. I suppose he has gone back to Virginia."

Mr. McBride's mouth was open, and he scratched at his beard, grunting in disapproval.

"That appears mighty ungrateful."

"He always said he should not be here, causing us trouble. I imagine he believes he was doing us a favor. It was within reason for him to think so."

Mr. McBride looked from Joetta to Robert.

"I reckon we got more to worry about at the moment than where that rascal went."

Joetta expressed her worry.

"Whoever did this might return."

Mr. McBride shook his head.

"Ain't nobody coming 'round here again. Those that done this think you and them boys were in the house. It'd be in your best interest to let'em keep thinking like that."

Chapter 28

News traveled fast they had perished in the fire. Joetta and Robert hid in the cabin, and the damage created an openness that allowed her to hear comments made by various sympathetic visitors. Some were sad and outraged, such as Mr. Spivey. He brought a block of Lucifers and some chewing tobacco for Mr. McBride, who immediately struck one of the matches and politely lit the other man's pipe. They talked while standing near the beech tree, and Mr. Spivey swiped at his eyes before speaking. Joetta sorely wished to ease his mind as he was quite upset.

"This is an outrage. Nothing but vigilante justice. You don't know who did it?"

"It was dark. I couldn't see'em. They run off like cowards."

"How'd your cabin come to be part of it? You're for the cause, aren't you?"

"Didn't seem to count. My daughter-in-law, she was kindly hardheaded about this war, and I suppose it was bound to cause problems for anyone related, whether or not they agreed."

"She was a brave woman. Stood up for herself."

"Helping that little fellow was the last straw, I reckon. That lieutenant had him pegged for a spy."

"Was he?"

"I heard his story. Sounded like the truth, so no, I don't think he was."

"Damn shame's what it is."

Joetta did not know if Mr. McBride defended her because he believed what he said, or was playing a part, perhaps not trusting even Sam Spivey.

She found it very difficult to remain out of sight when Mary came. Her friend sobbed and patted Mr. McBride's arm, and even he appeared discomfited at the farce. Joetta noted how, even here, away from her farm, Mary continued to cast her gaze about, her nature gone suspicious. She did not tarry, handing a bundle to Mr. McBride, squeezing his hand before hurrying away. Her gift of half a dozen eggs and two jars of milk had Joetta bowing her head, giving thanks, for just when it seemed they were at the precipice of suffering mightily, a small miracle would occur.

The day Bess and Thomas Caldwell came, Mr. McBride's voice rose to a staggering pitch of fury, and Joetta imagined it possible to have heard him in the next county.

"You got some nerve showing up here! Your boy caused this! Look at it! He might as well have set it ablaze himself!"

A fit of coughing quelled his tirade, while Bess sobbed and flapped a hankie about as if signaling surrender. Thomas Caldwell pointed to the ruins, emphatically refuting responsibility, his denial quite vigorous.

"No sir! No sir! This was none of our doing!"

Try as she might to come to some sense of forgiveness, Joetta, ousted from the comfort of her home, relegated to living conditions not much different from being outside, was too brokenhearted, and therefore apathetic toward their distress. After the Caldwells began a period of intermittent visitations from those who were curious, or those who felt justice had been served. They never stayed long, for there could be no comforting hospitality when made to stand in the cold amidst the ruins. Mr. McBride habitually gestured at the cabin, pointing out the damage while explaining his inability to be more cordial.

"Almost as cold inside as it is out. Smells something fierce, too, what with all the smoke, you see."

Joetta and Robert watched from behind a blanket hung over the window in the small back bedroom, peeking through the gap that afforded a narrow view and listening in as they could. There were strangers looking for a souvenir who would sneak pieces of wood, or even take some of the very ash left behind.

Joetta overheard one woman exclaim, "Her traitorous bones are part of this!"

Preacher Rouse and Elder Newell arrived, and Preacher Rouse pointed out how she had always been one to make it hard on herself, and others.

"The actions taken by our sister have brought sorrow and pain upon you, my brother. How unfortunate it led her down this narrow path and to such a tragic end."

Elder Newell's head bobbed and whether in agreement or from the palsy, there was no way to tell. Preacher Rouse could not seem to stop, perhaps wanting justification for his feelings.

"I knew that day in church she had set herself up for trouble. It was bound to catch up to her."

Joetta wished to march outside, as if resurrected from the dead, if for no other reason than to prove him wrong—again—however, at this point, she did not care much what anyone thought. Preacher Rouse said a prayer for Mr. McBride, who adopted a pious expression, and Joetta considered perhaps he was enjoying the attention a bit much. When Eliza Garner and Rebecca Hammond came, she did not know how she felt. Prone to gossip such as they were, it should not have surprised her. Perhaps they wanted to affirm rumors, to gloat with self-righteousness, or to judge for themselves she was, what they had always suspected, guilty of what she had been accused. She studied them with a discerning gaze. Were they her enemy? She too was born of the South, but because she did not express devotion to their cause, she was a foe. She could not decide if she perceived them in the same way. What she noticed was they did not look quite as well turned out as when they were at Bess's. Their clothing, less than pristine, revealed more about them than they would ever admit. War and its repercussions did not play favorites to those in its way.

Throughout the course of those who came to express condolences, whether genuine or not, Joetta experienced a variety of emotions, but one terrified her, and that was when the overseer Miller showed up. He rode down the path, dismounted, and barely spoke to Mr. McBride. He spent an uncanny amount of time examining the scorched land, hovering and poking about. He did not express sympathy, even when he eventually spoke to her father-in-law.

"They were in the house?"

"It was the middle of the night, where else would they be?"

Miller looked down his nose, and her father-in-law wilted under the other man's scrutiny.

"Uh-huh," said Miller.

Robert whispered, "Grandpa's scared."

Joetta jerked a finger to her mouth and frowned. Miller shifted his gaze from Mr. McBride to the cabin, scanning the front until it came to the window where they stood. Both were gripped by the man's look, even as they believed they could not be seen. After a few seconds, he shrugged, mounted his horse, and left. Mr. McBride limped to his chair and collapsed. They crept from the bedroom and waited for him to come in. It took a long time. After Miller, visits ceased altogether, and Joetta, in some strange way, felt free.

The winter of 1863 began in earnest, a period in their lives like no other. She and Robert escaped their prison at night, going outside to gather partially burned debris to use in the fireplace. Robert spent a lot of time searching for food, always a calamitous exercise, and most nights tried to fish or set traps, but with nothing to lure an animal, he relied purely on chance. Joetta was reminded of the article she had read, and began to understand eating whatever could be found was becoming a necessity. Hunger, like the war, would not spare them either. As the winter progressed, Mr. McBride tried to help, but could not move well and coughed frequently. Joetta was certain he was sicker than he let on, and this was proven one day when he coughed, and she saw blood-specked spittle on his handkerchief. Their eyes met, and he quickly wadded it up and stuck it in his pocket. They did not speak of it.

Depending on the whims of Mother Nature, sometimes the rain went in one direction and the room stayed mostly dry, sometimes not. They kept the fire going in the fireplace and like the wet, sometimes they were warm, oftentimes not. Mr. McBride's chair was brought in from outside, and a rocking chair from the small bedroom was placed near the fireplace for Joetta. Robert used a blanket and lay close to the hearth. They did not move unless absolutely necessary. This dull routine was broken only when Mr. Spivey brought news to Mr. McBride.

"Here's an article about Lincoln's speech in Gettysburg. It was a rather significant one."

"Gave a speech, did he?"

They walked off and their voices faded until Joetta could hear no more. After Mr. Spivey left, Mr. McBride presented her with a small bag, and a smile like she had never seen before. Somehow Mr. Spivey managed to confiscate a bit of cornmeal from a soldier who had saved his daily ration of meal and used it to barter for paper, ink, and covers to send his sweetheart and family letters. That night they had the corn bread, mixed with water and baked in the skillet. It was dry, but the best thing they had eaten in a long while.

Christmas Day arrived, and the struggle to find sustenance provided very little. They huddled around the fire and talked of old times, about Henry, Ennis, and mostly about the food Joetta used to prepare. She reminisced in painstaking detail how she prepared a hen, cramming it full of celery, onions, and seasoning it with salt and pepper, and roasting it to a perfectly crispy brown. She described mashed potatoes, served with butter pooling in the dips left by the spoon. Fragrant biscuits. The scent of spices in a raisin cake.

While she dwelled in this detail, Mr. McBride and Robert sat with rapt faces and glazed eyes, until Robert, his voice gone hoarse with hunger and want, said, "Stop."

She stammered and fell into a painful silence broken only by Mr. McBride's coughing fits. They ate a small portion of the fish Robert was able to catch, along with the few dried peaches. She did not tell them how few were left.

1864 came with little, if any, fanfare, and their domain remained strangely compressed, their view only what they could see beyond the cracks and gaps. For Joetta, the outside no longer existed as it once had, except to deliver a miserable rain or a cold wind. On an exceptionally frigid morning in early February, Robert came from checking his traps empty-handed and promptly fell asleep by the fire. She rose, her breath a cloud in front of her face, the air so cold she believed it would crack like ice as she moved about. Shivering, and with a ratty blanket about her shoulders, she stoked the fire. Mr. McBride had his blanket up to his chin, yet, as cold as it was, a sheen on his forehead revealed he was with fever.

She knelt and poked at the embers. They sparked and grew deep red, and she tossed a few pieces of wood on. Soon, there was a small blaze, and she sat warming herself until a pale-orange light announced a new day. She rose to her feet and looked outside. A strange pink and white shape lay near the cabin. Even in death, the broad mouth stretched into the notorious devilish grin identified it. Joetta gaped at the possum, knowing the thing had not crawled there and collapsed in that condition. Mr. McBride remained in a deep sleep, succumbing to his illness, whatever it might be.

She returned her gaze to the creature. This would give him what he desperately needed. What they all needed. Something with substance, and the bones, well, she could boil them until they were brittle and of no further use. She could make it *last*. In some distant part of her mind, the very idea of eating possum repelled her, but this was quickly gone with the reality of a full belly. She could dash out and back in, could she not? It was true the outside world believed them dead, but the possibility of getting caught like what happened with Charlie left her uncertain. She could not take the chance. She hurried over to Mr. McBride, tapped him on the arm and whispered, not wanting to wake Robert.

"There is a dead possum outside."

"Eh? What?"

"Someone has left a possum."

He sat up, a bleary look on his face.

"Possum, you say? I ain't ate one a them in years."

Joetta stood behind him as he peeked out.

"Why, it sure is."

He went out, bent down, grabbed the tail, and held the animal up. It was missing a hind quarter, and Joetta frowned. He hurried back in and tossed it on the table, then sat in his chair, his head hanging. Even that bit of movement drove the cough out of him in violent fits and spurts. Joetta hurried to break the ice on the pail of water, got a glass, dipped it into the cold water, and took it to him. He drained it, and wanted more. She refilled it, and this time he drank this slower. He was able to speak then, and whispered, "Prob'ly Spivey."

Joetta considered Mr. Spivey, but it was too cold and they were some distance away for him to have been there that early. The other mystery was the missing part. Someone had taken some for themselves and left the rest for Mr. McBride. Or, for all of them? Standing where she was, she noticed steam coming off the carcass, and a chill ran through her. This was a *very* fresh kill. She put a hand to her throat and became as motionless as the animal. Birds began their bright, morning song as the sun winked through the tree branches and set the countryside alight. It had been left while still dark. Possum were night creatures, and a good trapper could catch them.

Mr. McBride coughed again, and she stopped thinking about who it could be, or why they would do this. She began preparing it to go into her kettle while wishing for seasonings, like salt, pepper, and chopped onion. They would eat it despite how it might taste without those niceties and be grateful for it. The smell of boiling meat woke Robert, and he raised himself on his elbows and pointed at the pot.

"What's in there?"

"Possum."

"Possum? Where'd that come from?"

"I do not know. It was left by someone."

"Have I ever had it?"

Joetta thought for a moment.

"I do not believe so."

For the next several days, Joetta managed to do what she wanted; she made it last. When the meat was gone, she took the leftover bones and boiled them, and they sipped on the broth. Mr. McBride's coloring improved, and he got about a little more, appearing stronger. One afternoon, he even went to the root cellar of the old house and scraped about trying to find whatever he could, even though it turned out to be only wormy potatoes. She cut out the bad parts and boiled them, and the taste was off enough it was almost not worth the effort. Then, the same thing happened again. Another possum, trapped, skinned, and a hind quarter removed, was left dangling in a tree, hooked in the fork of the branch by its tail. Mr. McBride went out to gather more wood and came rushing back in holding it in the air.

"It's fresh again. Maybe it's Caldwell. He's closest. I'd say it's more than likely him. This here's guilt talking."

Joetta was concerned about the whole affair.

"If it is him, taking that one section is not be enough to feed their family. It would only feed one. Someone is leaving more than enough for one person. Someone is watching us."

Mr. McBride scratched himself, while Robert kept his eyes on the animal as if it would disappear. She cooked it like the last one, and they ate it, every last morsel, because they needed it more than any of them wanted to admit. Joetta also hated to admit they had become dependent on the mysterious hunter, and the random, yet scarce visits from Mary, who always brought Mr. McBride a bit of milk, eggs, and sometimes butter. Because Joetta knew what Mr. McBride did not, she understood Mary's reticent nature when he groused about her not coming enough.

"For all she knows, I'm over here barely hanging on."

"She is only being cautious. She is, after all, a woman alone."

"And I am a man alone, far as she knows!"

Mr. McBride, sick or not, could still act like Mr. McBride.

As the weather began to warm, Joetta took to sitting near the front of the cabin first thing in the morning, catching sunbeams on her hands and face through the slatted wood. It was quite enjoyable after winter's darkness and cold. It was on a day like this she sat in a patch of sunlight, eyes closed. There was little if any sound, although she was almost certain it was Fishing Creek she heard as water rushed over rocks from rain the previous day. She allowed her mind to wander to her favorite place on the embankment. Eventually she opened her eyes and straight in front of her, through a gap in the wood, was a dead chicken. Chicken! She did not know anyone who had chickens except Mary.

Joetta bolted out of her chair and darted outside, thinking only of how good it would taste, and not that she was making a grave error. As soon as she snatched it up, she saw him. Near the burned house and by the foundation he stood, this man, watching as if he had expected her. Stunned, she spoke with urgency, half yelling, hoping Mr. McBride was awake and would hear her.

"Someone is here!"

The man began running, coming at her fast. From within Mr. McBride groaned as he stood from his bed. Robert was still asleep, and she prayed he would wake up too. The man held a pistol, and when he was close, she recognized the overseer Miller.

He called out, "Less I'm seeing a ghost, I'm pretty sure I'm looking at Joetta McBride. Ain't that a miraculous thing coming out of that fire with nary a burn?"

Mr. McBride was suddenly there, and he stepped in

front of her, shotgun aimed at Miller. The effort to move so quickly left him gasping.

Miller said, "You don't appear to be doing so well, McBride."

"I'm fine." He had a fit of coughing, and when he caught his breath, he said, "You're trespassing, and by rights, I could shoot you."

"Sure. You could do that, but she's the one I come for. Ain't got to be complicated."

Miller rushed forward, shoving Mr. McBride out of the way. He stumbled and because of his bad knee, he fell and landed awkwardly. The sickening crack of bone stunned her, as did his bellow of pain. She dropped the chicken and rushed to help him, only Miller snatched her arm and dug his fingers in. For as much as he hurt her, she remained calm and quickly began telling him the story of Charlie's capture by the Union.

"Listen. You are mistaken. The boy you thought was a spy, his mother was killed helping a Confederate soldier. The Union took him, used him. He escaped."

"Save your stories for the judge."

He shoved her forward and put the point of his pistol in her lower back.

"Walk."

Mr. McBride rolled about on the ground, clutching his arm. There was no way he could get up on his own. She wanted to help him and could not.

"Mother!"

Robert, red-faced, his chest rising and falling rapidly, stood in the doorway of the cabin. He held his shotgun on Miller and the overseer paused.

"Don't be dumb. I'll shoot her 'fore you ever get me. Tend to your granddaddy. You're 'bout to learn a hard lesson today, but you'll get over it. We all do."

He pushed Joetta and she called out to Robert as she began walking.

"Do as he said. Help your grandfather. Everything will be fine. I promise."

"Please, mister. Don't hurt her!"

His voice rose into the air as if from another time when he was much younger, and she would wipe his tears and listen to his sorrows, such as they were at that innocent age. She sent him one last brave smile and did not turn around again. At the end of the path, they began walking east, into the sun, skirting the woods. The fact they did not get onto the plank road worried Joetta. Her mind went blank, her future in this moment as perilous and uncertain as a battle-front. After they had walked some ways, he pushed her toward the woods and into a heavy wooded area.

"Get over there and stand against one of them trees."

Joetta went light-headed with fear. She protested, despite her terror.

"I am to see a judge! That is what you said! That is what is fair!"

"Fair?" Joetta thought he might shoot her over those very words. He waved the gun about. "Hell, ain't nothing fair. The Garners' slaves took off, and suddenly there ain't no work for me. Me! Best damn overseer they ever had. I blame that on the likes of those like you."

"How am I to blame? I am impartial to these matters."

"You ain't impartial when you aid the enemy."

It was no use arguing. She stopped talking, but Miller kept on.

"Blame the old man. He didn't act right that day I come to pay my respects, so to speak. That was more of an inves-tigation, so maybe blame me and my skills of observation."

He came closer and she was forced against the trunk of a chestnut tree. She went into a freefall of despair, and the hopelessness that overwhelmed her made her avert her eyes. She did not want the last thing she saw to be this horrible man's face. She focused on a spot of color beyond Miller's left shoulder, the shade like that of a robin's breast. It moved and bobbed about, and Joetta thought she might be hallucinating when emerging quietly from the cover of trees, Charlie appeared, aiming at Miller's back. Charlie stared at her with an uncanny intensity and signaled her with a flick of his eyes to his right. Without hesitation, she bolted left.

Miller yelled, "Hey!"

A blast came, and the sound echoed through the woods, followed by a thud. She had already stopped, her flight stunted by uncertainty. She remained facing the direction of the farm, her breathing rapid, eyes shut. She prayed it was Miller who hit the ground.

"I ain't ever k-killed nobody d-directly."

Joetta spun around. Miller lay facedown in the dirt, blood already soaking the sandy soil beneath him. Charlie still held the gun on the man, his expression one of disbelief.

"I reckon I'm going to h-hell for sure now, or j-jail, one."

"Charlie, hell is certainly not the destination for you. Neither is jail."

He appeared tired, sad, and for some reason, unable to meet her eyes. Her legs still weak from fear did not stop her from going to him. She touched his shoulder.

"We thought you went home, to Virginia."

Charlie looked to be somewhere else, a faraway distant place, perhaps where he was from, and wherever that was, it gave him enormous sorrow.

"I only wanted y'all to think that's where I went, but I already knew won't nothing there for me, not with my mama gone. I thought maybe it would help if I won't around, except I still was, in a way. Kindly hanging out on my own and all. Been keeping watch on your place. I left y'all that meat. I know it must've seemed strange. I'll admit, I did what them soldiers did. I took some of it from them who said you were a traitor. Please don't tell nobody."

"Charlie. Because of you, we made it through the winter. And now, here you have gone and saved my life. We are indebted to you."

Joetta sought some positive reaction from him. He continued to look much too old for his age. He started to speak, and faltered. He finally looked at her, conveyed that same need of the past along with something new, gauging if he could trust her. She took it upon herself to spare him any doubt and told him what she had said to Robert.

"Everything is going to be fine. I promise."

Chapter 29

The war would be over in less than a year, but Joetta, Robert, and Charlie knew nothing of this. Their source of news dried up after Mr. Spivey informed Mr. McBride he could no longer make the trip. He began explaining why until the older man waved his hand in dismissal.

"Don't worry. Can't be helped."

Everyone was barely scraping to get by, even the Pooles, Garners, and Hammonds, something Mr. Spivey had shared during that last visit. Joetta's heart went out as she saw how thin he looked, as hungry as anyone else. She wished she could at least let him know they were alive, but it was best not to put him in a precarious position of knowing too much. The last piece of news he brought Mr. McBride regarded the mysterious disappearance of Miller. He said posters were plastered about town, but most suspected he had merely taken off, disgruntled as he was to lose his job. Joetta was not worried he would ever be found, not unless someone cared to look inside the bellies of the feral pigs who had somehow managed to escape being eaten themselves. This was the horrific scene the boys encountered when they went back to bury the man. Had they arrived much later, there would have been no trace of him. Joetta noticed neither Robert nor Charlie was particularly disturbed by this unspeakable encounter. This, the price of war, even on the innocent.

Mary's visits also ceased to almost nothing, and Mr. McBride worried out loud.

"She ain't coming, I don't reckon. I guess that's the end of the milk and eggs, too."

Joetta rocked in her chair, thinking of the perilous details in how they were living, but did not reveal these deep sentiments when she responded.

"I am sure she would make every effort to do so, if she could."

Joetta considered what might have befallen her friend. Maybe her livestock had finally been taken, or Hugh had been found out. Would the Browns suffer the same vigilante justice if so?

While these unforeseen circumstances contributed to their hardships, it would be the discovery of an old garden that would end up saving them and costing them terribly at the same time. The garden was a chance finding made on a warm day in the late summer of 1864, right after Robert's fifteenth birthday, as they descended into the worst of times. Isolation and deprivation had taken a toll. Because they were rather desperate, it was necessary the boys trap or fish as much as possible, a chance that was taken for survival. The need to exercise caution remained, but so did eating. It became most important, critical, in fact.

Robert and Charlie usually left before light, long gone by the time she and Mr. McBride crawled from out of their beds. It seemed their arising happened later each day, the lack of food contributing to a deep fatigue. He limped outside to sit while she remained in her usual spot, just inside the walls of the cabin, still unable to shake her nervousness over the encounter with Miller. Outside Mr. McBride coughed and waved flies from his face. He no longer whittled, having lost all interest in the pastime. Suddenly, he pulled himself up and began hobbling around to the back of the cabin. His breathing was labored and when he passed her, he wheezed a single-word question, the brevity born out of necessity due to failing lung function.

"Boys?"

"They are checking the traps, I imagine."

He leaned on his cane, his chest expanding and collapsing with effort. After a few seconds he spoke again with better control.

"Anna once had a garden. Over yonder." He pointed.

"Yes, I remember."

"Perennials. Could be something there."

"Surely not after all these years. It was so long ago."

Mr. McBride spat and continued in the direction he had pointed. Curious, she rose from the chair and at the threshold, she hesitated, then followed him. He waded into a thick area of weeds, struggling to lift his legs over the dense foliage. The area was so neglected, it was hard to believe anything of use could still be found. She looked about, dismayed by the tangle of brush.

"We should wait and let Robert and Charlie help you look."

He ignored her, of course, and it would be the last time he would do so. Joetta had always suspected his illness was tuberculosis, but she did not really know what he had. His coloring never seemed right anymore, and he kept a blue tinge to his lips and the tips of his fingers. As he fought to free one leg, then the other, another coughing spasm overcame him. She waded in to help.

"Hold still, I'm coming."

She made it to his side and began to beat on his back lightly, rhythmically, hoping to help clear his congestion. He continued making strangling sounds and she wished, as she had many times, that she could breathe for him. His legs were giving out, and Joetta's voice was high-pitched as panic set in.

"Can you walk?"

He faced her, eyes huge and pleading, his mouth a deep blue.

"Water," he croaked at her.

Dress held high, she stumbled from the brambles and ran as fast as she could. At the well she grabbed the dipper and scooped water from the pail. She clapped her hand over the top and ran back to where she had left him. In that short period of time, he had disappeared. She turned this way and that, looking and looking while odd displaced gurgling sounds sent a vague signal as to his whereabouts.

"Mr. McBride? Mr. McBride!"

Several feet away she spotted his boots. It looked as if he had stumbled about before collapsing. She rushed over and found him staring at the sky, his face and neck blue, and foamy blood bubbling from his lips. His eyes flickered, found hers, and he blinked rapidly. The dipper fell from her fingers and the water spilled down the skirt of her dress. Collapsing to her knees, she tried rolling him onto his side, hoping to help him breathe. His arms and legs jerked, and the arm he had broken, which had never healed properly and was permanently bent, was the arm he tried to push himself upright with. She grabbed his other hand to assist him, but it was no use. He was too weak, and he collapsed. His face went an even deeper shade of blue. A horrifying blue.

"No. No. Breathe!"

She dropped to her knees, swiped at his mouth with her sleeve and her hands fluttering uselessly as she willed his body to cooperate with her pleas. His mouth opened and closed as he struggled to suck in air.

"Come on! Dear God! Breathe!"

He fought to do as she wanted, all commotion and effort until he went still. His chest sank and did not rise again. In disbelief she watched life flee, surrendering to the battlefield of sickness. His gaze fixed on some distant object beyond her ken as she gaped down upon him, wide-eyed with distress. Her breath hitched, and she began rocking back and forth while humming a hymn. This was how the boys found her, knuckles and fingers red and swollen, and humming softly to Mr. McBride. They hovered over him, terribly upset, asking her question after question, while Joetta waffled between a sense of relief he was no longer suffering and the knowledge she had been unable to save him.

Eventually, Robert and Charlie carried him out of the thicket. From experience, they knew necessity outweighed sentimentality, given the heat, and immediately began to dig the grave, taking turns with a shovel head they had found nestled in the ashes where the tool shed once existed. They dug on into the evening, beside the plot of Anna Louise Hicks McBride, where wild pink roses grew as profusely as the briars and creeping jenny. It was while the boys dug they made the discovery of the very garden Mr. McBride insisted was there. Robert encountered the first sign and Charlie called out, addressing her in that way he had come to do soon after the incident with Miller.

"Mother, come look!"

She was back inside the cabin scouring the wooden floor with hot water where Mr. McBride had convalesced in his final days, trying to rid the area of a lingering odor of illness, while also trying to forget the dreadful images stuck in her head. She gladly left this sad and draining chore and went to the back of the cabin. There, Charlie held something against his chest, while Robert, no longer digging the grave, stabbed in the dirt furiously. Charlie held out his hands. Heaven on earth. Sweet potatoes! She clapped her hands together as Robert tossed two more on the ground beside his knees. They were in better shape than she would have believed. They dug until they had enough for supper. Only then did they return to digging the grave.

By evening, it was done. With their help, she wrapped Mr. McBride in a blanket, and the boys lowered him down. Joetta had found a verse from a hymn scrawled on a piece of paper and folded inside Mr. McBride's bible. She believed it must have held some meaning for her father-in-law, and it was those words she spoke.

> *"And when on earth I breathe no more,*
> *The prayer oft mixed with tears before,*
> *I will sing upon a happier shore,*
> *Thy will be done."*

Joetta asked the boys if they wanted to say anything. Charlie shook his head, while Robert kicked at the dirt and shrugged. As they began to fill the grave, Joetta gathered some of the wild roses nearby. When they were through, she laid them across the mound. Robert finally spoke.

"Grandpa told me he wished he'd never talked so much about the war."

"He said this?"

"Yeah."

"When?"

Robert would not, or could not, answer her. He was upset, so Joetta did not persist. She believed she knew anyway, the day Ennis was brought home. There had been a few concessions where Mr. McBride had surprised her. When the war began, he was nothing but bravado and talk. Then certain events happened, impacting the family and causing heartache. No one could come away from such unscathed—unless they were heartless. She did not believe Mr. McBride was heartless. She thought him ignorant, and foolish at times, but not that.

"May he rest in peace."

She noticed something in the soil near the toe of her shoe. She bent down and brought up another sweet potato. She held it up for the boys to see. Over the next few days a different hunt began, and soon they branched out, having found the pattern of the old garden. She dug alongside them. Joetta felt they were somewhat safe working in broad daylight since the backside of the cabin sat at an angle, hidden from the lane. She discovered tree collards, and leeks, while the boys found more sweet potatoes and wild onions. This bounty made her smile.

"How about that? In Mr. McBride's final hour, he provided for us."

With the boys trapping and fishing, and having some success, they bore the remainder of that year, not without sacrifice, and not always with full stomachs, but they lived.

1865 was upon them, and Joetta couldn't have cared less. To the best of her knowledge, the war in its perpetual, never-ending endeavor was not unlike their own days, each a replication of the one before, an endless struggle to endure what they must, and win. When she reflected on the past, on the time when everyone was together and the farm provided for their every need, she was certain they would never have that life again. She did not want to accept this. She did not want for who they had been or how they had lived to change. And yet, that alteration had already taken place and there was nothing she could do about it.

The repercussions of war, the loss of her beloved and her firstborn had collectively created this new world, and they were the ones left to make the best of it.

As the interminable cold winter waned, spring with its zest for new life appeared to hold promise, and Joetta soon believed something else was afoot and quite different. Unaware the South was making its last desperate stand, she began to witness random sightings of men who skulked about, and she did not like it, not at all. As if overnight, the brief yet alarming appearances of these scruffy-looking individuals, most spotted running into the woods, or at times seen from a distance traversing their barren fields, indicated something uncommon was taking place. She would spot a flash of movement, but the color of clothing was difficult to determine. She was certain, whichever side they were on, they were deserters. They skirted by the farm, clearly desperate, and furtive in their manner, and her only wish was for them to keep going and to not come snooping about. She did not want them rooting about the burned house or eyeing the cabin with curiosity.

Without Mr. McBride, their vulnerability felt like an exposed wound. When he had seen something suspicious, he was apt to barrel out of the cabin, shotgun visible with an attitude as inviting as a cornered skunk. Mr. McBride had that freedom. They did not, and she did not want the boys forced into a confrontation. It would signal there was no one but them. She made sure she had Mr. McBride's shotgun nearby at all times. She also made sure the boys understood they needed to be as careful as ever, if not more so. It would not do to be seen.

Chapter 30

Joetta desired to hear the latest news but could not merely walk into town, so it was like providence the day Mary Brown came down the path, holding a bunch of jonquils, the bright yellow like tiny bits of sunshine. It had been a while since she had seen her, and Joetta began cracking her knuckles wildly, worried about Robert and Charlie, who at that very moment were working at the back of the cabin, digging in the garden area. They could walk around to the front at any minute, and their hidden existence would be exposed. Mary tossed the flowers onto the remains of the old house's foundation, her shoulders shaking with grief. Joetta's heart went out. If there was one thing she was certain of, it was that Mary could be trusted. Needing companionship, needing to know something of the outside world, she left the cabin and crossed the yard.

"Mary."

Mary screamed loud enough to startle Joetta before spinning around to face her in astonishment. Joetta began talking fast.

"I know this is a shock. I am sorry to have made you think the worst had happened to us, but we thought it best." She gestured at the foundation. "As you can imagine, we wanted no more trouble."

Mary's color was off and Joetta feared she might faint. With a hand to her throat, she gaped at Joetta with owl-like eyes that did not blink. Joetta continued talking, her tone soft, explaining their rationale.

"It was horrible, but necessary. As you can see, they intended us great harm and were only satisfied once they thought us dead. We decided the safest recourse was to let everyone go on thinking it so."

Mary rushed forward and grabbed Joetta by her upper arms, continuing to stare at her as if she were seeing a ghost. Joetta gave her a tentative smile, a tiny nod of encouragement. Robert and Charlie, having heard the blood-curdling scream, came running from the back of the cabin and witnessed the reunion. Seeing the boys over Joetta's shoulders, Mary released her and spoke, her voice trembling with emotion.

"I *knew* it. There was something about the whole affair that didn't seem right." Robert went to her, while Charlie hung back. She hugged Robert, exclaiming, "Heavens, you've grown!" Mary let him go and smiled at Charlie. "I've heard about you. I'm Mary Brown, the neighbor from over that way."

"Charlie Hastings, ma'am. You brought milk and eggs."

"I did."

Mary grabbed Joetta's hand again and breathlessly spoke two more words. "It's over."

Joetta was not sure what she meant. "Over?"

"The war; it's over."

"How? When?"

"Lee surrendered to Grant a week ago."

As if testing the sound of the words to her own ears, Joetta repeated what Mary said. "The war is over."

"You didn't know? I thought Mr. Spivey was coming?"

"Mr. Spivey had to stop, and we lost Mr. McBride a few months back due to his illness."

Mary looked stunned. "I'm so sorry. How horrible to go through that by yourselves."

They showed her Mr. McBride's resting place, and Mary plucked a wild rose and laid it on the rock Robert and Charlie had brought from the creek to mark the grave.

Mary said, "I wish I could've helped more."

"It was quite daring what you did, as it was. That day at your farm, when you said we all have a secret or two, I understood the seriousness of yours."

Mary turned to study Joetta's face.

"You know? About Hugh?"

"When I visited you that day, I saw him come out of the barn."

Mary folded her arms, her expression brooding.

"He was to receive a monthly salary, food, a uniform, and what have you, to carry out his duties. They didn't provide like they said, so after a while, when he was so hungry and wearing rags, he came home. He said he was under no obligation as they'd forfeited on their agreement. Many left who thought the same."

"Do you think anything will be done to him?"

"We don't know. It's over, only no one knows what it means for deserters."

"Or those they deem spies and traitors."

"So ridiculous. Look at him," and she pointed to Charlie, who had gone back to work. "A baby still. And you? It's absurd."

"I suppose we will continue to be cautious, and wait and see."

Mary gestured at the dilapidated cabin.

"You and the boys ought to stay with us. This must be unbearable."

"We have become accustomed, and what if Henry were to come home?"

Mary's forehead wrinkled like an old woman's.

"You still think it possible?"

"I will always hold that hope. We never heard from him, so who can say? As a mother, I feel I would somehow know if he were not of this earth any longer."

"Yes, I imagine that's true. Hugh doesn't know how we'll recover from this. He said the South has been laid to waste. He's seen the devastation to the land, roads, and bridges. Our misery will continue for some time, I fear."

"It is not unexpected. Mr. McBride had said most of the fighting was done on Southern soil."

Mary looked up, gauging the position of the sun, and took Joetta's hand.

"I told Hugh I'd be back straightaway. Is it all right if I share that you and the boys are all right?"

"Yes, of course."

"I'll come back soon as I can."

After Mary was gone, Joetta felt relief at having told her friend. She had not liked lying, even if the intentions were sound. She remained outside, arms folded, thinking. The war was over, yet fear of the stain she bore as a traitor of the South would continue to affect the conduct of some. Robert must be made to understand, should anything happen to her, he was to go to his grandparents' farm in Hamilton, and take Charlie with him. She considered the road that led to Whitakers, and beyond it the road to Raleigh. If one kept on, North Carolina joined Tennessee, where her sister, Faith, and her husband, Marshall, lived. To the east was Hamilton, with her parents and brothers and their wives and children. While she loved and cared for them all, she began to think of another place, and another time, where a fresh start might be possible, and yet she had no way of knowing where that might be, or how to even begin. Joetta, now thirty-eight years old, very well understood such a large undertaking would not be easy, all alone, with two half-grown boys.

She decided as she was outside, she would risk the short walk to the front of the old house. She stood there with arms folded, toeing aside ashes where the front porch once stood. In the process she uncovered a stubborn stem working its way upward, seeking air and sunlight, and saw two familiar green leaves. She bent down and quickly brushed aside more debris. Hardly believable, but here it was. The jessamine had survived and was making a comeback, despite all. She cleared the ash away from the recovering vine, comforted immensely by the symbol of a previous life renewed. She sat back on her heels and considered the plant. It was hardy, tolerant, even in the most adverse conditions. Surely it was a sign for her, for all of them.

Before long, travelers, mostly Confederates, made their weary way home in earnest. Some stopped and picked fruit off their trees, some were in a great hurry and went by like they were on the run, while others meandered as if they had no purpose. Joetta would have preferred less proximity to the farm because she could never be certain if they would come nearer to investigate. She and the boys stayed out of sight while watching with heightened interest anyone who passed by, speculating on where they might be going and how long they had already been traveling.

Leniency was a word often used and argued over as the North began sorting out the postwar problems in the South. Some wanted the Confederates and those who supported them to pay for what they had done to the nation.

Others felt they had given their due; after all, the South was left in shambles. Joetta wished only to come out of hiding, but she wanted reassurances she and the boys would be safe. She did not know what sort of punishment might come, if those deemed disloyal could still stand accused. While she had never been formally charged, she did not want to reveal she was indeed among the living, only to be caught by the Home Guard or someone like Miller again. So, she waited.

One day Mary and Hugh came with news from the Union-occupied town of Plymouth that lay to the east. They had a first edition paper called *The Old Flag*, with Military Orders from The Headquarters Department of North Carolina, Army of the Ohio printed in a statement from April 27th, 1865. Mary seemed excited.

"Joetta! It's good news! Listen! *'All who are peaceably disposed are invited to return to their homes, and resume their industrial pursuits. Such as have been deprived of their animals and wagons by the hostile armies, will be temporarily supplied, as far as practicable, upon application to the nearest Provost Marshal, by loans of the captured property in possession of the Quartermaster's Department. The needy will also be supplied, for the time being, with subsistence stores from the Commissary Department.'* Isn't that wonderful?"

Joetta, along with the Browns, after reading it several times, stood quiet, even joyous, yet still guarded. They were not quite exonerated, but they were free to begin living their lives once more. Joetta imagined those in charge meant well. Did they not know they were starving and had nothing? Mary was elated, and pressed Joetta to stay with them.

"I meant what I said. Come and stay at our place. Why not? This land's not going anywhere. We can leave word in

Whitakers, should anyone come looking for the McBride family to come to the Brown farm. As things improve, you can begin again. There is help coming, from the sound of it, and that is good."

Joetta looked at the cabin in a different light than she had previously. It now signified, at least for her, a place of extraordinary hardship and worry. Living there, in conditions such as they had, honed her into a different person, and in that process she had somehow grown to detest and love it at the same time. Without Ennis, and her family the way they had been, she could not imagine a future here, but what she said to the Browns did not reveal this discord within herself.

"While I do not have the means to effect any great changes at the moment, I have found solace in the little things I can do here."

Even as she spoke these things out loud, the Browns patiently waited. She understood to refuse would be ridiculous, especially for the boys.

"All right. We are very grateful."

The few days away from the farm restored Joetta. She and Mary hauled buckets of water and dumped them into a large galvanized tub set up in the spare room, and Mary left Joetta to herself. Joetta took her hair down from its customary bun and found a jar where slivers of old soap were saved. Joetta chose lavender. She soaked her hair and lathered carefully, her fingers working their way up to her scalp. She gathered the soapy tresses and bent over the washtub to rinse with a bucket of cool water. She squeezed the water from her hair before sitting in the tub. She sighed and groaned her way through her ablutions, while not wanting to bear witness to the change in her body. She was painfully aware of bones jutting from shoulders and hips, ribs making a staircase of her middle, and hollowed cheekbones that gave her face a new, angular shape.

Her fragility was as unknown and foreign to her as their lives had been the past five years. She was weaker and more inclined to rest, almost unheard of in the past when she would get up at dawn and work until dark with nary a break. She finished washing and stepped out. She wrapped herself in an old sheet and stuck her head out the door.

"Mary?"

Mary came from the next room, a dress over her arm.

"I think this will fit, although it might be a little long on you as I'm taller, but it's clean.

Joetta took it and sat on the edge the bed. Mary watched her carefully.

"Are you all right?"

"I have been reminiscing on the times before the war. I should be looking forward, not backward. I cannot bring myself to do so."

Mary sat beside her.

"The past is where Ennis, Henry, and Mr. McBride dwell. To think ahead is to recognize a future without them in it."

Joetta turned to her friend.

"I have had this one persistent thought that perhaps a fresh start somewhere is called for."

Mary sat back and spoke with surprise and wonder.

"You would leave the farm where you and Ennis built your home and raised the boys?"

"He is not there, and neither is Henry."

"You must do whatever you think best, but I believe you could turn things around. It would make you see it in a positive light again."

"Perhaps. It holds such sorrow for me. It is as if the land itself is laden with it. Everywhere I turn, I see Ennis or

Henry. I see Mr. McBride under the tree. Their ghosts linger, as if waiting for me to join them."

Mary stared at her with concern and took hold of her hand. Joetta wished she had not said the last part, even if it did feel that way at times. They sat in silence, each lost in the moment of uncertainty.

Eventually she, Charlie, and Robert returned to the farm. Mary and Hugh escorted them there, and it was then Joetta learned what Hugh and the boys had been up to. With the tools he provided, he and the boys had worked to improve the cabin. Joetta had wondered where they got off to each day, and this was the answer. Robert and Charlie were eager to show her inside. They had built a small worktable and had set it near the fireplace. They created a platform in the corner that could serve as the base for a bed once she was able to make a new mattress. Folded over it was her mother-in-law's Rose of Sharon patterned quilt. Joetta remembered the elder Mrs. McBride placing it over her knees while she sat in the rocker. They pulled her into the small bedroom, where a similar platform had been added to go along with the bed already there. The room would do nicely to accommodate both boys now. She turned to Hugh and Mary.

"I cannot thank you both enough. When it is cold, we will pass the days in much greater comfort."

Mary glanced at Hugh, then spoke carefully. "I hope the winter will see you still here."

Joetta did not comment and to fill in the awkward moment, Hugh gestured at Robert and Charlie.

"These two are hard workers. They did most of it while I pointed."

He let out a robust laugh, and the moment was gone as everyone moved back into the main room and Mary held out a small sack toward Joetta.

"These are some late-season seeds I saved. It ought to be enough to get a small garden started. There's corn, beans, melon, and cucumbers in there."

Mary also provided milk, butter, potatoes, and onions and as Joetta began to express her appreciation again, Mary gripped her hand.

"You would do the same for us, and have, many times in the past."

The Browns left with the promise they would come back in a couple of days. Once they were gone, the boys went to check the traps and with the cabin empty, Joetta walked around, running her hands over the table, the bed platform, and becoming accustomed to the newly enclosed front section. She continued to reflect on the conversation with Mary, and even while the improvements made the dwelling more comfortable, the heaviness she held in her heart and mind stayed with her. She would stay busy, and heaven only knew there was enough to do. She held on to hope, as she always did, even when her future appeared as promising as the barren land surrounding her.

Chapter 31

Joetta awoke early, her sleep disturbed and unsatisfactory. As was habit, she got up, dressed, grabbed the shotgun, and went outside for a bucket of fresh water. She did not hear the man approaching until it was too late. He came quick and sure, as if he owned the place, and she barely had time to scurry into the shadows to hide behind the broad trunk of a longleaf pine. She quickly assessed what he had and what he did not. He was Confederate. That much she knew, but like many others, the tattered quality of his uniform indicated he had been traveling a long time. The shirt and pants were more rags than anything. The frock coat, she feared, had bloodstains. His shoes were open in the front, the soles having separated from the upper portion. *Lord, do not let him be a problem to me.*

He bent down and rubbed his leg. As he straightened up, he raised his arms to stretch, twisting slightly to the right, then the left. It was that particular movement that stopped her breath. She leaned forward, squinted, and quickly became light-headed. She must be hallucinating. He dropped his arms and looked around, eyes settling briefly in her direction before skimming by. The weight loss, the long, unkempt beard, the wild hair and grime all over his face did not help, nor did the years gone by. It was also possible she was overcome with wishful thinking because without a doubt, her beloved was dead. She had seen him in his casket.

Her memory of that moment resurfaced, and she recalled there had been significant decay and other natural setbacks of the body that might prevent someone from knowing with any amount of certainty, yet the box had distinctly carried his name. The man suddenly took off across the yard in the direction where the remainder of the old house's foundation still stood. It was his walk; she knew it well. It was him. She managed to speak his name, a question released into the air, unfurling between the here and now and the morning that had separated them.

"Ennis?"

He searched for the source and found her. She did not understand what was happening as she stumbled out from behind the tree and walked toward him, fighting both physical and emotional reactions. Under an onslaught of tears, her muscles would not cooperate. She was forced to stop, but kept her arms outstretched, beckoning him until the distance, no longer bound by forever, vanished. He scooped her into his arms just as her legs gave way. Unbelievably, miraculously, her beloved was alive.

The commotion of an exuberant reunion woke the boys, and Robert and Charlie exited the cabin, shotguns ready. Robert's first sighting of the strange man near his mother caused him to swing the weapon to his shoulder. He marched forward with determination, mouth pressed tight, ready to do whatever it took to protect her. She had not noticed him because her attention was solely on the man, her face revealing an uncommon and intense happiness. Robert studied this emaciated individual without the veil of danger clouding his eyes until puzzlement became disbelief and that became wonder. He dropped everything and ran and in the last moment, Ennis released Joetta and held his arms out to his son.

Joetta pressed her fingers against her mouth, overcome with emotion as they embraced one another. Charlie remained in the background while watching closely. Robert let his father go to stare at him as if making sure it was him, only to emit more exclamations of joy followed by more hugging. Finally, everyone settled down and Ennis motioned to Charlie, beckoning him forward.

"Who might you be?"

Charlie removed his kepi and tucked it under his arm as he approached Ennis.

"Charlie Hastings. Sir!"

Charlie snapped to attention and executed a brisk salute, which made Ennis raise his eyebrows at Joetta as she looked on with indulgence. Ennis returned his attention to the boy before him.

"Were you . . . ?"

"Taken captive, sir, by the Union, who used me as a drummer, among other things. Until I escaped."

Charlie gave him a devilish grin, and Ennis looked flabbergasted.

"How old are you?"

"Fourteen, sir. I was eleven when they took me. I think. Ain't ever known my exact birth date. Haven't. I haven't ever known."

Joetta told Charlie's story to Ennis, what happened to the boy's mother, and the condition she found him in. Next came the accusation of spy by the Confederate soldiers tracking him and confiscation of their livestock. He learned of the estrangement from the Caldwells. When he learned what Thomas Caldwell had done, he grew sad and disappointed, but even more so when Joetta told him of her persecution and how they were ostracized. Last, she finished with the actions of Harold and the burning of their home. Ennis took it in bit by bit until Joetta finally faltered into silence. He contemplated the ruin and asked the question everyone had.

"You don't know who did it?"

Joetta did not want Charlie to take on any burden of guilt as he was prone to do. She would fill Ennis in later on his proclivity toward blaming himself for their troubles, and altered the retelling of their plan to escape to safety.

"No. Your father thought it best we leave after Harold saw Charlie. Word had spread he was a spy and I was helping him. Your father could not make the journey. After a day's travel, Charlie took a route to return to his home in Virginia. Since he was no longer in danger, we thought it best to come back. When we got here, everything was gone. Whoever did it believed we were inside, asleep. We let everyone go on thinking that. It seemed safest. We have been in hiding since."

As Joetta explained, Ennis grew angry.

"This war made monsters out of some men, even those we believed we could trust."

She wished that was all there was to tell, except there was still the incident with Miller. She would have to speak of it sooner or later, so she quickly explained how Charlie happened to save her life.

"If not for him, I would not be here to tell you."

Ennis spoke to the boy. "It appears I owe you a debt of gratitude."

"No, sir. You ain't owing me nothing."

Charlie flushed, peeked at Joetta, and corrected himself. "Don't, I mean. Anything, I mean."

Everyone laughed, a moment of levity needed by all. Ennis turned to the cabin with a questioning glance.

"I'm sorely aware of a certain someone who hasn't joined us."

It pained Joetta to tell him about his father. She never considered this happening, so she had to search for the best way to explain the illness and how it slowly took him. She took Ennis's hand and led him to the back of his childhood home.

"He is right here, beside your mother."

She showed him the grave, and the garden of perennials nearby, now cleared of weeds.

"Having this garden helped us tremendously in these last few months."

"I remember it being here when I was growing up. Mother always was partial to what would return."

Ennis propped his hands on his hips, his back rounded with exhaustion. Joetta touched his arm.

"Let us go in so you can sit down and have some water. The boys caught a few fish and thanks to the Browns, I can make a stew."

"How are they?"

"Hugh, of course, was conscripted. He deserted some time back and stayed in hiding for a long while as well. Mary managed to hold on to her milk cow and a couple of her chickens."

"That's almost unheard of."

"Yes. Our livestock was taken for the sake of impressment, so it was called."

"It was nothing but acts of desperation."

Inside, Joetta placed a glass of water in front of her husband, wishing she could offer him more. She sat across from him and could not stop looking at his gaunt features, the gray that had come into his hair and beard. His eyes were clouded with the weariness of war and whatever other difficulties he had endured. When he lifted the glass, his hand shook, something new and worrisome. He drained it and set it back on the table. She wished to be patient, but there was one more thing that must be talked about, and the rest could wait.

"A man delivered a casket to me."

Ennis straightened up, a mixture of confusion and fear spreading over his face. He gave her his attention, waiting. She was quick to respond, to quell his fears it was not about Henry.

"I was told it was you. I asked that the lid be lifted. This person looked like you, although the passage of time for the deceased, as you can imagine, altered their appearance. I had to rely on the fact the box bore your name. Whoever this is, is buried beside your parents."

Joetta had pressed her hands into the folds of her dress, and Ennis now took hold of one and held it between his.

"You thought me dead all this time."

"Yes."

"I suppose without any letters you would. I was in prison."

"Prison."

He averted his gaze to look out the door, opened to allow a breeze, and he became very still. It seemed to her he did not want to talk anymore, that he wanted to dwell in the view of the farm and beyond. Even while the scenery offered only empty, ruined fields and a gap where their house once stood, one could yet see blue sky and hear birds singing. It was, if nothing else, peaceful. She watched him as she carefully asked another question.

"Where?"

He continued studying the land as he answered in a quiet voice, almost a whisper.

"Place called Fort Delaware."

"When were you sent there?"

Joetta hated being so persistent, but she believed he had been through something and she wanted to help, if she could.

"Late summer of '62."

He turned away from the open door, leaned forward, and propped his elbows on his knees. His eyes skipped to hers and away.

"It is not the sort of place to remember or spend time thinking about."

She rose from the chair.

"We will try to forget it, then. You rest. I will cook."

He stayed seated while she hurried to put together a meal. Later, after everyone had eaten, Ennis lay down. Robert and Charlie stayed close, and the only time they left the cabin was to get more wood to fill Joetta's wood box, or to retrieve water. Often, Joetta would find Ennis watching her. She would go to his side and sit with him, not speaking, simply being with him. Eventually, he brought up Henry again, a most painful subject.

"After I was taken captive, I kept on asking if anyone had heard of a young man by his name. When new prisoners came in, I asked them. If I overheard a guard talking about the latest battle, I asked, and I always got the same answer. 'We have no information on the whereabouts of a Henry McBride.'"

They were forced to accept it was possible he was one of the several thousand unknown dead buried in mass, unmarked graves right on the battlefields where they fell. As upsetting as this was to Joetta, she still held on to the hope that if he were truly gone, one day, they might at least be told of where his body rested. For Ennis, prison and its never-ending cycle of daily monotonous routines had taxed him mentally, and the poor conditions had stripped him of his vitality. She learned how he had spent time most of his time dreaming of making it home. Now that he had, what mattered was deciding how they would move on, how they could possibly put this horrendous time behind them and start over.

One afternoon after Ennis had been home for a few days, Mary and Hugh came along the path to the cabin. Before Joetta could intercede and tell them the wonderful news, Ennis rounded the corner from the back where he had been trying to fix some old fencing. Mary came to a standstill, while Hugh cursed, something he rarely did.

"I'll be damned! It can't be! Ennis?"

"Good to see you all," Ennis replied, as if he had been gone only a few days.

Mary's amazed stare went from Joetta to the man standing before them. She finally found a way to speak.

"Why, Ennis McBride, you are undeniably a miracle."

Hugh gripped Ennis's hand and pumped it up and down.

"How did this happen?"

While Mary and Hugh listened, Joetta found herself cracking away at her fingers with glee, her knuckle joints popping happily and no one heard or cared. Robert and Charlie came around from the back, where they had been helping with the fencing, and added to the scene of complete calamity and joyous chaos. Mary could not get over the fact Ennis was alive.

"I can't hardly believe it, Joetta. He made it home."

Joetta stared at her husband.

"It is a miracle."

"Guess who else made it home as well?"

"Who?"

"Benjamin Caldwell. He lost an arm, but he's alive."

"Bess must be ecstatic."

They sat together talking about the war, the hardships endured, and what the future might hold. The conversation lasted until the sky turned a deep purple and the stars were out, and only then did Hugh and Mary take their leave.

"Please come and see us."

"We will and soon."

The days following Ennis's homecoming fell into a routine. Joetta still had moments where she would stop her work to go find him, sometimes believing his return was a dream. Before too long, a very natural moment happened when they became acclimated to one another again as husband and wife. It reminded Joetta of their wedding night, as if they had never spent any time together in this way before. There were a few unintentional bumped knees and clumsy moves, but at least they did not have to worry about the boys, who in the heat of the summer had taken to sleeping outside. Ennis carefully traced her ribs and hips, as if detailing in his mind the new, leaner shape of her. She in turn found raised, puckered skin, the scars of war, tattooed on his left shoulder and his right hip. They had always known in some capacity, in spite of what might transpire between them, their love would endure, and it had.

For Robert, it was as if his father had never left. Sometimes when he would begin to do something, he would suddenly stop and look to Ennis, as if requesting permission. Ennis was quick to ease his mind.

"You've been the man of the house for a while. Do as you would."

The fact he was as tall as his father was something they joked about.

"Reach me that, would you, son?" Ennis would say,

pointing to the roof of the cabin or to an upper branch of a tree, not wanting a thing, and only making a joke.

The direction of Charlie's relationship with Ennis came one afternoon after he addressed Joetta as Mother, as he had been doing for some time. Ennis, while walking around the foundation of the old house, stopped to study the boy. Charlie, always intuitive and aware, ducked his head.

"I reckon I got no right to call her that."

"I believe you earned that right the day you shot Miller. Perhaps one day you will call me Papa."

Charlie made no sound, and searched out Joetta's reaction. She had witnessed the exchange and reassured Charlie of his place with them.

"My mother always said, 'God gives back what he takes,' and I think in this instance, that is you, Charlie."

Despite the healing on the McBride farm, Joetta remained worried over the complicated scenario she found herself in. Most everyone in town believed her dead, and while they believed this of Ennis too, her situation was highly sensitive. She did not know what might happen, even though *The Old Flag* news article had declared everyone free to go about their business. She finally told Ennis her concerns.

"Here I was watching from within the cabin while your father greeted those who came to pay their respects, although I suspect a few relished the idea of my death. Vile as it seems, I have never witnessed such behavior or attitudes until this war. From that back window, I watched people I did not know come to look and gloat. I must let it be known, I am here and well, at some point."

"There's only one way to do that."

She closed her eyes briefly and opened them to see that new, hardened Ennis before her, a side of him born from experiences he would not talk about.

"How?"

"Go into town and face them."

"When?"

"Today."

She squeezed her fingers tight. Ennis separated her hands.

"Don't worry. They can't do a thing. They won't. Not with me around."

Ennis and the boys got themselves ready as best as they could, which was to wash off their faces and wet their hair and slick it down, while Joetta also washed her face and re-did her bun. They were a ragged bunch, and while Joetta's dress was in a bit better shape, all of them still presented a poorly lot. They began the journey and it was depressing to pass by barren fields. Soon everyone was quiet, wishing to get there, to see what, if anything, was any better. Once they came into Whitakers, strangers mostly filled the street, and quite a few bustled about carrying a suitcase made of cloth. Ennis pointed at them.

"I heard about them while I was traveling home. They're called carpetbaggers. They're from up North."

Joetta noticed two of these men standing together. They were each counting money. Real money, like what she was used to seeing before the war.

"What do they want?"

"Anything and everything they can get."

His contempt was apparent. They went to the building that had once been Alice Atwater's milliner shop, turned bandage supplier, and now a provost marshal's office. The man behind the counter did not bother to look up, and spoke to Ennis quickly.

"I'm sure you're here for the same thing everyone else wants."

"What we were promised, and are owed, yes."

The longest sigh ever came from behind the counter.

"Fill this out. It'll take a while to get anything replaced."

"How long?"

"No way to know."

Ennis took the application, and they moved over to the window. He filled it out and returned it.

"What happens if I don't get what is owed me here?"

The man raised his head and stared at Ennis.

"If I were you, I'd take what is graciously given by the United States of America and call myself lucky to have it."

Ennis stuck his hands in his pockets and lifted his chin a little.

"Lucky." He turned to Joetta. "He says we ought to count ourselves lucky to get what's owed to us."

He spoke in a way Joetta had never heard, and she laid a hand on his arm.

"We should go see if Mr. Spivey's is open. You have done what you can."

Ennis looked down at her hand, and it worried her, this blank look, as different as his voice. She let out a breath when he placed his own hand over hers and led them out of the shop. As they exited, Joetta looked to her right. Eliza Garner and Rebecca Hammond, heads bowed in discussion, walked down the boardwalk toward them. Joetta felt a chill go over her, remembering the Garners' overseer. She and the boys stepped aside, while Ennis took off his hat.

"Afternoon, ladies."

He was invisible to them. Joetta, out of habit and manners, also spoke.

"Eliza, Rebecca."

At that, they stopped abruptly, their astonishment revealed in bulging eyes and mouths agape. Joetta shot an amused look at Ennis. Eliza actually reached out and touched her, as if testing whether or not she was real. Joetta frowned, moved closer to Ennis, and could not resist having a little fun as she gestured toward him.

"He is alive and well too, as you can see. One must have the mettle to put up with devilish acts, notwithstanding the tribulations of war, and dare I say, those who would harm the innocent. If one is in God's good graces, He is bound to protect them."

Robert and Charlie grinned in a rather maniacal way at the two women, and Eliza drew back as if she had encountered a pit of snakes.

"But we went to your . . ."

"Yes, I saw you."

Rebecca's breath sucked in, while Eliza's mouth matched the word she uttered. "Oh!"

Rebecca grabbed Eliza's arm and pulled her away.

"That woman is a disgrace, and deceitful!"

Joetta stared after them, a rage building in her she did not know she had. It overtook her, not unlike the flames that consumed her home, and then was gone as quickly as a fire that no longer has fuel. Ennis, a shrewd look settling over his features, turned to her.

"My dear, I believe I know what we should do, if you're willing."

Chapter 32

Joetta did not know what to think. Of course the boys were all for Ennis's idea as it meant a big adventure to them. Mr. Spivey came to tell Ennis he wanted in on it, while Joetta stalled. She recollected thinking about how she had wanted a fresh start too, had already spoken of something different to Mary, but what Ennis proposed sounded impossible and impractical. She quietly listened to Mr. Spivey talk about it.

"Folks been coming into the store asking me, 'Is it true, they're alive?' I tell'em, yep, seen'em with my own eyes. One of the first was the Caldwells."

Ennis looked puzzled.

"They could've come here for themselves and seen."

Joetta finally spoke and added her opinion. "They are ashamed, as they should be."

Mr. Spivey agreed. "Yep, I think so too."

Even though Joetta witnessed for herself how upset Bess had been, and how adamant Thomas was when denying any responsibility, their actions had put a deep wedge between them. Could she ever forgive them for what they had done, even if they were not directly responsible for the house? That question was not any easier to answer than making her mind up about what Ennis suggested they do.

As time went on, there was the need for routines to be kept. Even while this grand plan gave them something to think about, they still had to make the effort to ensure they would make it through the upcoming winter. Summer was waning, and there were still difficulties in getting supplies. Ennis walked in circles about the farm, unable to work, or do much other than look at unkempt fields. He took off one afternoon to see if the Browns would consider joining them in their latest endeavor, while Joetta worked herself into a frazzle over the fact he seemed more or less decided. He returned looking glum. He was quiet as he set items from the Browns on the table, a few eggs and some buttermilk.

"They are not interested."

The Browns did not want to take such a risk, and Joetta could not help but think, *Why should we?* She knew deep down in her heart she would follow Ennis anywhere, so she began to question why she was so reluctant and afraid. On a cool, yet sunny afternoon, she went down to her favorite spot on Fishing Creek, where she had not been in a very long time. After taking in the serenity and settling into deep thought, it came to her it was the unknown that scared her the most. When she went back to the cabin, she mentioned these feelings to her husband.

"It seems this will introduce more problems, and there is so much we would not know, Ennis."

"Remember, we would not be the first," was his response.

What she knew of her husband was that he would not consider something so drastic if he believed it would be a failure. He told her that while in prison, many others said they would not return to their land. They were going to set their sights on a different future, go where there was a chance at living with some sense of prosperity again. He spent a lot of time explaining his reasoning, and in many ways it had to do with how he had changed in the last few years. What he had seen and experienced. To come home and go about life as if nothing had changed left him unsettled. He was willing to wait for her to come around.

"I hope you will know by springtime next year."

"But we would simply leave all this behind?"

"A fresh start, Joetta. We would own land and farm as we always have, only elsewhere."

Joetta could see he was different. All of them had experienced or undergone change over these last five years.

Winter approached, and Ennis went along with the boys to trap and fish. He also created a lean-to structure so they could smoke what they caught to preserve it. Joetta took all she could from the tiny garden grown with the seeds from Mary, and stored a few vegetables in the old root cellar. Doing so brought back vivid memories, and if she closed her eyes while down in the dank, musty space, she could picture the house above her. Oh, how she wished to go up the steps, turn left, and enter the back door as it had been!

They settled in once the colder weather came, and The Big Dream, as Joetta began to call it, faded into the background, the subject approached only occasionally. The boys eventually let it drop altogether, as did Ennis. Joetta enjoyed the time with them in close quarters, where she could revel in their company. Ennis brought out a deck of cards he had acquired while in prison and taught the boys how to play. She was happy because for right now, no one was going anywhere, and she did not have to worry.

Time went swiftly. Joetta did not know if this was because Ennis was home, and she was content, or if it had to do with what loomed around the corner. Not long after the New Year of 1866, Ennis, Robert, and Charlie went into town to check on the progress of what had been promised them and when they returned, it was not with the news she expected. It was as if Ennis had been letting his notion hibernate during the winter.

"I have someone interested in the farm."

"What? I thought you went to see about supplies?"

"They are not here yet. It was while we were there this gentleman came in."

Ennis had a pleading look as he stared at Joetta.

"He's searching for land."

"A carpetbagger?"

"No, he owns a dairy farm in Ohio. His wife is ailing and her doctor said she would benefit from a milder climate. His name is Lawrence McAdams. He is staying in town. He's waiting to hear from me."

"Your decision is made then?"

"Of course not. I wanted to talk to you first. He will be there but a few days. He wants to come and see the place. I'm asking you to think about it."

Ennis went outside. Robert came to stand by her.

"I think he needs this, Mother."

Joetta stared after her husband as Robert and Charlie went out and the three of them headed into the woods. She was left to her thoughts and they did not give her much comfort. She began to think of another season to come and the struggles that would indubitably come with it. This did not sit favorably. Her recent life of privation did not give her much confidence or expectations for success. She went outside and walked over to the broken-down fence where she could look out across the land. There was a sadness to the place that was pervasive. Like an unexpected rain shower, the option Ennis had proposed began to seem like the smarter, better choice. This caught her off guard. Instead of shunning these thoughts, she took stock of what she knew and what she did not.

On this land she had borne two sons, lost three babies. She had raised those sons in the home built by the hands of their father and grandfather, along with their neighbors. She turned from the fence and walked toward the charred ground, randomly sifting through the rubble of the old homestead. She was without emotion, as if the events happened to someone else, a detachment from reality she thought curious. She tried to feel the old connection, and what became obvious was she no longer belonged here. She had not told Ennis how Henry haunted her at every turn. How, on occasion, she thought she caught sight of him working in the fields only to realize it was merely a branch moving in the distance, created by nothing but want for him to be there.

She needed to consider Ennis, and what he had been through, from the day he left to his futile efforts to look for their son. His forced decision to sign on, and his own expectations for it being only a few months, only to find himself caught in the war's grip for years. The squalid conditions, the hunger. The fighting, and seeing men die. His prison time. And there was Robert and Charlie, and what was good for them. They had endured so much, and she felt bound by her motherly instincts to turn it around, to give them something positive, a heritage without hate and animosity. If they stayed, how long would it be before they could live life as they had?

It dawned on her that might never be and before she could finish these musings, she was interrupted. A short man hurried toward her, waving his straw hat in front of his face as if he were hot even though the temperature was still cool. He spotted her and shouted a greeting. Was this the buyer?

"Might you be Mrs. Joetta McBride?"

"Who is asking?"

"Elmore Finley, ma'am, at your service, from Rocky Mount. I'm taking down written accounts of citizens and how they tolerated events of the past few years. I heard you have a different opinion, of sorts." This outlandish little newspaper man seemed entranced by her presence. "Well, ma'am, what are your thoughts on the war?"

"For heaven's sake, what kind of ridiculousness is this? What did you think of it?"

"If you please, I'm here to listen to *you*."

She had barely had the time to absorb what had taken place, and now here he was asking such fool questions as that. She pondered him for a moment.

"First, tell me what you have heard."

He told her, only he told her wrong. Of course she had to correct him. And she did, only he forgot to write sometimes, so riveted was he by the events she disclosed. When she was through, he stared at her for a long moment before speaking.

"You never changed your mind?"

She gave him a shrewd look.

"One either believes in one's morals and convictions, or they do not."

He scratched his chin.

"Did you not worry you might be hanged or shot for treason?"

She gestured toward the ruined homestead.

"What happened was close enough."

"Well, what will you and your husband do now? Rebuild? They say it's gonna take some time, for sure. It won't happen overnight."

Until her conversation with Mr. Finley, Joetta had not arrived at her conclusion. She faced him, and as soon as she uttered the words, she knew in her heart she was setting the course for their future.

"I believe we will head west, Mr. Finley. To Texas."

Mr. Finley looked duly impressed.

In the late spring of 1866, on a balmy day with a slight wind, others who would also go met them in Whitakers. Mr. Spivey and another family who heard of their plan, and would travel with them as far as the Mississippi River, sat outside the old general store, now owned by Elder Newell. They occupied two of the three large wagons, prairie schooners, purchased by the travelers a few weeks before. To Joetta, they looked rather grand and exciting. They each had a team of oxen, and plow mules tied to the back. Inside the McBride wagon were items from the cabin, such as Mrs. McBride's Rose of Sharon quilt, blankets, and the few pieces of furniture they could fit. Various new implements for farming were packed along with dry and canned goods. In one of the small chests was new material for additional clothing, the small blue bird given to Joetta by Mr. McBride, and the jessamine, uprooted from the soil and contained in a clay pot. Ennis and the boys had on new pants, shirts, and shoes for the journey. Joetta was in a new dress, the first store-bought she had ever owned.

One chest held the newspaper article Mr. Finley sent her, and her notoriety since it printed was proven by the growing crowd who came to see them off, some they knew and many they did not. She admitted, if only to herself, she liked the title, "The Rebellion of Joetta McBride." The South had been filled with Johnny Rebs, and she had undoubtedly been a rebel in her own right, just not the one they thought she ought to be. As she looked about the town, disturbing sights were everywhere. Men, old and young alike, drifted along the boardwalk, some without arms, legs, eyes, or revealing other hideous wounds. For her, it was the ones with the emptied out, hollowed eyes who were truly worrisome, the ones with the look of having left their souls on a strange battlefield. Everyone wanted to put their lives back together even while Union troops continued to occupy the town. This sowed resentment, especially from those missing some part of themselves, physical or otherwise, the ones struggling hard to fit back in. Joetta was relieved to leave it behind.

The Browns were there and the Caldwells, to her surprise. She did not know what to make of the fuss by Bess Caldwell, who grabbed her and hugged her. Perhaps her old friend was feeling magnanimous because of her Benjamin's return. Despite herself, Joetta felt tears coming. Bess held her at arm's length and carefully searched Joetta's face before she spoke.

"Dearest Joetta, we never meant you harm."

Bess seemed sincere, as did Thomas, but Joetta maintained her reservations. The truth was, they would never know. She and Ennis allowed the Caldwells their goodbyes, but neither could dispel the feelings of betrayal by their old friends. After the Caldwells had exhausted their good wishes, the Browns stepped forward, and from this exchange came a display of genuine affection and heartbreak at parting.

"Oh, Mary. How I wish you and Hugh were coming."

"Maybe one of these days, we will. Hugh is already talking as if he wished we were going along. Texas, Joetta! Think of it!"

"It is going to be an experience like I have never known. I have never left North Carolina."

She pressed several letters into Mary's hand.

"Would you please see these letters to our families are sent? They know we are going as I have corresponded with them, but they are to confirm our actual date of departure. As soon as we know what town is close enough for mailings and such, I will write and let you know where we are. And, Mary?"

Joetta's tone dropped as she fidgeted with her apron pocket and struggled to speak. Mary stilled her hand.

"What is it, Joetta?"

"Henry. Should Henry come, will you take him in and write to us immediately—will you promise?"

"Of course!"

"Tell Bess, too. He is apt to go there first anyway, looking for Benjamin."

The women clasped arms until Joetta let Mary go and invited her into the wagon.

"Come look inside. It is so big!"

While she showed Mary the interior, persistent whispers of "the spy" and "there he is!" could not be missed. Robert and Charlie, having already staked out their spots at the back of the wagon, flushed red and grew quiet. Joetta was certain poor Charlie would always carry this stigma if they stayed, regardless of how much time passed, and Robert would be apt to defend him, to his own detriment. This, and so many other reasons, reassured her what they were doing was right. Meanwhile, her own contingent of naysayers stood some distance away. The Hammonds, the Garners, Alice Atwater, and Preacher Rouse. Their curiosity had got the better of them, but they did not come forward with well wishes. With mouths behind their hankies, saying who knew what, they judged her still, of this she was certain. Eventually, Ennis motioned for her.

"It's time. We need to be on the way if we are going to make it to the first stop on our route."

Joetta turned to Mary, her throat tightening with emotion. She studied her friend's face, committing it to memory. With one last hug, she turned away and gave Ennis her hand to assist her up and onto the wagon seat. Mr. Spivey was in the lead wagon and leaned over signaling them with a wave.

"Off we go!"

His wagon lurched forward, the off-white cloth cover undulating in the wind. Ennis grabbed hold of her hand and squeezed it while giving her a lopsided smile.

"Ready?"

She nodded.

"Let us go see what the grand state of Texas holds for us."

He snapped the reins and their wagon followed Mr. Spivey's, and the other wagon followed theirs. Joetta kept her eyes forward, on what lay before them, a future as un-known as the new landscape they would inhabit. Wherever they ended up, she would replant the jessamine, and when it grew once again and revealed its bright yellow trumpet-shaped flowers, it would signify a new beginning, a home-coming. There could be no looking back now, and she did not, not even once.

Author's Note

The most common facts of why the Civil War happened are familiar to most; however, in looking more deeply into this troubled time, the position of neutrality and particularly one limited to a sole individual offered an interesting challenge. There are other Civil War novels where neutrality is an undercurrent in the story, but not necessarily the central focus. *When the Jessamine Grows* explores this very difficult time in our nation's history through the eyes of my protagonist, Joetta McBride, a woman bound by the neutral values of her family's lifestyle.

Many have heard of Southern states that didn't initially secede, called Border States. For their various reasons, they briefly took an impartial position. This isn't uncommon as the United States, in general and over different periods of time, has often adopted this view before being forced into conflicts—like with World War I and World War II, for example. You had to imagine these Border States had citizens who wondered what their state government would do while hoping they wouldn't become involved. It's also probable there were individuals or families in states that did secede more quickly who held secret unbiased views.

One of the reasons for some North Carolinians to think this way might have been the fact that the state in the nineteenth century was vastly rural. While approximately one third of its white population had slaves, only three percent was considered upper-class, meaning a status of gentry or planter. These individuals would've been lawyers, doctors, or business leaders who lived on plantations and owned large numbers of slaves. Another twenty-five percent of this white population would have been the middle class and would have consisted of men in the trades, suppliers, merchants, lower-level businessmen, and small farmers. They would've most likely owned fewer than twenty slaves. Next were individuals like my main character, Joetta McBride, and her family. They made up the rest of North Carolina's white population, equaling sixty to sixty-five percent of yeoman farmers, or skilled laborers.

Yeoman (or subsistence) farmers grew enough to feed themselves and their livestock. They weren't slaveholders, yet many of them would fight for that "peculiar institution" in the name of white supremacy and for state rights. Even so, I had to believe some of these non-slave-holding individuals (perhaps many) never wanted to be part of the fight at all. That bit of history is hard to find because those who held this opinion wouldn't have readily admitted it, given the hostility toward anyone against the "cause." This viewpoint was intriguing, and I decided to write a story from this perspective because I believed it would represent a lesser-known opinion.

Joetta McBride's beliefs pit her against the majority. This was not only dangerous, but complicated for her, and for me to write. To realistically portray how she might respond in various situations, and have the savvy to counter remarks that kept her out of the fray (and out of prison) while sticking to her values, proved tricky. Her honesty and sincerity, even in the face of danger, gave me much to work with, and to that end, I loved writing her story. While Joetta suffers a great deal, and loses much, she remains steadfast, a woman with strong convictions and an abiding love for her family. I hope she is a heroine readers will root for as they follow her complicated and treacherous journey.

Donna Everhart
February 2023

Acknowledgments

I am, and will always be grateful and appreciative for the people who share the extraordinary journey of publication with me. While an author creates the story, without the expertise and guidance of individuals I'm about to mention here, this accomplishment is only what it is because of the invaluable input provided and given graciously by professionals like these. I'm forever indebted to the following:

To my editor, John Scognamiglio, your confidence in my writing never fails to provide the enthusiasm or the courage I need to expand, explore, and grow as a writer. I appreciate every thoughtful suggestion, always given with care and consideration for my own creative visions.

To my agent, John Talbot, your dedication to my career, and my work, along with your dependable support are what allow me to focus on my craft. You're attentive, and always have my best interests in mind. I see you not only as an advocate, but as a friend.

To Vida, you leave no stone unturned when it comes to ensuring my books get noticed by the right people, in the right places. Thank you for always going above and beyond with boundless enthusiasm and positivity.

To Kris, you produce covers that captivate. It takes imagination, and vision, and what you create stands out with boldness and beauty. Thank you for the thoughtfulness you extend toward my stories.

To Carly, ever meticulous and precise, it takes a special person to do what you do.

To the rest of the Kensington team, thanks to each of you who work so hard in your varying roles during the publication process. You're passionate and resourceful, and I appreciate each of you.

To Lynne Hugo, thank you so much for the gift of your time reading and offering suggestions in the early drafts. Thank you for sharing the headaches, the angst, and hair pulling moments!

To my writer friends with NCWN and WFWA, who understand how important it is and what it means to provide support. Thank you for being on this journey with me.

To booksellers and librarians, you are the bedrock for writers. Without you, your stores, and your libraries, communities of readers and writers would never have the chance to connect on such an intimate level with one another and share in the common love of books.

To my readers who are incredibly special to me. You write and share your thoughts about my stories, how they affect you, and what they mean to you. These correspondences, whether personal email, or at events, are truly meaningful, and uplifting. I'm thankful for you. I'd like to also extend my sincere gratitude to a certain group of readers I've connected with in the realm of social media, who share their love of my books—Susan Peterson, Janet Smith, Susan Roberts, Dawnny, Denise, and those who come and hang out on my author page, thank you, thank you. There are always too many others to name, but I know each of you, and I appreciate you helping spread the word!

To Jamie Adkins, of the Broad Street Deli and Market, a true entrepreneur at heart, you've helped me in many ways, not only generously sharing space for my books, but allowing me a way to connect with local readers. Thank you!

Last, but never least, a huge, loving thank you to my children, Justin and Brooke, for sharing in various celebrations, book events, and book news. With extra appreciation and love to my husband, Blaine, your patience and unfailing support means the world. You're my true compass.

WHEN THE JESSAMINE GROWS

ABOUT THIS GUIDE

The suggested questions are included
to enhance your group's reading of
Donna Everhart's *When the Jessamine Grows*!

Discussion Questions

1. The Civil War was one of the most complex and contentious times in our nation's history, with both sides resolute in their beliefs. The McBrides were an exception and took a position of neutrality. Do you believe this was more prevalent than history would show? Could you have stuck to your values the way Joetta did?

2. Henry slips off to join the war, and Joetta wants Ennis to search for him immediately. He refuses, believing Henry should be held accountable for his decisions, while Joetta feels nothing but a mother's worry. This event creates an uncommon rift between them. Given their different opinions about Henry, who did you agree with, Ennis or Joetta, and why?

3. Joetta allows Union soldiers access to her well, and her father-in-law resents this immensely. He foolishly talks about it while in town, and soon, a handful of men from town arrive on the farm and ruin the McBrides' crops. Who do you think was most to blame for what happened, Joetta or Mr. McBride? What would you have done if you were in Joetta's position? How would it have made you feel?

4. Bess Caldwell, Joetta's friend, encourages her to join the sewing group created to help the troops and to show loyalty to the Confederacy. Given what took place with the crops, Joetta decides it might be a good idea. After a tense exchange with two wealthy members of the group, she's asked not to return by Bess, who's certain Joetta will bring trouble to the Caldwells. Do you agree

with what Bess did? Do you think Bess was betraying her friendship with Joetta, or do you think she was justified?

5. Robert resents his mother for many reasons. The moment she insisted his father go look for Henry, it seemed she could do nothing right from his viewpoint. How did you feel about Robert's behavior toward his mother?

6. Joetta takes in a young Union soldier, Charlie Hastings, who inadvertently gives Joetta something she desperately needs, someone to mother. In return, Joetta becomes a substitute mother to Charlie. What did you think of this special relationship?

7. Throughout human history, we've witnessed the lengths humans go to in order to survive. During the Civil War people ate almost anything for sustenance, were forced to hide for great lengths of time, and endured extreme weather, illness, and wounds. What is it about human nature that enables people to endure such hardships? What traits in Joetta and other characters enabled them to cope?

8. Joetta has a special place called Fishing Creek, where she goes when she's confronted by a difficult situation or is feeling troubled. Do you have a special place you like to visit when you're feeling upset or distressed? Is it a place no one knows about but you? How did you discover it?

9. Mr. McBride is oftentimes an irritant to Joetta and difficult to get along with. What did you think of the change in their relationship? How did you feel about what happened with him?

10. The war affected Joetta and her family in many ways. They endured multiple losses, setbacks, and privation. This creates a desire for change, even as the pull of the land and the memories of what they once had root them to that very place. Have you ever experienced a period of time when dramatic change was called for in your life, and if so, what did you do?

11. Which characters did you find yourself relating to the most? What did you find relevant or similar to your own personality?

12. If you could alter the course of one character's "life" in this story, which one would it be, and why?

13. There are multiple themes throughout the novel. Loyalty, betrayal, and family are the most prevalent. Explore these themes, and discuss which scenes brought them to light for you.

14. What did you think of the McBrides' decision to leave their farm? Were you surprised by it?

15. What does the title, *When the Jessamine Grows*, signify to you?

Visit our website at
KensingtonBooks.com
to sign up for our newsletters, read
more from your favorite authors, see
books by series, view reading group
guides, and more!

BETWEEN THE CHAPTERS

Become a Part of Our
Between the Chapters Book Club
Community and Join the Conversation

Betweenthechapters.net